PRAISE FOR ADAM

Dead Certain

"*Dead Certain* is dead-on terrific . . . It's an entertaining and riveting work that will more than hold your interest."

—*Bookreporter*

"Consistently compelling . . . Adam Mitzner is a master of the mystery genre."

—*Midwest Book Review*

"There are several twists and turns along the way . . . creating a big amount of tension . . ."

—*The Parkersburg News and Sentinel*

"[*Dead Certain*'s] leading coincidence, which is quite a whopper, is offset by an equally dazzling surprise . . . It packs enough of a punch to make it worth reading."

—*Kirkus Reviews*

A Conflict of Interest

"A heady combination of Patricia Highsmith and Scott Turow, here's psychological and legal suspense at its finest. Adam Mitzner's masterful plotting begins on tiptoe and morphs into a sweaty gallop, with ambiguity of character that shakes your best guesses, and twists that punch you in the gut. This novel packs it. A terrific read!"

—Perri O'Shaughnessy

"Mitzner's assured debut . . . compares favorably to *Presumed Innocent* . . . Mitzner tosses in a number of twists, but his strength lies in his characters and his unflinching depiction of relationships in crisis. This gifted writer should have a long and successful career ahead of him."

—*Publishers Weekly* (starred review)

"Adam Mitzner combines the real world insights of an experienced litigator with the imaginative flair of a fine novelist to produce a page-turner with deeply flawed heroes, sympathetic villains, and totally unexpected twists. I loved it."

—Alan Dershowitz

A Case of Redemption

"Head and shoulders above most . . ."

—*Publisher's Weekly*

Losing Faith

"Tightly plotted, fast-paced . . . Startling . . . A worthy courtroom yarn that fans of Grisham and Turow will enjoy."

—*Kirkus Reviews*

The Girl from Home

"An engrossing little gem."

—*Kirkus Reviews*

NEVER
GOODBYE

OTHER TITLES BY ADAM MITZNER

Dead Certain
The Girl from Home
Losing Faith
A Case of Redemption
A Conflict of Interest

NEVER GOODBYE

A NOVEL

ADAM MITZNER

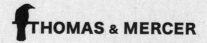
THOMAS & MERCER

Text copyright © 2018 by Adam Mitzner.
All rights reserved.

Published by Thomas & Mercer, Seattle

www.apub.com

Amazon, the Amazon logo, and Thomas & Mercer are trademarks of Amazon.com, Inc., or its affiliates.

ISBN-13: 9781542048378
ISBN-10: 1542048370

Cover design by Shasti O'Leary Soudant

Printed in the United States of America

For Susan, because there's nothing more important than being with someone you truly love.

PART ONE

1.

ELLA BRODEN

After the introductory applause dies down, and before the piano plays a note, I shut my eyes. It's a ritual I've adopted—to revel for a moment in the dark quiet where nothing exists except this feeling inside me.

Even though more than a hundred people are staring at me, I'm alone. Then I let a single person into my consciousness.

Charlotte.

In my mind's eye, my sister sits in the first row. She has on display that smile I remember so vividly from when we were little. The same one she flashed toothlessly when I held her as a baby—and every day afterward until the last time I saw it, six months ago.

I imagine mouthing *"Thank you,"* and she nods with understanding. She knows I'm grateful for her still being here, even after her life has ended. For giving me the courage to do this. For being proud of me.

Then I open my eyes.

"Thank you. Thank you all so much. My name is Cassidy. I appreciate you all coming out tonight."

That's the drummer's cue to call it out. *"One, two, three!"* And it's showtime.

The first time I took the stage as the opening act for Rescue Dogs, the clapping lasted ten seconds, tops. Polite, but certainly not enthusiastic. Karen, the Lava Lounge's stage manager, had warned me that this would happen.

"You're in the big time now, honey," she said. "On Tuesday nights, people pay to get in, so it's a different crowd than on open-mic night. Everyone comes to see the headliner, but you'll win them over, I promise."

The lack of enthusiasm was more than offset by the thrill of someone actually paying me to sing. Granted, I go on only one night a week, for which I receive a hundred bucks—a far cry from what I'd earned as a lawyer working in my father's law firm. Even my salary back when I was an Assistant District Attorney, which I'd always viewed as slave wages, was a princely sum compared with the pay scale for artists in New York City. But on the stage I feel truly alive, and that can't be converted to dollars and cents.

I do five songs. Lava requires that four of them be covers selected from a list compiled by management. It's heavy with female rockers—Heart, Joan Jett, Blondie. I'm allowed to perform one original number. I hadn't written a song since sleepaway camp, but after Charlotte's death I bought a used upright piano I found on Craigslist. For several weeks, I didn't get up from the bench except to eat, sleep, and go to the bathroom. "Never Goodbye" was the first song I wrote, and it's still the best. I suspect that most people listening to the lyrics think it's about a man, which is fine by me.

It's always a struggle for me to get through it, which is why I save it for my penultimate number. I'd prefer to close with it, but I know the club wouldn't have it. The closing number has to be loud. Really loud. Tonight I belt out Blondie's "Call Me."

The final applause is the most enthusiastic I've received to date. I even hear some whistles and a guy yelling, "More . . . More."

———

There isn't a backstage at Lava. The performance space is a red lacquer platform at the end of a large room. You exit from the left and join the paying customers, all of whom stand—at least until they start dancing. The only seating is at the bar.

When I step off the stage, Karen immediately approaches. She kisses me on both cheeks and then embraces me tightly.

"Amazing as always, Cassidy," she says with a wink.

Back when I was doing open-mic nights, she had no idea that Cassidy was a stage name. After I was promoted to a paying gig, I had to reveal my real name—and Social Security number—in order to get paid, but I swore Karen to secrecy and asked that she always call me Cassidy in public.

I never told her my backstory, but if she had any interest about the real me, a Google search would have revealed that Ella Broden is a former sex-crimes prosecutor with the District Attorney's office in Manhattan and the daughter of the country's most famous attorney. These days, that bio comes *after* the most noteworthy thing about me— I'm the older sister of Charlotte Broden, the grad student who was murdered six months ago. The cherry on top of my cyber footprint is the revelation that I'm a killer of sorts myself, on account of the fact that I stabbed Charlotte's murderer to death.

"I've been talking to Jake about you," Karen says.

Jake is the owner of the club. There's talk that he's backed by mob money, but I like to think that's all it is—talk—rather than consider the possibility that I went from prosecuting criminals to working for them.

"Good things, I hope."

"Only."

Not long ago, my greatest ambition was for Karen to elevate me from open mic to a paying gig. As soon as that happened, I turned my attention to climbing the next rung of the ladder—opening on a better night. I'm certain that when that comes to pass, I'll immediately start asking Karen when I can become a featured performer myself. In many ways, I'm still the same Ella Broden as I was in my lawyering days, looking for my next promotion. The main difference is that now I'm doing it in skintight Lycra and knee-high boots rather than a business suit and Ferragamos.

"And?" I ask hopefully.

"To be determined . . . but he's a fan."

Behind us, Rescue Dogs begins to set up on the stage. It's a band with six or seven members, depending on who shows. Their lead singer is a skinny guy named Liam. I'd bet anything that his parents actually christened him William, and I'd go double or nothing that he went by Billy right up to the moment he decided to be a rock star. Among the other ways Liam plays out his Mick Jagger fantasies is by constantly hitting on me, even though I'm at least ten years older. He actually thinks it helps his cause that he calls me "MILF."

Twenty minutes elapse between my set and theirs. The early setup is a trick Lava uses, making the crowd think the headliner's about to start so they'll down their drinks and order refills. Liam is too big of a star in his own mind to do roadie work, so he makes his way to Karen and me, leaving his bandmates to test the equipment.

"My two favorite ladies," he says, putting an arm around my shoulder. I remove it, and he laughs. "Aw, come on, MILF. I'm just being friendly."

"Be less friendly and we'll probably be better friends. Maybe you can start by calling me by my real name—Cassidy."

Karen laughs, and I give her a death stare. Now is not the time.

"You were really hot tonight . . . Cassidy," Liam says, exaggerating my name. "Hard act to follow."

"Maybe soon you'll be following *me*."

"Maybe," he says, although I know he doesn't fear that in the least. "But until then, I was thinking we should work you into one of the songs in our set. Might be a cool transition, you know?"

Even though I'm no longer a prosecutor, I can still read a liar from a mile away. He's not going to give me anything unless I "earn" it through some type of sexual exchange.

"I'd like that," I say. "How about we try it out tonight?"

"No . . . we need to discuss the terms first."

His smile is nothing short of disgusting. It's the kind of leer they'd use in a sexual-harassment training video. Even Karen looks offended, and that never happens.

Liam doesn't get the message. The fact that he's completely misread the entire exchange is confirmed when he puts his hand on the small of my back.

I'm about to reach for him again when I feel someone else do it.

"Hey," Liam says reflexively.

"I'm sorry. Did my removing your hand from the lady's ass startle you?"

My knight in shining armor is Gabriel, my boyfriend of the last six months. This is the second go-around for us. The first was years ago and lasted only a few dates because I was too impressed by fancy pedigrees in those days to think I could get serious with a New York cop when all my friends were marrying lawyers and bankers. Then he was put in charge of my sister's case and . . . well, the rest is history.

This is the first time he's come to Lava. I'd been resisting inviting him because no one who knows Ella Broden has ever heard Cassidy sing, and I wanted to keep it that way. I finally relented when he reminded me that even Batman let Alfred and Robin know his secret identity.

Even without Liam knowing that Gabriel's a cop, the look in his eyes clearly tells him that he would be wise to back down.

"I gotta go set up," Liam says, retreating to the stage like a frightened puppy.

When he's gone, Gabriel says, "You were wonderful." He kisses me on the lips.

"Karen, this is my boyfriend, Gabriel Velasquez."

Karen looks Gabriel up and down, the way she often does with me. I had previously been near certain that Karen was a lesbian, but by the look on her face after scanning Gabriel's body, I realize I can't rule out that she's bisexual.

"I've heard a lot about you," Gabriel says.

"Well, I hope I don't get . . . *Cassidy* into trouble by saying this, but she hasn't breathed a word about having a boyfriend."

"That's Cassidy. She's a very private person."

Karen looks up at the stage. Liam is chewing out his drummer about something.

"I think I better go deal with them." Karen turns and kisses me on both cheeks. "Again, awesome job tonight." She gives Gabriel the same pair of kisses. "Pleasure to meet you."

Gabriel holds his tongue until Karen is on the stage dealing with Rescue Dogs, and then he says, "Wow!"

"No, really. What did you think? The truth."

"You can't handle the truth," he says in a god-awful Jack Nicholson impression.

I squint at him to say that I'm waiting for an honest assessment of my performance. I can see the emotion bubbling up inside of him. So much so that it looks as if my tough cop of a boyfriend is actually tearing up.

"What's there to really say, Ella? The truth is that you're spectacular. Onstage. Everywhere."

2.

DANA GOODWIN

"You're home early."

My husband says this with a broad smile. He doesn't have to add that I'm a sight for sore eyes because I can see that sentiment all over his face. If I were married to a different type of man, I might be suspicious of such sentimentality after six years of marriage, but the one thing I know without any doubt is that Stuart is sincere in his love for me. Which is why, despite the fact that he longs for me when I'm away and I know I should be glad about it, it cuts me like a knife. A reminder of just how unworthy I am of his love.

My expression must betray my thoughts, because Stuart's smile fades. A wistful look crosses his face. "Did I mention that I'm very happy you're home so early?"

"I'm sorry I've been working such long hours lately."

"I get it. New job, new boss, new responsibilities. I mean, you can't be an elementary school art teacher for as long as I have without knowing what workplace pressure is all about."

A common joke Stuart tells is that he'd find another job if he could figure out an even more stress-free position than the one he currently occupies. I smile at his self-deprecation.

"Is Jacob still awake?"

"Yeah. I was just about to start the bedtime ritual."

"Mind if I do it tonight?"

———

I find my five-year-old son is sitting on his bed, talking to his stuffed tiger. It's bigger than he is. Jacob named him Mr. Big Tiger.

"Mommy!" he cries upon seeing me.

Jacob's excitement that I'm home is a further reminder of the late nights I've been spending away from him, and I feel the familiar stab of guilt that has accompanied me for the last several months. I'm determined to make it up to him, somehow. Him and Stuart.

"How's my favorite boy?"

"Good."

"Whatcha doin'?"

"Nothing."

"It looked like you were talking to Mr. Big Tiger. What does he have to say for himself?"

"He doesn't say anything. He's not real."

"Well, you're real. What do you have to say for yourself?"

"I don't know. You're real too, Mommy. What do *you* have to say for yourself?"

I suspect that every mother of a five-year-old thinks her child is a genius. If true, then I'm in good company, but I'm convinced that the label applies to my son. Jacob has a way of seeing the world, an intuition about things that I find absolutely remarkable. It's a trait he must get from his father, because for all my professional training, I seem not to be able to understand what's happening to me until it's too late.

"An excellent point and question," I say. "Let me see . . . I have this to say for myself. First, I love my Jacob very, very much. Second, I want to hear everything—and I mean *everything*—that happened to him today, starting with the moment he woke up."

I scoop my son into my arms and begin to squeeze him. He giggles and squirms, but not in a way that suggests he wants me to break the hold.

"I don't remember what happened when I woke up," he says when I finally let him go.

"Hm. Do you remember what happened when you came home from school?"

As he thinks about it, his eyes roll back and to the right. His little brows knit together tightly.

"Yes. I had a snack when I came home. Livie made it for me."

Livie is our babysitter. Olivia is how she's known outside of our family. When she joined us, Jacob was just eighteen months and he couldn't master her four-syllable name. Hence the nickname. Livie's a college student at Iona, charged with picking Jacob up at school and occupying him away from a screen until Stuart is done with his work-day, which is never later than 4:30.

"Was it . . . peanut butter and jelly?"

"How'd you know?"

I didn't, really. It was a guess.

"Because moms know everything."

"And what did you have for dinner?"

He can't remember at first. "Chicken fingers."

"Were they good?"

"Uh-uh."

I get up from my son's bed and open his dresser, fishing out the pajamas on top. Ironman.

"Time to get ready for sleep," I say, handing him his pj's.

I put Jacob to bed so infrequently these days that my son is visibly surprised that I'm doing the honors tonight. If that weren't enough to make me feel like the worst mother ever, my absenteeism over the past weeks—months really—is brought home when Jacob tells me that I have the ritual out of order.

11

"Teeth brushing, then pajamas, then story," he says.

I correct the mistake. After he's brushed his teeth and put on his pj's and we're back on his bed, I say, "What story do you want to read tonight?"

"*Mike Mulligan.* It's what I always read."

Although I wouldn't have thought it possible a minute ago, I now feel even guiltier. I should know the book my son *always* reads before sleep. The last time I read to him, which I swear couldn't have been more than a month or so ago, his favorite was something different. A book about trains, I think.

"Where is it?"

Jacob reaches over to his night table. He grasps the book with both hands and passes it to me as if it'll break if it hits the floor.

"Get all snuggly," I say.

He wiggles under his covers and then pulls them up to his shoulders. "Ready."

"*Mike Mulligan and his Steam Shovel,*" I say, then open the cover and begin to read.

After the story is finished, with Mike Mulligan and his steam shovel, Mary Anne, firmly ensconced in the basement of the new town hall, I ask Jacob if he'd like to read something else.

"No . . . I'm really sleepy," he says.

"Okay," I say, masking my disappointment that my time with Jacob is coming to an end. "Sweet dreams."

My son closes his eyes and turns away from me.

———

Stuart is waiting for me on the living room sofa when I return from Jacob's bedroom. He puts down his Kindle and offers to make me dinner.

"That's okay. I'll fix something for myself."

"Don't be silly. You just got home, and I've had three hours to unwind already. Besides, all I'm going to do is put the chicken fingers I made for Jacob in the microwave. Relax. I'll pour us both a glass of wine."

A moment later, Stuart places a plate of chicken fingers and roasted potatoes on the place mat in front of me and hands me a glass of white wine. As I begin to eat, Stuart talks about his work. It's a subject that has never interested me. It's all petty faculty disputes over the most trivial things, parents who think their kid is the next Picasso and don't understand why Stuart doesn't recognize true genius when he's in its presence, and pressuring even seven-year-olds to get into the "right" college.

Tonight he's going on about the school's new principal, a woman named Natalie Owens. The changes Natalie seeks to implement at P.S. 216 have become a recurring theme of Stuart's repertoire. It has something to do with sculpture, I know, but I was only half listening when Stuart mentioned it the first time, which means that I'm now uncertain whether the principal wants to introduce more or eliminate it. It's too late for me to ask Stuart for that clarification, so I simply nod as he speaks.

He segues from that topic to ask about my day. I tell him that everything is fine and smile to reinforce the point. In fact, my day was terrible. Thankfully, my lie is enough to end that topic of discussion, as Stuart doesn't inquire further. I breathe a sigh of relief that I'll be spared from having to provide him with any details. I take the opportunity to suggest we adjourn back to the living room.

Stuart settles into the club chair and immediately returns to his book. I take residence on our sofa and turn on the television. There's nothing good on, so I begin watching a rom-com I saw twenty years ago and didn't much like even back then. At least it's on a pay channel, so there won't be any commercials.

At ten, I tell him that I'm exhausted and get up to head to the bedroom. Most nights we head to bed separately, lately because I've still been at work when Stuart goes to sleep. On those nights when I am home, he normally stays up later than I can.

Tonight, however, Stuart follows me into our bedroom.

Even though in nearly every way Stuart appears to the outside world to be a beta man—slight in stature, balding, somewhat effeminate-sounding voice, working a job that is held in most schools by a woman—in the sack he's nothing but alpha. Tonight he dispenses with foreplay, gently enters me, and then rests his body on top of mine and establishes a slow, steady rhythm.

It's been quite a while since Stuart and I had sex. So long, in fact, that I can't remember the last time. I shut my eyes, trying to escape into the feeling, hoping to block out my pain for a few minutes. To my pleasant surprise, it works. So much so that when Stuart increases his tempo, I feel myself approaching the threshold. Stuart must sense that I'm close because he holds off his own pleasure. I climax, and he releases just a few thrusts later.

Before withdrawing, Stuart whispers in my ear, "I love you."

For the third time this evening, I feel guiltier than I had previously imagined possible.

3.

ELLA BRODEN

The transformation from Cassidy back to Ella Broden is akin to the way scuba divers ascend slowly to the surface to avoid the bends. Right now, I'm in the middle. I look like Cassidy—heavy black eyeliner, crazy tousled hair, and clothing that I might as well have painted on—but in Gabriel's presence, I always feel like Ella.

I never eat before I perform, which means I'm famished after my set. We select a pub a few blocks away from Lava. Actually, Gabriel chooses it after we walk by several much nicer places. His selection doesn't surprise me—I know Gabriel's aversion to fancy restaurants. It's not that he doesn't appreciate a good meal, but he believes spending $150 on dinner is obscene. It's just one of the many ways he's different from the other men with whom I've been involved.

Aside from the bar area, the space is relatively empty. We're seated in the back, and I ask the waitress for a glass of white wine—Ella's drink. Cassidy is a more of a whisky chick. Gabriel asks for a beer they have on tap, as he always does.

When the waitress walks away, Gabriel says, "I really liked the song you wrote. It's . . . very powerful." He chuckles. "I thought I'd heard it a hundred times through the bedroom door, but it sounds different onstage."

Sometimes, when I can't sleep—often, since Charlotte's murder—I sit at the piano and quietly sing "Never Goodbye." It feels as though I'm talking to my sister. I thought Gabriel was asleep during those sessions, but apparently not.

"I read this story once about Glenn Frey, you know, from the Eagles?"

Gabriel nods.

"When he was starting out, he rented a place on top of Jackson Browne's apartment. He claimed that he learned how to write songs because the ceilings and floors were so thin that he could hear Jackson Browne writing 'Doctor, My Eyes.' He went over the hook a million times, until he had it exactly right."

Gabriel smiles at my bit of musical trivia, but he's not going to let me change the subject so easily. "How does it feel, singing it?"

Another thing that differentiates Gabriel from all of my previous relationships is that he cares about my internal life. He claims it's an occupational hazard of being a police detective. They're trained to disregard the surface stuff, the signals the perp wants you to see, and delve deeper. To *detect*, he says, playing on the root word of his vocation.

"It's hard. Not gonna lie."

"Do you really feel the way you say in the song?"

Charlotte was an aspiring novelist. Despite her disclaimers about her work being fiction, I always assumed it was autobiographical. Apparently, Gabriel thinks that's true of my lyrics too. I can understand why, in this case, he finds that disconcerting. "Never Goodbye" is heavy with suicidal imagery. I suspect the line he's most troubled by is the one about wanting to swim down until I'm lost forever.

"Sometimes."

He nods, the interrogator in him trying to coax more out of me with his silence. It works.

"Less every day, though."

The waitress is back with our drinks. Gabriel lifts his beer to eye level.

"To it getting better each day," he says.

"Cheers to that," I say as I clink my glass against his.

Gabriel orders a steak. He likes them prepared well done. I shake my head every time he utters the words. For my part, I'm not in the mood for red meat. Although I usually think twice about ordering seafood in a pub, I throw caution to the wind and ask for the seared tuna—rare.

"Any more thoughts about an apartment?" he asks as we wait for our food to arrive.

My father wants to buy me an apartment. He first made the offer about five years ago, right around the same time he purchased Charlotte's place for her at Riverside and 108th. He said it was a good investment for him because he wouldn't be throwing money away on rent during her undergraduate years at Columbia. Claiming he didn't want to treat us unequally, he offered to buy me one too, even though I was already gainfully employed by the Manhattan District Attorney's office and supporting myself—albeit in far less luxury than I'd experienced as his dependent.

My father still hasn't put Charlotte's apartment on the market. It's sitting dormant, like some type of monument to her life. He dutifully makes the maintenance payments each month, although to the best of my knowledge he hasn't set foot inside since her death. Neither have I. I think he's hoping that if he can buy a home for *me*, it'll ease the pain of letting go of the one tangible piece of Charlotte's life that still remains.

"Not really. I just moved . . ." I say.

"Well, that was a matter of necessity. This would be by choice."

My sister's murderer went straight from my bed to Hell—right after I jammed a knife into his throat. I never spent another night in that apartment. After a few days of staying in my father's guest room—a lovely space overlooking Central Park—I returned to the West Village and the "comforts" of a fourth-floor, walk-up, one-bedroom sublet that looks out on an air shaft and smells of curry courtesy of the Baluchi's downstairs.

My lease expires in six months. At that time, I'll have to make a decision about where to live. Not just *where*, but *how* as well. With Gabriel? Off my father's charity? In a place I can afford on my own because I've cast aside my singing dream and gone back to practicing law?

But as I learned over this past half year, six months is a very long time. The world might look vastly different by then. Mine certainly did six months ago.

"It'll be an excuse to get new furniture, at least," Gabriel says with a sly smile.

"Are you saying you don't care for Jeffrey's interior decorating?"

Jeffrey is my ex-boyfriend. When we broke up, he left me his furniture as a parting gift. I've kept all his stuff to this day. Well, except for the box spring and mattress; they were soaked in blood.

"Did I tell you that he got passed over again?" I ask before Gabriel can respond to my question about Jeffrey's taste in furniture.

Jeffrey dumped me to fully dedicate himself to the effort of becoming a partner at one of those assembly-line law firms. The kind with thousands of lawyers working eighty-hour weeks, fifty-two weeks a year. Even though our breakup was one of the best things to have ever happened to me, I can't deny enjoying a little schadenfreude over his failure to make partner.

"No. How'd you find that out?"

"He called my father, looking for a job."

"Did he give him one?"

"No. I think my father's still hoping that I'll come back to work with him."

Gabriel nods, but I can see the wheels turning in his head. He's got his detective hat back on.

"Do you miss it?"

Once again, classic Gabriel. Most people would ask whether I'm considering going back to work for my father. Gabriel doesn't care about what I'm going to do for work as much as he does about what I'm feeling. I haven't been in enough relationships to establish a statistically significant sample size, but I'm still reasonably certain that Gabriel is an outlier in this regard.

"Not criminal defense," I say. "I could never do that again. But prosecuting. Yeah, I miss that. Thing is, I really *love* singing. And I've enjoyed having a break from a real job too, but a lot of the time my daily existence feels very self-indulgent."

It never ceases to amaze me how Gabriel is able to get me to divulge my innermost thoughts. Whenever anyone else asks about my life, I just tell them I'm living my dream. For some reason, I don't put on that show for him. Perhaps it's not for *some* reason, but for the *best* reason: I want him to know the real me. Even if I don't truly know myself.

"Is that why we're going on a double date with Lauren Wright and her husband tomorrow night?"

Lauren is my former boss, the chief of the Manhattan District Attorney's Special Victims Bureau. I was her deputy for four years, until I resigned nine months ago to join my father's firm. That job lasted only three months. My sister's murder made it abundantly clear to me that I didn't want to devote my life to defending the bad guys.

"My only ulterior motive is introducing her to you," I say with mock innocence.

Our dinner tomorrow night will be the first time Gabriel and I have gone out with others as a couple. He hasn't even met my father yet. At least not as my boyfriend, although they crossed paths during the investigation into Charlotte's murder. But Lauren is family too. She's much more than an ex-boss. She's my mentor, my role model, the woman I admire most. My mother died when I was still in college, so I never got to see her through adult eyes.

"Then I'd better be on my best behavior," Gabriel says as he flashes his A-smile, the one that never fails him with members of the opposite sex, including me.

"You'd better," I say. "If she doesn't approve, you're history, my friend."

———

After dinner we go back to my apartment. I suggest we take a cab, as the temperature has dropped to near freezing, unseasonably cold for pre-Thanksgiving New York City. Gabriel says the walk will be fun. He takes my hand, which, as cheesy as it sounds, is truly all the warmth I need.

We're at the point in our relationship where even though the sex is not new, it's still implied when we spend the night together. If my past is prologue, though, soon enough one or the other of us will claim to be too tired, or will have to wake up early, and that streak will be broken. For now, I try to enjoy the certainty of knowing it's going to happen.

I need to shed the last vestiges of Cassidy first. It's a hard-and-fast rule with me. I don't pretend to be her when I'm not at Lava, having learned the hard way never to blur that line.

I turn the shower to its hottest setting, letting my closet-size bathroom steam up before regulating the temperature so I won't be scalded. Then I step under the spray and wash Cassidy away. I watch the black mascara swirl around the drain.

4.

DANA GOODWIN

I give serious thought to calling in sick, even though no doctor or test would have validated my self-diagnosis. Still, I don't see how I can possibly function at work in my state. I feel certain everyone will be better off if I stay home today. Yet, at 7:15 a.m., when my snooze alarm goes off, I haul myself out of bed and into the shower.

Stuart always gets up earlier than I do. In the mornings, he's on "Jacob patrol," which is how we refer to getting our kindergartner ready for school. After I'm dressed, I cross paths with Jacob and Stuart in the kitchen. They each have bananas up against their ears.

"Mommy! Daddy and me have banana phones," Jacob says.

I decide not to correct his grammar, but Stuart does. "It's Daddy and I, not Daddy and me." Then to me, "It's the only way you can talk to the monkeys. The reception in the jungle is so bad that cell phones don't work."

"Say hello for me," I say.

"Why don't you get a phone so you can talk too?" Jacob asks.

I take the banana out of Stuart's hand. Into the end of the peel I say, "Mr. Gorilla, this is Jacob's mom. I just wanted to say hello. I hope you have a nice day swinging from the trees."

I hand the banana back to my husband and then kiss Jacob on the top of the head. After I kiss Stuart on the lips, I head out the door.

———

As soon as I log on to my computer, I see that the preliminary hearing being handled by one of the younger ADAs has been adjourned. I had planned on observing, but it's the prerogative of judges to cancel things at the last minute, which means that my morning has suddenly become free. On most days that would be grounds to celebrate, or at least to attend to the various matters that are piling up on my desk. Today, however, work is the last thing on my mind. I close my office door and ponder how things got to this point—and whether there's anything I can possibly do to make them better. Or at least different.

By 5:30, the only thing preventing me from leaving is my concern that Stuart will have a heart attack if I arrive home before eight o'clock two days in a row. So I sit in my office, still with my door shut, and play on the Internet. I decide to hide out here until at least seven. That way, I'll still make it home before Jacob goes to bed.

My cell phone jolts me back to the world of the living. I grab it out of my purse as if it's going to explode if I don't get to it in time. Still, I'm too late. The caller didn't let the phone ring long enough for me to answer and didn't leave a voice-mail message. No matter, it looks like a wrong number anyway. The caller ID indicates an 801 area code, which I recall from a case that I had years ago as being somewhere in Utah.

I sit at my desk with my iPhone in hand, trying to will it to ring again. If only I would get a text message. Anything to tell me that I'm not alone in feeling the way I do.

But when I lay the device on my desk again, it stays silent and black.

Less than an hour later, there's a knock on my door. I call out "Come in!" It's my boss, Lauren Wright, on the other side. She smiles at me, flashing her perfect teeth, and then moves ever so slightly to the side, revealing that she's not alone. Her husband stands beside her.

As man and wife, Lauren and her husband, Richard Trofino, are a study in contrasts. Lauren is tall and thin, with the look of a former ballerina, and her fair skin and red hair conjure the image of the all-American girl. By contrast, Richard's olive complexion tells you that his family tree is 100 percent Italian. Even in his finely tailored suit, his powerful appendages and thick neck make him look like a wrestler. Although he's barely taller than his wife, Richard conveys an intimidating presence—tempered by the fact that he's also extremely handsome.

He smiles at me in a way that's too familiar for my liking, especially in front of his wife. When I turn to gauge Lauren's reaction, she immediately breaks eye contact.

"Richard and I have a dinner tonight, and he surprised me by making a visit here before we head uptown," Lauren says by way of explaining her husband's presence in our office, which is rarer than a blue moon.

"We're dining with Ella Broden and her boyfriend," Richard says.

I look past Richard to Lauren, who's still standing at the threshold to my office. If looks could kill, I'm not sure which one of the three of us would be dead the quickest.

"Dana," Lauren says, "could I talk to you for a second? It's about the Dallenbach case."

She doesn't wait for an answer. Instead, she turns and walks out of my office, undoubtedly expecting me to follow. I look at Richard, who doesn't seem the least bit inclined to move. I suppose that's because Richard's reached a point in his life where he doesn't move for anyone. Everyone in his world either needs something from him or is afraid to cross him, and so he does what he pleases. In this instance, that apparently means he's not going to budge.

I, of course, do not have that luxury. When my boss tells me to come, I do.

In the hallway, I see Lauren fifteen feet ahead, just entering her office. I give chase, passing the secretary we share, Rita DeSapio, without saying a word. The usual protocol is to ask her permission before entering her boss's domain.

Lauren has left her door open, but when I enter I close it behind me. Anticipating my arrival, Lauren hasn't gone behind her desk. Instead, she stands right in front of me.

Neither of us says anything at first. I'm silent because I know that I'm *not* here to discuss Roger Dallenbach, a run-of-the-mill wife beater. Even though I've only been in Special Vics for nine months, this is the second time we've started a file with Dallenbach's name on it. The first case we dropped because his wife refused to press charges. A month later, the cops were back at the Dallenbach home, and this time the missus was down two teeth. Once again, she blamed the door rather than her husband. It's likely he'll go unpunished for this assault too.

The reason I'm actually here is because Lauren wanted to separate me from her husband.

"When is the Dallenbach trial set?" Lauren asks, just as the silence begins to get truly awkward.

"The *pretrial* conference is in two weeks," I say. "No trial date has been set yet."

More silence hangs between us. "Okay. Thanks," she finally says.

Without saying another word, Lauren turns and hurries out of her office. I have little doubt she's gone to retrieve her husband—and get him out of the building as quickly as she can.

5.

ELLA BRODEN

Lauren and Richard are already seated when Gabriel and I arrive at Sant Ambroeus, an upscale Italian restaurant that has been a mainstay of the Upper East Side since I was a kid. I instinctively check my phone to make sure we're not late, but we're right on time.

Even though I was only teasing Gabriel the other night when I told him that this was an audition for him, he's clearly nervous. So much so that he asked me to meet him at work so we could arrive together. When I entered his office, he looked like he was about to face a firing squad.

"It's just dinner," I said. "Besides, you carry a gun."

"Very funny. Is what I'm wearing okay?"

"Sure. It's the same thing you wear every day—gray pants, black shirt. Do you even have a change of clothes here?"

Gabriel gives me a sidelong glance when we first encounter our dining companions, undoubtedly because they're more dressed up than either of us. Yet, like Gabriel and me, they're also wearing their work uniforms. For Lauren, that means a dark blue business suit with a hint of a white blouse sticking out. Richard's suit is impeccable, dark blue and likely bespoke. The last button on his sleeve is undone, and his tie is knotted into a perfect dimple. I'm the most underdressed of the quartet—blue jeans and a cable-knit black sweater—befitting my status as a mostly unemployed artist.

"I hope you haven't been waiting long," I say.

Lauren stands and kisses me on the cheek. "We haven't even ordered drinks yet."

Lauren's fifty-two, maybe fifty-three, but most people are surprised when they learn that, assuming she's a decade younger. She certainly has the energy of a much younger woman, and the fact that her skin, hair, eyes, and smile all shine also contributes to the idea that she's not even approaching middle age.

Richard remains seated, but adds, "You came just in time. We were in the midst of a spirited debate: is it a bottle-of-wine kind of night or individual cocktails? Spoiler alert: my position is *both*."

Lauren is circumspect about her private life. That can be an occupational hazard for prosecutors, who seek to keep work and home as separate as possible. Among the few things I know about Richard, beyond what's been in the media for public consumption, is that Lauren thinks he drinks too much.

"I'd prefer wine," I say.

Lauren nods, as if to thank me for taking her side.

"I'm Gabriel Velasquez," Gabriel says, extending his hand to Richard.

"Oh, I'm sorry," I say, realizing my faux pas. "Gabriel, this is Richard Trofino."

As the men shake hands across the table, I say to Lauren, "I'd introduce him to you too, but I know you've worked together before."

"Indeed we have," Lauren says, "but this is our first social engagement. So very pleased to see you in this setting as well, Gabriel."

"Are you a lawyer too?" Richard asks Gabriel.

I'm surprised Lauren hasn't shared this minimal bit of intelligence with her husband.

"No . . . I'm a cop, actually. The *order* side of the law-and-order equation."

"Good man," Richard says. "I hate when I'm surrounded by lawyers. Being married to one is quite enough."

Gabriel smiles awkwardly, the way you do when a comment isn't really directed at you.

Gabriel doesn't inquire about Richard's occupation. Like everyone else in New York City, he knows that Richard Trofino owns one of New York's largest construction companies. That point was driven home during our short walk from the subway to the restaurant, when we must have passed three buildings with Trofino Construction emblazoned on the scaffolding. He also knows Richard's reputation as a man who often is on the wrong side of the law, but who is also so good at blurring that line that he's never been charged with a crime. And if the world of construction weren't rough-and-tumble enough, Richard added political kingmaker to his résumé by personally bankrolling the mayor's long-shot victory in the last election.

When I first told Gabriel that Lauren was married to *that* Richard Trofino, he voiced the same type of surprise I'd heard from others. Lauren herself has said more than once that they make an unlikely pair. Privately, she's told me that, despite Richard's take-no-prisoners business reputation, he is a different person with her.

A well-dressed man approaches and introduces himself as the sommelier. The wine list, a leather-bound volume, has been sitting open in front of Richard since we arrived.

"We're going to have a bottle of the 2014 Cakebread," Richard announces without consulting anyone else at the table.

"Excellent choice," the sommelier says, which seems to please Richard.

As the sommelier turns to walk away, Richard calls out to him. "You know something? I'm going to start with a Johnnie Walker Blue."

A waiter appears a minute later with the scotch. Richard is already halfway through his drink when the sommelier returns, a bottle of wine in hand. He pours a taste for Richard, who swirls it in his glass before taking a sip.

"Excellent," he declares.

"The waiter will be over in a moment to take your orders," the sommelier says.

"My friend," Richard says, "when the waiter comes back, make sure he's carrying another glass of the Blue."

Lauren looks at Richard, murder clearly on her mind. He is either oblivious to his wife's disdain or ignores it. His smile remains fixed, causing her abruptly to break eye contact with her husband. Turning to me, she says, "How's the singing going?"

I'm hesitant when people ask about my new career. I tend to expect a bit of snark, but there's none of that in Lauren's question. She's sincere in her interest, and I know she only wants me to be happy.

"Good. Slow . . . but good. At least I'm getting paid, so that's a step in the right direction. Plus I'm doing a fair amount of songwriting, and that's both rewarding and therapeutic."

"That's great. So, when can I—do you say to singers 'see you' or 'hear you'?"

"Either applies, and maybe soon. I finally broke down and allowed Gabriel to come. And you're the next person on that list."

"She was truly amazing," Gabriel says.

I feel myself blushing at his compliment. I decide to change the subject before Gabriel starts providing details about my life as Cassidy. Other than Gabriel and my shrink, no one knows that I perform under an alias. Even though Lauren will likely be the next person I let in on that secret, I'm not ready to do so just yet.

"Enough about me," I say. "Tell me about the office."

She considers the question for a moment and then says, "Here's something. I got a notice the other day that Donald Chesterman was just released. Remember him?"

"Jesus," I say. "That's a name I never wanted to hear again."

I turn to Gabriel. "Donald Chesterman is the devil incarnate. Raped his kids and his wife. His was the first major case I handled in Special Vics, back when I was a real newbie. I was technically second-seating Lauren, but she let me handle the key witnesses. A real baptism by fire. Three or four days into the trial, Chesterman took a plea." Turning back to Lauren, I say, "I thought he got fifteen years."

"Me too, actually. So when I got the notice of his release, I checked the file. The deal was from a *B* to a *C* felony, so the prison term was three and a half to fifteen. He apparently was a model prisoner, so he got out in eight."

The thought of Donald Chesterman on the loose is enough to weaken my appetite.

"On a hopefully happier note," Lauren says, "I've wanted to share something, but it cannot leave this table. Okay?"

"Okay," I say, obviously intrigued.

"I'm thinking about challenging McKenney for DA."

"Really?" I say. I realize the moment the words escape me that Lauren was undoubtedly hoping for something more supportive.

She chuckles. "Yes, really. It's something Richard has been suggesting for some time. I've always rejected it, but now might be the time for me to take the plunge."

Lauren always seemed disdainful of office politics, so the idea that she'd consider undertaking the soul-sucking commitment of a citywide race seems out of character. On the other hand, she'd make a spectacular DA. I know that she doesn't think much of the way McKenney is handling his duties. On top of which, she's a candidate made in heaven with her quick wit, good looks, and proven track record as a crime fighter. Not to mention that Richard's money would buy a hell of a lot of attack ads.

"I think that's amazing," I say. "Is there anything I can do to help?"

"You can keep it quiet for a little, until I make the announcement," she says. "And then, after I'm elected, you can take over the Special Victims Bureau."

I turn to catch Gabriel's eye, where I'm met by a dead-on I-told-you-so expression. He's confirming that he knew tonight's dinner was a job interview in disguise, even though he, like I, thought it was for the number-two spot.

6.

DANA GOODWIN

"Do you have any idea where my phone is?" I call out to Stuart.

Stuart pokes his head back in the bedroom. With a quizzical expression he says, "Is this a trick question?"

"What?"

"Isn't it in your hand?" he says hesitantly.

"No," I say, now annoyed. "That's my BlackBerry. I'm looking for my iPhone."

ADAs are the only people on earth who still use BlackBerrys. When the company filed for Chapter 11 a few years back, I thought the practice would end, but it's still the only device on which we're allowed to conduct business. The security features are apparently better than on a smartphone.

"Sorry. No, I haven't seen it," he says. "Maybe it's in Jacob's room."

That's a veiled jab. I spent the evening sleeping beside my son, leaving Stuart alone in our bed. It's something I do when I can't sleep, which is more often than not, unfortunately.

I return to the e-mail that I was reading on my BlackBerry. It's from the District Attorney. The big boss never—and I mean *never*—contacts me directly. If he has something of importance to say to the Special Victims Bureau, he reaches out to Lauren.

Nonetheless, today the e-mail is to me. His message is succinct: *Come to my office as soon as you get in.*

No one else is on the distribution list. Not unless they were bcc'd.

I forward the mail to Lauren, adding, "I just got this from Drake McKenney. Any idea what it's about? Will you be there too?"

I continue to get dressed, periodically gazing down at my BlackBerry, which is lying faceup on my bed. No response from Lauren.

Not that I'm surprised.

———

"Did you find your phone?" Stuart asks when I enter the kitchen. Jacob is beside him, munching on buttered toast. Stuart has a can of Diet Coke in front of him to satisfy his caffeine fix—he never acquired a taste for coffee.

"No. I remember taking it out yesterday and putting it on my desk. I'm guessing I just never put it back in my purse."

"Maybe it was the surprise of Richard Trofino showing up."

Stuart has met Lauren's husband twice. Once at a dinner party we hosted, and last Labor Day weekend, when Lauren and Richard invited us to their house in East Hampton. In that limited time together, Stuart developed a full-on man-crush for Richard.

I had told Stuart about Richard's appearance at my office and about his and Lauren's dinner plans with Ella Broden. I hoped it would soften the blow for what I expect to be coming shortly. Slapping a job posting for my position on my desk would have been less conspicuous than Lauren and her husband dining with my much-beloved, and currently unemployed, predecessor. Of course, Stuart lacked the facts necessary to understand that Richard's appearance in my office, yesterday of all days, meant that my career in Special Vics was likely coming to an end very soon.

"It truly wasn't that exciting," I say. "I really hope that my phone is in the office, though. I don't have time to wait in line at the Apple store.

I've got a meeting with the DA first thing this morning, and I imagine whatever we're talking about is going to occupy the rest of my day too."

I look at my son, who has as much butter on his face as the toast. I lean over to kiss Jacob on the head, and then Stuart on the lips.

"I love you both," I say and then race out the door.

———

Google Maps will tell you that I can make it from my house to One Hogan Place in forty-four minutes. It's wrong, as it almost always takes me at least an hour. More when there are subway problems, which is most every day.

One Hogan Place—building and address—are named for Frank Hogan, who served as Manhattan DA for almost thirty years and was known as Mr. Integrity. That descriptor wouldn't be applied to the current officeholder, unless it was meant ironically.

Manhattan District Attorney Drake McKenney is much more of a politician than a prosecutor. He practiced criminal law as an ADA for four years, but that was more than twenty-five years before he sought the top spot at the office. It's well known that he ran for DA because the job was open, not out of any desire to further the mission of the office. Now he makes all decisions with an eye toward how it will play when he runs for mayor in three years.

When I arrive at my office, I literally throw my coat and purse onto my desk. My purse hits the target, but my coat falls to the floor. I leave it there rather than make Drake McKenney wait another second longer.

Before I make my way upstairs to the eighth floor, his domain, I walk by Lauren's office, even though it's the opposite way from the elevators. Her door is shut, as it usually is before she arrives—but also any time she's in a meeting. Rita is attending to something on her iPhone.

"Is Lauren in yet?" I ask.

"Haven't seen her," Rita says, barely looking up from her texting.

"I got called into a meeting on eight. Any idea what that's about?"

Rita shakes her head.

"Do you know if Lauren was invited?"

"I don't. But maybe that's where she is now."

———

To get to the office of the District Attorney, I have to navigate a separate set of security guards. After clearing that checkpoint, I finally arrive in front of McKenney's assistant. She's the last gatekeeper.

"I got an e-mail that Mr. McKenney wanted to see me," I say. "My name is Dana Goodwin."

"He's in there," she says. "Go right on in."

I take a deep breath and then push open the doors.

The District Attorney sits behind his mammoth desk, looking as if he's posing for a portrait. For a man in his early fifties, McKenney could pass for ten years younger. The floppy hairstyle—Robert Kennedy on the campaign trail—has something to do with his youthful appearance, but the fact that he's tall and trim doesn't hurt either. He's bookended by the American and the New York State flags. Sitting in his guest chair is his deputy, Larry Kassak, a shorter, more swarthy individual I've never particularly cared for, although we haven't had enough encounters for me to have an informed opinion about the man.

"Good. You're here," McKenney says.

"I'm sorry for being a little late," I stammer. "I was . . . delayed on the train."

McKenney doesn't respond to my excuse. Instead, he gets up from his desk and walks over to his closet, out of which he pulls his overcoat.

We're leaving the building, apparently. I notice that Kassak is wearing his topcoat too.

"Are we going somewhere?"

"Yeah, grab your coat. We've got a car waiting to take us over to One PP."

One PP—One Police Plaza—is the address of police headquarters.

"Can I ask what this is about?"

"We'll brief you when we get there," Kassak says.

7.

ELLA BRODEN

On Thursdays at nine, I see Allison. Also on Wednesdays.

She's a psychiatrist.

Her office is located in a townhouse on Jane Street. There's a narrow staircase leading from the street directly to the third floor. I suspect Allison owns the entire house, either because she inherited the property or because her husband is a banker or an art dealer or something. It must be worth at least $10 million, and you don't amass that kind of fortune charging by the hour, even if it's in $400 increments.

The bills are sent to my father—the only bit of his charity I rely upon. I assuage my sense of entitlement with the thought that I'm doing it more for him than for myself. He insisted I see someone, emphasizing that it was necessary after the trauma I'd suffered. I might still have resisted, finding nothing wrong with sleeping all day and self-medicating with junk food, but for the fact that Gabriel echoed the sentiment.

Allison's office reveals a woman's touch. Lots of florals and pastels, with furnishings that tend toward the Victorian. My seat is a case in point—a long sofa upholstered in a mauve-colored velvet. It's a piece that might have been referred to in another age as a "fainting couch." Allison's chair is midcentury modern and black leather, which doesn't fit at all with the rest of the décor. So much so that I wonder if its presence isn't some type of Rorschach test.

At the start of our first session, Allison asked me why was I there.

"Because everyone said I should talk to a professional," was my answer.

"Do you always do what people tell you to do?"

I thought for a moment and gave her the truthful answer. "Yes. Pretty much."

She smiled. The way she did it reminded me a bit of my mother, which I quickly surmised was either a very good thing or a very bad thing in a therapist. "Good. At least honesty won't be a sticking point between us. So tell me, why does everyone think you need to be in analysis?"

"Because I killed a man," I said, knowing well that by phrasing it in that way I was baiting her. "I was sleeping with him, and he killed my sister. So there's that too."

She didn't let on that she already knew those things, although I'm sure she did. Even if there's some AMA prohibition about googling your patients, unless Allison had been living under a rock, she'd have heard about Charlotte Broden's disappearance and subsequent murder, as well as how I stabbed my sister's murderer to death. She probably even came across the articles published by lower forms of media, which speculated that the entire thing might have been a love triangle gone wrong.

"Then it does sound like we have a lot to talk about," Allison said.

The night after my first session, I had a very vivid nightmare. Oddly, until then, I was convinced that my subconscious had already been unfettered by Charlotte's murder and my role in avenging it. But, like clockwork, as soon as I opened up the Pandora's box of my psyche, I was bombarded by suppressed thoughts that I wished had stayed secreted.

In the dream, I was back in the townhouse that I lived in as a kid. Charlotte was alive. She was twelve, even though I was my current thirty-two years. My sister is terrified, her hands visibly shaking.

"What's wrong, Char-bar?" I ask.

"Oh my God, Ella. I'm so sorry," she says, crying.

"Just tell me what happened."

She can't stop crying. It makes me want to cry too.

Finally, she says, "Hannibal Lecter is upstairs. In Mom and Dad's room."

For some reason, the thought that Hannibal Lecter wasn't real didn't come into play in the dream. Instead, I ask a logistical question.

"How'd he get in?"

"It's all my fault," Charlotte sobs. "I'm so sorry, Ella. Please forgive me."

"It's okay," I say to comfort her. I take her into my arms, but she pushes me away.

"No! No, it's not okay! We're all going to die!"

In the dream, I know I have to do something or else Charlotte will be proven correct and we'll all die, but my solution is as ridiculous as the dream's premise.

"I'll . . . I'll go upstairs and kill him," I say.

"No!" she screams, even louder than before. "Please don't go. Don't leave me alone."

She holds me tightly, physically restraining me from carrying out my plan. I break our embrace.

"Stay here," I say sternly, then turn toward the stairs and slowly begin to ascend. I'm petrified, my knees shaking with each step.

On the second floor, I come to the kitchen—even though in our actual home the kitchen was on the ground floor. I step off the stairs and grab a large knife out of the butcher block. Then I continue to the third floor, to my parents' bedroom.

By now my heart is beating so loudly that my chest hurts. I am certain Lecter's going to kill me. But I don't even think to stop. Instead, I open the door to my parents' bedroom.

The room is pitch-black. I can't even see my hand. But I know from the way the hair rises on the back of my neck that I'm not alone.

In desperation, I begin to stab the darkness, the way Anthony Perkins killed Janet Leigh in *Psycho*.

The knife plunges into someone's body. Hannibal? My mother? My father?

I'll never know, because that's when I woke up with a jolt.

I told Allison about the dream at our next session, which was the following morning. Her reaction wasn't at all what I had expected. I obviously saw the parallels between my action in the dream and my killing Charlotte's murderer, right down to using a knife in both instances. But the questions she posed suggested she believed that more was going on than just an imaginative reenactment of how I murdered a deadly sociopath.

"How would you describe your reaction when Charlotte told you that Hannibal Lecter was in your home?" she asked.

"Terrified," I said.

"Of course, but it seemed in the dream that Charlotte had let him into your house. Were you angry too? I mean, she let the world's foremost cannibal and serial killer into your family's home, right?"

"It wasn't her fault, though."

"Oh? Why do you say that?"

Truthfully, I didn't know. I couldn't remember the dream any longer, at least not in enough detail to probe my thought process during it.

"I don't know. I just don't think I felt that way."

"Okay. So you protected your sister in the dream."

There was no question posed, but I knew she was asking me to contrast my dream with what happened in real life. Even though the thought that I failed my sister was nothing new to me, it still had the power to move me to tears. I expected Allison to comfort me, maybe even to apologize for upsetting me. Instead, she silently handed me a box of tissues.

As I was drying my eyes she asked, "What do you think of when you think of Hannibal Lecter?"

"I don't know . . . Anthony Hopkins, I guess."

"No. Not the actor, but the character. Who is he?"

"A cannibal."

"Do you know what he does for a living?"

"Eats people?"

"No, I think that's more of a hobby," she said, with a chuckle at her own wit. "If you remember the movie, Jodie Foster always calls him 'doctor.'"

"Okay . . ."

She didn't follow up. Psychiatrists are like prosecutors and cops in that way, using silence to draw out an admission.

"I don't think I remembered that," I said to end the quiet.

"Do you know what kind of doctor he is?"

I thought for a moment, then realized I *did* know.

"He's a psychiatrist."

She nodded. "Maybe your dream is a way of telling you that what you're truly terrified of is what you might end up revealing in here. In therapy. Maybe the monster that your sister let in is the *psychiatrist* on the third floor of the brownstone."

Today, though, I have nothing as revelatory to share with Allison as the dream in which I stab to death the stand-in for my psychiatrist using the same weapon as I used to kill my sister's murderer. Instead, I move in an entirely different direction.

"So I had a pretty good set the other night," I begin brightly. "And Gabriel was there."

"Good," she says in that noncommittal tone that I suspect all therapists use.

"Gabriel asked about my song, though. 'Never Goodbye.' Whether I actually feel the things I say in the lyrics."

We've discussed the song before. In fact, I sang it for her once. I wanted her to say that it was beautiful, but instead she used the word *torturous.*

"And what did you tell him?"

"The truth, like always."

She smiles. "And what is the truth?"

"That sometimes I feel like that, but not all the time?"

"And by 'like that,' to what are you referring?"

I find this to be a bit cruel. She knows what I mean but wants me to say it aloud. I suspect it's some type of therapist thing. If you articulate your desires, you're less likely to act on them maybe. Something akin to keeping a food journal so you don't overeat. Or perhaps Allison is simply a sadist.

"That sometimes I feel like I want to die."

8.

DANA GOODWIN

District Attorney Drake McKenney and Police Commissioner Calhoun Johnson usually only occupy the same space when television crews are filming. It's a not very well-kept secret that the two men don't like each other. The source of their enmity is a bit less clear, but it could be any one of half a dozen things, ranging from Johnson's animus toward politicians and those born with a silver spoon in their mouths—both of which apply to Drake McKenney—to McKenney's distrust of anyone he can't control, which pretty much sums up Calhoun Johnson. Yet despite their well-known hostility toward one another, as soon as we arrive in the Commissioner's office the two shake hands like old friends.

Like McKenney's domain, Johnson's office is a shrine to his greatness. The two workspaces share prominent displays of American flags, desks the size of compact cars, and photographs of luminaries shaking the occupant's hand. Johnson even manages to one-up McKenney: he's actually framed his medals and hung them on the wall.

McKenney introduces me to the Commissioner, and then Johnson does the honor of telling me that the short, balding guy with the mustache to his right is John Calimano, the Chief of Detectives, and the tall, wiry African American on his left is Henry Lucian, a police captain.

I nod at each of them, trying to act like being in the company of the highest-ranking officials in New York City law enforcement is something I do on a daily basis. I know better than to say anything, so I stand mute. Fortunately, the others are quiet too, although it creates an eerie silence in the room.

It's broken a minute later when the door swings open and a small woman, probably near seventy, enters. A step behind her is a handsome man, tall, dark-complexioned, close-cropped black hair, dressed in gray pants and a slightly darker gray shirt. He looks as startled by the VIP guest list as I was when I arrived.

"Everyone, this is Lieutenant Gabriel Velasquez," Lucian announces. "We can do the handshaking later."

The District Attorney finally explains why we've all assembled here.

"I have some very sad news to report. Lauren Wright, the head of the Special Victims Bureau, was found murdered this morning. Her body was discovered a few blocks from her home, in Central Park. Two gunshots to the head. At close range, we believe."

The others wear stoic expressions, as if this is merely another crime and not a personal tragedy. They didn't know Lauren. Not like me, anyway. Then again, few people did. I don't want to reveal any emotion, however. It's best to play this like they are and remain calm.

"I was just with them last night," Detective Velasquez says.

It seems like a non sequitur at first. Then I make the connection: Gabriel Velasquez must be Ella Broden's boyfriend. I'd heard she was dating the cop who handled the investigation into her sister's murder, and I remember Richard mentioning last night that they were meeting Ella *and her boyfriend* for dinner.

One of the cops, the taller, African American guy, Lucian, looks at Gabriel like a priest who's just heard blasphemy. "What did you say?"

Gabriel quickly explains. "My girlfriend is Ella Broden. She used to work for Lauren Wright, as her deputy. They're still friends, and last night the four of us . . . Ella, me, Lauren, and her husband, Richard Trofino . . . we all had dinner together."

"Jesus," Johnson says.

The Chief of Detectives, Calimano, asks, "What time did you leave the restaurant?"

Gabriel considers this for a moment. "Dinner was at seven, so I imagine we left by nine thirty, nine forty-five."

"Anything happen at dinner?" McKenney asks.

His tone is sharp. Like he's cross-examining a hostile witness.

"No, not anything of any consequence. Some marital bickering. Lauren thought her husband was drinking too much. There was some eye-rolling, that kind of thing."

"How much *did* he drink?" McKenney asks.

"I honestly wasn't counting, but he had a scotch before we ordered a bottle of wine. Maybe two, come to think of it. My guess is that he had two glasses of wine, and then an after-dinner drink."

"So, at least five," McKenney says, as if no one else in the room can do the math.

"Was he drunk?" asks Calimano.

"Not that I could tell. The restaurant was near their apartment. They walked home after dinner, so I wasn't that focused on his level of inebriation."

"He could have had a few more pops once they got home," says Lucian.

"Has anyone spoken to Richard?"

I startle myself with the sound of my own voice. Sometimes when I'm the only woman in a situation—which isn't infrequent—I end up being merely a spectator.

"The man's in shock," Calimano answers. "He's in Interrogation Two right now. Keeps saying that he didn't even know his wife wasn't in bed with him until we called."

There's a momentary lull. It's broken when Lucian asks, "Does Gabriel's personal connection change anyone's view that he ride point on this?" He looks over at Calimano for the answer, which reminds me of their ranks—Calimano is the Chief of D's, Lucian's boss.

"Your case, your assignment," Calimano says.

"Thank you, sir," Lucian says. "I hesitate to say this in his presence, but Gabriel is the best we have. So if there aren't any other objections, I want him on it."

The Commissioner nods. All eyes turn to the DA.

"That's fine by me," says McKenney. "I'd like Dana to work with him. If it's not Trofino, the odds are it's going to be work related. She knows the most about Lauren's caseload."

Gabriel makes eye contact with me and smiles. It makes me feel like a teenage girl being spied across the room. I nod but don't smile back at him.

"What about that?" Johnson says in my direction. "Was there anything out of the ordinary in the department? Threats by defendants, that kind of thing?"

The question is directed at me because I know what's currently on the docket of the Special Vics Bureau. "No, not that I'm aware of," I say. "I'll need to review all of our case files as well as any e-mails or voice mails that Lauren received. But we met once a week to discuss open matters, so I'd know if there was anything of particular concern. There wasn't."

Gabriel chimes in. "Lauren did say something about a guy who just got out. Raped his family."

This is not something Lauren shared with me. "Do you remember his name?"

"I don't, but Ella probably will."

That ends the general discussion, and no one says anything for a good ten seconds. It's the Police Commissioner who finally breaks the silence.

"At the risk of stating the obvious, this is our top priority. Blank check for overtime . . . manpower, you name it."

"Nobody kills an Assistant District Attorney," McKenney adds. "Nobody."

9.

ELLA BRODEN

An unseasonably cold November morning does nothing to lighten the foot traffic in the West Village. The streets are teeming with people when I emerge from Allison's townhouse. As I sometimes do during the day, I wonder where they're all going. I think about the fact that I have nothing on my schedule today. In fact, aside from Lava next Tuesday and my appointment tomorrow with Allison, I have nothing to do for the rest of the week.

I haven't gotten any farther away than the corner of Jane and Greenwich Streets when my phone rings. It's Gabriel. As he complains I often do, I start talking first, even though *he* called *me*.

"I just left Allison's. I was thinking about heading downtown later and watching my father argue my favorite case."

Gabriel knows I'm being sarcastic. The case in question is the money-laundering trial of Nicolai Garkov, a matter that has consumed my father for nearly a decade. Gabriel, however, doesn't respond to my comment. That's the first inkling I have that something is wrong.

"What?" I say to break the now-ominous silence.

"I'm sorry to have to tell you this over the phone, Ella, but I can't leave here. I wanted you to hear it from me before it's all over the media. Lauren Wright was murdered last night."

The news literally knocks me off my feet. As soon as Gabriel says the words, I sink to the sidewalk.

This can't be happening. Not again, I tell myself. And then those same words leave my mouth.

I don't hear anything Gabriel says back, because now I'm crying hysterically. Sitting on the curb, bawling my eyes out. A young man asks if I'm okay. I nod that I am, even as it's obvious to him that I'm not.

Not Lauren. Not now.

I learned that Charlotte was missing in stages. Her boyfriend called me before dawn saying she hadn't come home the night before and he was worried, but I assumed they'd had a fight and she was teaching him a lesson by staying out all night. Or I figured that she'd had a little too much to drink and decided to crash at a friend's place. The idea she might be in trouble, or dead, didn't occur to me until a few hours later, when she still hadn't returned my calls and I could no longer comfort myself with the thought she was sleeping it off somewhere.

And whom had I called for help? Lauren.

She put me in touch with Gabriel, who took over the investigation. By the time Charlotte's body was found washed up on the bank of the East River, she'd been gone for several days. Although the confirmation that my sister was dead was a jolt to my system, I had already assumed as much, so the reality only ended my prayers for a miracle.

This time, however, I haven't had any prior suspicions to soften the blow.

Lauren was alive last night, and now she's dead.

"What . . . happened?" I ask.

"All I know so far is that it was two gunshots to the head. Her body was found a few blocks from her apartment, in Central Park. They put me in charge of the investigation, so I can't leave the office right now. But come down to One PP. As soon as I get free, we can talk."

Who would want to kill Lauren?

The most likely murderer is always a lover. As the old expression goes, when you hear hooves, think horses, not zebras. When you see a murdered wife, think husband, not anyone else.

"Was it Richard?"

Part of me is hoping that Gabriel will say yes and then all this will be over. The other part of me knows that if Richard *did* kill Lauren, he'd never admit it. Worse still, he'd commit the crime in a way that would never in a million years link back to him.

"Richard is here, but I haven't spoken to him yet," Gabriel says. "I just heard about this and wanted to tell you right away. I'm told, though, that he claims he had no idea Lauren wasn't sleeping beside him when the bad-news call woke him."

Another Good Samaritan, an elderly woman, stoops over me. "Can I help you, dear?"

"Thank you, but no," I whisper. "I'm fine."

A chilling thought hits me like a smack to the head.

Donald Chesterman.

Like a Pavlovian reaction to the mere thought of the man, I feel a knot form in my stomach. If he killed Lauren, I doubt he'll stop with her. It's *me* he really hated. I was the one who did the stand-up work in court.

Donald Chesterman has been invading my subconscious from time to time ever since we put him away. Thoughts of him were like a squirrel that claws its way into the attic, wreaks havoc, and quickly leaves.

I sometimes wonder whether Donald Chesterman would have had such a lasting impact on me if he hadn't been my first major case. Lauren had already seen it all by then, though, and even *she* said she'd never had a case like his. Perhaps there are some crimes so horrible that it doesn't matter how grizzled you are, you simply can't imagine that type of evil. When you're confronted with its existence, it leaves an indelible mark on your soul.

Everything about the case seemed incongruent, starting with the man at its center. Donald Chesterman was a well-respected partner in a midtown real-estate firm. He lived in a prewar, three-bedroom apartment on Riverside Drive. He sent his children to private school. His wife, Donna, had a law degree from Fordham, although she didn't practice; she spent much of her time volunteering at the assisted-living community a few blocks from their home. I must have spoken to a hundred neighbors, business colleagues, and friends. To a person, each described a mild-mannered man and a family that was out of a Norman Rockwell painting. In other words, Donald Chesterman was the very last person who you'd think was terrorizing his family.

But terrorize his family he did. Over and over again. Beatings and rape—all three of them. Donna took the brunt of it, a conclusion I reached not based on anything she said but from the abject fear in her eyes. She steadfastly refused to testify against her husband. It might have ended there, or more accurately, the trial might never have even begun, if Chesterman's son, Donald Jr., who went by his middle name of Raymond, hadn't been so courageous. He was twelve, and adamant that he needed to do something to protect his sister, Jennifer, who was eight. That's why he called the cops.

Although in most ways that mattered the father and son could not have been more different, Raymond was also a bag of contradictions. He was a strong student, nearly all As, but had difficulty making eye contact. He was always looking down at his hands, which he more often than not kept in his lap, fingers interlocked. Taller than most twelve-year-old boys, he was still a stranger to puberty at an inch shorter than me, and so skinny that I was worried he might have an eating disorder. He was unfailingly polite, with lots of "Yes, ma'ams" that you don't normally hear from city kids. Our shrink said that Raymond was suffering from one of the worst cases of PTSD he'd ever seen—and that included soldiers who'd returned from Afghanistan.

Lauren and I met with Raymond for weeks before the trial, going over the questions and answers for his direct examination as if it were a play. When it came time for him to take the stand, he was spot-on.

"First it was just touching," Raymond said when I asked him to recount his sexual contact with his father. "I don't remember when that began, because it always seemed to have been that way. I was six or seven when he began putting his penis in my mouth. Ten when he started having sex with me."

During prep, Raymond's voice often quavered. Sometimes he cried. But on the stand, he was resolute. He even held eye contact with the jury, which was no mean feat for him—and something we'd practiced for hours.

The last question and answer still ring in my ears.

"Raymond, tell us why you agreed to testify against your father."

"Because my father is also raping my mother and my little sister. Jennifer is only eight, and I need to make it stop."

I had expected his father's lawyer, Michele Sutton, to rely on the standard playbook for crossing children—come across as a sympathetic friend so that you build trust with the witness and appear like a decent person to the jury, then point out all the ways that children are prone to manipulation by prosecutors and other authority figures.

Instead, she went for the jugular with the very first question: "Isn't it a fact that *you*, and not your father, are raping your little sister?"

Raymond looked at me from the witness stand, confused. I turned to Lauren, but she shook her head no. We couldn't help him. He was on his own up there.

"No, that's not true," Raymond said. "My father did that to Jennifer. Not me."

"So you say, but Jennifer hasn't accused him of raping her. Only *you've* said that in this trial. Same thing with your mother. You say your father raped her, but *she* doesn't say that. In fact, your mother is going to testify that you're lying. Your own mother, Raymond, is going to take this stand and swear an oath to God, punishable by the crime of perjury if she lies, and say that you—you, Raymond, not your father, but *you*—raped your baby sister. And the only evidence we have that you're *not* a rapist—in fact, the only evidence we have about anything you've said here today—is your say-so. The word of a person whose own mother says he is a liar."

I objected, telling the judge that there wasn't a question being posed. Before the judge could rule, Sutton said, "Here's my question, Raymond. Are you calling your mother a liar?"

"She's really scared," Raymond said.

"Why would she be scared?" Sutton said, as if the idea of a battered woman being so frightened that she would lie to protect her abuser was the most ridiculous thing she'd ever heard. "If what you say is true—that your father is a sexual predator who abuses his own family—she should be doing everything she can to send him to jail. But she's not, is she, Raymond? No. And you're right about one thing. She *is* scared. She's scared that your father is going to go to jail and then there won't be anyone to stop you from raping Jennifer. That's what terrifies her."

When his cross-examination was over and Raymond and I were in the hallway, he broke down. As he sobbed, I told him that I blamed myself for failing to see that line of attack coming. He didn't care about what had just occurred on the stand, however. Something much worse than being accused of rape brought him to tears.

"My father is going to come home with us," he said. "Isn't he?"

Later that evening, Lauren suggested that we offer Chesterman a plea deal.

"No," I said, almost instinctively.

"It's not that close a call," Lauren replied. "We're going to lose. The wife is going to testify that she was never raped and that Raymond was never raped, but that Jennifer was. She'll say Raymond is her abuser. For us to rebut that, we have to put Jennifer on the stand. And you know as well as I do that she won't hold up under cross."

That part was true. Our shrink had told me more than once that making Jennifer Chesterman testify would be like abusing her all over again. Besides, even if I could convince myself that the ends of putting Chesterman away justified the trauma to his daughter, Lauren was right: we'd most likely still fail. Jennifer would be sufficiently eviscerated by Michele Sutton on cross to ensure that the jury wouldn't believe her.

Still, I thought that anything less than a lifetime prison term for Donald Chesterman was giving up. "Then let's go to the jury without Jennifer," I said. "I'd rather lose at trial than live with the fact that I was responsible for allowing Chesterman ever to be free again."

I remember almost verbatim what Lauren said next, because it has guided me as a prosecutor ever since.

"This job should not be in any way, shape, or form about how *you* feel, Ella. It's about your clients, the people of the state of New York. And given that this is a family situation, I'm not all that concerned about the citizenry at large. But I am deeply worried about what happens to those children. How will *they* feel if Donald Chesterman goes free? Letting him plead to anything other than the max might not seem like justice for what he's done—and believe me, I agree with you, it's not—but with any luck, he'll be locked away long enough for them to become adults and be able to stay away from him when he gets out. In that context, we're giving these children their lives. Isn't that more important than taking away Donald Chesterman's?"

Chesterman took the deal. Maximum sentence of fifteen years, although he could get out sooner with good behavior, which is apparently what happened.

Shortly after he became a long-time guest of the New York Department of Corrections, Lauren received a letter. Typed, no return address, no name even, but we both knew it was from Chesterman. He must have had someone smuggle it out of prison, because prison mail is reviewed before it goes out. It was only one line, all caps, centered in the middle of the page:

THE MOMENT I GET OUT, I'M GOING TO KILL YOU.

As a prosecutor, you get a lot of death threats. Defendants live with a level of desperation unknown to most people. They're on the verge of being branded and caged. Even though they only have themselves to blame, they often look to foist it onto someone else. Who better than the person asking the judge to impose biblical punishment?

I scan the street. There are a dozen or so people in my line of sight, most making their way to the subway. Is one of them Donald Chesterman, preparing to complete his revenge? Or a man he hired to do his bidding?

Gabriel is saying something about the investigation, but I'm only half listening. Not even half. I tell him that I'll see him shortly, and then I break the connection.

10.

DANA GOODWIN

I settle into Gabriel Velasquez's guest chair and look around his office, trying to figure out what I can about my new partner by his surroundings. The room doesn't reflect my first impressions of the man at all. It's a mess. Papers are strewn about, and the mismatched furnishings seem to have been collected from different offices. He's very polished, with his monochromatic clothing and badge affixed to a chain around his neck. And he's handsome, almost painfully so, with large brown eyes and a smile that would be hard to deny.

"Sorry I made you wait," he says. "But as you heard in there, I've been dating Ella Broden for the last six months, and she and Lauren were very close. I just called her to break the news. Ella's sister was murdered six months ago, and, well, this is a lot to absorb in and of itself, but coupled with that . . . she's taking it very hard." He looks up and catches my pained expression. "I'm sorry. This must be terrible for you too. How are you holding up?"

I smile weakly. "It doesn't feel real yet, to be honest. I'm sure Ella has told you how wonderful Lauren . . . was. I mean, everyone loved her."

"Apparently not everyone," he says solemnly.

I wonder what he sees, looking across at me. My guess is that I'm five years older than Gabriel, which makes us contemporaries, but I'd wager he thinks of me as "older." Based on his involvement with Ella, I assume he's not intimidated by a smart woman, which isn't the norm among the men in the NYPD. At the same time, I suspect he's not happy to be teamed up with an ADA in the investigative stage. From past experience, I've learned that cops like to have a free hand in sifting through the evidence. Besides, whenever you have one of these inter-departmental matchups, the issue of hierarchy inevitably arises. Does Gabriel work for *me* because I'm the one who is eventually going to have to prove guilt in court? Or do I work for *him* because investigating crime is a police function?

I decide it's never too early to curry favor with a work colleague. It's been my experience that it's easiest to do that with men by sucking up to them.

"Full disclosure," I say. "I'm not at all experienced with what happens this early in an investigation. You guys normally do your thing, and then I'm handed a suspect and told to get a conviction. So you tell me. What's the first step?"

"We talk to her husband," Gabriel says.

———

Interrogation Room Two is not a place that anyone would feel comfortable, even if it weren't used exclusively for questioning criminal suspects. It's neutral in the worst way—gray paint, a small metal table pushed up against the wall, one metal chair on each of the three exposed sides. The fluorescent lighting is harsh, and there's an overhead camera with a blinking red light.

"Richard," Gabriel says upon entering, as if they're old friends. He reaches out to shake Richard Trofino's hand, which causes Richard to rise from the metal chair to grasp it. "I'm so very sorry for your loss."

If the story we heard is correct, the uniform cops woke him with a phone call. They must have given Richard some time to change before transporting him down to One PP. He looks like he just stepped out of a *GQ* ad for business-casual attire. He's clad in gray wool slacks, a well-starched white button-down shirt, and suede Gucci loafers.

Richard nods. In barely more than a whisper, he says, "Thank you."

I would not have thought it possible for a man's appearance to change so much in so little time. Less than twenty-four hours ago, Richard had stood in my office with his usual swagger, but now he has the look Jacob sometimes wears when he's frightened.

"I'm so sorry," I add softly.

I wonder if Richard is thinking clearly enough to understand that the next few minutes will determine everything. He hasn't been Mirandized because he's here voluntarily and Miranda warnings are only given to people in police custody, but I'm certain Richard knows that the smart move is for him to remain silent.

"Can I get you anything? Coffee, water . . . something to eat maybe?" Gabriel asks, still standing.

Richard declines the offer with a shake of his head.

This is Gabriel's cue to sit, and I immediately follow suit. A beat later, so does Richard.

"Dana and I will be leading the investigation into your wife's murder," Gabriel says. "Let me state at the outset that this is going to be a no-stone-unturned situation. We've been given every available resource to track down her killer. The first step in that process, however, is you. I know you've already answered some questions. You must be exhausted, but we need to start from square one."

I wait with bated breath for Richard's response. The next thing out of his mouth will tell me exactly how he plans to play this.

His mouth starts to contort as if he's about to say something.

Then he vomits all over my lap.

11.

ELLA BRODEN

I begin to walk to One PP. I'm not certain why I don't jump into a cab. It's still below freezing, last night's cold front not having moved on yet, and my destination is more than half an hour away by foot. After a block or two, I embrace the frigid air instead of letting it cause me discomfort.

It's begun to numb my face, and I want to feel numb all over.

When I finally arrive indoors, Steve Lassiter, the officer who more often than not mans the front desk, smiles at me. "Hey, Ella. Nice to see you again. Here to see Gabriel?"

He must not have heard the news.

"Yes" is all I trust myself to say.

"Sign in, and then go right on up."

I can't go "right on up," of course. There's a metal detector that requires me to remove my coat, my shoes, and my belt, and to place my phone and handbag on the conveyor belt. Even after I do all of that, I still set off the machine. A female police officer is tasked with passing the wand over me and then gently patting me down. Only after she's satisfied that I'm not a threat does she hand me a visitor's pass and tell me to have a lovely day.

On the sixth floor, I'm greeted by Ruth, the receptionist. I tell her I'm here to see Gabriel. She's not one for small talk—or smiling, for that matter. She tells me to have a seat.

"Is he in?" I ask.

"He's in the building," Ruth says curtly.

Although I've visited Gabriel at work a few times since we started dating, it's usually a prearranged lunch meet-up, and he greets me at the elevators. This is the first time I've been relegated to the unpadded wooden chairs set out in the hallway since I was a near-daily visitor six months ago, when Charlotte went missing.

I had been determined to hold it together. But being back here, once again to hear Gabriel tell me about a loved one being murdered, is too much for me to bear. I can't believe that I'm never going to speak to Lauren again. I go back through our talks, how much I've learned from her, how much I tried to be like her. It's all too much, and I once again break out into uncontrollable sobbing.

———

When he was leading the investigation into Charlotte's disappearance, Gabriel always maintained a positive demeanor with me. No matter how dire the circumstances, he somehow made me believe that a happy ending was still possible. I knew that was part of his training, but it nevertheless buoyed me when things were at their darkest. And then, when everything finally went black and Charlotte's body was discovered, Gabriel's presence assured me that I'd again see the light.

When he approaches me this morning, however, he's wearing the same horrified look that I've been carrying around since he told me the day's sad news. I can't imagine he's truly grieving—after all, Lauren was merely a work colleague to him, and not a particularly close one at that. Rather, he's worried about how devastated I am. He knows all too well the struggle it has been for me over these last six months, the slow and steady ascent out of the abyss. I'm certain he fears precisely what I do—that Lauren's death will push me back into that bottomless hole.

I fall into his arms, and he embraces me tightly. I revel in the warmth.

Until the noxious odor pushes me back, that is.

"You smell like—"

"Puke, I know."

"What happened?"

"Richard Trofino threw up, and I got hit with some splatter, I guess."

A minute later, we're behind the closed door of Gabriel's office. The privacy could allow me to break down further, but for some reason it causes me to collect myself. I'm conscious of my own breathing, a deliberate attempt to control my runaway emotions.

Gabriel has never lost anyone close to him. He's a thirty-eight-year-old man who still has all four of his grandparents. I've never met his parents, but in photographs they look to be the picture of health. Of course he understands plenty about loss from witnessing it on a daily basis. He's a wonderful consoler—in fact, I don't know how I would have survived Charlotte's death without his support—but no one who hasn't experienced grief firsthand can fully comprehend its power to overwhelm. It's the difference between watching the destruction of a hurricane on television and taking the full brunt of the storm.

"Can I get you anything?" Gabriel asks, ever the host.

"You know what I want."

He smiles to confirm that we can, in fact, read each other's minds. At least on issues like this one.

"Not much to tell you, unfortunately. Two GSWs. We think at close range, but ballistics will confirm. Lauren's body was found at five this morning by the duck pond in Central Park, which is between Seventy-Third and Seventy-Fifth Streets, so just a few blocks from her apartment. It's not clear yet if she was murdered there or shot somewhere else and then moved." He stops. "Anything I'm missing?"

"Richard's story is that he knows nothing?"

"He was in no condition to be questioned. We tried, but like I said, he threw up before we got started. The cops who were first on the scene told me he was a total Sergeant Schultz."

I've heard the Sergeant Schultz reference before, but I can't recall its origin. I only know it means that Richard is not giving anything up.

"You need to track down Donald Chesterman," I say.

"Yeah, I already mentioned that to Dana, but I couldn't remember the guy's name."

Gabriel is writing Donald Chesterman's name, so he doesn't forget again. I'm focused on something else entirely, however.

"Dana?"

"Dana Goodwin. She's partnering with me on this."

"Really?"

"Yeah. Do you think she's not right for this?"

Dana Goodwin replaced me as Lauren's deputy. Before she got my job, I'd met Dana over the years only a handful of times—a consequence of the Manhattan DA's office having hundreds of ADAs in its ranks—because Dana spent her career in General Crimes, whereas I had been a lifer in Special Vics. But I knew her by reputation. In fact, I'd wager *every* ADA knew her that way. She was universally recognized as the best trial lawyer we had. On top of which, she was beautiful. Her large eyes and slender neck conjured the image of a Golden Age movie star.

Lauren's natural inclination had always been to reject long-term line ADAs for management roles because they had a difficult time transitioning from trying cases to acting as supervisors. "Once they've seen Paris, you just can't keep them down on the farm" was how she put it. With Dana, Lauren said she made an exception because she saw something special in her. "Something like I saw in you," she explained to me in that way parents sometimes do so you don't think they like your sibling better.

I spent some time with Dana before I left, helping her transition into the job. It didn't take me long to conclude that Lauren had made an excellent choice. Aside from being whip smart, Dana had an easygoing way about her and a sharp, cynical sense of humor that I've always found fun to be around. Of course, all of that only made me more jealous.

"It's not that. She's a great ADA. Maybe the best there is. But McKenney should have appointed a special prosecutor. Someone from outside the office."

"Why?"

"To avoid the appearance of a conflict of interest. I was special prosecutor a few years ago when some Queens ADA was gunned down. Turned out to be a mistaken-identity thing, but the Queens DA made the designation as a matter of course."

"I'm sure McKenney did it just so he can maintain some level of control over the investigation. Nothing better for him than Richard Trofino going to jail for murder, right?"

"I don't know," I say. "It doesn't sound right to me. Especially if McKenney knew that she was thinking of challenging him for DA. That makes *him* a potential suspect."

"I actually wasn't thinking about that," Gabriel says.

He looks like he's contemplating it hard when a knock on the door startles me. Gabriel calls out that whoever is on the other side should come in.

A uniformed cop sticks his head in. "Sorry to interrupt, Lou, but we got something during the search of the apartment."

It takes a second for it to register that the cop is referring to Gabriel as "Lieu," as in Lieutenant.

"I'll step out," I say.

"No," Gabriel says quickly as he follows the officer out of his office. "You stay. This'll only take a second."

Gabriel returns about a minute later. In his hand is a plastic bag. I can't see what's inside it.

"What's that?"

"We might have caught a pretty significant break. Lauren left her cell phone in the apartment."

"Her cell or her BlackBerry?"

He looks down at the bag. "It's an iPhone."

"She never used it. That's why she left it behind. She only used her BlackBerry."

He looks at me curiously, as if he can't imagine someone who wasn't glued to their iPhone. Or maybe it's because he thought BlackBerrys no longer existed.

"For ADAs, all work communications have to be done on a BlackBerry," I explain. "Phone, text, and e-mail. In fact, my BlackBerry was my only phone for quite a while. I finally bought an iPhone because I wanted to listen to music when I ran. I'm surprised Lauren even owned an iPhone, to tell you the truth. She didn't when I was her deputy. And I'm sure she rarely used it."

"And here I thought we found the Holy Grail. Her phone's passcode protected anyway. So right now, it might as well be a paperweight."

"Richard doesn't know the code?"

"I don't know. But you can bet we'll be asking him."

"I'll go double or nothing he claims he doesn't," I say. "That'll be your first indication that he's the guy. If he killed her, there's no way that he'll want you knowing what's on her phone."

12.

DANA GOODWIN

After Richard got sick all over me and Gabriel sent him home, I headed back to my office for a change of clothing. I have a spare suit and blouse stowed there from the last time I was on trial. Sometimes it makes more sense to stay in a hotel rather than to hike back to Queens at two in the morning.

The first face I see upon my return to One Hogan is Sandra Wittcamp, the most junior lawyer in the group. I'm still covered in remnants of Richard's last meal—at least what I couldn't wash off in the One PP restroom—but she doesn't seem to notice.

"I was looking for Lauren," she says. "Any idea where she is?"

It occurs to me that I never discussed with Drake McKenney how to break the news to the members of Special Vics. I can't get too far out in front of the boss on something like that, so I obfuscate.

"Is there something I can help you with?"

"Maybe . . . It's about the Gutierrez case."

The name means nothing to me. "What's the issue?"

"It's a domestic," she says, trying to sound casual with the lingo even though I can tell she's uncertain whether she's using it properly. "The vic was pretty badly beat up. Broken nose. Anyway, now she says she fell. Doesn't want to press charges."

This is the most common obstacle in sex-crime prosecutions. We could easily bring in ten times as many cases if it weren't for recalcitrant—or, more accurately, *petrified*—wives and girlfriends.

"Did you explain to her that it's not going to get any better if she does nothing?"

This is what the newbies are taught during orientation. When the victim wants to forget the whole thing, you play the role of understanding friend, advise her to pursue the matter and remind her it's going to be more of the same until she does.

Virtually no victim ever changes her mind. That's when it gets tough. The DA's office doesn't *need* the victim's cooperation to prosecute, but it's often a matter of resource allocation. Why knock ourselves out to protect someone who won't accept our help, especially when the case is likely unwinnable if the victim is going to deny under oath that any crime occurred?

"Yeah, but she's insisting she fell," Sandra says.

"Right. Did you talk to the husband?"

"The wife?"

"No, I know you talked to the wife. Did you talk to her husband?"

"There is no husband," Sandra says, trying to maintain a straight face. She knows she set me up and is now trying to show she's enlightened.

"Two women?"

"Yeah," Sandra says with the hint of a smile.

This is actually a first for me, but I'm not going to share that with Sandra. Better that she think I've seen it all.

"Did you speak to the battering wife?"

"Not yet. I didn't know what to say."

"First complaint?"

Sandra nods.

"Any chance that the injuries *were* actually the result of a fall?"

"No. The vic was pretty clear with the cops on the scene that she'd been hit."

"Any weapon?"

"The cops didn't think so. Punches. Maybe some kicks too."

I conclude that this case isn't going to be prosecuted. It'll likely take at least two more beatings before the victim is ready to go that route. And she may never get there.

"Here's what I'd do. Bring them both in. Have a uniform with you. Meet with the vic first. Go over the options with her. If she sticks to the slip-and-fall story, tell her that it's your experience that it's not going to stop and it's likely going to get worse. Then, when she won't change her mind, tell her that if it happens again, she should call you right away. Make sure you give her your card, and tell her to keep it somewhere safe. Her wallet. Inside her phone case. Someplace she has ready access to it in case she needs it, and where her wife won't find it. Then I'd meet with the perp. Just you and her. No cops. You emphasize to her that she should consider this a gift from God, and that she should pray that her wife doesn't 'fall' again, or 'walk into a door,' or have someone mistakenly 'drop' something on her head. Because if you hear that anything like that has happened, you're going to make sure that it's a jail situation—even if her wife doesn't want to press charges."

Sandra nods as I go through this explanation. "Okay. That sounds good," she says. "Thanks, Dana."

"You're welcome. One last thing."

Sandra looks at me with wide eyes, no doubt expecting me to impart some additional pearl of hard-earned wisdom.

"After you send them home, say a prayer that they don't end up killing each other."

———

Back in my office, I shut the door and change into my spare clothing. Then I call the District Attorney.

McKenney's assistant says that her boss is behind closed doors and left instructions not to be disturbed. I tell her that it's important I speak with him as soon as possible because I need to alert the people in the bureau before the news hits.

"What news?" she asks.

"Just give him the message, please," I say.

I don't get a return phone call. Instead, Drake McKenney shows up at my office twenty minutes later.

Even though I've worked for the man for fifteen years, this is only the second time I've been in a room with the District Attorney. The first time was this morning.

"Terrible news today," he says. "Lauren was . . . quite simply, what we all aspire to be as prosecutors."

I get the feeling he's workshopping this turn of phrase for when he has to deliver a more public eulogy. I know that Lauren wasn't as big a fan of Drake McKenney as he's now professing to have been of hers.

"Yes. Just terrible." I pause in case he wishes to express more of his sadness, but he doesn't say another word. "The reason I called you is because one of the lawyers in the group just asked me where Lauren was, and I realized that we need to make some statement before the news becomes public."

"That's why I'm here," McKenney says. "Bring everyone into a conference room, and I'll address the troops."

———

We don't actually have a room big enough for addressing the troops. The largest space on the floor is used for document review, but it has a long conference table that seats thirty. The entire Special Vics Bureau numbers more than a hundred, so it's a standing-room-only situation, with many outside the doorway, in the hall.

Some in the room wear nervous looks, but I'm certain no one knows why the entire bureau has been assembled. This type of all-hands meeting has never happened in my tenure, but that's been all of nine months. My guess is that most of the ADAs think they're about to hear something about layoffs or a salary freeze.

"Thank you all for coming on such short notice," McKenney begins. He doesn't see the need to identify himself, even though I'd be shocked if anyone present has ever formally been introduced to him. Then again, everyone knows who he is. "I'm going to be brief. I'm here today to share with you some very tragic news. Lauren Wright was found murdered this morning. News of her death will be released to the media shortly. As you know, I often talk about this office as a family. Like a family, we share each other's triumphs. And like a family, we pull together when we suffer a tragedy. Today is the saddest day of my tenure as District Attorney. The one small measure of comfort I take from Lauren's murder is knowing that we will work together and not rest until we bring the responsible person or persons to justice."

McKenney looks over to me. I'm not sure if it's because he wants me to say something. It would be highly uncharacteristic for him to share the stage, so I stay silent.

"I know that the last thing on any of your minds at a moment like this is work," McKenney continues, "but it is vitally important that we continue our mission of speaking up for victims. Now more than ever, we have to live up to the standard that Lauren Wright set for all of us. The best thing you can do to honor her memory is to go back to work and do your job in a way that would make Lauren proud. Dana Goodwin will serve as acting chief. Any questions, please direct them to her. We'll be holding a memorial service for Lauren in the coming weeks." He surveys the room. "Okay. That's it. Thank you, everyone."

The population of the Special Victims Bureau scuffles out. After the room clears, I approach McKenney.

"I think that went very well," he says.

"Yes," I say, because everyone knows Drake McKenney likes to be complimented.

"Dana, one of things that has always impressed me about you is that you're a straight shooter. So let me return the favor for a moment and give it to you straight. What I said in there, I meant every word of it. One of our own has been killed, and we need to do everything we can, not only to bring Lauren's murderer to justice, but to keep doing our jobs. The sad reality, however, is that there are going to be others who will use this tragedy for their own political ends. I gather you know that I'm thinking about challenging Lubins next time around. I have no doubt that our fearless mayor is going to use Lauren's murder to score some political points. Which means that the longer the case goes unsolved, the better it is for him and the worse it is for me. That's why I need someone loyal to this office on top of this investigation. To make sure we get the guy who did this, even if he's one of hizzoner's asshole buddies. And if all that happens, you will have my eternal gratitude."

"I understand," I say.

And I do. He doesn't want someone loyal to the District Attorney's office. He wants someone loyal to *him*. And he thinks that's me. The quid pro quo he's offering is that if I do his bidding on this, I can remove the "Acting" from my new title and become Chief of the Special Victims Bureau.

In the last twenty-four hours, I've gone from the near certainty of being unemployed to being promoted to one of the most powerful legal positions in New York City—at least in an *acting* capacity.

All I have to do to make it final is to ensure that Richard Trofino is arrested for his wife's murder.

13.

ELLA BRODEN

Most federal cases in Manhattan are litigated in the Daniel Patrick Moynihan Courthouse. Completed in the mid-1990s, the building is twenty-seven stories of marble. It's the second-biggest courthouse in the country—surpassed only by one in Missouri, of all places.

When I was an ADA, I rarely set foot in federal court. My beat was the New York State criminal court, which is located down the street. On rare occasions, I'd be hauled in by some federal judge on a jurisdictional argument, and I'd always feel like Little Orphan Annie when she first walked through the door of Daddy Warbucks's mansion. I couldn't believe that anyone could practice law in such luxury. The federal courtrooms are enormous, with thirty-foot ceilings and furnishings that could be in the lobby of a five-star hotel—inlaid, solid cherry tables and high-back leather chairs.

My speculation about Donald Chesterman taking his revenge on Lauren was enough for Gabriel to insist that I have a police escort to the courthouse. But upon our arrival, I tell Officer Santiago that I'll be safe inside without him. I point out the fact that the court has its own police force, not to mention that everyone goes through a metal detector to gain entry.

The gallery is full when I enter Judge Paulson's courtroom, which means that there are more than a hundred spectators—ten times as many as are present during most court proceedings. I take a position along the back wall. There, I spy several reporters and at least two sketch artists doing their thing.

My father is at the lectern, his back to me, but his booming baritone fills the cavernous space. He makes point after point about how the prosecution's approach should be disallowed, that Nicolai Garkov is entitled to the same due-process rights as anyone else, which include the right to be tried *only* on the charges set forth in the indictment, the right to confront his accusers, and the right *not* to have the jury unfairly prejudiced by innuendo about other crimes for which he does not stand accused.

Twenty minutes later, Judge Paulson says that he disagrees. And, of course, his opinion is the only one that counts.

I catch my father's eye as he's heading out of the courtroom.

"Ella," he says, stopping to embrace me.

For a man who just lost a major motion, he doesn't look the least bit upset. I know it's not because he doesn't want to win—in fact, I've never known anyone more competitive than my father. Even when Charlotte and I were little, he never let us win at anything, no matter what the contest. In court, he has an especially vicious kill-or-be-killed mentality.

But one of his great strengths, I think, is that he's able to let go of a loss. It's something that eluded me in my own professional life. I wore my defeats on my sleeve, no matter how trivial.

"This is a pleasant surprise," he says. "I thought we were meeting at my office." He grins. "Did you come all the way down here just to tell me that you told me so?"

I want to tell him that Lauren's death is the reason for our change of plan, but this is not the time or the place for such a heavy discussion. So I force a smile and act as if nothing is amiss.

"I had to visit Gabriel for something, so I was just down the street anyway. I thought I'd watch the motion before lunch. But, just so you know . . . I told you so."

My father explains that he had made a reservation for us to have lunch at Cipriani, which is among the priciest restaurants in midtown. But because we're already downtown, he suggests that we go to Cipriani's downtown location, which is also among the priciest restaurants in the neighborhood. It's about a ten-minute walk from the courthouse, but my father keeps a car and driver waiting, so we're chauffeured there.

The hostess frowns when my father tells her that we're there without a reservation. Looking past her, I can see why. There's not a single empty table.

"Tell Ricardo that Clint Broden is here, and I've brought my daughter."

The hostess turns to do as requested. She returns a few minutes later with a man by her side. He's about my father's age, with silver hair and a regal bearing.

"Welcome, Mr. Broden," the man says. "Please follow me to your table."

I assume the man leading us through the restaurant is not the aforementioned Ricardo, because my father doesn't address him by name. Whoever he is, he finds a spot for us in the center of the restaurant at a table that I would swear wasn't empty a moment ago.

As soon as we're seated, a waiter comes over and hands us each a flute of champagne. "Compliments of Ricardo," he says.

"Who's Ricardo?" I ask after the waiter leaves.

"A man who knows how to repay a favor," my father says.

My father hasn't detected that anything's off with me, but he's never been particularly attuned to my moods. He has also been cut off from the outside world for the last hour or so. One of the post-9/11 rules is that you can't bring any electronic devices inside the federal courthouse, which means he doesn't know yet that Lauren Wright has been murdered.

I've been looking for an opportunity to break the news to him, but our initial conversation is dominated by how Judge Paulson's decision is going to change his trial strategy regarding the Garkov case. When he takes a moment to peruse the menu, I seize the opportunity.

"I have something to tell you."

My father lifts his eyes away from the page to look at me with concern. "Everything okay?"

"No. No, it's not. I heard this morning that my former boss, Lauren Wright, was murdered."

He grimaces as if to convey that he disagrees with *anyone* being murdered. "I'm so sorry, Ella," he says in the tone I'd use if he told me that his barber died. Someone you've known for a long time, but with whom you share no real intimacy. I can't blame him for not knowing how important Lauren was to me. Through the years I've probably downplayed it, fearful that he might take personally my efforts to find a surrogate for my mother.

"Lauren and I were very close. She wasn't just a boss to me but . . . well, much more than that. A really good friend and a mentor. I saw her just last night. Gabriel and I had dinner with her and her husband."

My father doesn't say anything; even though he is more facile with language than anyone I've ever met, heartfelt discussions with his daughter have never been his forte. Still, I know that he, more than anyone else, knows this pain. He does his best to always wear a smile in my presence and to allow me to lean on him with my grief—without burdening me with his own sorrow—but I'm well aware he hasn't recovered from Charlotte's murder either.

"I feel . . . I feel like I'm cursed," I say.

My father is shaking his head in disagreement. "No, of course you're not. It's not you. These things happen sometimes."

"Do they? I mean, Charlotte is murdered and now Lauren? Within six months of each other? Do 'these things' really just happen?"

My tone is sharp, like I'm trying to pick a fight. It's misdirected, of course. I'm not mad at my father. My beef's with God, or the universe, or maybe life in general.

"I think you know the answer to that," my father says soothingly. "Because it *has* happened."

"That's not very comforting."

"Don't I know it," he says.

He's fighting back tears now, a losing battle he acknowledges by rubbing his eyes. After a deep breath, he says, "But there's another thing I know too, Ella. And this I know with more certainty than anything I've ever known." He reaches over and puts his hand on top of mine, offering a gentle squeeze. "And that is that you are most certainly *not* cursed. You have years and years of joy out there, waiting for you. Trust me on this."

I know my father means well, but I can't see his optimism about my future prospects as anything more than wishful thinking.

14.

DANA GOODWIN

I spend the rest of my workday reviewing Lauren's current docket. It was full of rapists, child abusers, and general sadists. At Gabriel's request, I also reach back into the archive to pull out Donald Chesterman's file. That guy was a seriously sick puppy, although perhaps not any more so than the others. The bigger issue for me is that if I'm going to have to consider everyone Lauren prosecuted who's now out of jail as a potential suspect, I'll easily have to review a thousand more case files.

I think back on my promise to Stuart of only yesterday to keep saner hours. Yet another way I'm going to fail him. Investigating Lauren's murder means I'll be logging long hours for the foreseeable future.

It's after eleven when I finally arrive home. Stuart has been waiting up for me. The moment I enter our house, he jumps from the couch and gives me a long hug.

"I'm so sorry," he says into my ear.

"I . . . just can't believe it, you know?"

I called Stuart earlier to break the news of Lauren's murder. I told him I was too emotional to discuss it over the phone and that I'd been put in charge of the investigation, which meant that I'd likely be home late. That was my passive-aggressive way of telling him not to wait up so that I could avoid discussing Lauren's murder with him when I got home. He obviously didn't get that message.

He leads me over to the sofa, where we sit side by side. Stuart's holding my hand, caressing my thumb with his. "I know it's early, but do you have any idea who did it?"

"Just the usual knee-jerk reactions. Her husband is a person of interest. And Drake McKenney is praying that's how it turns out. Indicting Richard allows him to kill two birds with one stone: he ties the mayor to a wife murderer *and* cuts off hizzoner's chief funding source. He probably figures it'll make the mayor easy pickings when he throws his hat into the ring."

"Do you really think it could be Richard?"

Politics has never interested Stuart. As a result, I know he couldn't care less about Drake McKenney's mayoral aspirations. The thought of uxoricide, however, visibly troubles him.

"He's the statistical best bet," I say, which isn't actually a response to Stuart's question.

"They seemed so happy together," he says.

"I don't know" is all I can think to say in response.

That's not true. I do know, for a fact, that Lauren's marriage to Richard was not as advertised. Another thing I know is that being the boss of the New York City construction world puts Richard in close proximity to many men who freelance in the criminal world.

"I'm reviewing about a million old case files on the alternative theory that it's some creep she prosecuted," I add. "Gabriel told me about this guy—"

"Who's Gabriel?"

His interruption is a reminder of just how little I've shared with Stuart. "Oh, sorry. He's the cop I'm partnered with on the investigation. Gabriel Velasquez. And get this: he's dating Ella Broden."

"*That* Ella Broden?"

"I know, right? They met when Ella's sister went missing. It's all much too incestuous for my liking. On the plus side, he does seem like a decent guy, and the police brass love him. Anyway, he told me that Ella worked with Lauren on some case like a million years ago and the guy just got out after a long stretch. Apparently he had made some threats against Lauren. Long story short, in addition to Richard, our suspect list includes the current crop of psychopaths we're prosecuting—and *everyone else* Lauren had a hand in sending to jail over the last *twenty years*. So about a thousand people, give or take."

"Is that your way of telling me that you're going to be working late for a while?" he says with a smile.

I smile back. "It's my way of telling you that I'm not happy about it."

He smiles, pleased with my answer. I don't think he minds my burning the midnight oil at the office so long as he thinks that I don't like being away from him.

"Enough murder talk. How's Jacob today?" I say.

"Good. He's been asleep for about two hours."

Even though he's asleep, simply being in his company will be a godsend for me.

"I'm going to check in on him," I say.

When I enter his bedroom, Jacob is snuggled under his blankets. Sometimes he likes to put the top sheet over his head to completely insulate himself from his surroundings. Tonight he's hiked it up to only a few inches above his shoulders. His long, soft curls flow down his cheeks. His breathing is shallow, his eyes shut. I try to imagine what he might be dreaming.

Jacob's in the throes of a superhero phase. His bedroom resembles what I would imagine a conference room would look like in the Justice League. A fathead Batman is on one wall, staring down Superman on the other. His linens depict Ironman, and his pajamas tonight are Spiderman's costume.

I never thought I'd have a child. In large measure, that was because I never thought I'd marry. I can't imagine what my sixteen-year-old self would think if she could see me now. In fact, I'm sure that my thirty-year-old self would be disappointed too. But I'm certain that every iteration of me would love Jacob with the same type of reckless abandon that I do.

I kick my shoes off and lie next to my son. I take in the floral scent of his hair and feel the curly wisps against my own cheek.

My presence causes him to stir, and he softly says, "Mama."

"Shh," I whisper into his ear. "Stay asleep, my sweet boy."

I want to stay like this forever, to hold on to the person I love most in this world. I know hoping that my five-year-old can protect me is as misguided as his faith that Superman would come to his rescue if monsters appeared from under his bed. But I shake away rationality and wrap myself in the security of his Ironman top sheet.

15.

ELLA BRODEN

Since my return to the apartment after lunch with my father, I haven't left the piano bench. At first I wasn't very productive, just playing with a few melodies and every once in a while going through the chorus of "Never Goodbye." But after a few hours, I came upon an arrangement of chords I liked, and then I started adding some lyrics.

Gabriel opens the door moments after I've done a run-through of what I have so far. I'm certain the timing is not coincidental. He was undoubtedly lingering in the stairwell, not wanting to interrupt me because he knows I'd stop playing as soon as he entered.

Recently, he told me that this is the closest he's ever come to living with someone, the four nights or so a week that we cohabitate. He also shared that he's already broken his personal record for relationship length. I knew better than to ask him his *number*, assuming that he'd lie, or worse, tell me the truth—which must be that he's either in or approaching the three-figure range. I wonder if these are things that should give me pause about considering a lifetime of monogamy with him. There are certainly aspects to Gabriel that read as if he's untamable. Nonetheless, whenever we're together, I don't sense longing on his part to be anywhere else.

We kiss on the lips.

"New song?" he asks.

"Just something I'm playing with."

"I like it."

"Yeah . . . I don't know."

He waits for me to explain, to elaborate about the song's meaning perhaps, but I don't intend to divulge more. In the song, the narrator is not sure whether love can save her. My lyrics are not so opaque, and he surely heard enough to realize that the narrator is me.

Still, he's not one to press. Especially not tonight, after I've lost a loved one.

"How are you holding up?"

"Barely," I say. "Maybe not even that well. I saw my father after you. He lost the Garkov motion *in limine*."

"The what?"

"The motion about whether the prosecution can introduce the Red Square evidence. I told him he'd lose it, and he did. Afterward, we went to Cipriani."

I'm reasonably certain that Gabriel has never heard of Cipriani. If he has, I'm even more sure he's not impressed.

"Did you tell him about Lauren?"

"Yeah. He gets it. I mean, as much as anyone can. He's the only person who really understands what I went through in losing Charlotte. Still, I don't think he can fully grasp what it's like to lose a second person so soon after, but . . . it's hard to hold that against him."

A sad smile comes to Gabriel's lips. "I hope you don't hold it against *me* that I don't have the first clue as to how awful this really is for you."

"You know. You know because you know me."

"Thanks for thinking that. I just wish . . . I don't know, that I could be of more help, I guess."

I can't imagine a partner being more there for me than Gabriel has been these past six months. Of all the things in my world that I question, that I'm lucky to have him is not one of them.

"The only way you could possibly be more support is if you told me you found Donald Chesterman and he was holding the gun he used to kill Lauren."

"No such luck, I'm afraid."

"What do you have so far?"

"Unfortunately, not a whole helluva lot. We're checking the surveillance footage around their apartment and on the way to the park. There are no cameras in the park, so that's a dead end. We're also going to do a deep dive into Lauren's finances, e-mails, that kind of thing."

"Good luck with that," I say. "You know when Richard Trofino buries a body, it stays buried."

"I know. The odds of finding anything linking him to the murder are not good. She was dead for hours before the police got to him. More than enough time for him to rid himself of gunshot residue and ditch the murder weapon."

"You have a time of death?" I ask, noting that it's new information to me that hours elapsed between Lauren's murder and the police telling Richard she was dead.

"Yeah, one twenty-seven a.m."

"Well, that's rather precise."

"Shot Spotter doesn't lie."

I'm less than a year removed from the DA's office, but technology moves on. I have no idea what "Shot Spotter" is. Slightly embarrassed, I ask.

"It's this new pilot program. A technology, really. Little microphones are placed throughout the city. The way it works is that these microphones have sensors that somehow ignore ambient noise, but when there's a loud boom—like a gunshot—the information is immediately transmitted to the Shot Spotter manufacturer in California. They review it . . . I don't know what kind of review they do, but their algorithms have some way of determining that it's a gunshot, not a car backfire or whatever, and triangulate the location. There's also a time stamp. It's like DNA—infallible."

"And what does this infallible technology say?"

"That Lauren was shot at one twenty-seven a.m., right where her body was found."

"Wow. A brave new world of law enforcement."

"New toys, same crimes. Just because we know the *when* doesn't put us that much closer to the *who* or even the *why*. It could be that someone lured her out to her death, or it could be a random crime. Maybe she couldn't sleep, went for a walk, and it's a wrong place wrong time kind of thing."

I nod, but Gabriel knows as well as I do that there's no way the head of Special Vics was gunned down in a random act of violence. This crime was about someone wanting to murder Lauren Wright.

"Oh, and the murder weapon is a Glock 19," he says.

"So, a cop gun."

In New York City, cops are given a choice of three service weapons. The vast majority of police, including Gabriel, go with the Glock 19. The primary reason is that it's the cheapest, and cops have to pay for them out of their own funds. It's also the smallest, which appeals to the women on the force, but also to many of the men, because most cops carry their weapons when they're off duty, and the Glock 19 is most easily concealed.

"Yeah, but I'm not aware of any cop having an issue with Lauren. I think it points to Richard."

He's saying that Lauren got the gun from a friendly cop, and Richard used it to kill her.

"I don't think so. Lauren was always very by the book," I say.

"I've known plenty of ADAs who wouldn't jaywalk and still asked me for a piece, just so they could sleep well at night without going through the rigmarole of getting a permit. In Lauren's case, it might not just have been to expedite the process. Maybe there's something in

Richard's background that would have denied them a permit. Or, more likely, he balked at providing years of his tax returns."

Even though the media is full of stories about how anyone can get a firearm with virtually no effort, in New York City it's a time-consuming process, and does actually include disclosure of financial records, including years of tax returns. Gabriel's theory makes a lot of sense. I'm certain Richard Trofino would never let anyone see his tax returns.

It's only been a little more than twelve hours since Lauren's body was discovered, but the first twenty-four hours are critical in any investigation. If the first day doesn't point in the definite direction of a suspect, the odds of ultimately apprehending the killer become exponentially greater.

Which is why I'm hoping with all my might that Lauren procured a cop gun and then her husband used it to murder her. At least that way, there's *some* evidence pointing to the person who killed her.

PART TWO

16.

ELLA BRODEN

Lauren Wright is laid to rest on a sunny, bitterly cold Monday morning. The cemetery is on Long Island, more than an hour outside of Manhattan. The grounds are expansive, tombstones as far as the eye can see. It snowed the night before. Nothing major, just enough to dust the landscape white.

Gabriel is wearing his dress blues. I've never seen him in uniform, and if it weren't for the circumstances, I would have commented that I'd like to see him dressed like that more often. As good as he looks, I can tell he's uncomfortable. He's tugging at the collar like it's choking him.

Among the four hundred or so mourners, a sizable percentage are cops. They form a veritable sea of blue. Henry Lucian, Gabriel's captain, is near the front of the chapel. Gabriel tells me that the shorter man with the mustache standing beside Lucian is Chief of Detectives John Calimano, his boss's boss. I recognize from television the African American man who completes the triumvirate—Calhoun Johnson, the New York City Police Commissioner.

Directly across the room, similar higher-ups from the District Attorney's office congregate. Drake McKenney centers their group. He's studying what appear to be index cards. His deputy Larry Kassak goes on tiptoe to whisper something in McKenney's ear, while Dana Goodwin looks on as if she's bored.

I know it's a petty thought, but I'm hoping that Dana doesn't deliver a eulogy. I'll understand if Richard asked McKenney to say something. He's a public figure, after all. But I'll feel aggrieved if Dana, rather than I, was tasked with extolling Lauren's virtues as a boss and a mentor.

I strain my neck looking around for Richard the way you rubberneck to see a car accident on the shoulder of the road. I don't see him anywhere. Then I remember that at Charlotte's funeral, my father and I waited in a side room until right before the service began. No doubt that's where Richard is holing up now.

A few moments later, Lauren's body is wheeled into the well of the chapel. The casket is closed—I suspect because her wounds were too gruesome for the mortician to make her presentable. That's probably also the reason there was no prior public viewing either. Richard walks beside her coffin, a minister across the box from him, a Mutt-and-Jeff juxtaposition. The minister, white haired and bespectacled, has a tall and thin elegance about him; the widower's head doesn't rise much above the casket. He's looking just as Richard Trofino usually does—like he's itching for a fight.

When they reach the front of the chapel, Richard finds his seat in the first row. The minister takes the three steps up onto the stage and situates himself behind the lectern.

I didn't know Lauren to be a religious person. In fact, I would have been surprised if she attended church at all. Still, I think she would have liked this setting, with its formality. Charlotte's funeral was much more of a bohemian affair, befitting her life. Lauren was a public servant in a relatively high office, so the pomp strikes me as appropriate.

The service begins with the minister welcoming everyone. I'm not looking at him, though. My eyes are fixed on the coffin. I can't help but wonder what Lauren is wearing, imagining her the way she looked in court in one of her smart blue suits. Of course, it's far more likely that Richard selected an outfit for her to wear for all eternity that was more in keeping with his wife's life outside the office.

I lose myself in more macabre thoughts. How much her body has already decayed. Whether it's cold to the touch like a piece of defrosting meat.

I don't focus again until I see Drake McKenney walking up to the stage. Once he's in place, he removes from his breast pocket the same three-by-five index cards I saw him fingering earlier and lays them down on the lectern.

"One of the great honors in being the District Attorney for New York County is that you meet the finest lawyers in this city," he begins. "That, by definition, means you meet the finest lawyers in this country. And among this elite group, the best of the best, Lauren Wright stood out. It was not only her intellect, which was second to none. Nor her judgment, which I relied on time after time. It was her *compassion* that made her so special. Above all else, Lauren Wright was a woman who dedicated her life to speaking for the weakest members of our society—abused women, children, the elderly—those who, in our office, are called special victims."

McKenney goes on like this for five minutes. It's a good speech, but it's still a speech rather than thoughtful remembrances of a friend.

After McKenney, Lauren's sister, Leslie, speaks very briefly. Less than a minute. She's obviously not accustomed to addressing a crowd. I met Leslie once when she visited Lauren at the office, maybe a year into my deputyship. I don't recall at the time noting how much Lauren resembled her sister, but it's eerie—both of them possessing a striking contrast of soft smiles and intense eyes framed by a curtain of reddish-blonde curls.

Richard's eulogy is the last. The stories he tells describe a happy marriage, much closer to what I always imagined Lauren's home life to be than what I observed firsthand at dinner the night she was killed. Or what I've imagined since, as I've become more and more certain that he murdered his wife.

"Lauren and I communicated on a level that was all our own," he says at one point. "I remember once, fairly recently, in fact, we were at a friend's house playing a game called Apples to Apples. I don't know if you're familiar with it, but it's a card game. The way it works is that a leader for each round pulls a card that's descriptive. For example, it might say 'awe-inspiring.' Everyone then plays a card from their hand that they think the leader will select as best matching that description. For 'awe-inspiring,' someone might play a card that says 'Sistine Chapel.' Another player might throw down a card that says 'Michael Phelps.' And someone else might play a card they think is funny, like 'my pants.' The leader selects the one that appeals most. So there's no correct answer. The point of the game is to play the card you think the leader will choose. If your card is chosen, you get a point.

"Anyway, on this particular round, Lauren was the leader. The descriptor word was *selfish*. We all throw in our cards, and I announce that I'm definitely going to win. Our fellow players dispute this, thinking that they've played the card Lauren will select. The first card that Lauren turns over says 'my daughter,' and Lauren chuckles. The next one says 'Kim Kardashian,' and this time everyone laughs. The third card reads 'millennials,' and there are nods of approval. When she turns over the last card, Lauren breaks out laughing. Not a little guffaw either, but like she's never seen anything so funny in her entire life. She can't even read the card, she's laughing so hard.

"One of the other players reads it for her. 'Lobster,' he says. He looks completely confused. Then he says, 'I'm sorry, I don't get it. The clue was *selfish*, right?' The others also seemingly don't understand. But Lauren finally stops laughing long enough to say, 'That was Richard's! I know it was Richard's!' Then another of our friends says something like, 'Does someone want to let the rest of us in on the joke?' And that's when Lauren yelled out, 'Don't you get it? Lobsters are *shellfish*.'

"My point in sharing this story is that I knew without a shadow of a doubt that Lauren would get the pun instantly, and she'd know just as quickly that I was the only one who would have played that card. That's the kind of connection we had."

Richard smiles at the memory, looking a bit too happy to be there.

———

The graveside ceremony vividly reminds me of the day we laid Charlotte to rest. The coffin balancing on the bands over the grave, the ritualistic lowering of it into the ground, the tossing of fresh dirt on top of the casket until the wooden box vanishes.

I'm crying with the first shovelful. I don't know if I would have reacted the same way if it hadn't been for Charlotte, but I think that about a lot of things—maybe everything—in the aftermath of my sister's murder. I'm not the same person now as I was before. Gabriel pulls me to him, and I muffle my sobs against his chest.

The minister concludes the service by saying that he took considerable time to select an appropriate final passage. He then announces that he will read from 1 Corinthians:

> And when this which is corruptible
> Clothes itself with incorruptibility
> and this which is mortal
> clothes itself with immortality,
> then the word that is written shall come about:
> "Death is swallowed up in victory.
> Where, O death, is your victory?
> Where, O death, is your sting?"
> The sting of death is sin, and the power of sin is
>   the law.

As we're making our way back to the parking lot, while I'm still thinking through the meaning of the closing phrase—*the power of sin is the law*—Dana Goodwin catches up to us. Beside her is a man who I presume to be her husband, based on the fact that he's holding her hand.

We all stop near the funeral office, where the earlier service occurred.

"This is my husband, Stuart," Dana says. "Stuart, meet Gabriel Velasquez and Ella Broden."

"The famous Ella Broden," Stuart replies.

Amid the sea of cops and Richard Trofino's construction cronies, Stuart's less-masculine variation of the male species stands out like a sore thumb. He has a slight build and a fair complexion bordering on pasty: the kind of guy who would play an accountant in the movies. Then again, looks can so often be deceiving in such matters. Gabriel could probably kill Stuart with his bare hands without breaking a sweat, but I also assume that Gabriel's a more nurturing partner solely because I've never met any man who is Gabriel's equal in that regard.

"I talk about you too much, apparently," Dana says. "But it's not my fault. Lauren went on about you all the time." Dana offers a shallow laugh. "Sometimes it made me mad."

I smile at her attempt at humor. I'm certain Dana never felt the least bit threatened by me. She exudes pure confidence.

Her phone rings, but she doesn't move to answer it. It takes Stuart saying, "I think that's your purse ringing, honey."

She startles. "I'm sorry. I didn't realize it was me. I lost my phone and I haven't had the chance to program my old ringtone into the new one yet, so I still don't recognize the ring."

After she answers, she tells Gabriel that it's the office. We all wait as she says "uh-huh" a few times. Then, "This is good work. Check to see if there's any connection between Detective Papamichael and Lauren. Maybe they worked on a case or something."

As she's putting the phone back in the purse, Dana looks about, most likely to make sure that no one can hear what she's about to impart. Apparently, she views spouses as within the investigation umbrella because she says, "That was O'Dell. They found the gun. In the sewer a block away from Lauren's home. It was registered to a Detective Gregory Papamichael—and he died two years ago."

"Papamichael . . ." says Gabriel. "I remember him. Over at the one-six, I think. Does the name mean anything to either of you?" He looks between Dana and me. "Any connection to Lauren?"

"I've heard the name before," I say. "An old-timer. But I don't remember if he ever worked any of my cases or had any overlap with Lauren."

Dana's brow is furrowed. "You know, I think Lauren did mention him. It's an odd name and it kind of sticks. I'm trying to remember the context, but I'm pretty sure his name came up between us."

"If Lauren knew him, that shines a pretty bright light on Richard," Gabriel says.

Stuart's eyes move back and forth like he's a spectator at a tennis match. I've always thought that prosecutors and cops have a rhythm to their thinking and a specialized jargon that make it difficult for an outsider to fully grasp. I've had more than one past boyfriend ask me to translate discussions like the one we're having now.

"I can't say that I cared very much for McKenney's eulogy," I say. "Especially given that Lauren was thinking about running against him."

This disclosure apparently takes Dana by surprise. "Really?" she says. "She didn't mention that to me."

There's a bit of a proprietary air about the comment. As if Dana is insulted that I was the first to hear. Apparently the sibling rivalry cuts both ways.

"It was very preliminary," I say.

"When did she tell you this?" Dana asks, apparently still trying to get her arms around the fact that I knew something about her boss that she didn't.

"We had dinner the other night. She mentioned it then."

She looks over at Gabriel, her ire now directed at him for not sharing this information as part of the investigation. It then clicks for me why she's so upset: she realizes that Lauren was going to make me bureau chief if she won.

Gabriel says, "I'm sorry I didn't say anything. I wanted to wait until a little more evidence was developed. Quite frankly, I wasn't quite sure how you'd react to your boss being a suspect."

She smiles as if he's making a joke. "You're serious? You think Drake McKenney committed *murder* to avoid a primary challenge?"

"I don't know," Gabriel says, "but the one thing I *do* know is that everyone always says Drake McKenney would kill to keep his job."

17.

DANA GOODWIN

After the funeral, I head back to Hogan Place. Stuart goes home to relieve Livie at the usual time. Before saying our goodbyes, Gabriel and I agree to connect later in the day to compare notes.

Lauren's decision to run for DA against McKenney has me confused. Not Gabriel's suggestion that it makes McKenney a suspect, but the idea that Lauren actually was going to run for DA. And, of course, that she didn't tell me. Win or lose, that meant that she was going to leave Special Vics. That's what her dinner with Ella Broden was about. She apparently wasn't thinking of firing me after all.

At six, Gabriel calls. He tells me that a team of cops has already been through all the surveillance footage available. It's a goose egg. Even though every building along Park, Madison, and Fifth Avenues has security cameras, each one only films its own entryway. Anyone walking down the side streets goes undetected.

"The cameras don't even pick up Lauren. Aside from when she leaves her building at around ten after one, she's not seen again. And the worse news is that Richard Trofino *never* appears."

"He could have left through another exit," I say. "One without a camera."

"I know," he says, then sighs. "With that bit of positive news, I'm going to call it a day. Let's meet first thing tomorrow and strategize for a bit about how to approach Trofino."

"Sounds like a plan."

———

I've now lived in New York City for nineteen years, the longest stretch I've spent in one place. For the first eighteen years of my life, I called suburban Virginia, right outside of DC, my home. It was a nice enough place to grow up, but boring as hell. For reasons that I still don't understand, I chose to go to college and law school in similarly low-key environments, which meant that by the time I had my JD degree, I was more than ready for city life.

I started out in the East Village, because that was the place young professionals ended up. Back then, I called a run-down one-bedroom walk-up home. Two of us shared the bedroom, and a third paid a share of the rent to sleep on the pullout in the living room. After a few years, I wanted a place of my own but couldn't cover the rent in Manhattan anywhere south of 110th Street. Commuting from Harlem or above didn't make sense because I worked downtown, so I migrated to Brooklyn. First to Park Slope, and then, after Stuart and I married, we rented the garden floor of a townhouse in Carroll Gardens. Jacob's arrival necessitated a second bedroom, and Brooklyn proved too up-and-coming for us to expand our living quarters and also pay for a regular babysitter, so we relocated to Queens—the "new Brooklyn" as it's sometimes called in the press.

My neighborhood in Astoria is an eclectic mix of working-class families, land speculators, actor types—which is why it's referred to as "Actoria"—and people like Stuart and me, priced out of a family home in Brooklyn or Manhattan. The broker described the place in the real-estate listing as a "jewel box," which really just means that it's small.

Stuart and Jacob are in the living room when I come through the front door. As he invariably does when I enter, Stuart jumps up to greet me with a kiss on the lips. In this way, he reminds me a bit of when I was a kid and Harry, our cocker spaniel, would start wagging his tail the moment I stepped into the house. Jacob, by contrast, remains on the sofa, his eyes glued to the television. I wonder if he even knows I'm home.

I plop down next to Jacob, which at least breaks his focus from the screen. If only for a second.

"Whatcha watching?" I ask.

"It's a movie."

"I know. Which movie?"

He looks over at his father.

"*Jungle Book*," Stuart says.

"Is it good?" I ask Jacob.

He doesn't answer.

"Your mother asked you a question." Stuart reaches over for the remote and with the press of a button freezes the screen. A boy wearing a red loincloth is talking to a much bigger black bear. "Jacob, please tell Mommy about your day."

I brace for my son to object to this interruption in his viewing pleasure, but he takes it in stride. Jacob is like his father in that way. Very even-tempered. Rarely prone to crying or tantrums, which I hear from other parents and the child-rearing websites is pretty unique among little boys.

I now have a small window in which to engage my son. Our conversations are often terse—especially when initiated by me. I've learned the trick to get him to talk more is to be specific in my questions. Asking "How was your day?" invariably results in a one-word response: "Good." Regardless of whether his day was actually positive. But if I ask who he sat with at lunch, the answer often gives me a peek into what transpired at school. It's actually a technique that works with suspects too.

"Tell me one thing you learned today." Tonight's query.

"I don't know," he says, an answer that tells me he wants to get back to watching the movie.

"It doesn't have to be something you learned in school. It could be from a friend. Or a teacher. Or even something you learned about yourself maybe. Maybe a new food you tried. Just something about your day that I don't know. Let's see if you can stump Mommy."

He looks at me with a scrunched-up face, rising to the challenge. "Did you know that Owen is going to get a puppy?"

"No, I did not know that." I don't tell him that I also don't know who Owen is.

"Owen is going to get a puppy."

"That's nice."

"Can we get a puppy too?"

I want so much to say yes, to be a hero in my son's eyes. What I don't want so much is to walk a dog in the rain at eleven o'clock at night.

Stuart saves me from the being the killjoy. "I told Jacob that a dog is a big responsibility and that when he gets a little older, we could certainly revisit the topic. Owen has a brother who is ten. That seems like the right age for a boy without an older brother to get a dog."

Stuart at his best. My weakness, as a parent and perhaps a human being, is that my first instinct is to confront. It serves me well in the courtroom, less well with my family. But Stuart is a natural peacemaker, knowing exactly how to defuse even a situation as fraught as denying a boy a dog.

I nod at my husband, both to denote my agreement and to thank him for being the heavy. "Your father is right. I think a few years from now we can certainly add a new member to our family. Would we get a big dog or a little dog?"

"Big dog."

"Of course," Stuart says, more to me than to Jacob.

"What would we name this big dog?"

Jacob shrugs. "I don't know. I'd have to meet the dog first."

"Maybe Mr. Big Dog," I say, "to go with Mr. Big Tiger."

Jacobs laughs. "That's a silly name for a dog, Mommy."

This time Stuart smiles at me. I suspect it's because I've been able to put aside the tragedy in my day to engage our son about the trivial. Although it wasn't Stuart's intent, of course, realizing that's what I've done quickly erases my smile.

I press the play button, and the man-cub is once again talking to the big bear. Stuart takes the opportunity to engage me.

"Do you want to talk?"

I look over to Jacob. I could scream "Fire!" and he wouldn't look away from the movie. Still, I'm not going to have a discussion about murder in front of our five-year-old.

"Not now," I say. "I really just want to spend some time with Jacob."

"Do you want to do the reading honors again tonight?"

"Yeah," I say, "that would be great."

———

"What shall we read?" I ask Jacob once he's snuggled under his blankets.

"*Mike Mulligan*."

"Again? Don't you want to try something new?"

"No. *Mike Mulligan*," he says emphatically.

It's a repeat of the other night. I read the same words, and Jacob asks the same questions, almost verbatim: "What happens to steam shovels when they're not needed anymore? Why doesn't Mike realize that he hasn't left a way out? Can we go to the place where they live?"

I patiently answer each query, remembering what I'd told him the other night so that I'm consistent in my explanations. That's all children want. To feel like the world is safe for them and they can anticipate what is coming next. Not to be surprised.

I try not to focus on just how much I've failed my son in this regard. God willing, he'll never know.

———

Stuart offers to microwave the leftover Chinese food he and Jacob had for dinner. I take the opportunity to change into my home clothing, which amounts to sweatpants and a Mickey Mouse T-shirt I've had since college. The chicken and broccoli is already on the table, steam rising off it, when I return to the kitchen.

We have a small, square table in our kitchen with three chairs around it. It's my favorite place in the apartment because it fits only our family. There's something I find comforting about outsiders not being permitted here. We use the dining room for visitors, but the kitchen feels like home to me.

I take my seat across from Stuart and scoop up a forkful of chicken. It's bland, the way Jacob likes it, but I still enjoy the warmth in my mouth.

"Did you know about Lauren running for DA?" he asks.

"No," I shake my head.

"What would that have meant for you? I mean, if she ran?"

"I don't know. I suspect she would have resigned as bureau chief. Maybe McKenney would have fired her. I don't know what that would have meant for me, though."

He looks at me with as much sadness as I feel. I know what he's going to say next, and I don't want to hear it.

"I'd rather not talk about it, Stuart. It's all just too much."

"I understand. If you change your mind, I'm here."

I nod to accept his offer, even though I know that I'm not going to ever feel differently. There's nothing about Lauren Wright that I want to discuss with Stuart.

18.

ELLA BRODEN

Gabriel walks through the door to my apartment and, after kissing me hello, announces that he's hungry. I tell him I had a grilled cheese about half an hour ago and offer to make him one, but he tells me not to bother. He heads over to the pantry. After removing a box of Cap'n Crunch, he pours half of it into a large bowl that I usually use for tossing salads, then adds nearly half a carton of milk. Still standing, he begins to spoon the crunchified-sugar bits into his mouth.

"Do you want to sit down and eat that?"

I don't wait for him to answer. Instead, I walk over to the small wooden table in the corner of the kitchen. It's pushed against the wall on two sides, but that allows for two chairs. I take one of them, and Gabriel follows suit.

"Did you stay inside after the funeral?" he asks.

He's still worried about Donald Chesterman. They haven't been able to find him, as the man evidently left prison and the grid simultaneously. I've already told Gabriel several times that I couldn't live with police protection, and that I'd be safe without it, but I appreciate his concern nonetheless.

"Yes. I came right home after the funeral. But don't you think we can relax about Donald Chesterman? He has no connection to Papamichael."

"I know, but stolen guns go through a lot of hands. It'd be a hell of a coincidence if a felon got hold of a police detective's gun, but stranger things have happened."

"But if he's the killer, that would be the *second* pretty big coincidence. He'd also have to have known that Lauren would be in the park that night."

"That I'm less troubled by. He could have been stalking her, waiting for a time when she was alone. When she left the apartment, he could simply have followed her into the park."

I disagree, but there's no reason to debate the issue. I'd much rather focus on whether the evidence supports Lauren obtaining the gun from Papamichael, which would tighten the noose around Richard's neck.

"Did you find out whether Lauren and Papamichael ever worked a case together?" I ask.

"He had a bunch of cases with Special Vics. A few with you, actually, and some others in the unit. But he also had cases with virtually every other ADA. So I'm not sure it's a real connection to Richard."

"But *any* case with the unit means access to Lauren. She was pretty hands-on."

"Since when do you hate Richard Trofino so much?"

"Since he killed his wife. But the better question is: since when are you such a Richard Trofino defender?"

The two types of people Gabriel despises most are millionaires and politicians. I suppose criminals would be a close third. Richard fits the first two bills, and quite possibly the third too—even before the murder.

Gabriel shrugs. "I'm just trying to keep an open mind, that's all. Besides, the two doormen on duty that night both say that they remember Lauren leaving at around one a.m., and they never saw Richard. And he doesn't show up on any of the security cameras in the building either."

"I've lived in doorman buildings, Gabriel. There are always exits that don't bring you past the doormen. And I'm sure there are ways of avoiding the cameras."

"I know. That's what Dana said too."

"Listen to the women in your life, Gabriel. You might just learn something."

This at least gets a smile out of him. "Did Lauren ever mention to you she wasn't happily married?"

"No, but . . . well, I'm not sure she would have. But if you're looking for motive, there's always one when it's the husband. Especially a husband like Richard Trofino."

"What's that supposed to mean?"

"It means what I said. You know the guy's capable of it."

Gabriel nods that he agrees. "What about Drake McKenney?"

"What about him?"

"Like I said at the funeral, everyone always says he'd kill to keep his job. Do you think that's a legit motive?"

Drake McKenney's even higher on Gabriel's shit list than Richard Trofino. Maybe at the very top, in fact. McKenney has focused on prosecuting cops as a way of burnishing his image with the political left, and cops don't forgive that kind of thing. Perhaps that's why Gabriel doesn't want to focus on Richard Trofino. He'd rather bring down the DA.

I shrug. "I've heard better."

Gabriel gets up from the table and heads for the cupboard. The Cap'n Crunch comes back off the shelf. I'm tempted to tell him that the box is supposed to have ten or fifteen servings, but I don't. I've never been that type of girlfriend, and I don't see any reason to start now.

When he rejoins me at the table, I ask for a taste. He holds his hand underneath the spoon to catch any dripping milk and guides it into my mouth.

I had forgotten just how sickly sweet children's cereal tastes. I didn't even like it much when I was a kid.

"Mmmm," I say.

He knows I'm mocking him. "You don't have to eat it; I only ask that you stock it."

"And that I do."

He takes another spoonful. "Delish."

I listen to him chomp. He's enjoying his Cap'n Crunch as if it were manna from heaven. I like this side of Gabriel. Jeffrey was always so serious. Not just about work, which on some level I understood—even though I didn't know how anyone could get so worked up about litigation between two giant corporations—but about everything. He found no pleasure in life other than his own success, and that's a tough row to hoe. Gabriel, on the other hand, understands that it's the small joys that make life worth living.

"I've been thinking a lot about how the minister ended the funeral. The biblical quote," I say.

"I don't remember it. What was it?"

"I googled it. It was from First Corinthians. The part I wanted to understand better was the line about how sin was the law."

"Was that really what it said?"

"Not exactly." I pull out my phone. I'd done some research from it earlier in the day, but the search was no longer on my Google page. I rerun it while Gabriel inhales more cereal.

"Here it is. The exact quote is 'The sting of death is sin, and the power of sin is the law.'"

"The power of sin is the law," he repeats. "What does that mean?"

"Funny you should ask, because I was reading some commentary on it . . ."

"And?"

"You know, a lot of mumbo jumbo. But one of the interpretations I thought was interesting was that if it weren't for the law, no one would know that they'd sinned. You only actually realize what you've done is wrong *because* it's prohibited."

"That's a little backward, don't you think? It's not the illegality that makes something wrong. It's inherently wrong first, so it's made illegal."

"I suppose that's the conundrum that's being posited in the scripture. One of the commentators made the point that sometimes you don't even think about sin until you're told it's sin, and then it's all you can think about. The example he used was a group of kids walking by an abandoned house. If there's no sign, they would probably just walk by. But put a 'No Trespassing' sign out in front and all of a sudden they're tempted to sneak inside. And, whether they go inside or not, the damage is already done. They've sinned because they're thinking about going inside, and they want to go inside. The only thing stopping them—if they are stopped at all, that is—is the fear that they'll get caught. Which means that they're no longer pure of heart. In other words, now they're sinners."

Gabriel considers this for a moment. Then he smiles. "With all due respect to the Apostle Luke—"

"This one was Paul."

"Same difference. I think that's a load of crap. On this, I'm just a simple cop. There's right and there's wrong. And . . . you know, lusting in your heart or whatever, that's not wrong. That's being human. It's whether you choose to *act* that matters. The law punishes action, not thought, and not sin. If God wants to punish sinful thoughts, so be it. But the NYPD does not."

"You want to know what's a load of crap?"

"Please, enlighten me."

"The notion that you're a simple cop."

19.

DANA GOODWIN

Richard Trofino lives on Park Avenue between Seventy-Third and Seventy-Fourth Streets, in a limestone-clad, prewar, elevator building. A white-gloved doorman wearing a full uniform, including jacket and tie, holds the door.

It was Gabriel's decision not to question Richard before the funeral. As a result, his only contact with the police since the vomit incident was when he told Gabriel over the phone that he didn't know his wife's iPhone passcode. I didn't voice any objection to giving Richard some time to mourn. I understand the strategy behind it—allow the suspect to relax a bit. Maybe he'll get a false sense of security, infer that our lack of interest in him means that he's not a suspect.

Of course, I have my own reasons for not wanting to question Richard until he's good and ready to talk. Not the least of which is to avoid being on the receiving end of his last meal.

Gabriel called ahead to set up the appointment. I half expected Richard to tell us that he'd lawyered up, but he said he was available at our convenience.

As soon as Gabriel and I enter the building, a second white-gloved doorman, this one with a mustache to match, asks who we're here to see.

"Richard Trofino," I say.

"And who may I say is visiting?" the doorman asks.

"You may say it's Dana Goodwin and Gabriel Velasquez," Gabriel says, flashing his badge. "But before you do, I'd like to ask you a few questions."

The doorman looks like he's just smelled something foul. I suspect he's under strict instructions by the co-op board not to speak to law enforcement or the press.

Gabriel doesn't give him the chance to decline. "How many other exits and entrances to the building?"

"We're going to get the building plans," I add quickly, "so it's not like you're giving us information we won't have by the end of the day. But we'd rather hear it from you. If you're wrong, no worries. No one will know you were the source of the information."

That does the trick. He says, "Four. The service entrance is manned from six a.m. to eleven p.m. The others are always locked. There's a door out to the garage, and then two fire exits, one on the north and one on the south."

"The ones that are locked . . . does anyone other than staff have keys?" Gabriel follows up.

"Everyone in the building."

"What about security cameras?"

"Yeah, but the north one is busted. We're waiting on a part."

"Who knows about the busted camera?" I ask.

"The board."

"Is Mr. Trofino on the board?" Gabriel asks.

"Yes. He's the chairman."

"Thank you," Gabriel says. "Why don't you tell Mr. Trofino that he has visitors now."

———

Richard greets us at his door. He looks better than he did during our last one-on-one encounter, but that was a particularly low bar. The sharpness that I associate with him—the look in his eyes that he's one step ahead—is once again front and center.

Richard leads us into the living room. The furniture befits grown-ups who don't fear children's messes—lots of white and beige surfaces. Under the picture window is a long sofa, and that's where he decides to sit. He motions with his hand that Gabriel and I should take the chairs opposite him.

"We're starting to develop some more information," Gabriel says once we're settled. "Most important, we found the murder weapon."

Gabriel had told me not to share with Richard that it had been tossed a stone's throw from his residence. We want to avoid Richard lawyering up. Indeed, given that Richard has a dozen lawyers on retainer, it's somewhat surprising he hasn't played that card yet. Although, as Gabriel pointed out, it's one thing to stand behind lawyers in a business dispute and quite another when it's about your wife's murder.

"It was registered to a man named Gregory Papamichael."

Richard seems confused, which is not a look he wears comfortably. "Why would he kill Lauren?"

"Have you ever heard that name before?" I ask.

"No. I don't think so. Should I have?"

"He's a former police detective," Gabriel says. "He's been dead for two years."

"We think that he supplied the gun," I explain. "Which is why we're trying to track down anyone who has any type of connection to your wife and who knew Detective Papamichael well enough for him to give them a gun."

Richard sighs in a way that makes clear he knows we were trying to trick him into an admission. "Well, *I* didn't."

"Did Lauren?" Gabriel asks.

"I said I never heard the name before," he says sharply, visibly upset by the path we're pursuing. He has correctly deduced that it leads to him as his wife's murderer. "That means I have no idea whether Lauren knew the man."

"We also heard that your wife was considering running against Drake McKenney for DA," I say, moving the suspicion away from Richard and on to McKenney for the moment. "Is that true?"

He blinks, and for a moment it seems as if he doesn't understand the relevance of his wife's future political plans. But then he shows a subtle twitch that indicates he's fully caught up.

"Yeah," he says. "She was a few weeks away from making it official."

"How widespread do you think the news was about your wife's potential challenge?" Gabriel asks.

"I don't know. It wasn't a state secret. We'd put out feelers to potential staffers, to see if they'd be interested in coming aboard, that kind of thing."

I follow up. "Do you think Drake McKenney knew?"

"He knew," Richard says without hesitation. "He actually chewed me out over it. He thinks being DA is his God-given right."

"When was this?"

"Just last week."

"What did he say?" Gabriel asks.

"I don't remember his exact words . . . but it was along the lines of how he'd bury Lauren, and then he'd come after the mayor and me. Something like that, but with more profanity."

This is enough to put Drake McKenney on the suspect list. Right alongside the man who just placed him there. But if it's true that misery loves company, then it's even truer for murder suspects.

"There's something else, and this type of thing is always delicate," Gabriel says. "Did you have any suspicion or knowledge that there might have been someone else in Lauren's life?"

"Like . . . a lover or something like that?" Richard asks.

"Yes," I say. "We're asking because . . . well, she *did* leave the apartment after midnight. We thought it might have been to meet someone."

He looks at me with contempt. As if he's saying that I should know better than to ask such a question. He'd be better served keeping such thoughts to himself, however, because right now he looks as if he has murder on his mind.

I can't deny that it frightens me to see Richard's anger so raw. But I hold my ground. It's critical that he commit to a position on this now. So I prod him.

"I know it's hard for you to imagine, but whenever a spouse is murdered, that's always the police's first line of inquiry. Of course, we know that she wouldn't have told you about an affair or anything like that. But we're asking if you had reason to suspect. Was she out more than usual lately? Any changes in her demeanor toward you? That kind of thing."

Richard processes what I've just said for a moment, and then I see it register in his eyes. Like a switch that's been flipped. Men like him see the angles before the straight lines, and he's just connected the dots. If he knew his wife was unfaithful, he had motive to kill her.

"No. Lauren would never do something like that. And it wasn't that uncommon that when she couldn't sleep, she'd go for a walk. I must have told her a million times it wasn't safe so late, but she always reminded me that we lived on Park Avenue."

I look over to Gabriel to see if he's buying what Richard Trofino is selling. By the narrowness of his eyes, it's obvious that he's not. It's a viewpoint that I wholeheartedly endorse.

20.

ELLA BRODEN

When Allison initially told me that she'd like to meet every Wednesday *and* Thursday, I assumed I must be in much worse psychological condition than I'd thought.

"No," she assured me. "I just find that the work is really jump-started when you double up for the first little bit."

I wasn't sure if I believed her then, and I'm even less certain now. That's because the "first little bit" has lasted six months so far, and there's no end in sight. The last time I asked her if she thought we could go to one day a week was about a month ago. She said we could discuss the topic whenever I wanted, but her advice was to keep this schedule for "a little while longer."

After I'd resigned myself to the fact that we'd be meeting two days a week for maybe forever, I asked her why we met on back-to-back days. It seemed to me I would have more to discuss if we met on a Monday and then a Friday, for instance.

"The work we do here," she said, "is not about you telling me what's happened in your day or week. Rather, we're trying to dig down into your subconscious, which requires breaking down the various walls and other defense mechanisms you've established so you don't let anyone— even yourself—go there. The reason I like to meet in close succession is because it's the normal human reaction to begin to rebuild those walls right away. So the pattern is that we chip away at them here, and then you start rebuilding when you leave. If we meet the next day, the walls are still weak, so we can make much better progress."

"Then why don't we just meet for three hours on one day?"

"Because the chipping away, if you permit me to continue the metaphor, loses its effectiveness after a while. Think about the ax blade becoming too dull to continue the work. It gets sharpened overnight."

Today I have a lot of wall breaking to do. In fact, I'm going to need a goddamn wrecking ball.

Allison shows me an off-kilter smile when she opens the door. I wonder if that's because she already knows what I'm going to share. Although Lauren's murder was a full-fledged media event, especially on cable news, I sometimes question how closely Allison pays attention to what I'm saying. I can't be certain she even made the connection that the murdered ADA and the ex-boss I've talked about during the past six months are one and the same.

If she does know, Allison doesn't raise the topic. Instead, after we're seated, she begins the session as she always does: "How are you today?"

"Cursed," I say.

She doesn't recoil, which reveals that she listens to me more carefully than I've given her credit for. Still, she feels the need for me to provide the exposition because she says, "Tell me what you mean by that, Ella."

"I'm assuming you know about Lauren Wright being murdered."

"Yes. I read about it. I'm very sorry for your loss."

"Thank you. So . . . what I'm saying is don't get too close to me. You might end up on the murdered list too."

Allison sniffles, the way you do when someone tells a joke that isn't at all funny. "Is that how you feel?"

"No. I think that's the undeniable reality. Whoever I love gets murdered. End of story."

I know I'm laying it on thick, but I feel as if it's my prerogative in a setting where I'm paying by the hour.

"I see," she says, one of her prompts for me to elaborate.

"I know that the tragedy here belongs to Lauren and her family. It's not about me. But . . . my sister was murdered six months ago, and now the woman I was closest to aside from Charlotte has been too. It's not fair."

"You're right. It's not fair," Allison says in her soothing voice. "And I know it may feel as if it's directed at you, but tragedies sometimes don't space themselves out. I have many patients who've lost two loved ones in close succession."

"Were your patients' loved ones murdered?"

She smiles tautly at my challenge. "No. That's . . . statistically speaking, very unlikely. I agree. But it still doesn't mean you're some meaningful common denominator in both deaths. That part is a coincidence."

"Lucky me, I guess."

———

When I leave Allison's, I get on the number one train heading uptown. Even though it's the local, I take it all the way to 155th Street, as I'm in no hurry to get to where I'm going.

I haven't been to Charlotte's gravesite since she was laid to rest. Given that I was just at a cemetery the other day, I'm not sure why I thought it would be beneficial to be here today. I just wanted to talk to my sister, I guess.

Everything about the grounds looks different than it did on that rainy day six months ago. Back then, I remember feeling an almost magnetic pull toward Charlotte's open grave, but today I'm having difficulty even remembering the location of the burial plot.

I find it in the back of the cemetery. The placement seems so unfamiliar that I momentarily wonder if they've moved it. Ridiculous, of course.

I peer down at my mother's tombstone, which stands beside my sister's.

ANNE BRODEN
OCTOBER 24, 1953–MAY 9, 2004
DEVOTED WIFE AND MOTHER

I've always hated her epitaph, ever since my father first showed it to me, handwritten in his illegible scrawl on a yellow legal pad. I was twenty, a junior in college. He said, "I don't know what to write. How's this?" I said, "It's fine," because I couldn't process anything at that point. Even today, I can't. But I'm sorry that we defined my mother's entire life by her relationship to us. The saddest part, however, is that I still don't know what would have been more fitting.

My sister's tombstone is the same size and shape as my mother's. Side by side, they look like pillows atop a king-size bed.

CHARLOTTE BRODEN
AUGUST 8, 1995–JUNE 1, 2017
NEVER SAY GOODBYE BECAUSE GOODBYE MEANS GOING AWAY
AND GOING AWAY MEANS FORGETTING

I picked the quote. I scoured the Internet for potential quotes, and that one spoke to me. So much so that I also used it for my ode to Charlotte set to music. Reading it now, I feel a twinge of guilt that it's no better than my mother's. It's still about us, not her. Maybe that's the way it always is with death.

"Hi, Char-bar." The cold air turns my breath to vapor. "Lucky you're bundled up down there. It's freezing up here." I chuckle, then look around the cemetery nervously, worried someone will find my laughter inappropriate. No one else is around. Apparently harsh winter days are not optimal for visiting dead loved ones.

"I'm sorry I haven't been here since the funeral. I know you don't care. It's not like we don't talk all the time. I hope you're with Mom. I bet she really missed you and is much happier now that you're together. Not that she wanted you to die, of course. But . . . lemons into lemonade, amiright?"

And just like that, I start to cry. I was hoping to avoid a total meltdown, but once that dam breaks, I put up no resistance and let the tears run down my cheeks.

"I'm sorry, Char. I know that I'm the lucky one. I had you in my life and I get to *have* a life. I'm so sorry for you. God . . . the things you're never going to experience. It's so terrible. I wish you and Gabriel and I could go out to dinner. You'd like him. I mean, all girls like him. He's gorgeous. But, you'd see what I see in him. He's . . . a really good man. Can you believe that? There's one out there. And he's mine. The fact that he's beautiful and smart and great in bed . . . I mean, what did I do to deserve that?"

21.

DANA GOODWIN

Despite the pileup of work on my desk, I've come home before Jacob's bedtime. I know that in the next few days I'll have to burn the midnight oil, but I feel the need to be with my son tonight.

As soon as I enter, Stuart shouts, "We're up here!" I hear Jacob's laugh, followed by a splashing sound. I make my way upstairs to find my son and husband in the bathtub, surrounded by bubbles. When it's dry, Jacob's curls fall lightly onto his shoulders, but now Stuart has sculpted his hair with shampoo so it sticks straight up, like a Mohawk.

"Lieutenant Stuart and Captain Jacob, reporting for duty," Stuart says with a mock salute. Then to Jacob: "Skipper, salute our commanding officer, Rear Admiral Mommy."

My son raises a soapy hand to his forehead and mimics his father's salute. I play my part, returning it. "You two get good and clean. That's an order."

"The captain and I were at the officer's mess at . . ." Stuart pauses to do the calculation. "Seventeen hundred hours. Mac and cheese. But with the Rear Admiral's permission, I would gladly join her for a glass of wine and second dinner, after the captain settles into his quarters for the evening."

"That sounds good," I say.

———

I retreat to Jacob's room. My son runs in a moment later, as naked as the day he was born. His hair is damp, and the sweet floral smell of his shampoo fills the room.

"Jammie time," I say as I toss a pair of pajamas beside him.

"No. I want to wear Spidey," he says.

I look back at what I selected—Ironman. I rummage through the drawer a bit more. Batman and Superman are present, but not your friendly neighborhood Spiderman.

"I don't see Spidey," I say.

"I wore him before my bath."

I glance over to the hamper. They're right on top.

I know that better parenting would be to explain to my son that just as he is now clean, it is important that his pajamas get laundered too. But I'm not willing to risk his being disappointed in me, so I scoop out the pajamas he wants and hand them to him.

He pulls the web-slinger's shirt over his head. I try to help him with the arms, but from under his shirt he tells me to stop because he can do it himself. When his face reemerges he's wearing a satisfied grin of independence.

I don't even ask Jacob to choose a book. Instead, I reach for *Mike Mulligan* as he wiggles his way under the covers. When he's all set, I begin to read.

After the story is completed and Jacob rolls away from me, I lie in bed beside him. Tonight Jacob rewards me by falling asleep in my company, and I spend a few minutes watching his little chest rise and fall with each breath. And thinking about what I've done.

"I keep meaning to ask whether the school moved that boy away from him," I say to Stuart when I return to the living room.

"Which boy?"

A week or so ago—before Lauren's murder, which now seems like ages ago—Jacob came home crying because of some altercation with a boy who sat next to him during story time. Among the boy's other infractions, he tapped on the desk as if it were a drum, and Jacob found it annoying. I wanted to call the teacher, but Stuart convinced me to give it a day. Then Lauren was murdered and I had a more serious crime to investigate than tapping with intent to annoy. Now I fear that nothing has been done to rectify the situation—yet another failing in my son's life for which I'm culpable.

"The tapper."

"Oh . . . Ross. It turns out that he and Jacob share a love of some video game, and now they're besties."

"Really?"

"Yup. If only all problems could be so easily resolved, right?"

On our third date, Stuart told me that his father had taught college mathematics, and that as a child he imagined professional mathematicians to be the kind of people who live in the abstract ether, detached from the rest of humanity. The kind of misanthropes who would rather work a good proof to completion than have a discussion with another human being.

"He was never home," Stuart explained. "Always logging long hours at the university. So I developed this worldview where I saw mathematics as a kind of calling, like the priesthood, compelling its chosen few to pursue it above all else, including family."

We were sitting in front of a restaurant fireplace, drinking bourbon. I hadn't considered Stuart to be particularly handsome before that night, but there was something about the way his profile was illuminated by the flame, the warmth I felt from the alcohol, and the way he was opening up to me that caused me to realize he was much more attractive than I had previously thought.

He took a sip of the bourbon and shook his head with a laugh. "So then I leave for college, and everything is good. But when I come home for my first Christmas break, my mother tells me that she's kicked my father out—*finally.* I remember how she said that word. As if it had been a long time coming. And I swear I didn't have the first inkling that my parents were unhappy. I just thought my dad worked all the time, but I considered that to be the price of being a mathematical genius. I figured my mother had made peace with it long ago. I don't remember exactly what I said to get her to explain the reason to me. Maybe I asked where he was living, but the upshot was that my father had a *second family* in the same town where we lived."

Stuart stopped then to take another mouthful of bourbon. His eyes looked as sad to me as I imagine they must have when his mother first told him this truth.

"What do you mean, another family?" I asked.

"Like you hear sometimes about these guys who are traveling salesmen or truckers or whatnot, and they have one family—you know, kids, a wife, a dog, a house with a mortgage—and then in another town there's the same thing. Just like that, except my father didn't see the need to leave town to have both. He had literally married someone else—of course, not legally, but the other woman didn't know that. They also had a little boy—my half brother, Stephen, six years younger than me. And a house, and, yes, a dog too. So there you have it. My father wasn't this genius closed off from the actual world staring at a blackboard late into the night. He was a guy juggling two families."

"Is he still alive?"

"No. He died four, maybe five, years ago. After my mother threw him out, he downsized to one family and that suited him just fine. I didn't talk to him for the rest of the time I was in school, but a year or two after I got out, it occurred to me that everything I knew about the man was a lie. I wanted to know the truth. I didn't tell him this, but the reason I sought him out back then was so that I could learn how to avoid becoming him."

"And did you?"

"I sincerely hope so," he said with a chuckle. "One of the things he said, which I remember quite vividly, was that he became a mathematician because it is the only discipline where utter perfection is achievable. He said that a great poem or piece of music could never be perfect because it was always subject to the eye, or ear, of the beholder."

"And so you became an art teacher," I said.

"Well, first an artist, then a teacher. But the point's the same. I wanted to create things of beauty, not strive for perfection."

Stuart never wavered from being the man he was that night. A hopeless romantic, looking for true beauty in the world.

I was drawn to that optimistic worldview like a moth to a flame, even though I was never truly a holder of the faith. Prosecuting comes with the occupational hazard of seeing people actually become their worst selves. On some level, I always knew that would someday be true of me too. But I was thirty-seven and realized that the window for starting a family was fast closing. Stuart seemed to be my last, best chance at having a regular life, and he loved me with more passion, more ferocity, than any man I'd ever known. It was almost as if I thought that love in a marriage mattered in its totality, so that Stuart's overabundance would make up for whatever I lacked.

22.

ELLA BRODEN

I always begin the transformation to Cassidy with music. My phone even has a playlist entitled "Cassidy." Three such playlists, actually. Tonight I put on the one that starts with "Sympathy for the Devil" and wonder why I've never covered that at Lava.

With the music blaring, I start by applying makeup. It's the eyes that make Cassidy. Smokey and dark. Tonight I decide to make them metallic too. The first time I did Cassidy's makeup, I actually followed a YouTube tutorial. By now I'm an expert, and it takes me less than five minutes to establish that sultry-and-dangerous look that Cassidy rocks. Once my lids are fully painted, I put on false eyelashes. They're the longest I could find. The lipstick tonight is blood red. That's actually the name on the tube. I paint my nails a matching color and then hold my finger to my lips to admire how closely I've matched the hues.

My face and nails done, I do Cassidy's hair. It's actually the easiest part because it amounts to little more than shaking my head vigorously. The idea is that she should look as if she's just finished having great sex. I haven't cut it since I began performing, and in another month or two it'll actually be the length I've always imagined Cassidy would favor.

Last is the clothing, or more accurately, the *costume*. Tonight I want to wear color. That narrows it down quite a bit, as most of Cassidy's wardrobe is black. But there are two items of a different palette in my closet to choose from: a body-hugging gold minidress, and a backless red dress with a plunging neckline. I reach for the red.

———

Lava is hopping when I enter. The bar is full and the crowd is already thick, even though I'm not scheduled to go on for another twenty minutes. I'm wearing a long, black coat over my costume, so I don't draw too much attention to myself as I push through the patrons to check in with Karen.

"There she is," Karen squeals like a teenager.

She kisses me on both cheeks, as she always does. Then she looks me up and down, her other greeting ritual.

"Show me," she says, as lasciviously as any man might utter that line.

I open my overcoat. First one lapel, then the other, the way I might if I were trying to seduce her. Rather, if Cassidy was trying to seduce her. Ella wouldn't play this game with anybody, much less her boss.

"I like it," Karen says, literally licking her lips. "I like it a lot."

"Thank you kindly," I say with a slight curtsy.

"After you blow the roof off this place, come find me. I have some . . . news."

She looks at me mischievously, obviously enjoying knowing something I don't. I assume her news has to do with Liam's offer last week to let me transition into their set. I'd thought Gabriel scared Liam sufficiently to put the kibosh on that, but maybe not.

"Sure," I say. "You'll be the first person I'll come to after I . . . blow the roof off."

———

Most of my set is a blur. One moment I'm being introduced by Karen— or rather, Cassidy is—and a second later, I'm beside Karen again, my thirty-minute performance completed.

The only part I actually remember is doing "Never Goodbye." I thought about not doing the song at all, fearful that I wouldn't be able to get through it. I felt as if I owed it to Lauren to sing it in her honor, but from the first words I could feel the words fighting me. Three minutes later, I breathed a sigh of relief when the last note was played.

"Keeps getting better and better, Cassidy," Karen says, after once again kissing me on both cheeks.

"Thanks. It was a tough one tonight. I had a death in the family earlier in the week."

"Oh, I'm so sorry. Is everything okay now?"

"Yeah," I lie. "Thanks."

"Well, maybe my news will cheer you up," Karen says.

I had forgotten that Karen had teased some news before I took the stage. Now I await her reveal.

"Want to open Saturday night?"

"*This* Saturday night?"

"The very same. You'll be opening for Onyx. They're awesome. They wanted a female lead-in, and I thought of you, of course. But wait . . . there's more. The money is twice what you're making now, and I hear that there'll be some record people in the audience."

She's waiting for me to accept on the spot. And she's right that this should be a no-brainer. It's the break I've been waiting for. The break *every* singer waits for. Still, old habits die hard, and for a moment I hear myself turning her down. I'm on the verge of telling her that while I appreciate the opportunity, I don't know if I'm ready. That I've suffered this personal thing, how tonight was a struggle just to get through my set, and I don't want to go on if I'm not completely mentally prepared for it.

But I catch myself. That would be Ella talking. Cassidy knows to leap at the opportunity and not look back.

"Sounds amazing. Thank you so much, Karen."

She kisses me on both cheeks yet again. This time it ends with a strong hug.

"Thank me by blowing the roof off like you always do," she says.

———

It's slightly past eleven when I arrive home from Lava. Gabriel is still awake, lounging on my sofa.

After I remove my coat, he says, "Jesus. I can't believe any self-respecting man would let his woman out in public wearing that."

He wasn't here when I left, so this is his first time seeing tonight's outfit. I know that he's kidding. At least, I think I do.

"It was a tough one tonight," I say. "Give me a few minutes to morph into Ella. She's got some good news to share."

In my bathroom, I transform back. First by washing away Cassidy's mascara and eyeliner, then taking special effort to rub the lipstick off her mouth, and finally by tying my hair back. From the hook in my bathroom, I grab my flannel PJs, put them on, and return to being me.

When I reenter the bedroom, Gabriel is sitting in bed shirtless, the rest of him under the covers.

"That's the woman I love," he says.

He's begun saying it like that. Not quite an "I love you, Ella," but always as a slightly indirect aside. I'll say something funny and he'll say, "That's why I love you." It's as if he's trying it on for size, getting comfortable with the idea of love before committing to it. For my part, I'm an all-or-nothing person when it comes to such declarations. I won't say anything of the sort until I'm absolutely certain that I'm in love with him. I expect that to be soon, however. Very soon, in fact.

"Karen offered me the opening slot on Saturday night. There may be some record people there too."

"Ella . . . that's truly amazing. I'm so proud of you."

Gabriel is the easiest man to read that I've ever known. It's as if he can easily detect deceit in others but hasn't the first clue how to pull it off himself. I've never seen a false emotion come out of him. When I first complimented him on his authenticity, he deflected, telling me that if he was truly out to be a master prevaricator that was exactly how he'd seem.

"Thanks. I almost turned her down. I was worried that it's too soon after Lauren."

"I'm glad you said yes. You worked hard for this."

I climb into bed. When he comes closer to kiss me, I realize that he's not wearing his boxers.

He leans over and kisses me deeply. Part of me wants to pull away. Since Lauren's murder, I've felt guilty experiencing pleasure, which put an end to our streak of lovemaking. But I want this now—to be swept away from my grief—if only for a short while.

23.

DANA GOODWIN

Gabriel arrives at my office at nine sharp. This is the first time I've hosted, as we've previously met at One PP. The reason he's here is because the first item on our agenda today is to tell Drake McKenney that we consider him a suspect in Lauren Wright's murder.

With an outstretched arm, I invite Gabriel to take a seat at the small table I use for in-office meetings, but he must not catch the cue. He moves toward the collection of Jacob's drawings I have taped on the wall next to the window. The largest of them depicts three semi-stick figures, none of which have feet or hands. It's our family. I'm in the middle, drawn the tallest even though Stuart's got me by a couple of inches.

"Is that your son's masterpiece?" he asks.

"Yes. I also have a photograph if you want a more accurate representation." I make my way back over to the desk and grab a silver frame that I keep angled away from guests. "This was taken last year, I think. That's Stuart, who you met at the funeral, and our son, Jacob. He's in kindergarten now."

"Does your boy like Batman?"

At first I think Gabriel must be psychic, but then I remember that, in the photo, Jacob is wearing his Batman shirt, complete with cape.

"If it has the suffix 'man,' he's obsessed. Spiderman, Batman, Superman, Ironman. At the kindergarten Halloween parade at their school, there were twenty-five superheroes and twenty-five princesses. Everyone gushes about how cute they all are—and don't get me wrong, they're friggin' adorable—but nobody ever asks, 'What's wrong with this picture?'"

"And here I was just making random conversation," Gabriel says with a smile. "Didn't mean to hit a nerve."

I can't help but smile back. "Sorry."

"No need to apologize. You don't want your son to grow up to be a crime fighter. I don't blame you at all."

"It's not that, it's—"

"Really, Dana, I get it. If I could do it all again, I'd definitely be a princess too."

"Exactly," I say, now laughing. "I'm glad we're on the same page on this. Why on earth would anyone want to risk their life and have to keep their work a secret when they could live in a palace, have beautiful gowns, and be married to a handsome prince?"

He laughs too. "Let's go see the great man," he says.

———

It's long struck me as odd that as people rise to senior ranks in any organization, the larger their desks seem to get even though the amount of paper they actually deal with decreases. Aside from a thin sheaf, nothing burdens Drake McKenney's desk except for trophies—the kind lawyers collect, like acrylic paperweights enclosing miniaturized court decisions.

His secretary lets us in, but McKenney doesn't move from behind his desk to greet us. Not to open the door or even to stand to shake our hands.

I don't have a strong opinion about the District Attorney. I know I should, as seemingly everyone does. Lauren certainly wasn't a fan, often complaining that McKenney prioritized chasing headlines over the real work of the office. But I've always treated our DA like the weather—something in my life that I have no control over. So complaining when it's bad seems like a waste of time. Besides, like the weather, he's not *always* bad.

I suspect Gabriel doesn't agree. Most cops loathe McKenney on account of the fact that he has not shied away from prosecuting them. On top of which, McKenney comes across as an asshole most of the time. His little power play of not getting up to greet us is a case in point.

"Thank you for seeing us, sir," I say.

"Of course," he says with a politician's smile. "I don't have much time, though. I've got to meet Judge Lawson in about ten minutes. I meant what I said before, though. This investigation takes top priority over everything else, so you have my undivided attention until I have to leave."

This is Drake McKenney's way of limiting our discussion. It's likely something he does with everyone, to make sure he isn't trapped in a meeting. I know that Gabriel is going to assume that it means McKenney has something to hide.

"How'd it go with Richard Trofino?" McKenney asks.

Another power-play move. We only have a few minutes with the man, and *McKenney's* selected the first topic of discussion.

"Not too much there," I say. "He says that everything was good between him and Lauren. No third parties involved. No money problems. And he claims that he never heard of Gregory Papamichael."

"Who?"

"The murder weapon was registered to him," I say. "Dead now, but a former detective over in the one six. He never reported it stolen. It's possible it was and wound up in the murderer's hands that way, but we think it's more likely that Papamichael gave his gun to Lauren for protection—and then Richard used it to kill her."

McKenney nods to confirm that he believes that this is definitely a plausible scenario.

"On the other hand," says Gabriel, "we don't have anything that links him to the murder scene. No evidence of motive either. On top of which, Richard is cooperating with us fully and without lawyering up, even though he's got half a dozen high-priced sharks on speed dial."

"The lack of evidence *is* evidence," McKenney says. "Husbands don't need motives to kill their wives."

Gabriel doesn't seem put off by McKenney's tone. I'm not sure if that's because McKenney isn't his boss or because Gabriel doesn't sweat anybody.

"Even so, the primary reason we're here is to get *more* evidence," Gabriel says. "Specifically, we'd like authorization to turn Lauren's iPhone over to an outside group and see if they can open it."

When Syed Farook made national headlines in 2015 by killing fourteen people in San Bernardino, California, he probably had no idea he'd also change law enforcement. Before the attack, Farook completely destroyed his two personal phones. No one even attempted to access the information he had stored on them because they knew it was a lost cause. But for some reason, Farook left in pristine condition the iPhone issued to him by his employer. Because the iPhone was passcode protected, the FBI had to seek a court order to compel Apple to unlock it, but Apple resisted, claiming it didn't have that ability. Ultimately, the FBI used a third-party vendor to crack it. The FBI has never detailed publicly how they did it, but there are private security firms who claim to be able to hack their way in. For a price tag that runs into six figures, of course.

"Trofino is claiming he doesn't know the passcode?" McKenney asks.

"That's right," Gabriel says.

McKenney chuckles. "Fucking Richard Trofino," he says to neither of us in particular. I'm sure Gabriel understands, as I do, that McKenney thinks Richard is hoping her phone never gets opened. "Lauren primarily used a BlackBerry, right?" he asks, this time looking at me.

"Yes," I confirm.

"So cracking her iPhone will cost about a hundred grand," McKenney says, "and it's still not likely to yield much information beyond her taste in music."

I don't say anything, but I know Gabriel is not going to let McKenney off the hook so easily. "We won't know that until we crack it," he says.

"All right," McKenney says with sigh. "Let me think about that. I've got a drawer full of cell phones that we haven't cracked because I don't want to spend the money. I've got to consider the optics of spending the money here and not there."

Gabriel gives me a sidelong glance. I know what he's thinking. That this is part of a cover-up. Before I can silently signal him not to go there, he does.

"We've heard that Lauren was going to throw her hat into the ring for District Attorney."

Drake McKenney may not be a real lawyer anymore, but that doesn't mean he doesn't know the tricks of the trade. I can almost see the wheels spinning in his head.

"Is that so? I hadn't heard that. Then, again, I'm usually the last to know about potential political challengers."

I need to show Gabriel that I'm on the team, even if the game we're playing places me adverse to my boss. "Richard Trofino said he discussed it with you. More than that, actually. He claimed you two had a screaming fight about it."

McKenney puts on a confused expression. Even though I think it's sincere, it looks false. It's almost as if McKenney has perfected the most common facial reactions he needs in public office—confidence, honesty, sincerity—but he hasn't learned how to look surprised, even when the sentiment is authentic.

"Richard said that *he* told me she was running?"

Every lawyer knows that when the witness repeats your question, he's stalling. Trying to think through an answer to a question that was unanticipated.

"That's what he said," I confirm. "And that you were angry about it and chewed him out."

"More than that," Gabriel adds. "He said that you threatened to *bury* her. That's a direct quote."

McKenney smiles as if now he finally understands. "That never happened. I mean, I talk to Richard from time to time. Every elected official in this city does that. Even before he became the mayor's asshole buddy. He has the kind of juice that when he calls, you answer the phone. But he never discussed Lauren with me. I think even a guy with his reputation would know that's something that would cross the line."

"So he's lying?" I ask.

"He's lying. Not too hard to figure out why, right?"

Neither Gabriel nor I answer, even though we both know that McKenney is suggesting that Trofino made the entire encounter up to throw suspicion on a political rival.

McKenney takes the momentary lull to mean we're finished. He gets up from behind his desk and makes his way to his closet. As he's putting on his overcoat, he says, "Appreciate the update. I'm sorry that I need to run, but I really can't keep Judge Lawson waiting."

Gabriel and I follow him out of his office and into the hallway. I think we're done, but then Gabriel decides to spell out for McKenney what I'm certain the DA has already surmised: that we consider him a suspect in the murder of Lauren Wright.

"Just so no one accuses us later of not doing our jobs . . . where were you the night of the murder?"

McKenney stops in his tracks. After a beat, he turns to face us. He's still all smiles. But this time I can see rage behind the grin.

"With my wife," he says. Then he turns on his heels and walks away.

24.

ELLA BRODEN

Before Allison can officially begin our session with her customary "How are you?" I blurt out my news about my getting a Saturday-night gig at Lava.

"What a difference a day makes. Yesterday you thought you were cursed," she says with a smile.

And just like that, the guilt crashes over me again. "I'm still cursed," I say. "I mean, the Saturday-night thing is nice, but I'd turn it down in a heartbeat if it would bring Lauren back. And let's be real about it. Nobody is declaring me Beyoncé just yet. All that's really happened is that I've been given a better night to sing five songs in front of a hundred people."

"Don't do that, Ella," Allison says, sounding a lot the way I imagine my mother would say those words. "Diminish your accomplishment. You've worked hard, and now it's being rewarded. What I find interesting is that you were excited about it too—that is until I connected it to Lauren's death. Once I did that, you sought to minimize it. Why do you think that is?"

"Her *murder*," I say. "I hate when people use the term *death* or *passing* or whatever as a synonym for *murder*. It's not the same thing."

Allison nods at my rebuke. "Fair enough, but my question still stands."

"I guess it's because . . . I felt like you were trying to balance out Lauren's murder with something positive. I just can't go through life thinking like that. How could every good thing that happens to me make my mother's death, and Charlotte's and Lauren's murders somehow less tragic?"

After a moment's reflection, she says, "I understand your point, but I'm not sure you fully understand mine. I don't want to patronize you, but I think some things require being said, even though I know that you, probably more than most people, already know the truth of what I'm about to say. You're a fortunate person, Ella. You're intelligent, attractive, and talented. You're financially secure, and you have people in your life who love you. Many, many people do not have even one of those things, and you have them all. Now, I know, there's much more to your life than that. You've also experienced suffering that is extreme. You lost your mother at a young age and then your sister in the most horrible circumstance imaginable. And to top it all off, you experienced something extremely traumatic: having to fight for your life and taking a life to save your own. Now a mother figure—Lauren—has been murdered. So, no, I'm not going to tell you that any of that was normal. Like the blessings you have, the . . . *curses*, as you call them, also seem to be abundant. And I'm also not going to tell you that they balance themselves out. Life doesn't work that way. Some people get many more blessings than curses, others get the opposite. You're still young. That means I'm both delighted, and sorry, to say that many more blessings and curses will come your way. And there's no way of knowing whether, when you take your last breath, you'll have accumulated more of one than the other. All you can do, all any of us can do, is be happy when happiness is to be had, and suffer through the tragedies as best we can."

I've given myself this little speech before too. All those starving people all over the world, or those in chronic pain or who are blind or refugees . . . the list of those who have it much worse than I do is endless.

The counterargument is that I only experience my own life. So while others most certainly have it worse than I do, that reality is true of everyone on the planet except one person. Should the second-most-tragic figure on earth not complain because another person is suffering more? And when a billionaire or movie star loses a child, isn't his or her loss just as wrenching as anyone else's?

"Gabriel has been asking about the apartment," I say.

The segue to a different topic is sharp enough that I expect Allison to call me on it, but she lets its slide. She likes it when we discuss Gabriel, so I shouldn't be surprised.

"Tell me more about that," she says.

I recount our discussion from a week or so ago, struggling to remember if we had it before or after Lauren's murder. I think I impart it faithfully, although perhaps Gabriel would disagree.

"What do you want to do?" Allison asks, getting right to the point without the usual detour into why I might have said whatever I said.

"I don't know."

"Tell me how you feel about the decision, then."

"That I'd rather not have to make it."

She looks at me with comfort in her eyes. It's a maternal look if ever there was one. "What's holding you back?"

"It makes me feel . . . I know this is silly, but like I'm being disloyal to Charlotte."

"Tell me more about that," she says in her therapist tone.

"It's a simple equation, really. I'd never be with Gabriel if Charlotte hadn't been murdered, so I'm directly benefitting from her death. You know the way couples have these great meeting stories? 'We were both on line at the bakery and fighting over the last black-and-white cookie when we decided to share it. He wanted to give me the chocolate side, but I said we should each get half of each . . .'" Allison finds this amusing, perhaps because I said it in a whiny voice. "My origin story with

Gabriel is that my sister was murdered and he was in charge of the investigation."

"To me, that's far more compelling than sharing a cookie. Gabriel was there for you at the worst time of your life. You saw how he could be nurturing and compassionate and a true partner for you. What's wrong with that?"

"If Charlotte were still alive, I wouldn't have any of it. I told you, didn't I, that I dated Gabriel briefly a few years ago?" Allison nods to affirm that this is not new information. "So, I had a chance with Gabriel earlier, but I threw it away because I was too . . . high and mighty to date a cop. It took Charlotte being murdered for me to come to my senses."

"Ella, you're not the same person after Charlotte's murder. Every way you see the world is different now. That includes how you deal with men and what you're looking for in a partner. But I'm curious as to why you view this as some type of betrayal. As I see it, it's a wonderful gift Charlotte has bestowed on you."

I don't have an answer at the ready. That's not for lack of trying, as I've considered the issue many times before. I know Charlotte would be happy for me. In fact, the very last thing I can imagine is that she'd want her death to deny me anything.

"I just do" is all I can think to say.

25.

DANA GOODWIN

After our tête-à-tête with Drake McKenney, I accept Gabriel's invitation to lunch. He selects a place two blocks away from his office. It's packed when we arrive. Gabriel apologizes, as if it's his fault he didn't call weeks ago for a reservation. He offers to go somewhere else, and I think it's cute that he feels responsible.

"Not after you built up the pie so much," I say. "I'm willing to wait until rapture."

"I can set you up at the bar," the hostess says. "It's the same menu."

Gabriel looks at me to confirm that this is acceptable.

"Sure," I say.

The diner's bar is as 1950s middle America as you can imagine. At least to my imagination, having never actually set foot in middle America. I'm assuming Chicago doesn't count. The stools are vinyl upholstered, each in a different primary color. I take red, and Gabriel opts for the yellow to my left rather than the blue to my right. In front of us, in a glass case, waits a single slice of apple pie bigger than my head.

"Hey there," the woman behind the bar says to Gabriel. She's in her early twenties, probably a wannabe model or actress. She clearly likes what she sees in Gabriel. "What can I do you for?"

"I'm going to have some coffee," he says. Then, looking at me, he adds, "And for the lady . . ."

"The lady would like an iced tea," I say.

"Alrighty then," the waitress says. "Be right back with those, and then I'll take your food orders."

When she makes her way to the coffee pot, I lean closer to Gabriel. "Alrighty then?" I whisper. "Are you a regular here or something?"

"Nah. They're friendly to everyone."

"Right," I say with the utmost sarcasm.

He doesn't respond to my banter, so I shift back to work mode. "So what do you think?"

"About what?" he asks.

I roll my eyes. "Whether the waitress thinks you're cute isn't much in doubt. I was asking about McKenney."

"McKenney definitely doesn't think I'm cute," he says.

Our waitress returns, a coffee in one hand, an iced tea in the other. For the first time it occurs to me that she looks like she's dressed for a dude ranch—blue jeans, a rope belt, cowboy boots, and a chambray shirt under a fringed leather vest. She gives Gabriel his coffee first, then sets the tea in front of me.

"And what can I get you for lunch?" she asks, looking only at Gabriel.

At least he knows the woman should order first. He nods in my direction. Still, it takes a second for the waitress to break her focus from Gabriel's smile. For this, I can't blame her. It's a heck of a smile.

"I'll have the chef salad, Russian dressing on the side," I tell her.

Gabriel gives me a look.

"What?"

"Nothing. I wouldn't have pegged you for a chef-salad-dressing-on-the-side type of woman."

The waitress laughs, but it comes out as a bit of a snort. "Sorry," she says. "And for you?"

"Grilled Swiss and bacon."

"Fries with that?" she asks.

"Yes, please," Gabriel says.

"Coming right on up," she says as she walks away. *Struts* away would be more accurate.

"I think I'm impressed," he says.

"With Miss Rodeo here?"

He chuckles. "No. You asked what I think about McKenney, and I said that I think I'm impressed. With you, I mean. It's not easy to take on your boss in that way, and you did it well."

"Thanks . . . I think."

"You think?"

"Well, I know you meant it as a compliment, but it's a bit condescending. Lauren was my friend, and I'm after the son of a bitch who murdered her. If that's Drake McKenney, then God help him."

———

After lunch, we return to Gabriel's office to find an extremely tall man waiting for us.

"Lou, I think I got something," he says.

"Vincent, meet ADA Dana Goodwin. Dana, this is Vincent D'Angelo. He's making the initial cut of the financial evidence we're collecting. And in case you're wondering, yes, he did play college basketball."

D'Angelo holds a black loose-leaf binder. The label on the spine says "Bank Records." He remains standing after we enter the office, even though Gabriel takes his position behind his desk and I settle into one of his two guest chairs. D'Angelo must think this will only be a short visit. Still, by standing beside me while I sit, his head is practically in another zip code.

"So what do you have?" Gabriel asks.

D'Angelo opens the binder and then turns it around so it's facing Gabriel, upside down to me and him. Still, I can tell that the first page he's opened to is not actually a bank record at all. Instead, it's a calendar for the month of August. Dollar amounts are listed in a few boxes, in $200 or $300 denominations, but the figure "$300" is written in red on every Tuesday.

"The credit cards went nowhere," D'Angelo says. "All routine stuff. But it's the cash withdrawals that caught my eye. Husband and wife kept separate checking accounts, and the missus's withdrawal pattern was to take out two or three hundred bucks on Monday, you know, cash for the week. Occasionally she'd take another two hundred in a month, but that was pretty rare. That pattern goes back more than a year. But then, about five months ago, in addition to these Monday withdrawals, she started withdrawing three hundred bucks every Tuesday. On rare occasion, on a Wednesday. But it's like clockwork." He waits a beat, then gives the big reveal. "Gotta be an affair, right?"

Before either of us can answer, another man is at the threshold of Gabriel's office. He's heavyset, with a smoker's yellow teeth.

"Lou," he says, "the uniforms just brought in a homeless guy. Claims he saw the Wright murder. He's in Two."

"It seems that our cup runneth over," Gabriel says.

———

Two uniformed cops are waiting outside Interrogation Room Two. They're big men, made to seem even bigger because they're wearing bulletproof vests.

Gabriel introduces himself, extending his hand to the older of the two cops, although both must be less than thirty years old.

"Al Mitchell," the cop says as he shakes Gabriel's hand.

The other one, the younger guy, reaches over to me with an outstretched hand. "Joe Roman," he says.

"So what's the story?" Gabriel asks.

Mitchell does the honors. "No ID on him. Says his name is Franklin. Homeless guy. We know him from the area. Sleeps a lot of nights in the shelter provided by a church over on Lexington. Anyway, he says that on the night the DA lady got killed he was in the park loading his sack full of empty soda cans, and he heard the shots."

"Did he see the shooter?" I ask.

"He's a little fuzzy on that," Mitchell says. "He saw someone, but he can't say for certain that it was the shooter. But the guy he *did* see was the only person in the vicinity, and he was in a hurry to get the fuck out of Dodge."

"Described the guy as wearing dark clothes," Roman adds.

"White or black?" Gabriel asks.

Roman answers. "Claims he didn't see the face. Saw the guy from behind."

"This is good work, officers," Gabriel says. "Anything else we should know?"

Roman shakes his head to indicate we've been told everything, but Mitchell adds, "Only that the guy smells something awful."

———

Mitchell wasn't kidding about the stench. Worse than the puke smell from my last visit to Interrogation Room Two.

Franklin has long greasy hair, an unkempt beard, filthy jeans, and a ripped shirt that, once upon a time, was probably white. He could be anywhere from thirty to sixty-five and is fretfully thin. His vacant eyes are a dull gray.

Gabriel seems totally at ease with both the offensive odor and the unwashed appearance of our guest. He extends his hand. For a moment Franklin looks confused, as if he's never seen the ritual before. Then he grasps Gabriel by the fingers.

"Franklin, I'm Gabriel, a police lieutenant here. Thank you for coming down. This is my partner, Dana Goodwin."

Franklin nods and smiles. "Okay."

"I want to talk to you a little bit about what you told the other police officers," Gabriel continues. "But before we do that, can we get you anything? A sandwich maybe? Or some coffee?"

"A sandwich would be nice. Do you have roast beef?"

"I'm sure we do. Excuse me for a moment so I can have someone get you that sandwich. While we're waiting, we can talk. Sound good?"

"Okay," he says again.

Gabriel steps out, leaving me alone with Franklin. I smile, and he smiles back.

"What's your last name, Franklin?" I ask.

"Pearse. But I don't spell it like the twelfth president."

I nod. "So how *do* you spell your last name, Franklin?"

"P-E-A-R-S-E."

Gabriel returns during the spelling bee. "Sandwich will be about five minutes or so."

"Gabriel, Franklin just told me his last name is Pearse, but not spelled like Franklin Pierce, the president. He spells it P-E-A-R-S-E."

"That's right," Franklin confirms.

"Good to know," Gabriel says with a smile. "Thank you for that, Franklin. And like I said before, even though I know that the questions we have for you are going to be the same types of questions the other police officers asked, it's important that I hear the answers directly from you, okay?"

Franklin doesn't say "okay" this time. In fact, he doesn't acknowledge that Gabriel has said anything at all.

I decide that, because my rapport with him thus far has been good, I'll ask the first question. "As I understand it, last Friday night, you were in Central Park at about one in the morning. Is that right?"

"Don't know the time. Don't remember the day either. Could have been Friday or Saturday or some other day. Also don't know if it was near the duck pond or some other place in the park. I always go to a bunch of places because the bigring can take two hundred and forty cans at a time."

"I'm sorry, what's a *bigring*?" I ask.

Franklin laughs. It's the first time I've heard that sound coming out of him. "It's not a big *ring*, like you put on a big finger, or something. The *big* . . . *green*, like the color. It's what the machine you put the cans and bottles in is called."

Gabriel looks at me and smiles as if to say "Everybody knows that."

"I understand. Sorry for interrupting. Please continue," I say.

"Okay. So I'm loading it up. Now, you can only get twelve dollars, and so that's two hundred and forty cans, right?"

He waits for me to confirm his math. I say, "Right," even though I have no idea how much he might get for each can.

Gabriel puts him back on track. "While you're loading up the cans, what did you see?"

"Didn't see nothing at first. But what I did was hear something. It was like *boom boom*. Sounded like firecrackers, but not as loud."

"You heard two of them?" I follow up.

"Yeah. *Boom boom*. Like that. One right after the other."

"What happened after that?" Gabriel says.

"Nothing. I didn't know nobody was dead. I just thought . . . I don't know what I thought, but I kept filling up my bag. But then I saw someone . . . they was running away. I know I should have checked to see what was happening . . . maybe that poor lady would be alive if I did, but I had the cans and I didn't want someone to steal them. I didn't know they were gunshots neither. I just thought . . ."

His voice trails off, as if he's embarrassed. Even though he hasn't shown the slightest trace of indignity about being homeless, how he smells, or what he looks like, he recognizes that not helping someone in need is shameful.

"You didn't do anything wrong," Gabriel assures him. "You didn't even know that you heard gunshots, right? I'm glad you didn't go to look. If someone has a gun, you need to stay clear of them. The best way for you to help that lady is to tell us what the person you saw running away looked like."

"I saw them from behind. Didn't see any face. Just somebody wearing a black sweatshirt with a hood."

"Could you tell if the man was white or black?" Gabriel presses.

"You need to see their face to tell that. Like I said, I didn't."

"Okay," Gabriel says. "How about how tall he was?" Gabriel stands up. "Was the person you saw as tall as me?"

"No. More like me," Franklin says. "At least I think so. He was far away."

He means someone closer to five and a half feet tall. In other words, much shorter than Drake McKenney—but still very much in the ballpark for Richard Trofino.

26.

ELLA BRODEN

After my session with Allison, I return to my apartment and spend some time at the piano. All the while, I mull over Allison's contention that my relationship with Gabriel is a gift from Charlotte rather than something forever tainted by her murder. I know Charlotte would like me to think of it that way. I can almost hear her say it: "If I'm going to have to be murdered, at least you should get a handsome man out of it."

Then Lauren chimes in. "And I'm glad *my* getting killed helped remind the universe that it owed you one, which is why you're getting the Saturday-night gig at Lava."

I laugh to myself, envisioning my Grammy Award acceptance speech: *I'd like to thank the people in my life who were murdered, without whom I would never have had anything good ever happen to me.*

After I've spent enough time feeling sorry for myself, I decide that it would be therapeutic to do something productive. I begin playing the song I had started to write the other day.

———

Gabriel walks through the door like a beaten man. His face has a drawn, haggard cast to it that I remember all too well from when he was working Charlotte's case.

"You look like you've been ridden hard and put away wet," I say. He laughs. "Long day."

He retreats to the bedroom to put away his gun, a ritual he follows religiously. Even though I'm wearing pajamas, I know Gabriel isn't going to change clothing. He doesn't keep anything here except his work clothes and some underwear. He sleeps in boxer shorts, if that.

Sure enough, a minute later he's back, still dressed exactly the same.

"You want me to make you something to eat, or to order something in?"

"No," he says, heading to the kitchen. He opens the refrigerator. "I'm just going to have a beer for now."

He settles into the armchair that sits beside the sofa I'm occupying. After taking a long slug of beer, he asks, "So how was your day, dear?"

"I had Allison this morning. We talked a little about how I should see your presence in my life as a gift from Charlotte."

"And here I thought I was *God's* gift to you."

He says it with a smirk, which tells me he's kidding. Sometimes I wonder if he doesn't on some level know it's true. After all, you can't get as much attention from the opposite sex as comes Gabriel's way and not have it go to your head at least a little.

"If you're not interested in hearing about my inner life, you should tell me about your day." I say it with enough edge that Gabriel knows I'm mildly annoyed.

"No, I'm sorry. I am interested. Why am I a gift from Charlotte?"

"I'm struggling with the idea that if Charlotte hadn't been murdered, we wouldn't be together. How can anything good come out of something so awful?"

He doesn't initially respond. Even though we'd never expressly discussed it before, I'm certain that other comments I've made over the past few months have been sufficient for Gabriel to surmise that I find this cause-and-effect link a harbinger of our future unhappiness.

"And Allison told you not to think of it that way, but as a gift?"

"Yeah. She's a glass-half-full kind of shrink, apparently."

"You know she's right, don't you?"

Do I know that Allison's right? Isn't that a self-answering question? If I knew she was right, I wouldn't be raising the issue in the first place. On the other hand, of course I know she's right. I don't believe that everything that occurs in the universe is because of me.

All I can muster in response is a shrug.

"Well, even if you don't know, *I* know," he says. "Allison *is* right, at least partly. Maybe I'm not a gift for *you*, but you are certainly the best thing that has ever happened to *me*. And . . . I didn't have to suffer a tragedy for us to come together. The tragedy for me would be if somehow I lost you because you thought you couldn't be happy with me on account of the way we met . So . . . how does that work with your worldview?"

"It hurts my head to think about it. Let's table the discussion about my tortured psyche for now, if that's okay. Tell me about your day?"

Gabriel's eyes narrow. That's his way of saying that the discussion about my tortured psyche is only going to be just that—tabled. It won't be forgotten.

"It was a big one, actually. First we met with McKenney, who claims he hadn't heard about Lauren challenging him. He flatly denied getting into any kind of yelling match with Richard Trofino."

Gabriel had previously shared with me Richard Trofino's claim of a profanity-laced shouting match with the District Attorney, with McKenney making threats. I took it with a grain of salt. Richard could be counted on to use whatever means necessary to cast suspicion on McKenney.

"Just a flat-out denial?" I ask.

"Yeah. McKenney says it never happened. He doesn't just deny that he made threats. He denies that the conversation with Trofino about Lauren running for DA even occurred."

It does give me some pause to learn that McKenney denied even *knowing* about Lauren's potential challenge. It's a common fact pattern in criminal investigations for different parties to have differing views of an event—the archetypical he said/she said. But it's rare not to have any common ground at all. I had expected McKenney to deny Trofino's claims that he threatened Lauren, but not that the encounter ever occurred. One of them is lying. It makes sense that Richard would concoct a story about McKenney making threats, but the only reason that McKenney would deny it outright is if he thinks he might be a suspect. Then again, I suspect that lying is woven into Drake McKenney's DNA. It's possible he does it as a reflex, rather than with any long-term objective in mind.

"There's also a homeless guy who claims he saw Lauren's murderer," Gabriel says. "Or somebody near the scene. Or maybe no one at all, because he could be hallucinating. But if it's that, it's not even a particularly good hallucination. Although he claims he *heard* the shots nearby, all he *saw* was someone running away. Claims he didn't see a face, so there's no ID. Because nothing is easy, the one thing that the homeless guy is sure of is that the shooter was much shorter than McKenney."

"Lucky for you that Richard is five eight, tops," I say hopefully.

"Donald Chesterman is short too," Gabriel says.

"Thanks for the reminder."

"But that wasn't even the big break of the day," Gabriel continues. "We also learned that Lauren might well have been having an affair, which puts the spotlight back on Richard. It also gives some context as to why he might be working hard to shine it in McKenney's eyes."

Gabriel has said this part without thinking it through. If he had, he would have realized that I'd react poorly to the news that Lauren was having an affair. Charlotte was having an affair too, and it led to her murder. To this day, a feeling persists inside me that I never really knew my sister. Now I can add Lauren to the group of people I love whom I apparently don't know the first thing about.

Gabriel can tell I'm upset. He leans over to me and reaches to take my hand.

"I'm sorry, Ella. I should have been more delicate in telling you that."

"It's okay. You didn't have an affair. Lauren did. And she wasn't cheating on *me*, so I really have no grounds to take it personally. What leads you to think she was?"

"Cash withdrawals. Each week, three hundred bucks. Like clock-work. Started in late July."

That does sound like an affair. The other reasons for needing cash—drugs, bribes, gambling, hit men—weren't in Lauren's wheelhouse.

"Any idea who Lauren might have been involved with?" Gabriel asks.

I shake my head. Lauren's sex life was not a topic that we ever discussed. Mine took up all the air.

"I wish I did, but I'm kind of shocked to learn about it at all, to be honest. So, no, I don't have the first clue. I don't remember her ever even saying that so-and-so was attractive."

Gabriel nods. "We're flashing her photo around the hotels in the neighborhood near the office. If someone recognizes her, maybe they can work with a sketch artist to come up with her guy. A better bet is her mystery lover showing up on the surveillance tapes from the ATMs where she made the withdrawals. But you know how the banks like to take their time getting those over to us." He pauses for a moment. "It's a little weird that she'd be the one paying, though, right? I mean, I'm all for gender equality, but I think that when you're having an affair with a married woman, the guy should pay."

The way he says it suggests that this is not a hypothetical in Gabriel's life. I wonder how many times he's paid for hotel rooms to spare a married woman from doing it.

"Maybe they went twice a week," I say. "Or maybe the guy wasn't a multimillionaire or married to one, so Lauren felt like it was only fair that she pay."

He nods. "I didn't think of the twice-a-week thing, but yeah, they might have alternated paying. Because even if he wasn't a millionaire, I still think the guy would pay sometimes, no matter how much money the woman has. Otherwise, I don't know, you feel like a hooker."

I'm not going to debate the etiquette of who should foot the bill for adulterous affairs with my boyfriend, so I change the subject to something more relevant. "What does Richard say about the affair?"

"We talked to him before we had the bank records, but he told us that he didn't think there was another man in her life. Dismissed it out of hand, actually. We haven't gone back to him with this evidence, but I'm sure it's not going to change anything. He's a smart enough guy to realize that admitting he even had an inkling his wife was cheating gives him motive."

I couldn't agree more. Richard Trofino's no stranger to peril—legal or otherwise—and those experiences undoubtedly taught him the importance of establishing a defense early and sticking to it, no matter what. On top of which, he's most definitely *not* the kind of man who would play the cuckold well. If he had learned that Lauren was cheating on him, he very well may have killed her.

27.

DANA GOODWIN

The next morning, I receive a text from Gabriel asking me to meet him at the Commissioner's office. I assume that, now that we've briefed McKenney, Gabriel wants his boss to be up to date.

I arrive at One PP and go directly to meet up with Gabriel. His surly assistant tells me that he's already gone to the meeting, so I head up to Calhoun Johnson's office.

When I enter his office, Commissioner Johnson is sitting behind the desk and his number two, a guy I haven't met before but who I remember seeing at Lauren's funeral, is in one of the guest chairs. Off to one corner are the two other cops who were present at the meeting when we were told about Lauren's murder—the lanky African American who is Gabriel's boss and the short, mustachioed guy who is the Chief of D's.

I can't remember either of their names, and neither introduces himself to me. Drake McKenney stands off to the side, and Gabriel is leaning up against the wall. I smile at my partner, but he doesn't return the gesture.

It's when I see the four uniformed officers—three men, one woman—in another corner, that I realize what this meeting is actually about. There's only one reason uniform cops would be here.

"I'm going to get right to the point, Dana," McKenney says. "You're under arrest for the murder of Lauren Wright."

This must be the cue for the uniform cops. The four of them move in tandem, as if all 140 pounds of me might overpower them with any less manpower. My fight-or-flight response kicks into overdrive, but I tell myself to stay calm. Everything unfolds before me in what feels like slow motion.

One of the cops pulls a set of handcuffs from his belt and in a stern voice says, "Put your hands behind your back."

I'm being arrested for murdering Lauren Wright. The words actually play again in my head, this time in my voice, repeating what McKenney said a moment before.

I do as directed and put my arms behind me, wrists together. One of the other cops clips the cuffs around my left hand and then my right. The handcuffs are much colder than I'd assumed they would be, and they dig uncomfortably into my wrists. If I had a free hand, I'd rub the spot where the contact is most painful, but of course I can't.

The sole woman in the group, a Latina with long, dark hair, begins speaking. "Dana Goodwin, you have been arrested for the murder of Lauren Wright. You have the right to remain silent . . ."

I know I should listen to her and remain silent. I should also invoke my right to counsel, which will prevent them from questioning me right now. I've seen literally hundreds of people end any chance they had of acquittal by speaking in exactly this situation. Yet despite my training, I can't help myself.

"What the hell is going on?" I say, looking squarely at McKenney.

No one answers me. Instead, the cop continues reading me my rights aloud.

"If you do not have the means to pay for an attorney, one will be provided for you."

"I asked you a question, goddammit!" I shout at the DA.

McKenney holds my stare. "We cracked Lauren's iPhone. You must have thought that was never going to happen, because I can't for the life of me understand why you didn't leave the country when you knew we found that phone. Did you actually think we were never going to get around to hacking into it?"

I want to answer his question, to deny my guilt, but my better judgment has now taken over. I need to be smart about this—and that means not to make it any worse by speaking.

The cop finishes her Miranda speech. "Ms. Goodwin, do you understand your rights as I have just explained them to you?"

I crane my neck at the others, looking for an ally in the room. My gaze bounces from person to person until it stops on Gabriel.

We only met eight days ago, but in that time, we've spent nearly every waking moment in each other's company. During that time, I've come to think of him as a friend. I thought the feeling was mutual. Does he think I murdered Lauren Wright too?

"I'm sorry, Dana," he says.

"I understand," I say as defiantly as I can. And then I add, "About my rights."

It's equal parts liberating and horrifying when the thing you've feared most in the world finally occurs. Secrets I've kept will soon be offered up for public consumption. And while that once seemed the absolute worst thing that could ever happen, it's now the least of my worries.

PART THREE

EIGHT MONTHS EARLIER

DANA GOODWIN

28.

I hadn't prepared a résumé since George W. Bush was president. That was the résumé I'd used to secure my employment with the DA's office, but it had long ago been lost to outdated word-processing systems. To apply to be deputy chief of the Special Victims Bureau, I created a new one from scratch.

Lauren didn't even look at it when we met, although she might have glanced at it before my interview. Then again, maybe she couldn't have cared less about where I went to college or law school, or what I wrote my law review article about. Certainly, she already knew that I'd spent the last eighteen years in General Crimes.

My boss in General Crimes was Eugene Stickleman, who everyone in the group referred to as "Stick-Up-His-Ass Man." He was the kind of person who never smiled and had no family—or interests—as far as I could tell. He lived alone in a garden-level studio apartment in a building owned by this old lady he referred to as Mrs. Golitto. All I knew about Mrs. Golitto was that she owned lots of cats. Stickleman was forever complaining because the cats used his patio as a litter box. He pretty much wore the same suit, shirt, and tie combination—gray two-button suit, white button-down-collar shirt, solid-blue tie—every single day.

Lauren Wright was his antithesis in every way, starting with the moniker people used behind her back: "Lauren Always Right." Not the cleverest nickname, but it fit. Her reputation was that she was infallible. In her judgment about cases, about people, about everything.

It was big news when Ella Broden stepped down. Not a shocker, given who her father is, but a deputy doesn't often leave the job. When one does, it triggers a rush of would-be successors, something akin to what happens when a politician in a safe congressional district decides to seek higher office.

I had gone on the interview on something of a lark. I knew that there would be at least half a dozen people vying for the spot, and I assumed that Lauren would promote from within her group. Lilly Weitzner, the head of the Sex Crimes Division, or Sara Sadinoff, the leader of the Elder Abuse Division, were the odds-on favorites.

Lauren and I met in her office. Whereas Stickleman's work space was cold and off-putting, like its occupant, Lauren's office was thoroughly inviting. The décor was light: a pale yellow sofa and sky-blue chairs surrounded the conference table. Impressionist prints in white frames adorned the walls, and her desk was a warm cherry wood—obviously one that she purchased herself, because the standard-issue DA's desk lacked even a hint of style. A needlepoint picture on the wall behind her chair read: "A Woman's Work is Putting Away Sex Offenders."

I couldn't even remember when I first met Stickleman, but I knew instantly that my introduction to Lauren Wright would be indelible. That my career and my life would never be the same.

She got up from behind her desk and seemed to glide toward me. That was the sense I had, that she moved with the grace of a dancer. She was dressed in typical ADA attire for women—blue suit, white blouse, sensible shoes, a simple rope necklace, and small gold earrings—but somehow she made the ensemble appear to be elegant rather than workmanlike. But it was her gaze that froze me in her orbit. Lauren had the most piercing blue eyes I'd ever seen.

"I've heard so many great things about you, Dana," she said. "And I can't believe that we've never met before. How can that be?"

"I've had my head down in General Crimes for a long time, I'm afraid."

"Well, I'm very glad that you popped up to meet with me today. But I have to ask the most obvious question: Why? You've made quite a reputation for yourself over in GC. Eugene can't stay chief forever. Why not wait him out? In another three, four . . . at most five years, you'd be chief. And, full disclosure, I'm not going anywhere in that time frame."

I had a prepared answer for this question. I was going to wax on about how I'd never wanted a management role, explain that I came to the DA's office to try cases. How, after nearly twenty years, I had accomplished all I set out to achieve in the courtroom and thought it was time to take on new challenges. My lack of deputy experience would hinder my being picked to take over for Stickleman when the time came . . . blah blah blah.

For some reason, however, when the time came to deliver this speech, I deviated from my script and actually told her the truth.

"You," I said. "I don't mean to be a suck-up, but I'm not here because becoming a deputy is a box I need to check on my way to getting a bureau chief job. I'm here because I want to work with you."

My revelation caused Lauren to sit up straighter. I suspect the other applicants had all answered that question with a variant of the same speech I had prepared about seeking out new challenges.

"Okay, I'll bite," she said. "Why do you want to work for me?"

"I want to be inspired. Not to get all new-agey about it, but I'm looking to work with someone who can help me become the best version of myself. To become something more than I have been up until now."

"That's a high bar for a boss."

"With all respect, I'm not looking for a boss. I'm looking for a partnership. I understand I'm not going to be an equal partner, but

I want to feel like my point of view truly matters in all decisions, big and small."

I left Lauren's office without the slightest indication of whether she liked me or not. Then I didn't hear from her for two weeks and assumed that was that. The call came on a Friday at 6:30.

"Is this a test?" I asked, throwing caution to the wind. "I mean calling on a Friday after working hours to see if I'm still here."

"No. If you hadn't answered, I was going to leave the job offer on your voice mail. Welcome aboard, partner."

29.

A month into my deputyship, Stuart suggested we host a dinner party and invite Lauren and her husband over. He said he wanted to get to know the woman I spoke about all the time. I did not think it was a good idea.

"I want her to think that I'm a superstar," I explained to him. "She's going to come here and see that I can barely boil water."

He dismissed my concerns out of hand. "You *are* a superstar. You can do anything, even host a dinner party for your boss. Trust me. It's going to be a huge success."

I took comfort in the idea that there'd be others present to serve as buffers. I also invited my closest friend, Kate, and her husband, Ed. They're the smartest, most interesting people I know, and very New York City. Kate and I met at college. She was a vegan even then—she introduced me to the term. She teaches feminist political theory at Sarah Lawrence and is the kind of intellectual who probably hasn't seen a movie without subtitles in a decade. I'm not entirely sure what Ed does for a living, even though he and Kate have been married for more than ten years. I know it has something to do with economics—the subject of one of the two PhDs he holds from the University of Chicago—and that he could make ten times as much money if he did whatever it is that he does in the private sector. They have no children, but two dogs. Needless to say, they live in Williamsburg, Brooklyn.

I cooked a lamb roast. Much to my surprise, it turned out perfectly. For my vegan guests, I added pretty much every vegetable I could find at the farmers' market. The result of my culinary efforts was displayed atop the buffet in our dining room—platters containing roasted root vegetables, cauliflower sautéed with mushrooms, a pasta primavera, and a potato recipe that I'd tried for the first time. It contained a ton of chili powder.

Kate and Ed arrived early, while I was still in the kitchen. I remained secluded while Stuart sat with them for about ten minutes, until I heard another knock on the door, when I left my station to greet Richard and Lauren. Whereas Ed and Kate were both outfitted in clothes from the Gap—jeans, sweaters, sneakers—Lauren wore a little black dress with a V-neck revealing her considerable cleavage. I noticed Stuart taking in the view. Richard was wearing what he must have considered casual wear: an expensive-looking sports jacket likely made of silk, and gray trousers.

I had previously told Kate to make sure that Ed knew Lauren was my boss and Richard was the Trofino of Trofino Construction, but she must not have passed that information along.

The first words out of Ed's mouth were, "How do you two know Dana and Stuart?"

"Dana and I work together," Lauren said graciously.

"And by work *together*," I said, "Lauren actually means *for*. She's my boss. My very new boss, in fact. So say nice things about me."

Everyone laughed, but I felt uneasy nonetheless. To calm my own nerves, I offered Lauren and Richard some alcohol. Lauren opted for the already-open bottle of red wine, but Richard asked if we had any scotch. To my surprise we did, so I poured him two fingers' worth, neat.

"The smell from the kitchen is heavenly," Lauren said after she took a sip of the wine.

"Thanks. You look beautiful."

"I'm sorry if I'm overdressed. I just . . . I like to dress up when we go out."

"No, don't apologize. Like I said, just beautiful."

"Thank you. Your house is so charming."

"Would you like a tour?"

"Of course."

I turned to Richard. "I'm about to give your better half the nickel tour. Care to join?"

"If it's okay, I'm just going to enjoy this very fine scotch."

"It's just us, then," Lauren said. "So lead the way."

Our home is barely more than fifteen hundred square feet. By virtue of walking in the door, Lauren had already seen most of it: the living and dining rooms. I opened the door to the kitchen and said the obvious.

"This is the kitchen."

"Smells so good," she said again.

Next, I led her up the staircase to the bedrooms. I pointed at the closed door to the office and said, "That's Stuart's man-cave-slash-art-studio. It's quite the mess, so we're going to bypass it." As I said it, I worried that I hadn't made the bed in our bedroom either, but when I opened the door to the master, I saw that, thankfully, I had. "Here's our bedroom."

"Very nice," Lauren said. "I especially like the photograph. Is that Jacob?"

She was pointing to a black-and-white shot in a silver frame. Stuart had taken it when Jacob was two. It was still my favorite picture of Jacob, capturing an impish smile that he has to this day.

"Indeed it is. Come, let's visit the model."

I knocked lightly on my son's half-closed door. "Jacob? Sweetie, I want you to meet someone."

I pushed the door open. Jacob was staring intently at his iPad. He didn't look up.

"Please put your screen on pause and say hello to Mommy's boss."

He didn't move. I felt a flush of embarrassment, prayed that he wouldn't make me say it again. Or worse, require that I be the heavy and actually remove the iPad from his clutches in order to get his undivided attention. Thankfully, the wait was short. He put the device down.

"Jacob, this is Ms. Wright. She's Mommy's boss at work."

"Hi," he said, as disinterested as a four-year-old boy could be.

"What are you watching?" Lauren asked.

"Thomas the Tank." Jacob decided that he'd had enough social interaction and returned to the iPad.

"Sorry," I said to Lauren. "Little boys are not great conversationalists."

"He's so sweet," she said.

———

At dinner, the candles flickered on my dining table, giving our guests a glow. Kate was talking about a play she had recently seen in a basement space in Bed-Stuy that accommodated an audience of fifteen—and in which the six actors onstage performed in the nude.

"Men or women?" Richard asked.

"Three of each. And the weird thing was that the nudity really had nothing to do with the plot. I mean, there was nothing sexual about the play at all. It's like the characters, you know, went to work, came home, etcetera. But they were all naked. No one commented on it in the play. The playwright was apparently making some symbolic point about how we're all naked or something."

"Not very subtly, of course," Ed added.

"Do you go to much theater, Lauren?" Kate asked.

"Not as much as I'd like. Richard isn't a fan."

"Maybe if the actresses were naked, I'd reconsider," he said with a loud laugh.

The others all smiled, but Lauren's grin appeared to be strained. You can tell an awful lot about a marriage by the silent expressions spouses share when they think no one is looking. Hers communicated that she was unhappy and had been for some time. She tried to mask it as best she could, and I wondered how much longer she could continue the charade. You might think that was a lot to glean from a single reaction, but it was one that I know all too well, since I wear it myself on a daily basis.

The dessert was all store-bought. The chocolate cake was from my favorite bakery and particularly decadent—and vegan to boot. I also put out vanilla Häagen-Dazs and Ben & Jerry's Chunky Monkey vegan ice cream. To my surprise, Stuart broke out the one bottle of cognac we owned. Richard was more than happy to accept his offer of an after-dinner drink. Ed gave in to the peer pressure and joined them.

"Ladies?" my husband asked, waving the bottle.

"No thank you," Kate said. "I've had enough."

"I'm game if you are," Lauren said to me.

"Sure, why not?" I said, even though I was already tipsy.

I couldn't remember the last time I had cognac, except to recall that on that prior occasion, I didn't like it. It tasted too strong, too alcoholic. It was likely because of my inebriation, but this time I found it to be utterly delicious. Like a warm bath completely enveloping my body. Although I knew I should resist the feeling of being swept away, I couldn't help but welcome the relief my buzz was delivering.

From the looks on the faces of my guests, it was clear that I was not the only one feeling no pain. Lauren's cheeks were flushed, and there was a calmness in her eyes that I'm not sure I'd ever seen before. She was no longer looking over at her husband every thirty seconds, as she had been earlier in the evening.

She and I had fallen into a discussion about work, excluding the rest of the table as they talked about a recent national political scandal.

The others were loud, but Lauren and I spoke in a stage whisper, as if we were involved in a secret conspiracy.

Without any segue, Lauren broke from talking about the Humphries case, a particularly disturbing child-abuse situation in which the mother had been burning her daughter's backside, and said, "This was wonderful. I'm so glad that you thought to invite us."

I leaned in closer to her; I could feel the warmth radiating off her skin. "I was nervous about it. You know . . . worlds colliding and all."

"Don't be silly," Lauren said. "Tonight only proved to me what I've suspected since we first met."

"Oh, and what's that?"

"That you're a woman not only of extraordinary ability, but also of secret talents."

30.

For some reason, the DA's office does performance reviews in the middle of the calendar year. Lauren referred to the exercise as "the black hole of being a supervisor."

"If I had my way, we would never do written reviews," Lauren said. "The good ADAs know they're good, and the bad ones are even more self-aware of their shortcomings. All reviews do is upset the good ones because they obsess about the one area of constructive criticism you provide and disregard all the positive things that are said. The bad ones inevitably respond by giving up altogether. I have never, and I mean *never*, seen anyone turn around a bad review."

We had twenty-seven to do.

I suggested that the process would be aided by some alcohol. Lauren agreed quickly, and fifteen minutes later we were off campus at some hole-in-the-wall Mexican place around the corner from our office with a pitcher of margaritas in front of us and a stack of performance reviews in a Redweld folder.

"Is this what you dreamed it would be like when you decided to be a lawyer?" I said in jest after we'd gotten through the first five.

"I actually wanted to be a nun," Lauren said in a much more serious tone. "Really. And not just when I was eight. I thought about it in college, even. Do you know what Richard says about it?"

"No, what?"

"He says it's because I was searching for the perfect man even then, and nothing less than God would do for me." She smiled, but not without effort. "Did I ever fall short of that," she added with a chuckle. Then she downed the rest of her margarita—her second.

I followed suit, throwing back my own drink. Then I reached for the pitcher and refilled both of our glasses.

"I sometimes wonder what the world would be like if marriages weren't forever," I said. "If your marriage license was kind of like a driver's license. You have to renew it every few years. If you don't, no big deal. You take the bus for a while."

"That's brilliant," she said. She raised her glass in a toast. "To taking the bus for a while."

We clicked together our margaritas and then both took healthy slugs. This time she refilled the glasses, even though they were only half-empty.

"I think we'd better do some more work while we're both still semi-sober," she said.

We plowed through the rest of the reviews, checking boxes, making jokes, and drinking our margaritas. Ninety minutes later, we were left with an empty pitcher and one sheet of paper still to complete.

"This one is yours," Lauren said. "I suppose I should fill it out in private—and when I'm not drunk."

"What fun would that be?" I replied. "I'm a big girl, I can take it. How am I doing?"

If I'd been any less inebriated, I wouldn't have said that. Not only because I was putting her on the spot, but because I wasn't sure I *could* take it.

Lauren's drunken smile quickly vanished. It was as if she could will the alcohol out of her system and seamlessly reenter boss mode.

"You know, Dana, I never thought I would have another deputy after Ella. I figured that she'd stay with me until I passed the mantle of leadership to her. And I liked the idea, to tell you the truth. But the dynamic between us was a mother-daughter-type thing. I brought her in when she was very junior, and there was so much she had to learn. Not just about the Bureau either, but about navigating her way around . . . life, really. I talked to her about her boyfriends, her relationship with her father, and how she felt about losing her mother so young, which gave her responsibility for her younger sister. And . . . well, you know how that story ended, with the tragedy concerning her sister's murder. Don't get me wrong, I liked being a role model for her. I see now that, with you, exactly what you told me you wanted when you interviewed is what I've been missing too—being part of a true team. Not a chief and deputy, but equals running this group. And I swear to you, Dana, the bad guys better watch out, because we're going to be unstoppable."

She made quick eye contact with me, but when I smiled back at her, she turned away, clicking her pen and looking down at the paper in front of her. "But now we have to put it down on paper."

She began to read from the form. "Rate subject one to ten on the following . . . first . . . intelligence." She looked up at me. "That's a ten."

"You're not really going to do this in front of me, are you?"

Lauren smiled and then looked back down at the evaluation form. "Number two . . . dedication to her job. Gotta go again with . . . ten."

"Are you sure you want to do this?" I said although I knew I wasn't going to stop her.

"Number three. Relationships with coworkers."

Lauren looked at me as if she wanted me to grade myself.

"Well, considering I'm drunk with my boss filling out my evaluation . . ."

"Right . . . maybe I need to give you an eight there."

"Hey!" I shouted.

"Just kidding. I already put down ten. Okay, last one. Overall, how do you rate this person?"

I waited, feeling my heart race even though I wasn't the least bit nervous about her evaluation. She teased me by withholding her rating for a minute. Then, when her mock deliberations had gone on so long that I was about to beg her to tell me, she said, "I'm going to keep that to myself for a little while longer, I think. Can't give everything away on the first date, right?"

She paid the check by snapping down her American Express card and dismissed my offer to pay my half with "Don't be silly." Then she ordered an Uber, telling me that she didn't want me on the subway drunk.

"I'll be fine," I protested.

"Nope. The car will drop me off and then take you home. And, before you say another word, all that stuff I said about our being partners and equals, that was the tequila talking. I'm still your boss, and this is an order."

"Yes, ma'am," I said.

———

The Uber pulled up less than a minute after we exited the restaurant. Once we were in the back seat, the driver turned around to us. "Good evening, ladies. First stop is Seventy-Fourth and Park, correct?"

"Yes," Lauren said. "Then you're going to take this lovely woman to Queens."

The driver smiled, which I took to mean that he could see that we were both drunk. He turned around, and we began making our way through Lower Manhattan.

"Shall I take the FDR?" he asked, now looking straight ahead. "It's probably fastest."

"No," Lauren said. "I like watching the city go by at night."

For the rest of the ride, Lauren looked out the window. I sat quietly, alternating my gaze between my view of the cityscape passing before me and my boss, captivated by the same view. The neighborhoods changed every ten blocks or so—the Lower East Side to the East Village to Gramercy Park to Murray Hill to Beekman Place.

The traffic on Third Avenue approaching the Fifty-Ninth Street Bridge was heavy, so the driver crossed over to Madison. A few minutes later, the car came to a stop at the near corner of Park and Seventh-Fourth Street, a good twenty feet from the building's entrance.

"This is me," Lauren announced.

"Come out my side so you don't get killed," I said.

I opened my door and stepped out. It had begun to rain, a light mist.

We would joke about it after, each of us taking credit. But I know the truth. It wasn't her. It could have never been Lauren. This was all me.

I kissed her. On the lips. When she didn't break the seal immediately, I parted my lips slightly and allowed my tongue to make contact with hers.

It was an out-of-body experience, with conflicting sensations—the cold rain juxtaposed with the warmth of her mouth, the softness of her hair against my cheek. It made my entire being tingle.

I broke the embrace. When I did, I knew Lauren wanted more.

———

The next morning, Lauren appeared at the threshold to my office. She looked perfectly put together, as if last night's alcohol had had no effect on her. Her cheeks had a rosy glow and her eyes glistened. She was even having a good hair day. I, on the other hand, felt like I'd been hit by a truck.

I knew that there were really only three ways she could play this: pretend the kiss never happened, claim it was a big mistake, or set up a situation for us to finish what we'd begun.

"I . . . I can't remember the last time I drank like that," she said.

"I couldn't tell by looking at you. I'm feeling it today, though."

"I feel . . . great, if you want to know the truth," she said with a broad smile. "Was your husband upset?"

I wondered if Lauren had intended for her simple query to have so many meanings. Was Stuart upset I came home late? Drunk? With my boss's lipstick on my mouth?

"He was fast asleep. It's not uncommon that I come home really late from work. My boss is a real hard-ass—he knows that."

"Yesterday we were 'partners,' and now I'm back to being your boss, huh?"

Even though Lauren said it with a laugh, I knew that I'd upset her. That hadn't been my intent, at least not consciously. But once my words were out there, I couldn't deny that I might have intended them as a warning for both of us to consider the price we'd have to pay to go down this path.

We agreed to meet after work—to "talk." She selected a poorly lit bar around the corner from the office. We sat at a table at the back, and I ordered a Heineken because you have to order something, even though the last thing I had on my mind was consuming more alcohol. Lauren seemingly needed the liquid courage, however. She asked for a vodka cranberry right off the bat.

As soon as the waitress brought us our drinks, Lauren said in a low voice, "To . . . one of the great kisses of my life."

I could feel my eyes moisten in response to her compliment. I clinked my beer bottle to her vodka cranberry, and then we both drank.

"It was a first for me," Lauren said as if she were in a confessional. "I mean, not even in college."

"It's been a while for me," I said, and left it at that.

She scanned the room. Apparently it was empty enough for her liking, because she put her hand on top of mine.

"Tell me about it," she whispered.

"It's not important, Lauren. Past is past. What matters is what you want to do now."

She lifted her hand but didn't break eye contact. "It's my choice?"

"Only because I've already chosen. This is the kind of thing that needs to be unanimous."

This time she didn't even look around the pub. She immediately leaned across the table and placed her lips on mine. It was *that* kiss, not the drunken one from the previous night, that ranks at the very top of *my* list.

Lauren wasted no time in calling for the check, then paid it in cash. She led me by the hand out of the bar and across the street to a Best Western hotel. She'd obviously planned ahead, because the room was already booked.

The room was no-frills, but more than adequate for our intended purpose. Clean, with a king bed and a flat-screen TV.

As soon as the door closed, I took matters into my own hands. Literally. Before she could say anything, my lips were on hers, my tongue in her mouth, my hand on her breast.

———

When we were finally satiated, neither of us said anything. The first quiet of the last hour fell in the room. All I could hear was Lauren's breathing and my own beating heart, as if they were engaging in a two-part harmony.

Stuart liked to talk after sex. To recap what went on. I always hated when he did. I was there. I knew what happened. I much preferred to be alone with my thoughts. Lauren appeared to be like me in this regard. She wordlessly curled up beside me and placed her head on my shoulder. I lost myself in her sweet scent. Mixed with the rawness of the sex we'd just enjoyed, it was nothing short of heavenly.

31.

Every Tuesday that summer, Lauren and I met at the same Best Western. It became the center of not just my week, but my life. A few hours when I no longer existed as the woman I'd come to despise. I recognized, of course, the circularity of my reasoning. I hated myself precisely for what I was doing with Lauren—for the betrayal of Stuart, and Jacob too. And yet I couldn't pull myself away. It was as if the only antidote to that feeling was more time with Lauren. I suspect that anyone with an addiction knows the cycle all too well: self-loathing, the desperate need for relief that brings on even greater self-loathing, inextricably leading yourself back to that relief.

In August, Lauren invited Stuart, Jacob, and me to visit Richard and her at their East Hampton home for Labor Day weekend. Summer homes in the Hamptons were virtually unknown to ADAs, save for those, like Lauren, who had spouses with seven-figure incomes.

"Are you kidding?" I replied.

"No. I find the weekends intolerable."

I understood the sentiment all too well. It was as if time stood still on Saturday and Sunday. Before Lauren, like most people, my working life had been dedicated to a countdown to Friday afternoon. Now, however, I couldn't wait until Monday mornings, when I could see her again.

"This seems like a colossally bad idea."

"No worse than any of our others recently," she said.

And so, Stuart, Jacob, and I headed to East Hampton. Stuart was excited about seeing how the one-percenters lived, and Jacob couldn't stop talking about the fact that our hosts actually had their own swimming pool.

Throughout the drive east, I considered feigning some type of illness as justification to ask Stuart to turn around. But I didn't say a word.

After more than three hours on the road—the last hour in bumper-to-bumper traffic along a single-lane highway—our beat-up, ten-year-old Hyundai rolled onto Lauren and Richard's circular white-pebble driveway. Their perfect house, complete with large picture windows, a long sloping roof, and a wraparound porch, stood before us.

"They live here all alone?" Jacob asked as we got out of the car.

"It's different outside the city," I said.

"It's different, all right," Stuart said.

Lauren greeted us at the door. She was wearing flowing white linen from head to toe and looked positively angelic. I was in jeans, as was Stuart, and Jacob was wearing his Aquaman T-shirt and shorts.

We embraced. She kissed me on the cheek, holding me tighter than an introductory hello of a coworker warranted. When the hug ended, I nervously looked at Stuart, but he was oblivious, staring up at the double-height ceiling and the enormous crystal chandelier that hung from it.

"Quite a place," he said in a way that sounded more envious than complimentary.

"We like it here. An oasis from the city," Lauren replied. "Come in. Let me get you situated in your rooms, and then you can change into swimsuits. We can all sit out back. Richard went to the market for provisions for tonight. We thought we'd grill, if that's okay with you both. And you too, of course, Jacob. Do you like burgers?"

"Mmm hmm," my son said.

"Excellent," Lauren said. "Come, follow me. I'll show you to your rooms."

She led us straight to the sweeping staircase that dominated the entry. When we began up the stairs, I caught a glimpse of the living room, which looked like it was right out of *Architectural Digest*—virtually the entire space was white, right down to the rug. I shuddered thinking about Jacob even passing through it.

At the top of the landing was a long hallway. We turned left.

"There are five bedrooms upstairs," Lauren said, sounding a bit like a real-estate broker. "Obviously, that's four more than we actually need, but you'd be surprised at how you just expand to fill whatever space is available. Our bedroom is on the other end of the floor, but I figured you'd all like to be close to one another and far away from us for privacy, so I decided that the two on this end would be best. I hope, Jacob, that you like a room with bunk beds. I know a lot of boys like to climb the ladder."

My son's face lit up. Bunk beds were about as exciting a proposition as he could imagine.

All of the doors were closed. Lauren pushed one open. Inside was a tranquil blue room with white bunk beds occupying one wall and a twin bed opposite it. The rug was a beige sisal.

"This is the room that children normally stay in," Lauren explained. "And Jacob, I'm going to tell you a secret. Are you ready?"

He nodded to indicate that he was.

"Okay. When we decided how to decorate this room, we wanted it to feel like you were at the bottom of the ocean. So the carpet is supposed to be like sand. When you take off your shoes and socks, you'll find out that it feels a little rough on your feet. We painted the walls blue, like the ocean. And you see here?" She pointed at a chest that was consistent with the nautical theme, looking a bit like what a pirate might bury treasure in. "That's where you can put your clothes, if you want. And here . . . this clamshell has some toys and stuff you might want to play with."

Jacob made a beeline for the toys and immediately pulled out a truck. He looked to me for permission.

"Why don't you change into your swimsuit, Jacob? Then you can take the truck outside," Stuart said.

"That sounds like a great idea," Lauren said. Then she added, "The grown-ups should follow me."

Stuart and I entered the room next door. It reminded me of a bed-and-breakfast in Maine we once stayed in. Four-poster bed, colorful needlepoint quilt, a claw-foot tub in the bathroom.

"Here you guys are," Lauren said. "I'm sorry, no toys in your room—although you do have an en suite bath."

Lauren left us alone to change, at which time Stuart said, "Not too shabby."

———

The house was beachfront, but we spent the day lounging by the pool, with occasional trips to the beach for Jacob to collect sand. It was a tough call as to who was ogling me more—Richard or Lauren—even though I kept my cover-up over my one-piece when I wasn't in the pool cooling off. At four o'clock, Richard announced it was happy hour. He called on Lauren to mix up a batch of gin and tonics. Lauren asked if I could help, and I followed her to the kitchen.

She opened the refrigerator and pulled out a bottle of Bombay Sapphire, then poured almost half of it into a large pitcher. To that she added two handfuls of ice. From the shelf above she pulled out two bottles of tonic and poured them in. For a moment, she rummaged through the refrigerator before announcing, "Last, but certainly not least," while waving a lime.

After slicing the lime into wedges, her concoction was complete. I assumed we would return to the outdoors, but instead Lauren peered out the window. From my vantage point, I could see Richard reading on his lounge chair. Stuart had joined Jacob in the pool.

"Come here. I want to show you something," Lauren said, reaching for my hand.

I walked with her into the next room, a bright red dining room. A table that easily could seat twenty was in the center, a series of gold-framed mirrors on the wall. It was in the reflection of a mirror that I saw Lauren lean toward me.

Her kiss took me by surprise. "Not now," I said, pulling away quickly. "Not here."

"I just miss you. I thought having you here would make the weekend pass without the heartache I usually feel, but it's worse having you so close but not being able to . . . well, you know."

I nodded. I did know.

———

Richard drank nearly the entire pitcher of G&T on his own. I had just enough to make it look like I was participating, but I wanted to make sure above all else that I kept my wits about me. Stuart isn't much of a drinker, so he had even less than I, and Lauren was too busy preparing dinner to have more than one glass.

Dinner was a feast. Grilled steak and tuna, roasted potatoes, a kale salad, and a burger made especially for Jacob, even though I told Lauren that he'd eat whatever the grown-ups were having. She opened a bottle of white wine and poured it equally among the four of us.

After cleanup, Lauren announced that she and I were going to take a late-night stroll. It was clear from her tone that the men were not invited. Not that Richard cared, as he had already excused himself to his study. Stuart kissed me on the top of the head and said he was going to put Jacob to sleep, then turn in himself.

Before I headed out, Stuart said, "Be safe. It's dark out there."

———

It was indeed pitch-black outside, nothing like nighttime in the city. I literally could not see my feet as we walked.

As soon as we reached the beach, Lauren kicked off her shoes and instructed me to do likewise. The sand was cool underfoot, and I could feel my body relax as my toes acclimated to the soft terrain. The only sound was the crashing of the waves.

We walked for a few minutes. The houses dotting the landscape provided enough illumination for us to be reasonably certain that we were alone, but it was too faint for anyone to see us from a distance. At a point where the footing became firmer, Lauren declared that we had arrived at our destination. She lowered herself onto the sand, pulling me down beside her.

The temperature must have dropped ten degrees just during our walk across the beach. After an entire day of feeling like I was near heatstroke, I found myself pulling my hoodie tighter around me. Lauren sought warmth by nuzzling her head under my shoulder and wrapping an arm around my waist.

"Jacob is wonderful," she said. "He looks so much like you."

"You think? Most people say he favors Stuart. Around the eyes."

"No. He's you."

"I think he had a nice day. He still can't get over that you have your own pool and beach. Tomorrow I'd like to take him into the ocean before we have to head back."

"Don't talk about heading back, okay?"

She craned her neck up at me and placed her mouth on mine, pushing me back onto the sand. Then she repositioned herself directly on top of me. Her eyes were shut tight, and she looked like she was praying, as if she had found some holy communion with my body.

We kissed for a few minutes. Her hands all over me, and mine on her in the same way.

At one point, she inched away from me, just far enough that our lips were not touching, but still close enough that we could resume with only the slightest movement by either of us. Her eyes were wide open, however, glistening. For a moment, I thought she might cry.

Instead, she said, "I love you."

It was almost as if she was telling herself, rather than sharing the sentiment with me. I had been playing out this exchange in my own head for the last few weeks, afraid to say the words first. But I knew exactly what she meant. I loved Lauren Wright in the way people dream of being in love—with that all-encompassing, how-can-I-live-without-you, swept-off-my-feet commitment to another human being. A sense so overwhelming that oxygen, water, and food became meaningless to existence. I believed that I could easily survive on this feeling alone. It was a drug more powerful than any controlled substance, and just as hallucinatory. It warped your mind, made you do things a sane person would never consider.

I had never reached that height with Stuart. I loved things *about* him—his calmness, his love for Jacob and for me—but I did not love him like *this*. Not like I loved Lauren.

It made me both feel sorry for Stuart and understand him better. I finally realized why he looked at me the way he did. He knew this type of love.

Once you love someone like this, other love is revealed to be nothing of the sort. Which makes it not simply a lesser emotion, but a lie. Worse than that, even. It's an inhibitor of true love, tricking you into forgoing the real thing for a pale imitation.

———

When I arrived back at the guest room, Stuart was still awake. He said Lauren and I had been gone long enough that he'd become worried.

I apologized and told him that Lauren and I had got to talking at the beach, said we had lost track of the time.

"What were you talking about?" he asked.

"What people talk about. Work, a little. Life, a little."

"She certainly likes you."

I searched Stuart's face for some clue that he was suggesting something closer to the truth. As usual, he was impossible for me to read.

"What makes you say that?"

"Just a feeling. But no need to get defensive. It's a good thing, right? Your boss should like you."

He reached for me. I could not have felt any lower, kissing him. I braced myself for the fact that it was going to get worse.

Then he pulled away abruptly. "Your hair is full of sand."

I instinctively reached up to feel my scalp. It was gritty, as I should have expected from the last hour writhing around on the beach with Lauren on top of me.

"We were looking up at the stars," I lied. "I should take a shower so I don't get sand in the bed."

32.

There were times during my affair with Lauren when I imagined how it would end. I never envisioned any tears, or even raised voices. Neither of us threatened to ruin the other's life, and our husbands never became the wiser. In fact, in this fantasy, it was as if my relationship with Lauren had never occurred. The only evidence of it was my memory. I even wiped Lauren's clean.

The reality could not have been more different. Not only from that best-case scenario, but the worst-case one as well.

In mid-November, Lauren asked me to share a taxi home with her. We had done this before. A half hour in the car together, an hour if we were lucky enough to hit traffic, making out in the back like teenagers. I knew, however, that there'd be none of that tonight.

"What's wrong?" I asked.

"I don't want to talk about it here. I'll explain on the ride," she said.

As soon as we got in the cab, Lauren took my hand. Hers was cold on account of the weather, which had hovered around freezing for the last few days. I wanted to ask her again what she had to tell me, but I was afraid to say a word.

As the car rolled uptown, I kept Lauren's hand in mine. She was looking out the window, undoubtedly trying to summon the courage to tell me that we were over.

Finally, I couldn't take it any longer. "Just tell me," I blurted out.

She turned to face me. I could see the beginning of tears in her eyes.

"I . . . need to stop because . . . because I'm just dying inside, Dana. I've been telling myself that for weeks, but I'm . . . I'm just too weak when I'm around you, and I can't help myself. So I've decided that tonight, when I get home, I'm going to tell Richard and beg him to forgive me. I don't know any other way that I'm going to be able to stay away from you unless I burn the bridge so I can't go back. Telling Richard will do that."

She broke eye contact, peering again outside the window, as if the answer to why she was breaking my heart could be found on the city streets. The cab was moving swiftly, a rarity of no traffic, and we were making every light. We'd be at Lauren's building in only a few minutes.

A sense of panic began to take hold. "Stop here," I called out to the driver. "We're going to get out right here."

"No," Lauren said, countermanding my directive.

For a moment, I thought that was it. She was going to do what she said—go home and tell her husband about our affair. This would be the last time I ever held her hand.

But then she said, "Go to Fifth and Seventy-Second. We'll get out there."

———

As we walked through Central Park, the air was frigid, and I could see my breath with each exhale. After the initial shock of the air's chill, though, I no longer felt any physical discomfort. It was as if my entire body was bracing for the deathblow I knew Lauren would deliver.

"Let's sit at the duck pond," Lauren said.

The body of water before us didn't look much like a pond. It was clearly made out of cement, and the water was less than a few inches deep at the edges. Bits of ice floated on top, and there was not a single duck in sight.

Benches lined the western side of the pond. As soon as we reached the first one, she sat down, leaving me ample room to sit beside her without touching.

There was no one else in sight. That was hardly a surprise, given the weather and the late hour. I knew Lauren had chosen the venue for just that reason. Speaking at a Starbucks in her neighborhood ran the risk of being seen by someone who might report back to her husband.

"Did you ever read *Catcher in the Rye*?"

The question was so random that I almost thought I imagined it.

"What?"

"The book *Catcher in the Rye*. By J. D. Salinger?"

"Yeah, I read it in high school."

"Remember when Holden Caulfield asks, 'Where do the ducks go in the winter?' It's supposedly some great existential question. In the scene, he's actually here. I think it's summertime, though. And as you see, the ducks aren't here in the winter."

"I don't care where the ducks go, Lauren."

"Right," she said.

I reached for her hand. She grasped it, and then a moment later pulled away.

My heart burst. It truly felt that way. As if I could feel it shatter in my chest.

"I love you," I said. "I love you so much, Lauren." I was crying now, begging for her not to leave me.

But somehow, my declaration of love seemed to have the opposite of my intended effect. She stiffened and look at me coldly.

"You say that like it matters," she said. Her tone was angry, as if *I* were ending it with *her*, rather than the other way around.

"It's all that matters, Lauren."

"Really? Are you going to divorce Stuart to be with me? Are we going to get married and raise Jacob, like a real family? Do you see that as a possible future? And what about work? You think McKenney is going to let us work together and be together? That's never going to happen."

During our affair, from time to time, we'd talk about a future together, but it was a fairy tale. I thought we both understood that. I couldn't imagine leaving Stuart, although I also couldn't put into words why I felt so bound to him. For some reason, it seemed like I'd be leaving Jacob too, even though Lauren reminded me repeatedly that's not how divorce worked.

What we had never discussed was what would happen if we broke up. How could we work together? And if we couldn't, which one of us would leave? Those things were never far from my mind. Nor I assume from Lauren's either. I assume that, like me, she found them too depressing to consider, which is why we never spoke of them aloud.

I followed that approach now too, remaining silent in the face of her challenge. That was all the answer Lauren needed.

She shook her head. I'd never felt lower. She wasn't conveying disappointment as much as contempt.

"Yeah, that's what I thought."

I couldn't believe how quickly my life was unraveling, even though I should have been prepared for it to unfold in exactly this way. If she told Richard, he'd never tolerate my continuing to work with his wife. I could involve HR, or even sue, but that would only make everything worse. If I did that, Lauren would be fired for sleeping with a subordinate, but my career would be over too. McKenney would never make me bureau chief—not after I'd slept with my boss and then turned on her. He'd appoint someone outside the group, and that person would replace me in short order with someone he or she could trust. In the end, all I'd accomplish by going public would be hurting a lot of people, especially Lauren, and delay the damage to my career by a few short months.

Which meant that I'd have to be the one to leave Special Vics. But for where? Stickleman wouldn't take me back, not after he seemed so insulted when I left. I could try the private sector, but it would take months. If Lauren told Richard about us, he wouldn't wait patiently while I looked for new employment.

Then I thought about Stuart, and everything got even worse. If Lauren was fired, it would be a public matter. Our affair would be known to everyone. But if I was the one to leave, even if I told others it was to enter the private sector, or to go back to General Crimes, Stuart would know it wasn't true. I'd told him too many times how much I loved it at Special Vics. If I left, he'd know it was because of Lauren.

I racked my brain for a way out of the mess that I'd made. It didn't take me long to seize on it—the only way that I could keep my job and my marriage.

Lauren would have to die.

PART FOUR

33.

ELLA BRODEN

Gabriel looks as if he's seen a ghost. I've never seen him shaken before, and it's more than a little disconcerting.

I had come to One PP this morning with him to review some old case files. The police brass still thought it was possible that Lauren was murdered by someone she had prosecuted, and wanted to expand the search beyond Donald Chesterman. Gabriel thought it was a waste of time, given that the murder weapon had come from Detective Papamichael, which meant whoever murdered Lauren had to have some connection to him, and an ex-con wouldn't fit that bill. Still, an order is an order. Gabriel thought I'd be better than Dana at recognizing which of the rather lengthy list of people Lauren sent to prison during my tenure as her deputy, and who had since been released, might have sought revenge. As soon as we arrived, however, Gabriel was summoned by Calhoun Johnson. He hadn't been gone more than fifteen minutes, but it was obvious that something monumental occurred during that time.

"What happened?"

"They arrested Dana for Lauren's murder," he says.

"What?"

"I just left the Commissioner's office. It was quite the scene. All the brass was there, and far more uniforms than needed. They arrested her. Handcuffed her right in front of me and led her out of the room."

I'm still having trouble processing. It doesn't make any sense.

"They got into Lauren's phone," Gabriel continues. "Dana sent Lauren a text at 1:03 in the morning, asking her to meet in Central Park. Lauren was dead less than a half hour later."

It still doesn't make any sense. "Why would Dana kill Lauren?"

"*Dana* was the one Lauren was having the affair with," Gabriel says, as if this information would clarify things for me rather than confuse me even more. "I literally begged Lucian to hold off on the arrest. I asked him to let me go back to Richard with proof of the affair to see how he'd react, or to let me wear a wire with Dana to see if I could get a confession out of her. He said it was above his pay grade. Drake McKenney apparently wanted the headline—today."

As I'm listening to Gabriel suggest that something is wrong here, I can't get my head around the one fact that Gabriel doesn't contest: Lauren and Dana were lovers. Aside from the obvious—that both were married to men—I couldn't imagine Lauren being so reckless as to have an affair with her deputy.

I think back to Charlotte, the parts of her life that she hid from me, and the way she wrote about passion causing you to do things that previously would have shocked you to your core. I recall telling Lauren how I felt betrayed by Charlotte for not confiding in me about that part of herself. She told me that it wasn't my place to judge because I didn't live Charlotte's life. I had accepted that. Now I wonder if she was really talking about herself.

I was completely unaware of Lauren's sexual preferences, and Dana's proclivity to commit murder is even further beyond my ken. But I've been a prosecutor long enough to know that crimes of passion—even the premeditated kind—defy rational thought. Dana Goodwin is certainly not exempt from being hurt so badly by a lover that, in a moment of insanity, murder might have seemed a proportional response.

The press room at One PP is at least twice as large as the space devoted to that use at the DA's office. The back wall is wood paneled and the requisite American and New York State flags flank the podium. A sign reading "Police Department of the City of New York" is front and center, in case anyone didn't know where they were. It's already a standing-room-only crowd when Gabriel and I arrive, which means that the invitation to the press must have gone out even before Dana was arrested.

The police department's press liaison, a thin, thirtysomething blonde I recognize from her prior job as a reporter on the local news, calls everyone to attention. Speaking into the microphone so her voice comes out of the speakers on the sides of the room, she introduces Calhoun Johnson and Drake McKenney. Apparently, no one else is going to get billing aside from the two top dogs.

Johnson steps to the microphone first. Even in civilian clothing, the Commissioner cuts a military figure. McKenney stands off to the side, mentally rehearsing whatever he's going to say when it's his turn. I wonder if McKenney has index cards tucked into his suit jacket pocket for this occasion too.

"Earlier this morning, the New York Police Department arrested former Assistant District Attorney Dana L. Goodwin for the murder of Lauren Wright, who was the Chief of the District Attorney's Special Victims Bureau," Johnson says. "We are unable to release all of the evidence that brought about Ms. Goodwin's arrest, but she and Ms. Wright were engaged in a sexual relationship that led to this horrific crime. At this time, Ms. Goodwin is in custody and will be arraigned later today. I want to thank the members of the NYPD who worked nonstop on this investigation, as it was their diligence and dedication that allowed us to make this arrest. And with that, I would like to introduce the District Attorney for New York County, Drake R. McKenney, to say a few words."

I can almost see McKenney's smirk. Although arresting Richard Trofino for the crime might have been marginally better for the DA's future political career, I suspect he's deriving immense personal satisfaction from the fact that—despite Richard's manly swagger—the world will now know that his wife preferred the opposite sex. I bet the DA wishes he could revisit their earlier screaming match about Lauren's candidacy, but this time with McKenney unloading on Richard about his sexual inadequacies.

"I also want to thank the men and women of law enforcement, as well as the men and women from my office, who worked with them on this investigation, for their superior work," McKenney says. "But I also want to focus once more on the human side of this tragedy. Lauren Wright was a friend of mine, and a model of what prosecutors in the Manhattan District Attorney's Office strive to be: fair, compassionate, hardworking public servants. We are thankful that, with today's arrest, we are able to bring some measure of closure to her family."

He doesn't once mention Dana Goodwin. Not that I'm surprised, of course, but I do see the irony. By murdering his political rival, Dana Goodwin has done more for Drake McKenney than he ever could have hoped.

34.

DANA GOODWIN

It is an occupational hazard for prosecutors to wonder what it's like to be a criminal defendant. To have your life stripped naked so that people you've never met can render a verdict about something that only you know for certain.

I have seen the process countless times from a different vantage point, and yet, from this side, it is still nothing like I imagined. The feeling of helplessness from being confined is far more overwhelming than I'd considered. I'm acutely aware that if I trip—which is a real possibility given that I am being pushed at all times from behind—I'd certainly break my nose, if not my neck. With my hands cuffed behind my back, I'd have no way of bracing myself before I hit the ground.

I'm escorted from Calhoun Johnson's office by all four uniform cops. The Latina who read me my rights holds onto my arm but doesn't say a word. We don't stop walking until I'm delivered to booking. It's a process I've also seen numerous times—without recognizing the abject humiliation of being catalogued. The fingerprinting, the mug shot, the confiscation of my belt so I lack the means to take my own life.

After booking, I make my one allocated phone call to Stuart. I'm determined not to break down. It's important to me that I'm handling this turn of events. So, in as matter-of-fact a tone as I can muster, I tell my husband that I've been arrested for Lauren's murder. I detect a brief moment when he chokes up, but I don't give him enough time to become completely overwrought before I say, "Call LeMarcus Burrows. He'll tell you what to do."

———

Four hours after my arrest, I'm ushered into the courtroom from the side entrance, which is used exclusively for those in custody. Until the moment before the doors opened, my hands were cuffed behind my back.

LeMarcus Burrows is sitting at the table for defense counsel. I first met LeMarcus when he was an ADA in General Crimes, what now seems like a million years ago. I knew from the get-go that he was putting in his time as an ADA to learn the enemy's secrets, and that as soon as he'd mastered them, he'd switch sides.

One of the first conversations I ever had with him was about the TV show *Law & Order*. He said, "You know the beginning, the thing they say about two separate-yet-equally-important groups?"

"Yeah," I said.

"You know it's wrong, right?"

"No. What's wrong about it?" I said with a laugh because we were actually discussing the accuracy of a television procedural.

"I don't know the lines by heart, but it's basically about how the police investigate crimes but the prosecutors try the offenders."

"Yeah, so?"

"So, we *don't* prosecute the offenders, Dana. We prosecute the *accused*. They're only the offenders *after* they're convicted."

He was right, but it didn't stop me from laughing. "You're not going to last three years here," I said. "But if I'm ever in trouble, I'm making my one phone call to you."

LeMarcus has always been a very handsome man. He has a coffee-colored complexion and he's gifted with a smile that can either draw you in or cut you down, depending on whether you're friend or foe. In the years since we first met, he has added *debonair* to that description. Back in the day, he didn't seem to care much about his appearance, which might have been because ADAs were paid just enough to cover their rent and food—stylish clothing was something to put off until we entered private practice. Today he's decked out in a glen plaid three-piece number with a blue tie that captures the hue in the pattern to a T.

He greets me with a smile practiced for just such occasions. By rote, without considering whom he has for a client in this particular instance, he tells me that I need to answer "not guilty" when the judge asks for a plea. Before I can ask him anything, the presiding judge, Phillip Tomasso, does exactly that, shouting out just the one word: "Plea?"

Tomasso likely has a dozen cases to hear this morning. Apparently he's not even going to allow the presence of an ADA accused of murdering another ADA to slow down his docket.

I say my line: "Not guilty."

"Bail, Ms. Serpe?" Judge Tomasso says.

Silvia Serpe is the ADA handling today's arraignment calendar. I know her, but not well. She hasn't yet looked at me.

"Your Honor," she says, "the People request that Ms. Goodwin be held without bail. As the court is I'm sure aware, the defendant is accused of a terrible crime. Lauren Wright, the chief of the District Attorney's Special Victims Bureau, has been murdered. It's important to send a message to the public that no favoritism is shown because the defendant has connections to the District Attorney's office."

LeMarcus offers the predictable counter. That the prosecution's case is weak, that I have strong ties to the community, including a young son, that I not only have never before been accused of a crime, but have devoted my life to prosecuting criminals.

"If anyone—*anyone*—believes in the criminal justice system, it is Dana Goodwin. She is no risk of flight and certainly wants to be vindicated in a court of law," LeMarcus says, his voice rising in that theatrical way he frequently adopts in court.

For the first time since I was brought before him, Judge Tomasso makes eye contact with me. I wish he hadn't, for all I see in his expression is disgust. Then he takes a deep breath.

"One million or bond equivalent," he says, and bangs his gavel.

———

After my hearing, I'm again handcuffed and then deposited back into lockup. The one bright spot is that I'm put in the group that's transported to Rikers Island, the jail that houses defendants who are confined pending trial.

I can't touch a bite of dinner, which is a good thing because I'm sure if I ate whatever gray slop is on my plate, I'd feel sick tomorrow. By eight, I'm growing worried that Stuart can't come up with the money, and that I'll be spending tonight in a cell. In the morning, I'll be on the first bus out to Rikers.

But at ten, I'm told to collect my belongings.

As soon as I cross the threshold into freedom, Stuart embraces me tightly. Into my ear, he whispers, "I love you."

I'm back home a little over an hour later. Our babysitter, Livie, says Jacob fell asleep without any fuss. She doesn't ask anything about my circumstances, even though it's obvious to me that she knows. Probably more than I do, in fact, because I haven't been online yet. I'm not certain if the source of Livie's knowledge is Stuart or the Internet, however.

After Livie leaves, Stuart and I sit across from each other in our kitchen. Stuart has made me tea, and I am enjoying the warmth of the cup as much as the mint flavor, all the while attempting to come to terms with the fact that I am now an accused murderer.

"I didn't tell Jacob anything," Stuart says. "But the reporters were already outside our house when he came home from school. I told him that it was about a big case you were involved in, and he seemed to be okay with that."

Those same reporters had been lying in wait upon our return. It was a terrifying experience for me, a hardened prosecutor. I shut my eyes and try to shake away the nightmare that awaits my five-year-old son. No matter how hard Stuart and I try to shield him, my son's blissful ignorance will not be a permanent state. Soon enough, he'll be able to navigate the Internet. He also has friends whose parents talk about scandalous topics in front of their five-year-olds.

"We'll have to tell him something soon," I say. "Before he hears it elsewhere."

"Maybe it'll be best for him if he's not in the city when all of this happens," Stuart says. "I don't know . . . He can go stay with my parents, or your sister."

"No."

The force of my declaration seems to surprise Stuart. If anything, I wish I'd said it louder. There's no way in hell I'm giving up what may well be the last months I'll have with my son. He is the flesh-and-blood reminder of why my freedom—indeed, my life—still matters to me. I need to keep him close, or I'm certain I won't survive.

I allow myself a moment to imagine life on the run. How much worse would it be than my current predicament? Just Jacob and me, living off the land somewhere tropical. I fantasize that he might even see it as something of an adventure, between the different animals we'd encounter and the prospect of swimming every day. But then reality invades even my efforts at escapism. Jacob won't be five years old forever. He'll need to go to school and have friends, and I'll need to be able to feed, clothe, and shelter him. I have a limited skill set outside of the American justice system, a lack of fluency in any language other than English, and no idea how to create a new identity for us. I flash on going it alone, but I won't abandon my son. That would be worse than prison. Worse than death.

"LeMarcus told me that he normally asks for a quarter-million-dollar retainer, but as you and he go way back, he agreed to take the deed on our house," Stuart says, snapping me out of my own thoughts on the futility of escape.

"Awfully kind of him," I say.

"Yeah. So when all this is over, we're probably going to be homeless."

"Speak for yourself," I say. "The odds are very good that I'm going to have free room and board for the rest of my life."

He looks at me with tears in his eyes. I know what he's going to say before the words come out.

I stop him cold. I just can't go there now.

"I don't want to talk about it, Stuart. I . . . I just need some time to think all of this through on my own."

35.

ELLA BRODEN

"Hi, Ella. This is Drake McKenney."

The call woke me, even though it's after ten in the morning. I quickly try to shake the grogginess out of my voice.

"Oh . . . hello . . ."

I've never spoken to Drake McKenney one-on-one. I've shaken his hand a few times and even shared the platform with him at press conferences, where I stood off to the back while he, front and center, would take credit for the accomplishment that was usually my doing. He never stopped by my office, although I worked one floor below him for five years. Never even called. Not after I won at trial, or when I was given the office's highest commendation, or when I resigned. Not even after Charlotte went missing.

"Did I catch you at an inopportune moment?"

"No . . . it's fine. How do you know my cell number?"

"Ah, you'd be surprised what we know about our former ADAs."

I'm sure he meant for the remark to sound witty, maybe even charming, but it comes across as creepy, as if I've been under surveillance.

"Let me get right to the point," he says, perhaps because he too realizes that his effort at humor fell flat. "Can you find some time to meet with me today?"

"Okay . . ." I say, tentatively.

"Great. I'm going to put you down as my eleven thirty. I'll see you then."

I ask him what we'll be discussing, but he doesn't respond. When I pull the phone from my ear, I see that our call has ended.

It hardly matters. I've already deduced the reason Drake McKenney wants a private audience with me. It's the only thing that the DA could be calling me about, now that the chief of his Special Victims Bureau is dead and her deputy under arrest: he wants me to run Special Vics.

I jump into the shower and blow-dry my hair straight, like I did for work back in the day. Then I pull out my lawyer clothing—a dark blue pantsuit and lighter blue silk blouse—which hasn't been called into service for more than nine months.

Looking in the mirror, my image seems strange to me. I'm so accustomed to seeing unemployed Ella Broden—no makeup, in jeans and a T-shirt—or Cassidy, with her heavy mascara and skin-tight clothing, but not this totally put-together lawyer staring back. I haven't seen her for a long time.

An hour later, I'm back at the District Attorney's office for the first time since my last day as an ADA. When I left, the joke among my colleagues was that I'd be back all the time to meet with them on behalf of clients. My father's practice, however, is nearly all federal-based, so during my three months of employment with him, I logged time in the United States Attorney's office, talking to the prosecutors there. I didn't have any cause to visit my old stomping grounds.

Being back at One Hogan is like returning to high school after you've graduated—it's an odd feeling. I no longer belong in the place that defined me for so long. That point is made clear when I don't even recognize the security guard—a guy who looks like he's still in high school himself. I apparently don't register with him either, because he asks to see my identification and instructs me to put my belongings on the conveyer belt.

"Where's Richie?" I say, a reference to the man who had his job for at least thirty years.

"Who?"

"Richie . . . he had this job when I was an ADA."

"When was that?"

"I left about nine months ago."

"I've only been working here for three, so I don't know."

He hands me a blue visitor's decal with the number eight circled. Everyone refers to the DA's domain simply as the Eighth Floor. It's the DA equivalent of the Oval Office.

"Please affix it to your outer clothing," he says, then points to where the elevators are located.

I get a similar pang of familiarity when the elevator doors open to let someone off on the seventh floor, my old stomping grounds. I crane my neck to see if there's anyone loitering in the halls whom I might know, but then the doors shut again. A few seconds later, they part at my destination.

McKenney greets me at the threshold to his office. Although the DA's work space lacks the panoramic view that my father's boasts, as well as the museum-quality art, it's no less a kingdom. There is certainly no shortage of places to sit—four guest chairs opposite his desk, twelve others around a conference table, two sofas and three armchairs. The walls are covered with photographs of Drake McKenney and A-listers from politics and the arts. Everyone from President Trump to Jay-Z is represented in the pantheon of famous people who have shaken Drake McKenney's hand.

McKenney arranges himself behind his desk, then directs me to occupy a chair opposite it by pointing. When we're both situated, he gets down to business.

"Thank you for seeing me on such short notice," he says.

I suspect he doesn't have the first clue as to what I've been doing with my life since I left the office. Like everyone in the legal community, he knows my father. Like everyone in the English-speaking world, he knows about Charlotte's murder. I don't flatter myself into thinking that he's given me a second thought in the last nine months. More to the point, I doubt he gave any thought to me at all even during the years I worked for him.

"Not every day the District Attorney asks to speak to you."

"Your circumstances are going to become even rarer in a moment," he says. "People sit where you are every day and ask me for a favor of one type or another. But today, you're going to receive such a request, because I have a favor to ask of *you*. And like they're always telling me, I wouldn't be asking if it weren't important."

For years, I thought about my career path at the office. And now, after I've given up on being a lawyer altogether, the promotion I long dreamed about is at hand. Talk about irony.

"I'm all ears, Mr. McKenney."

"Please, call me Drake."

"Drake."

"The reason I've asked you to come down here is that, quite frankly, when Lauren was murdered, I made a mistake allowing Dana Goodwin to handle the investigation."

One thing that everyone knows about Drake McKenney is that he never admits a mistake. Any failure is always someone's else fault. Of course, it would be hard to find a scapegoat regarding his decision to put Lauren's murderer in charge of the investigation to find her murderer. Up until a second ago, I wouldn't have put it past McKenney to try, though. That's why I don't expect his mea culpa to go beyond these walls.

"What I should have done was go outside the office and appoint a special prosecutor to handle it," he explains. "At the time, I thought it was more important that we keep it within our family here, but . . . well, I'm not going to make the same mistake twice."

It takes me a moment to realize how dramatically I've misinterpreted his call. Thirty seconds ago, I was sure I was about to become the bureau chief of Special Vics. But Drake McKenney isn't offering me that job. Instead, he wants me to prosecute Dana Goodwin.

McKenney goes on to tell me that he's selected me because I'm the finest non-Manhattan DA out there, but I'm not so naïve as to buy what he's selling. He's bowing to political pressure to do this by the book. But I've been granted this assignment for one reason, and one reason only: McKenney still wants to control the situation. Even though the whole point of a special prosecutor should be to wrest that oversight from him, he figures that, as long as he can dangle a potential bureau chief spot before me, I can be counted on to do his bidding. It's a win-win for him. He gets to say that he appointed someone independent to prosecute the case, and yet he'll still be manipulating the strings. It's the exact same thinking that caused him to select Dana to partner with Gabriel, but now I'm the one playing the part of his puppet.

"Can I have some time to think about it?"

"Of course. I realize that this will be a big-time commitment and a lot of pressure. Media attention, that sort of thing. So you should give it some thought."

He smiles the way I've seen him do at rallies. A politician's smile.

"Let me leave you with this, Ella. And I realize that I run the risk of seeming heavy-handed, but I wouldn't say this if I didn't truly believe it." He pauses for dramatic affect. "I'm quite certain that it would make Lauren happy to know *you're* the one who's going to bring her killer to justice."

36.

DANA GOODWIN

I'd stayed away from the news and social media since my release, but it would have taken immersion in an isolation chamber for me to completely block out my case. It's everywhere: tabloid headlines, cable news shows, Twitter. From every window of our house, I can see the reporters continuing their vigil. I know that even more will await me when I arrive at LeMarcus Burrows's office.

For that very reason, LeMarcus offered to meet me off-site. I declined, recognizing that being stalked is my new reality and it's better to face it than to hide. LeMarcus coached me on how to act as I made my way into his building—look straight ahead, smile but not like I'm enjoying myself, don't run but don't dawdle either.

An hour later, I traverse the press gauntlet in front of LeMarcus's building. Reporters shout out questions that they couldn't have expected me to answer.

"Did you kill Lauren Wright?"

"Were you in love with her?"

"Why'd you do it?"

It takes all my self-control not to run away, but I walk straight ahead into the building. Not too fast or too slow, with a half smile front and center.

The nondescript midtown high-rise that houses the law offices of LeMarcus Burrows and Associates is one of the many buildings in this city that is more than forty floors tall, but it was built without a household-name anchor tenant or owner, so it has no descriptor. Unlike, say, the Chrysler Building or the Seagram Building, or anything called Trump.

I take the elevator to the twenty-fourth floor. When the doors open, a sign points to the left. At the end of the corridor are glass doors with the firm's name in large, gold letters.

In my prior life, I never visited defense attorneys. It was a point of principle in the DA's office that defense lawyers traveled to see us, not the other way around.

The firm's name also graces the entry wall, this time in silver letters each about half a foot high. Beneath them is an African American man sitting behind what appears to be an antique desk. He's immaculately dressed in a gray, three-piece tweed suit, his tie held in place with a shiny silver tie bar. He looks like he could otherwise be a lawyer, but for the fact that he's in the position occupied by the firm's receptionist.

"LeMarcus is on a conference call with a court right now, so he asked me to bring you back to the conference room," the man says without introducing himself.

The room he leads me to is small, with a large picture window providing a view of another building's twenty-fourth floor across the street. The table has only six chairs, which is three times as many as we'll need for this meeting. In the center is a single banker's box. The side label reads: "The People of the State of New York v. Dana L. Goodwin."

I sit alone, staring at the box, afraid to open it as if inside lurks something deadly, like a poisonous snake that only LeMarcus should handle. After five minutes of me staring at it like Pandora, the door swings open and LeMarcus rushes in. He's also wearing a three-piece suit. I wonder if it's a coincidence or part of the uniform at the firm.

Although LeMarcus and I were friendly when we served together as young ADAs, we weren't the kind of friends who stayed in touch after his goodbye dinner. I'd seen him through the years, sometimes as an adversary, more often at functions honoring some judge or a fellow colleague. During those meetings we were always cordial, suggesting that we should get lunch or dinner and catch up, but neither of us ever extended an actual invitation. It was the relationship I had with nearly everyone I worked with—until Lauren.

"I'm so glad that the bail's all worked out," he says while taking the seat across from me. "This will be so much easier now than if you were still inside."

"Yeah, I like living at home more than sharing a cell at Rikers too."

He nods at my joke, but it apparently only merits a thin smile. I take LeMarcus's demeanor to suggest that he's not going to get more attached to me than any other accused murderer who pays him to set them free.

"I'm going to get right to it," he says, "if that's okay with you."

"Please do. I've read that they have Lauren's iPhone, but is there anything else linking me to her murder?"

"I'll get there in a second. Before I do, I wanted to get some pre-liminaries out of the way. The first is to discuss the pros and cons about our pulling Judge Gold."

The book on Arthur Gold goes something like this. Back when I was in middle school, he was a personal-injury lawyer of limited success, which caused him to seek the pay raise the state judiciary had to offer, even though for most lawyers a judge's salary—which amounts to less than large law firms dole out for last year's law-school graduates—is a disincentive to taking the bench. He might not have had a chance but for the fact that he was openly gay in 1987. This endeared him to the Greenwich Village Democratic Club, and they used their growing clout to make him a judge.

Since the first day he donned the black robe, Judge Gold has been one of the system's outstanding jurists. One of the few—maybe the only—whom both defense lawyers and prosecutors are equally glad to appear before. Defendants take comfort in his jaundiced view of police power that only comes with having experienced discrimination first-hand, and prosecutors like that he doesn't fall for the games defendants try to play, including endless adjournments and novel legal theories to reduce responsibility. *Fair, decent, thoughtful,* and *smart* are the usual words used to describe him.

Gay never comes up. Not anymore, at least. Strike that. It hasn't come up for years. But once the media hears his name rolled out of the wheel to preside over my case, I have little doubt that in some media circles he'll be rebranded as "Gay Judge Gold."

"My advice is that we stick with him," LeMarcus continues. "But I do have some reservations. I have enough respect for Judge Gold to know that he doesn't engage in identity jurisprudence. At least not on a conscious level. But if some of that does seep in, he's going to bend over backward to seem strict so people don't think he's favoring you because of the perception that you share a sexual orientation. I say that without any disrespect, but as a black man, I think I get some latitude here. Judge Gold's years on the bench have made the fact he was the first openly gay judge at most a footnote. And he likes it that way."

I'd surmised this much on my own. I'd also concluded that there was very little I could do about picking my own judge. Even if LeMarcus objected to Judge Gold on the grounds he knew Lauren personally, every judge in New York County fit that bill. Maybe the chief judge of the court would assign someone from one of the outer boroughs, but that was even a bigger wild card. Besides, if we objected and Judge Gold decided to stay on despite our concerns, my fate would be in the hands of a judge who knew I didn't want him.

"I've never lost in front of him," I say.

"But you've never lost, period," LeMarcus says, this time with a real smile. "I'm zero and two with him, but neither was a triable case."

Triable case is a defense-lawyer term. Most of the people who seek defense services are not only guilty, but are swimming in overwhelming evidence for conviction. A guy who sold drugs to an undercover cop, or someone that has laid out the particulars of a crime on wiretaps. For that reason, defense lawyers don't put much stock in their overall win-loss record. Rather, the subset of how they do in *triable cases* is all that matters.

A case is *triable* when there's something they can tell the jury in furtherance of a not-guilty verdict. I've always found the term amusing because it makes clear that guilt or innocence is beside the point.

"Is my case triable?" I ask.

"The evidence they have is solid," he says, looking me straight in the eye and now without any smile. "I'm not going to lie to you about that. I don't know if it's enough all by itself for a conviction, but it's close. So, to answer your question, as far as I know right now, yes. You have a triable case. But that could change in a hurry. If the prosecution gets anything else—and I suspect they're hard at work looking for it—it won't be triable. And, as I'm sure you know, I don't expect them to offer a plea."

This I do know. Limiting the damage by accepting responsibility in exchange for receiving a reduced sentence—say pleading down to manslaughter in the first degree, which carries with it a penalty of ten to thirty years—thereby leaving some possibility, however remote, that I could be out in time to see Jacob graduate from high school, is not a possibility. Not for killing an ADA. A guilty plea now and a guilty verdict after trial are going to lead to the same result: twenty-five years to life, the maximum penalty for murder in the second degree in New York. I only avoid mandatory lifetime incarceration because murdered ADAs aren't defined as "peace officers" under the statute. Kill a cop and you're charged with murder in the first, but an ADA only merits a second-degree murder charge. Lucky me, I guess.

"The reason they made the arrest is because they cracked Lauren's phone," LeMarcus continues. "Gabriel Velasquez confirmed to me what's in the press—that on the night Lauren was killed, you texted her asking to meet you in the park."

I begin to reply, but LeMarcus puts up his hand, instructing me to stop. "I should have said this before we began because it's part of my standard spiel. I thought you might have found it patronizing, but it's important that you not tell me anything that I haven't asked. I don't want you to taint me with information that makes a particular defense outside the ethical boundaries. Understood?"

I nod that I do. He wants to leave open the possibility of presenting a defense that doesn't conform with what actually happened. In other words, he is open to my committing perjury so long as he's not guilty of suborning it.

"Good. Aside from the phone, they also have evidence corroborating the affair," LeMarcus says rather solemnly. "Gabriel didn't tell me exactly what they had, but I'm guessing it's surveillance footage at the hotel that captures you and Lauren together. It's also likely that one or more hotel clerks remember you. Two women checking into a single hotel room regularly is semimemorable. Even in New York City."

In my head, the loop plays of what this is going to look like in court. Stuart sitting in the gallery's first row, hearing people testify about my weekly appearances at the Best Western hotel, hand in hand with Lauren.

"Let's talk for a second about the gun," LeMarcus says. "As you know, it was registered to Detective Gregory Papamichael. The good detective is no longer with us, but I'm sure they're trying to find a connection between you and him. If they do, that'll be another bridge we need to cross. But until they disclose what they have, I don't want to hear anything from you about it. Papamichael was on the force a lot of years. He must have worked cases with a lot of ADAs, and so my working assumption is that he never gave you a Glock Nineteen."

I want to affirmatively deny that Papamichael ever gifted me the gun, but I hold my tongue. In part that's to follow my counsel's directive not to say anything he hasn't expressly asked me to impart, but the primary reason is that I know he's not going to believe me. He's probably never had a client who didn't swear innocence, and my bet would be that every single one of them was guilty.

"Also, they have your current phone. The one they took from you when you were arrested, but it has nothing on it that predates the murder. I know that's because your communications with Lauren were on your prior phone, and you lost that."

I'm amazed LeMarcus is able to keep a straight face. I can't even imagine the number of defendants who told me that some vital piece of evidence had been lost or conveniently stolen—guns, cars, credit cards.

"What's their theory of motive?" I ask.

"They haven't said. Can I assume from your question that there is nothing on Lauren's phone that indicates a recent breakup, or a fight of any kind?"

I recognize the carefulness of the wording. He doesn't want to know if Lauren and I actually *had* a fight or *had* broken up. He only cares about whether there's proof the prosecutor can find of either on her phone.

"That's right," I say. "There won't be anything on her phone like that."

"Good. That, in a nutshell, is what makes your case triable: the age-old question of why."

37.

ELLA BRODEN

I step outside McKenney's office in a post-dreamlike state. Part of me wonders if I just imagined the entire encounter. To make it real, I call Gabriel.

"You'll never guess who I just met with," I say.

"Oprah," he replies without hesitation.

"Drake McKenney."

Gabriel doesn't say anything back. That's his standard MO—to stay quiet until I get to the point.

"He wants me to be the special prosecutor on the Dana Goodwin case."

"What did you say?"

"I told him that I wanted to take a day to think about it. But I honestly don't see how I can say no."

I hear him laugh. "Well, that part would be easy. What's the line . . . you just put your lips together and say no."

"I think the line is 'blow.'"

This time it's not a laugh I hear. It's a deep sigh.

"Is this something you want to do? Not something you think you *should* do? But *want* to do?"

"That sounds like you think I shouldn't."

"You couldn't be more wrong about that. Think about how much I'm going to enjoy working under you."

It takes a second for the full meaning of his double entendre to sink in. By taking over the prosecution of the case, I'll become his boss. When Dana and he were investigating, Gabriel was in charge, but now that a defendant is in custody and the matter is going to trial, I'd be calling the shots, and his job as the detective in charge of the investigation is now to assist me. I'm surprised that this hadn't occurred to me sooner. It's another reason my assignment might have appealed to McKenney. It gives him control not only over me, but also the NYPD.

———

After getting off the phone with Gabriel, I seek advice from the only other man I trust: my father. I call ahead to secure time on his schedule, though I know my father won't have an open slot: nobody ever cancels an appointment, not with the nonrefundable $1,500 an hour he charges. Some client or other must be bumped for him to see me.

Ashleigh, his far-too-shapely secretary, greets me at the door to my father's eponymous law firm. "So nice to see you again, Ella. The place just hasn't been the same without you around."

During my brief foray in criminal defense, when I worked with my father, I suspected that he might be seeing Ashleigh. At the time, I did not approve. She's too young for him, and even though she is actually pretty smart if you engage her, the first impression she makes is of being a bimbo. Allison and I have spoken about it a few times; the one tangible change I can see in my life from therapy is that I'm less judgmental about whom people choose to love.

Ashleigh leads me to my father's corner office. I know that he would have come out to greet me himself unless he was otherwise occupied, so I'm not surprised to see him on the phone when I enter. He raises a single finger, telling me that he'll only be a moment more. If I had a nickel for every time he's made that gesture to me in my life, I'd be sitting on a mountain of nickels.

As he speaks, I scan his work space. Nothing, but nothing, makes me feel more like a child than being in my father's office. Although the room is furnished with antiques and fine art, he still displays on his bookshelf the carousel full of crayons that Charlotte and I used whenever we visited as children.

He brings his call to a swift conclusion and takes a moment to beam at me before saying anything. He's done more of that since Charlotte's death, as if he's thankful for our every encounter. For nearly all my life, I felt the pressure that comes with being the firstborn. More than anything else, perhaps, it has shaped my destiny—for better and for worse. Yet now I realize that the role of "only child" is even more laden with potential for parental disappointment.

"This is truly an unexpected pleasure. I only wish I had some advance notice. I would have jettisoned my lunch plans for you in a heartbeat, but at this point, it's something noncancelable, I'm afraid."

"This shouldn't take long, but I need some advice. I've been offered a job."

"That's great, Ella. With anyone I know?"

"In fact, yes. Drake McKenney. He wants me to prosecute Dana Goodwin for Lauren Wright's murder."

My father is like me in that we're both careful when we speak. An occupational hazard for lawyers, he's always said. A misstated word can mean that someone goes to prison. The stakes here aren't quite so high at this moment, but by his silence, my father recognizes the measure of import I'll attach to his next utterance.

"Congratulations. It is quite an honor that Drake would assign to you what I don't think it's any exaggeration to say is the most important case he's had as DA. From what I read in the papers, this will not be the easiest case to win. Without putting too much pressure on you, I'll say that McKenney's *got* to win it if he wants to be mayor someday. He probably has to win just to continue being DA after next November."

"I haven't accepted yet," I say. "That's why I'm here. I'm . . . not sure what to do."

"I don't believe that, Ella. You know what you want. You always have. I think sometimes you're as unfair to me as you think I am to you, if you know what I mean."

I say I don't, but of course, I do.

"You want to share responsibility for your choices with me. Now, I don't mind—it comes with the job of being your father. But it also makes me wonder if I'd done a better job whether you might not need for me to do it at all."

This is another recurring theme in my sessions with Allison: my decision to follow in my father's career footsteps rather than pursue music back when such a choice made sense for a twentysomething with dreams. I've held it against him ever since, despite the fact that, deep down, I know it was my decision, even if I was motivated by pleasing him. And he's probably right that I'm here now to get his blessing to accept the job so I will have someone to blame if I fail in the end.

"I'm working on it," I say with a smile.

He smiles back. "I know you are. I'm working on it too. Which is why I'm not going to tell you that if you take the case it will make you the most famous prosecutor in this city. Or that you will be able to write your own ticket after that."

"Not if I lose."

He chuckles. "Even if you lose. Think about the A-list lawyers in this city. They're known for their famous clients, but they almost always end up either losing or pleading them out. I mean, look at me. I haven't won an acquittal in . . . I don't know, four or five years, at least. Hasn't hurt my practice any." After a beat, he continues, "I'm also not going to say this: it is perfectly acceptable for you to decline. Cases that are personal, they're always the toughest. There's enough pressure on you to win besides having to feel that you've failed to avenge the murder of someone you love if you lose."

There's a knock on the door. Even before my father can respond, the door slides open slightly. Ashleigh's head pokes in.

"Your one o'clock is here," she says.

"Thanks, Dad," I tell him. "For everything you said—and everything you 'didn't' say."

———

Since Dana Goodwin's arrest, Gabriel has kept to a saner schedule, but he still rarely comes home before seven. Today he arrives at six, undoubtedly because he wants to finish discussing the conversation we started earlier.

I sometimes can't believe how much I miss him during the day. I've never felt this way about a man before, and it both frightens and exhilarates me.

Tonight I've cooked, which is something I've been trying to do more lately. Not so much to prove to Gabriel that I'm domestic, but to give some structure to my day.

"Something smells delicious," he says.

"It's just the sautéed onions. I honestly didn't expect you to be home so early. In a half hour or so it'll be chicken fajitas. I'm also going to make some spicy guacamole."

"I'll make us some margaritas, then. Give me a minute."

Gabriel retreats from the kitchen, no doubt heading to the bedroom to stow away his weapon. He returns quickly and opens the cabinet where I keep my alcohol.

"I see tequila, but no margarita mix," he says, his head stuck in the cabinet.

"This is a from-scratch operation, my friend," I call back.

He stands up straight. "I talk big," he says with a chuckle, "but I don't know how to make a margarita without margarita mix."

"That's why God invented the Internet."

He rolls his eyes but reaches for his phone. A few taps later he says, "Okay. Two ounces of tequila . . . check. One ounce of lime juice. Do you have that much?"

I laugh. "Yes, but you'll need more than that if I'm having any. Luckily, I have a whole container, so we're good there. What about the Cointreau?"

"You're good. I was just about to ask you what that is."

"It's a kind of liqueur. Check the cabinet. I think I have some. Or at least I did once."

I can hear the bottles clacking against one another. "I don't see it. Can you make it without it . . . Oh wait . . . Yup, you have some."

He walks the bottle into the kitchen with a proud look on his face, as if he's Indiana Jones extracting some ancient artifact from a secure crypt. "Two margaritas coming up."

He opens the freezer and plunks two ice cubes into each glass, then stirs the ingredients together and sets the finished product on the counter in front of me.

"To . . . a new challenge," he says, raising his glass.

I clink my glass to his. "Is mixing a margarita a new challenge for you, Gabriel?"

He takes a sip of his creation. "I was referring to your new job."

I take a sip. It's good. Perfect, even.

"I still haven't told McKenney I'm taking it."

"I'm not McKenney. What are you telling *me*?"

I take another swallow of the margarita. Then one more.

"Yeah, I'm going to do it."

Gabriel looks down at his drink. I know this expression: he has something to say but doesn't think it's his place to say it.

"What?" I say.

He sighs. "What what?"

"What aren't you telling me?"

"I don't think Dana killed her."

"Who, then?"

"Richard. The affair gives him a strong motive."

"But the texts from Dana's phone—"

"I know, but I bet she comes up with some explanation."

"Good luck to her on that."

He shakes his head in disagreement. "She's going to say that she texted Lauren to meet her for a happy reason, a lover's rendezvous for some make-out time in the park. Richard was suspicious and followed Lauren. He hid while Dana and Lauren did their thing. Then, after Dana left, Richard put two bullets into Lauren."

Gabriel hadn't shared this theory before, but it's a good one. In fact, I'm disappointed that this didn't occur to me on my own. Perhaps I have a blind spot here. As much as I might try to keep my personal feelings at bay in bringing Lauren's killer to justice, I can't deny that I've *wanted* Dana to be guilty from the moment she was arrested. I've told myself that's because I believed she is guilty, but maybe my desire to be Lauren's favorite plays a role too. I know that, in life, Lauren obviously preferred Dana—but if I can prove Dana's guilt, then I'll regain my favored position, albeit posthumously.

38.

DANA GOODWIN

"Right before you arrived, I received a call from Ella Broden. She's been designated as special prosecutor for the case."

LeMarcus says this to open our second meeting. It's Saturday morning; by meeting on the weekend, we've avoided the press barricade, at least at his office. There are still a few die-hards camped in front of my house, unfortunately.

My instant reaction to this news is negative, although it takes me a moment to organize my feelings so I understand why. It's not that I'm concerned Ella Broden is too worthy an adversary. In fact, I can think of a few ADAs I would consider better in the courtroom, not to mention that Ella must be a little out of practice. As with an athlete, it's hard to take a year off and then come back for the toughest game of your career.

And then I realize the reason for my opposition is right in front of me. I'm concerned about Ella's connection to Lauren. Although that might work in my favor, making her too close to be objective, it also means she'll work twice as hard to secure a conviction as someone not personally invested.

"We don't want her," I say.

I expect LeMarcus to inquire further, but my reaction must be consistent with his own take.

"Agreed. What grounds do you propose we allege to make that happen? I don't think her friendship and working relationship with Lauren will be enough."

The most common grounds used to disqualify the other side's lawyer is to cite a conflict of interest. Traditionally, that can happen when the lawyer once represented the other side on a similar matter. The thinking goes that in such circumstances, the lawyer has acquired inside information about the adversary and therefore cannot now appear on the other side. Obviously, that happens far less in a criminal setting than in civil cases. Ella Broden has never been my lawyer, so there's no clear conflict of interest in having her prosecute me.

The only other basis for disqualification would be if she could be considered a witness in my case. I'm certain that consideration was vetted before her appointment, and the powers that be must have concluded that she has no inside knowledge to add to the prosecution's case.

From my prior discussions with Gabriel, I know that Ella would have nothing to add to my defense. Still I say, "The night Lauren was killed, she and her husband had dinner with Ella and Gabriel."

LeMarcus seems surprised by the revelation. "Hold on. Gabriel Velasquez? The police investigator working the case with you?"

"Yeah. He and Ella are boyfriend-girlfriend. Small world, right?"

"Was Ella ever alone with Lauren that night? I mean, even if it was just to visit the ladies' room?"

"No. Gabriel would have told me if Ella learned anything in a one-on-one that was relevant to the case."

"All right. Even so, I think that'll be enough to disqualify her. We can say we want to call her as a witness. It's not like there aren't lots of other people who could prosecute the case without denying the defense the opportunity to call to the stand one of the last four people to see her alive."

I like what I've just heard. Ella's as good as out.

"Which brings me to the next issue," LeMarcus says. "Who do we tell the jury actually *did* murder Lauren?"

Working as a prosecutor, I cared only about what really happened. I always took for granted that I could demonstrate the truth to a jury. Defense lawyers like LeMarcus see the world differently. The truth doesn't matter as much as how he can spin the evidence he can present. Evidence and the truth are distant cousins.

I don't provide him with a scapegoat, at least not quickly enough. My hesitation causes LeMarcus to answer his own question.

"Richard Trofino is the obvious choice. Was there anyone else in the mix?"

"Do we have to decide this now? I'd prefer to see how the prosecution's case comes in before committing to that kind of defense."

"Unfortunately, we don't have that luxury. The moment the jury hears about your affair with Lauren and sees that last text, every single one of them is going to believe that you killed Lauren Wright. And they're going to hear that in the prosecutor's opening statement. That means they very well may make the decision to convict before I even get a chance to speak. The only way we can fight that is if we tell them equally early who actually killed her."

I nod in agreement. *It's the only way,* I tell myself.

"There were only two other people we looked at," I say. "This guy Lauren prosecuted ten years ago named Donald Chesterman. She tried the case with Ella Broden, actually. He made some threats and just got out of prison, but we didn't see a way of linking Chesterman to the gun. Besides, we had no idea where he was."

"Okay. Who's behind door number two?"

"Drake McKenney," I say. "Lauren was going to run against him, and Richard claimed that McKenney reamed him out over it, even making some threats. McKenney denied it, though, and then the homeless guy said the man he saw was shorter than McKenney."

LeMarcus considers this for a moment, no doubt trying to figure out whether it will be easier to get the jury to believe that Drake McKenney murdered Lauren than to convince them Richard pulled the trigger. I don't point out that my lawyer's careful consideration of accusing Drake McKenney gives the lie to the idea that we're going to tell the jury *exactly* who killed Lauren. More accurately, we're going to try our damnedest to blame whomever we can most plausibly sell to the jury. In fact, that's LeMarcus's job. My freedom depends on his doing it well.

"I'm not worried about the ID," he says. "The least of our problems is the homeless guy. The jury's not going to convict on his partial sighting. After I'm done with him, they'll sooner believe he saw the Easter Bunny. But you can't cross-examine a cell phone. McKenney has some appeal in this regard because he got custody of Lauren's phone after the arrest. That means we don't have to claim that someone else sent the text. Instead, we argue that he framed you by somehow putting that text on her phone *after* the murder."

"How could he do that?"

"I have no idea. But, I expect that if we pay enough, we'll find some expert to say it's possible. That would go a long way toward establishing reasonable doubt. And I like going after McKenney because he's not very popular with the minority community. You gotta figure that at least three of our jurors will be people of color."

I nod to indicate that he's made a good point. It takes only one person to hang a jury.

"But I still think Trofino is the more attractive choice," he continues. "It's a hard sell that a sitting DA commits murder to avoid a potential primary challenge. People lose elections all the time. In his case, the worst-case scenario is that he'll end up making millions of dollars in the private sector if he's voted out of office. Besides, when a woman having an affair is murdered, it doesn't seem plausible that her murder is completely unrelated to that. By contrast, everyone on earth will believe that Richard Trofino had an obvious motive for killing his wife.

And I suspect the jury will hate him every bit as much as McKenney. A multimillionaire who can't take no for an answer. My thinking is that we explain away the text by claiming that Lauren mistakenly took *your* phone home the night of the murder. That kind of mix-up happens sometimes. Richard read the texts, flew into a jealous rage, and then decided that he could kill his wife and frame you for the murder just by sending a text from your phone. As part of that theory, we'll need to demonstrate that you didn't have a passcode on your phone. Otherwise, Richard wouldn't have been able to access it, even if he did have it in his possession."

"I really didn't have a passcode," I say, understanding that this fact is essential to any defense that involves someone else sending the text from my phone. "And I can do you one better on your theory about how Richard came into possession of my iPhone. On the night Lauren was killed, Richard was alone in my office. He could have taken the phone then."

LeMarcus smiles like he's hit the lotto. "That's good. Very good, in fact. Now tell me, who can testify that he was in your office alone?"

I think for a moment. Then I realize I know the answer to this one.

"Rita DeSapio. She's the secretary that Lauren and I shared. Her desk is between our offices. Even if she doesn't remember, I'm certain we can prove Richard was in the building that evening, because he must have signed in downstairs."

"Excellent. Now, about the phone. How can we prove that you didn't have it that evening?"

I know that this is going to be more difficult. "I bought a new one the next day," I say.

He nods but isn't convinced. "Okay . . ." he says, pausing, most likely in the hope that I'm going to give him something better to work with. We both know that if I did send the text and then murder Lauren, the first thing I'd do is get rid of my phone, so a purchase the next day doesn't prove very much.

"Stuart and I can both testify to it," I finally add.

"Let's put a pin in the idea of your testifying for the moment. Stuart will be enough to get us closer to reasonable doubt. Who can support that your phone wasn't passcode protected?"

He means other than me, another indication that he's not so much putting a pin in the discussion regarding my taking the stand as tabling it indefinitely.

"Stuart," I say, because he'll be my stand-in on any evidence that I can't put in myself.

"Good. Now, the last piece is about the gun. They're going to try to link *you* to Papamichael, but we're going to do our best to link him to Lauren. My guess is that, given Papamichael's seniority, he crossed both your paths. I suspect we'll end up fighting to a draw on which of the two of you he could have given a gun. But that's fine by me, because they bear the burden of proof."

"I'd be willing to testify that Lauren mentioned his name to me," I say, trying to put my thumb on the scale so that my testimony helps my defense.

"Noted," he says, "but it won't help very much. The jury isn't going to believe you just because you say so. They're going to believe the case files."

The primary reason LeMarcus does not want me on the stand is that the jury will think I'm lying. He doesn't care if they reach that conclusion because I am committing perjury, or because that's what jurors usually think when the defendant takes the stand. Either way, my testifying makes a guilty verdict that much more likely.

"So, let's see where that leaves us," LeMarcus asks, but I can tell it's a rhetorical question, with that point driven home when he keeps right on talking. "The secretary testifies that on the evening Lauren Wright was murdered, her husband, Richard Trofino, entered your office and was there alone for several minutes. Your husband testifies that when you got home, you did not have your phone, and that he knew from prior experience that it was not passcode protected, because it was often handed to your son to play with. The next day you bought a new phone, and the Apple store confirms that, which further drives home that your phone was stolen the night before by Richard. And, as for the gun, Lauren Wright knew Detective Papamichael, so he must have given her his weapon some years back. Richard used it to kill her."

LeMarcus offers me a satisfied grin. He looks exceedingly pleased with the world we have just constructed. Richard Trofino murdered his wife after sending messages on the phone he stole from me and using the Glock 19 his wife procured from Detective Papamichael. Simple.

———

Stuart kisses me on the lips the moment I return home from LeMarcus's office.

"How'd it go?" he asks.

"LeMarcus didn't say that if I'm convicted he'd serve the time."

He grimaces at my gallows humor.

"We came up with a defense today. It's a good one too."

"Yeah? Care to share?"

"Richard Trofino. We're going to claim that he took my cell phone when he was in my office, read the texts between Lauren and me, got insanely jealous, but realized that if he killed his wife in their apartment he'd go to jail. He decided that the better play was to frame me by sending her a text from my cell phone. Oh, and we're reasonably sure that Lauren worked cases with Papamichael at some point, and that connects Richard to the gun. So it all fits together rather nicely."

Stuart nods that this makes sense to him too.

"I think it's my best defense," I say. "I've considered all the other options. Believe me that I have. This one is the most likely to result in my acquittal."

Stuart nods again, even though I appreciate that he isn't professionally equipped to make an informed decision about trial strategy. I decide to change the subject to something much dearer to my heart.

"How's the little boy today?"

If Stuart is put off by my abrupt segue, he doesn't show it.

"He's good. He's working on a special project in his room. "Why don't you go check on him? I'll start dinner for you."

———

When I open the door of my son's room, I see Jacob hunched over his desk, so involved in whatever he's doing that he's oblivious to my presence. He's had that desk since he was born, but I don't remember him ever sitting at it before. Another reminder that my little boy is growing up. Whereas that reality would previously not have been the source of any distress, now I can't help but take it to the next step and think about him going the rest of the way through life without me.

I kiss him on the top of his head. If I've startled him, he doesn't show it. In fact, he doesn't react at all.

"Whatcha working on?" I ask.

"I'm writing a book," he says matter-of-factly.

"What's it about?"

"A boy and a computer. The computer's name is Jane. The boy's name is George. And they're best friends. But the computer . . . it's old and it doesn't work as good as the new computers. Oh, and George's job is working with computers, so he really needs a good computer or people won't give him money."

My son has updated *Mike Mulligan*. In place of a steam shovel, he's using a computer. I couldn't be more proud if he'd written *War and Peace*.

"That sounds really interesting. What does . . . George do about it?"

This causes my son to turn to face me. His expression shows he's worried, perhaps for Jane the computer.

"I'm not sure yet," he says. "I want there to be a happy ending, so Jane and George can still be friends. But . . . I don't know what you do with old computers. Do you?"

I actually give this some thought, hoping that I can solve the problem. In the actual *Mike Mulligan*, the author has a footnote crediting the person who gave her the idea for the ending. Maybe Jacob will do me that honor as well.

"How about . . . I don't know. Maybe Jane is perfect for teaching little kids how to use a computer? And maybe George can become a teacher and they can work together in the school."

Jacob smiles with the power of a thousand suns. I smile even more broadly.

"I'll make George an art teacher like Daddy, and Jane can be used to teach kids how to draw."

"That sounds perfect."

"Thanks, Mom."

And then he turns away from me to continue working.

39.

ELLA BRODEN

Saturday night at Lava looks as different from my Thursday-night gig as those performances do from open-mic night. It seems as if each type of show draws an entirely different crowd. Tuesdays are for the bohemians, the slackers, the ne'er do wells. People who can't afford to buy tickets to see live music but are happy to listen to wannabes play. Thursdays bring out the millennials, but Saturday is for grown-ups.

The median age appears to be above my own. The patrons are, for the most part, coupled up. No doubt more than a few have hired sitters and refer to the excursion as "date night." Some of the men are even wearing sports jackets.

For my own attire, I picked the very first outfit I ever wore to perform as Cassidy. I purchased it on eBay, and the label sewn inside the collar bears a designer's name that I could never have afforded new, although I'm well aware that the dress could be a counterfeit. When that thought first occurred to me, it only made me cherish the garment that much more. We were kindred spirits in that way. It's black and short—too short to be worn by anyone but Cassidy. It actually shows less skin than most of her costumes, but I think it's the most provocative, on account of the fact that nearly the entire front and back are see-through black lace.

Gabriel's reaction when he saw me in my Cassidy outfit was an eye roll followed by a smirk.

"No?" I asked.

"No . . . I mean, *yes*. You look . . . spectacular. I just . . . I still can't believe you get up in front of people wearing that, is all."

"Not me," I said. "*I'd* sooner die. Cassidy."

———

I'm wearing my overcoat when I enter Lava. I've asked Gabriel to come with me this evening. Ever since I broke that taboo and allowed him entry rights to Lava, I've realized that it had been a mistake to try to separate my worlds. His hand is on the small of my back, but as soon as we're a step inside, he moves in front to clear the crowd. I walk behind him. He must spot Karen before I do, because he abruptly zigs. A few steps later, I see that he's heading straight for her.

It's hot in the club, and Karen's dress bares her shoulders and arms. It gives me the best view I've had yet of her impressive body art, the main feature of which is a serpent that curls around her arm from her bicep to her wrist.

Gabriel gets the first double kiss, and then me. I can feel Karen's hand on my back; it's almost as if she's trying to ascertain the contours of my outfit beneath my coat.

When our embrace ends, she says, "Need to see the merch."

This time I don't do the stripper routine. With Gabriel beside me, I can't pretend I'm Cassidy, so I simply remove my coat and hand it to him. He drapes it over his arm like he's a coat-check boy.

"Me likey," Karen says.

"Thanks," I reply.

"You're going on at ten sharp. I've looked at your set list. Good choices, all of them. I think you should move the one you wrote up a slot, maybe two. Don't get me wrong, I love that song, but closing with two up-tempo numbers is better."

A minor change in song order usually doesn't faze me. For some reason, however, my legs suddenly feel like jelly.

"You okay?" Gabriel asks as soon as Karen leaves us.

"Yeah . . . all of a sudden . . . I don't know what just came over me."

"Do you want a drink?"

I do. I'm badly in need of something to calm my now-runaway nerves.

A man vacates his stool the moment we reach the bar, and Gabriel motions for me to sit.

"Relax. You're going to be great," Gabriel says. "You always are, Ella."

I want to tell him not to call me that. Not here. But instead I ask the bartender for a whisky. Once it's poured, I reach eagerly for the drink, and finish it in two gulps.

"One more," I say quickly.

"Take it easy," Gabriel says. "You want to be relaxed. Not smashed."

He's right. I take his advice, nursing my second whisky. Gabriel's attuned enough to my needs that he knows to be quiet now, allowing me to stay in my own head. As I'm collecting my thoughts, it occurs to me that Gabriel's use of my name wasn't by mistake, but design. He wanted to remind me of who I really am.

———

Karen's introduction lasts longer than it does on Thursday nights. She spends nearly all of it finding different ways to communicate what a thrill it is for her and for Lava to host Onyx. It's obvious from the screaming that the crowd is here to see them perform. It makes me even more nervous, and I finish the last drops of my second whisky.

"But before Onyx gets up here, you all are in for something that you'll not soon forget. There's only one woman who I think can match the intensity that Onyx brings to the stage, and that's Lava's very own . . . Cassidy!"

Karen's introduction garners enthusiastic applause, although it's not nearly as loud as when Onyx was mentioned. When I reach the stage, she hands me the microphone. With her hand covering the top of it, she whispers, "Blow the roof off this place like you always do."

A moment later, I'm alone before the crowd. I shut my eyes. To my surprise, tonight it's neither Charlotte I see in my mind's eye nor Lauren, but Gabriel. I open them quickly and focus on the genuine article.

"Thank you," I say. "Thank you all so much for being here tonight."

The introductory chords to "Light My Fire"—the cheesy organ riff that lets you know at once that you're going to another place—fills the room. I go with it, and am all too happy to be swept away.

After "Light My Fire," I sing The Pierces' "Kissing You Goodbye," which is new to my repertoire. I like that it sounds spooky and has the word *goodbye* in it. Then I take it down a notch with "Nothing Compares 2 U." I do that one because I read somewhere that Sinéad O'Connor sings it in honor of her mother, despite the fact that it was written by Prince, who was undoubtedly thinking about a woman gone for seven hours and fifteen days. Then I bring it back up to eleven with Fiona Apple's "Sleep to Dream." I disregard Karen's advice that "Never Goodbye" should follow and keep the original playlist, with Bruce Springsteen's "Brilliant Disguise" next.

Even among the throng before me, Gabriel stands out clearly. He holds a clenched fist above his head, his way of telling me that I'm doing great.

"Thank you, all of you. I've got two songs to go. My next one is not a cover, so don't feel bad if you don't know who sang it." The crowds laughs. "Someday maybe someone *will* cover it somewhere and say this is Cassidy's 'Never Goodbye,' but right now, it's only mine."

I hadn't given any prior thought to where I was going with this. In fact, until this very moment, it never even occurred to me to change the arrangement.

"Usually when I perform this song, the band backs me up," I continue. "But if it's all right with you all, tonight it's just going to be me. I want you to hear it exactly the way it sounded in my head when I wrote it."

My declaration of independence is met with a rousing cheer. I make my way to Jonah, who is one of the best piano players I've ever met, and ask him to slide down a bit on the piano bench. "The rest of you guys," I say to the band, "just stay put. I'm going to do this old school. Just me and the piano, but I would greatly appreciate it if all of you would stay up here onstage for moral support."

To a bandmate, they smile. A few offer nods of encouragement, which is enough to start my fingers playing the melody. Even though this is by far the largest crowd I've ever played, it's as quiet as it was when I first laid down the chords alone in my apartment. I don't hear so much as a breath coming from the audience. My voice is the only sound in the room.

It's not until the applause breaks out that I'm awakened from the trance. Jonah, who I had completely forgotten was less than six inches from me, leans into my ear. "Oh my God," he says.

My knees wobble when I get back up, but I make it back to the center of the stage. Then I close my set with Alicia Keys's "Girl on Fire."

After I've sung the last lyric, I can't hear my own voice thanking the crowd above their applause. It hits me that I won't be taking the stage for a few weeks now, while I'm performing on that other stage I call home: the criminal courtroom. As I'm wondering how much longer I can straddle this dual persona, I see the one constant in my life, my own personal North Star in my constellation of confusion. Gabriel. I leave the stage and follow that beacon right into his embrace.

"I love you," he says.

No qualification. No trying it on for size. Just a declaration.

"I love you too," I say without missing a beat.

40.

DANA GOODWIN

I didn't want to invite anyone for Thanksgiving. My parents offered to fly in from Arizona, but I told them not to come. I also said that I didn't want them to come for the trial. I just couldn't bear them seeing me that way. Stuart's mother is too ill to travel, and it's a condition of my bail that I can't leave the state.

I suggested to Stuart that we treat the holiday like any other Thursday. I have nothing very much to be thankful for this year, after all. He said that he would do whatever I wanted, but then he put his thumb on the scale by offering to do all the cooking.

So it's just the three of us.

The thought has never been far from my mind that this may be the last Thanksgiving I will spend with my son. Prison is worse than death in that way. Thanksgivings would continue to come, but I'd never be with Jacob.

Although I've rejected the idea of jumping bail, suicide has never strayed far from my thoughts. The last way I can achieve freedom, if everything turns against me.

As far as I can tell, Jacob still knows nothing of the hurricane swirling around me. As Stuart toils in the kitchen, my son and I watch the Macy's Thanksgiving Day parade, challenging each other to be the first to scream out the name of the character balloons when they appear on-screen. He wins with each character he knows, and I'm surprised how many he does—SpongeBob, Hello Kitty, Pikachu, Thomas the Tank Engine. He thinks Paddington is Winnie the Pooh, but I don't correct him. To my surprise, he has no idea who Snoopy is, but comes back strong with the Power Rangers, Ronald McDonald, and the prehistoric squirrel from the *Ice Age* movies.

"Scrat," Jacob tells me his name.

He's sitting in my lap, and I'm holding him tight. So tight that he tells me that I'm squeezing him too much. Although I don't want to, I relax my grip ever so slightly.

I know in this moment that I will not be able to live without Jacob. He is my oxygen, and without him I will suffocate.

———

Stuart does a lovely job with dinner. The turkey is browned perfectly and juicy. The side dishes look like they should be in a magazine.

He deliberately did not carve the drumstick so that Jacob can eat it like a caveman. My son looks to me for approval. I nod, telling him that because this year Thanksgiving is just the three of us, he can do it that way, but when others are present, he needs to use a fork and a knife.

He tears off a chunk with his teeth, his grin visible behind the hunk of meat. "I'm glad we don't have anyone else here," he says, still chewing. "I really like it when it's just our family."

"That's an excellent thing to be thankful for, then, Jacob," Stuart says. "Don't you think?"

"Uh-huh," Jacob says, taking another bite of his drumstick.

After dinner, Stuart says that he'll do cleanup. He invites me to watch television with Jacob. Christmas shows are in heavy rotation on the networks. I have a choice between *Frosty the Snowman* and *How the Grinch Stole Christmas*. I opt for Dr. Seuss.

"Have you ever seen this?" I ask Jacob.

"I don't think so."

"You're going to like it. It was my favorite when I was a little girl."

I sing him a little of what I remember from the main song. About the Grinch being so mean that I wouldn't touch him with a forty-five-foot pole, although I'm guessing as to the length that's actually in the song. Jacob giggles and asks me to sing more. I don't recall the stanzas, so I sing the chorus again. He stares at me as if he's never heard anything as beautiful in his entire life.

He watches the program with his mouth agape. The wonder of bearing witness to my son experiencing something new never gets old for me. When the program ends, he predictably asks how long until it's Christmas.

"About a month," I tell him.

He looks sad. I think he expected it to be tomorrow.

"What is Santa going to bring me for Christmas?" he asks, apparently not taking the moral of the *Grinch* to heart.

"I don't know. That's between you and Santa. Make a list, and if you've been a good boy this year, I'm sure that some of what's on your list will be under the tree."

"I think I've been a good boy," he says. His big brown eyes beg me to confirm his self-assessment.

"The best," I say.

I allow Jacob to stay up later than usual. After the *Grinch*, we switch the channel to *Frosty Returns*, but then I remember that times have changed since I was a child. I can simply order the original *Frosty* from Amazon for his viewing pleasure. When the snowman vows to return next Christmas, I'm tempted to queue up *Rudolph the Red-Nosed Reindeer*, but it's late. Jacob doesn't have to see every Christmas classic tonight.

After Jacob is asleep, I join Stuart in our bedroom. As soon as I'm in bed, he reaches over and takes my hand. When I accept the gesture, he follows it up by kissing me deeply, leaving no doubt where he'd like this to go.

I consider pulling away for a moment. We haven't been intimate in weeks—not since the night before Lauren's murder, in fact. But when Stuart's mouth moves down my torso, I don't resist. He stops exactly where I want him to and stays there until I'm over the edge. I climax a second time during the main event. As soon as my orgasm has subsided, Stuart speeds up his tempo, moving ever faster until he lets out a deep groan, at which time his entire body becomes rigid. He stays that way for a few seconds, and then he relaxes.

"I love you," he whispers into my ear.

As I'm catching my own breath, I realize that I've had a nice day. The first in . . . I don't know how long. Certainly since my arrest. But even since before then, when the highs I enjoyed in Lauren's company were always juxtaposed with the guilt that brought me low when I returned to Stuart.

After feeling nothing but guilt around Stuart for months over my affair with Lauren, I realize all it took was her murder to relieve me of that cloak.

41.

ELLA BRODEN

We are the third case on the court calendar. The appearance is designated as the initial pretrial conference, but it's more akin to a meet and greet so the judge can say hello to the lawyers. The only thing we'll actually accomplish is the selection of the trial date.

That's good for me. I need more evidence, and that means I need to give Gabriel time to find it. Of almost equal importance is that I need a few months, at least, to regain my footing. I've been a prosecutor again for a week now, and I'm finding the adjustment back to working full time more difficult than I anticipated.

Normally there wouldn't be any opposition from defense counsel about setting a distant trial date. For most defendants, especially those out on bail, delay is the next best thing to acquittal—both represent time spent out of prison. But my guess is that LeMarcus Burrows is too smart to fall into that trap. He knows I don't have much evidence, which means that, in this rare instance, time is not on his client's side.

I get to court early, an old habit of mine. I like to see the judge in action before my case is called. I scan the courtroom, but I've arrived before Dana Goodwin and her team.

Judge Gold is bald as a cue ball, with the exception of a few hairs that sprout up on his forehead, of all places, giving him a slight resemblance to Charlie Brown. I've entered in the middle of another preliminary conference. From the arguments being made, grand larceny seems to be the charge, but neither lawyer has said exactly what was stolen. Judge Gold sets their trial for July 11, eight months away.

I breathe a sigh of relief that he's giving out July trial dates. That should be enough time for me to get my ducks in a row.

Out of the corner of my eye, I see Dana Goodwin enter the courtroom. LeMarcus Burrows stands beside her, almost like a protector. They take a position against the wall. For the briefest moment, I catch Dana's eye. We both instinctively look away.

The bailiff calls out the name of the next case, and a different defendant enters the courtroom from the side door, behind which is the holding pen for those unfortunates who are held over pending trial. The man who enters is wearing the orange prison jumpsuit and is shackled at the ankles. He looks like a criminal—long, knotted hair and tattoos on his neck.

The prosecutor on this case is someone I don't recognize. He's a younger guy, no doubt out of narcotics, which is where a lot of the newbies wind up. He announces that the defendant is ready to enter a guilty plea to a Class C felony, and then reads: "Defendant did knowingly and unlawfully possess a controlled substance—to wit, crack cocaine—with intent to sell it. He is thereby guilty of a criminal possession of a controlled substance in the fifth degree, a Class C felony."

The defendant must have priors. Conviction on a Class B for a recidivist normally gets you twenty-five years. By pleading down to a Class C felony, Mr. Neck Tattoo is likely going to cut his sentence in half.

Judge Gold goes through the ritual of accepting a guilty plea, beginning by asking Mr. Neck Tattoo whether he wants to change his previously entered plea.

"Yeah, to guilty," he says.

Then the judge reads from a script, getting a "yes" answer to each question.

"Are you pleading guilty because you are guilty? Do you understand that by pleading guilty you are forfeiting a right to a fair trial by a jury of your peers? That you have the right to be provided with counsel if you cannot afford counsel? That you have the right not to testify in your own defense? That by pleading guilty, you also give up the right to appeal?"

In response to: "Has anyone offered you any inducement or promise to enter this plea?" Mr. Neck Tattoo finally says, "No."

"Good," Judge Gold says. "I accept your guilty plea and sentence you to twelve years."

I watch Mr. Neck Tattoo shuffle out, his shackled legs clicking together as he walks. I can't even begin to imagine what goes through your mind when you're told that nothing awaits you in life but misery and loneliness for the next twelve years. Which causes me to look over to Dana again. It's as if we shared the thought, because she's looking right back at me.

That's when the clerk bellows out, "People of the State of New York against Dana L. Goodwin. Counsel, please state your appearances on the record."

The players make their way onto the stage, which in this case amounts to walking through the swinging gate that separates the spectators from the well of the court. As the prosecutor, I always go first.

"Ella Broden for the People of the State of New York, by special designation," I say.

"Ms. Broden, a pleasure to see you back in my courtroom," Judge Gold says.

"LeMarcus Burrows of the law firm LeMarcus Burrows and Associates, New York City, for the defendant."

"And Mr. Burrows, my warmest welcome to you too, sir. Now, before we commence with today's conference, I must get some things out of the way. This is obviously an unusual matter. A first for me, and I dare say, perhaps any justice on this court. I knew the victim of this crime. Lauren Wright appeared before me numerous times, as did the lawyers who worked for her in the Special Victims Bureau of the District Attorney's

Office. And I also know the defendant, Dana Goodwin, in that same professional capacity. I can say that outside of professional functions, I do not recall ever socializing with either Ms. Wright or Ms. Goodwin, although, Ms. Goodwin, you should feel free to correct me on that point. Even though my relationship with all the participants has always been purely professional, if anyone thinks that association is grounds to believe I cannot impartially preside over this case, or that an appearance of impartiality would not benefit the cause of justice, please make that position known now."

I knew all this before Judge Gold's speech, but it's still music to my years. I want a judge who knew Lauren so he'll be as upset as I am about her murder. And the fact that he knew Dana professionally only means that he's that much more disappointed that she could commit such a heinous act.

"The People see no conflict or even the appearance of a conflict," I say.

I wonder if Burrows will agree. My guess is that, if he had his druthers, he would have selected another judge. Maybe a woman. Certainly someone younger. But there's always a risk in telling the judge you don't think he's up to the job, so I suspect Burrows will ultimately fall in line too.

"The defense likewise believes that Your Honor can impartially preside over this case," he says.

"Very well, then," Judge Gold says. "It's always nice at the beginning of a case when everyone thinks the judge is fair. It's only when I start ruling that one side or the other starts complaining. Of course, I know I've done my job well when each side complains equally."

Some titters come from the gallery. Burrows and I laugh too, even though the Judge's remark was not very funny. Dana manages only a grim smile.

"As you might have heard," Judge Gold continues, "the case right before you just pled out. I had that trial on my calendar for next month, and blocked out two weeks for it. I'm going to slide you into that slot.

If need be, I can open my calendar for the week after that too, although that runs some risk of taking us into the Christmas and New Year's period, but I think that'll give us more than enough time to get through everything. I realize it's fast, but would starting on December fourteenth work for everyone?"

I have never in my career gone from indictment to prosecution on a felony charge, never mind a murder case, in less than four months. Judge Gold is proposing that I do it in less than four weeks.

Burrows knows not to look a gift horse in the mouth. As quickly as he can, he says, "The defense will be ready on the fourteenth."

I'm not so accommodating. "As the court is aware, I have only recently been assigned to this matter, and am acting as a special prosecutor. I do appreciate the court's desire to move this case along as quickly as possible—"

I know from my first words that I've made a mistake. Judge Gold is looking down at me with a scowl.

"Let me stop you there, Ms. Broden. The answer I'm looking for is 'yes.' I make it a hard and fast rule not to allow the prosecution to delay a trial. You people on the left side of caption can take as long as you want to prepare your case prior to obtaining an indictment. As a result, I presume that when the District Attorney obtains one, the office is ready to go to trial on that day, and only the defense needs time to prepare. Are you telling me that was *not* the case with regard to Ms. Goodwin?"

I have no choice but to take the tongue-lashing. When he's finished, I say, "My apologies, Your Honor. The People are ready to proceed on the court's schedule."

"Excellent," Judge Gold says. "Anything else on either of your agendas today?"

"Nothing for the prosecution," I say.

"Nor for the defense," Burrows adds quickly.

"Very well, then," Judge Gold says. "I will see you all on the fourteenth for trial."

42.

DANA GOODWIN

The United States Constitution prohibits a defendant from being tried in absentia, but my physical presence is almost a technicality. I'm ignored by the participants and powerless to interject. I might as well be a wax figure. But that's going to be my life every time I set foot in a courtroom from here on out. Victims' families sometimes made the same complaint to me, and I always told them not to worry because I was their voice. That makes LeMarcus Burrows my champion, but it doesn't mean that I like what I just heard in there.

I know better than to have a discussion with my lawyer within anyone's line of sight or hearing, especially with so many members of the press about. So I hold my tongue until we're in the back seat of a taxi leaving the courthouse. We shouldn't talk here either, because if the taxi driver were later subpoenaed, he could testify about what we discussed. Attorney-client privilege is broken by the presence of a third party, even one who is simply driving us from court to LeMarcus's office. Still, good luck to Ella Broden or Gabriel ever finding Mr. Ram Furpah to get him on the witness stand.

"What happened with Ella Broden? You told me that you were going to move to disqualify her," I say, not attempting to hide my displeasure.

"The early trial date wouldn't have held if we switched prosecutors," LeMarcus says calmly. "I know you'd prefer that the prosecutor not have a personal interest in the matter, but let me tell you something: *every* prosecutor will have a personal interest in this matter. Maybe he or she won't be as close to Lauren as Ella was, but they're going to want to string you up just as much, believe me on that. Now, I would have been more than happy to knock Ella off the case if there was no price to pay for it, but pushing back the trial date is the absolute worst thing that could happen to you, and that's the only thing we'd get by disqualifying her. So it was a no-brainer to let that go."

"December is too soon."

LeMarcus looks up at the driver, who hasn't moved his head. I'm sure he doesn't have the slightest interest in our confidential communications.

"For the prosecution, it's too soon," LeMarcus says. "They're not ready. For us, it's a godsend."

"It's not all about trial strategy, LeMarcus. Trial on the fourteenth could mean I'm convicted and rotting in jail by Christmas. I want to spend Christmas with my son."

He unclicks his seat belt and slides closer to me. Whatever he's about to say, he wants to make sure it is not overheard by the driver. Leaning in, he whispers, "You have an important decision to make, and you have to make it right now. If you want to go for an acquittal, this is the only way. We force the prosecution to put on a case it hasn't yet completed investigating. But if you're conceding the verdict is going to go against you, then you're absolutely right that the calculation is completely the opposite. Right now, you're free. You won't be after trial—*if* you're conceding conviction."

He stops and waits a beat. Then, after another, he says, "I'm not ready to concede. Are you?"

———

That evening, I explain to Stuart what occurred in court, including the news that my fate will be known before New Year's. Stuart nods but doesn't otherwise respond to the moved-up timetable for a good thirty seconds.

"That's good," he finally says. "We can be in . . . wherever by the first of the year."

This is Stuart's way of saying that I'm going to be acquitted, and that after I'm found not guilty, we're going to escape New York and leave all of our troubles behind. It's a topic he's raised before, telling me that he'd like to relocate to a place where his salary alone will be enough to support us, which will allow me to spend as much time as I want with Jacob. Preferably somewhere warmer, he says, like a southern college town. He references Charlottesville, Virginia, and Columbia, South Carolina, as places with good public schools and interesting people. He imagines us in an old Victorian house, one with a drawing room and a fireplace crackling in the library, a small garden out back that I can tend while Jacob plays in the tree house beside it.

It's a seductive fantasy at times. So much so that there are even days when I imagine myself puttering around in that garden, a baseball cap of some college team I've never heard of shielding me from the sun, with Jacob on the swing set beside me.

When Stuart first broached this idea, I asked him if he truly believed that a happily-ever-after ending was possible for us. He didn't waver.

"I'm certain of it. I love you, and I think you love me. And I know we both love Jacob. Nothing else really matters besides that."

But of course, a lot of other things matter. Not the least of which is whether I'm found guilty of murder.

PART FIVE

43.

ELLA BRODEN

I begin as I always start an opening statement, by saying, "The People will prove that the defendant, Dana Goodwin, is guilty." Then I point at the accused.

It was Lauren who taught me the importance of pointing. On my first day, she told me and the other new arrivals to the Special Victims Bureau that you need to show the jury that you're not afraid to stand in judgment. It tells them that they shouldn't be either.

With my arm still outstretched, I continue, "Dana Goodwin was engaged in an extramarital affair with Lauren Wright. You will see proof and hear testimony that Ms. Goodwin and Ms. Wright met on a weekly basis for months, always in hotel rooms, so that neither of their husbands would know about the affair. The most compelling evidence of Ms. Goodwin's guilt will not come from a third party, however, but from the defendant herself. Her text messages to Lauren Wright, and Lauren's messages back to the defendant, show that they were two people who, if not in love, were definitely in lust with each other. And one of those texts—the last text that Ms. Wright ever received—was sent by Ms. Goodwin at 1:03 a.m., asking Ms. Wright to meet her in Central Park. The very place where she was found dead a few hours later."

I tell them that Franklin Pearse's ID matches Dana Goodwin's physique, that she owns a black hoodie, and that the murder weapon was registered to the late Detective Papamichael, a cop who worked a case that Dana prosecuted four years earlier.

I think it sounds compelling. But midway through my opening, I can feel that I'm losing the jurors. I'm not connecting the way I need to, which is evident by the vacant expressions I'm seeing from the twelve people who are charged with adjudicating Dana Goodwin's guilt.

Part of it is that I'm rusty. It's been more than a year since I've tried a case. But I thought I'd handled jury selection well. The men and women who are seated are pretty close to the collection I was hoping for—older people, who I thought would be less willing to accept both the extramarital affair and its being of the same-sex variety; and no African American women, who jury consultants repeatedly told me in the past I do not connect well with. Moreover, I only need my eyes to know that women of all races love LeMarcus Burrows. My jury-selection strategy was vindicated by the fact that Burrows operated on exactly the antithetical premise, trying to fill the jury with African American women and millennials.

I suspect the real weakness in my opening has nothing to do with my being out of practice, and far more with the fact that when it comes time for me to connect the dots for the jurors, I fall short. Although I've told them the *who*—Dana Goodwin—and the *how*—two gunshots to the head—I haven't delivered on the *why*.

Of course, there are really only a few options. Either Lauren ended the affair and Dana killed her in anger, or Dana ended it and then killed her because Lauren threatened revenge, most likely related to Dana's continued employment—but it also might have been to prevent Lauren from telling Dana's husband. A third possibility is that Dana decided to end it by killing her lover rather than risking the possible reprisals that would follow breaking up with her boss. This last scenario has the added benefits of not only ensuring that she remain gainfully employed but also probably securing her a promotion.

The problem is that I have no idea which of those alternatives is true. The second-to-last text exchange they had—the last one being the text that drew Lauren into Central Park and to her death—suggested two people who couldn't get enough of each other. In other words, not people on the verge of a nasty breakup.

Rather than advance a theory that I can't prove, I'd opted to leave the question open. It seemed like the smart move, as motive isn't an element of murder—intent to commit the crime plus an overt act is all that's required for conviction, and I have ample evidence to support each.

The jurors' faces tell me that I'm wrong. They want to know *why*. I can't blame them. It's hard to send someone—especially a young mother who has devoted her life to putting criminals behind bars—to jail for the rest of her life without knowing that.

"That was good," Kayla Kirk whispers to me when I return to counsel table. Now that Gabriel is a testifying witness, he'll be sequestered from the courtroom during witness testimony, so Kayla has been added to the trial team to second-seat me. "You made a lot of strong points. I think the jury was engaged."

This is Kayla's first jury trial, so her opinion doesn't mean that much to me in any event. But knowing it's not true makes her praise sound like a criticism. Worse still, I can hear Lauren's voice in my head, telling me that I'm failing her.

The sequester order doesn't apply to opening statements. As a result, Gabriel is seated in the gallery's first row. When our eyes meet, he smiles, but even though I'm sure he's trying to convey that I've done well, this is not the smile he shows me at Lava.

Judge Gold's voice snaps me back to the trial. "Mr. Burrows, please present your opening statement."

44.

DANA GOODWIN

I'm sick to my stomach after hearing Ella Broden explain to the jury how I murdered Lauren.

My reaction has nothing to do with surprise. Through pretrial discovery, I've seen the hotel registries and the photographs from the ATMs that Lauren and I visited together. I also knew that Ella would refer to the text message sent from my phone to Lauren on the night she was murdered as a smoking gun, and that I had worked a case with Papamichael a few years back, which linked me to the murder weapon. But every other time I considered the evidence, it was with a ready rebuttal thrown in, which allowed me to find solace that each piece was easily explainable. So I reasoned that many people have affairs—more than 50 percent of married people, according to some studies—but that only a statistically insignificant number end in murder. And I took comfort in knowing that Stuart would testify that I lost my phone before the text was sent, which explained that evidence away, and that Papamichael and I had only one case together, which was years ago; he had cases with hundreds of ADAs over his career. And Lauren and I were in love. And . . . and . . . and . . .

When the evidence was presented by Ella, however, it sounded compelling. I'm reminded of LeMarcus's concern that the jurors would make up their mind right after her opening. I pray that's not true, because if it is, I'm going to be convicted.

After Judge Gold tells him it's his turn, LeMarcus stands and buttons his suit jacket. He cuts an impressive figure. Tall and trim and handsome as all get-out. By the smiles on their faces, it seems clear that the women jurors certainly like what they see.

"Thank you, Your Honor," LeMarcus says to Judge Gold, then pivots a half turn so he's facing the jury. "The prosecutor—Ms. Broden—claims that Dana Goodwin killed Lauren Wright. But she never said *why*, now did she? And that is because there is no motive here. No fights. No breakup. It doesn't make sense that a woman in love—and clearly Dana and Lauren *were* in love, as evidenced by their texts—would murder her lover for no reason. But let me tell you something that *does* make sense. It makes all the sense in the world. Lauren Wright was murdered by her husband."

The courtroom is eerily quiet at the dropping of this bombshell. The jurors, who had undoubtedly expected another long examination of the evidence, seem surprised that something so noteworthy has occurred so suddenly.

"The defense agrees with quite a bit of what Ms. Broden said," LeMarcus says. "We're not going to pour water in your ear and tell you that it's raining, after all. So, let's get that stuff out of the way right now. It's true that Ms. Goodwin was Ms. Wright's second-in-command. It's true that they had an affair. Also one hundred percent correct that a text from Ms. Goodwin's phone caused Ms. Wright to leave her home late at night and enter Central Park. And there's no denying that Ms. Wright was shot twice at close range while she was there."

He stops and looks into the eyes of each juror. To a person, they hold his gaze.

"But," he says thunderously, "the evidence will show that Lauren Wright's husband, a man named Richard Trofino, was in Dana's office on the day of the murder. For several minutes, he was there alone. *Alone*

in the office of the woman he knew was having an affair with his wife.
That's when it all clicked for Richard Trofino: a way he could solve all
his problems. He no longer would be the jealous, humiliated husband.
He would extract his revenge by killing his wife and framing her lover
for the murder. All he had to do to carry out that plan was to take Ms.
Goodwin's cell phone. Once he had the phone, the rest was easy. He
sent the text, snuck out of their building, fired two bullets into his wife's
head, grabbed her phone, returned home, and then put his wife's phone
back on the night table so that the police would be sure to discover the
evidence that would lead them to arrest Dana Goodwin."

Richard sits in the gallery's first row. Like all the witnesses, he'll
be sequestered when the testimony begins, but he is permitted to hear
the openings, closings, and legal arguments. Out of the corner of my
eye, I catch his profile. Although he's trying to remain expressionless,
it's a thin mask. He's obviously furious that my lawyer is branding him
a murderer.

"All of the evidence mentioned by Ms. Broden points much
more at Mr. Trofino than at Ms. Goodwin. The gun was found near
Mr. Trofino's home, a borough away from where Ms. Goodwin lives.
The prosecutor, Ms. Broden, she didn't mention that, now did she? And
the *one* case that Ms. Goodwin worked on with Detective Papamichael?
That was more than four years ago. Besides, here's another thing Ms.
Broden didn't tell you all: Lauren Wright had more than *twenty* cases
with Detective Papamichael. If he was going to give someone a gun,
who do you think it would be? Someone Detective Papamichael had
one case with, or someone he had twenty cases with?

"Ms. Goodwin's phone, you ask? What about her phone? Well,
Ms. Broden left out the part about Ms. Goodwin buying a new phone
the next day, which tells you she didn't have it the night of the murder—because it had already been stolen by Mr. Trofino. Of course, she
just thought she lost it. You'll hear Ms. Goodwin's husband testify that
his wife didn't have the phone that night—that it was lost *before* the

text was sent. And the ID by that homeless guy? Oh, what homeless guy? That's right, Ms. Broden also didn't tell you that her star witness, Mr. Franklin Pearse, is a homeless man. Here's another thing she left out of her opening statement: Mr. Pearse's description of the murderer's stature exactly matches Mr. Trofino's."

LeMarcus lets his accusations sink in. The silence as is as powerful as his argument.

"In a murder case, to know the *who* is really a function of learning *why* they did it," LeMarcus says. "But in her opening, Ms. Broden didn't tell you the why. Why would Ms. Goodwin want to kill her lover, her work partner, her best friend? Ms. Broden didn't tell you why because there is *no reason* that Dana Goodwin would do such a thing. But I'll tell you why Richard Trofino killed his wife. He found out about the affair. He found out that his wife was in love with someone else—and that someone else was a *woman*. And for someone like Mr. Trofino—a mover and a shaker in this city—that was something that he could not abide.

"The only reason—the *only* reason—that Ms. Goodwin is on trial here is because Ms. Wright's phone was found," LeMarcus continues, now nearly shouting. "The prosecution claims that she just 'forgot' it at home when she went out into the park. Lucky break for them, they say, and bad luck for Dana Goodwin. But I don't believe in lucky breaks, not in a murder case. And neither should any of you. The reason Lauren Wright's phone was not found on her dead body was because, after he murdered his wife, Richard Trofino took his wife's phone out of her pocket and brought it home to make *sure* that there would be evidence pointing to Dana Goodwin. After all, who *doesn't* take their phone with them after receiving a text to meet? And it's that phone—and that phone alone—that links Dana Goodwin to the murder. Without it, well . . . Richard Trofino might as well be sitting at the defense table for murder."

It's good theater, no doubt about that. The jurors are on the edge of their seats, hanging on LeMarcus's every word.

But it comes at a high price. It's no longer going to be sufficient for us to argue that a faceless *someone else* murdered Lauren, or even that I should be acquitted because the prosecution has not sufficiently proved my guilt beyond a reasonable doubt. The trial has now become an election. The jurors will either vote guilty to convict me or not guilty to condemn Richard Trofino.

45.

ELLA BRODEN

Gabriel is my first witness. I call him to the stand at the start of the day on Tuesday morning.

At my insistence, he's wearing a dark suit with a crisp, white shirt and a tie. Gabriel has testified more than a hundred times, but he told me this was the first time he's ever been told what to wear—and then added that he usually only dons a suit for weddings.

"Good morning, Lieutenant Velasquez."

"And to you, Ms. Broden."

"Lieutenant Velasquez, can you explain to the jury how you and I know each other?"

I've scripted it this way to get the most damning part of the examination out of the way with some humor. My hope is that the jury will find it charming that the prosecution's first witness is sleeping with the prosecutor. A Hepburn-and-Tracy thing, rather than a conflict of interest.

"We have been dating for the past six months."

"And in that relationship, do I refer to you as Lieutenant Velasquez and do you call me Ms. Broden?"

"No. We're on a first-name basis," he says with a smile.

This generates the hoped-for chuckles from the jurors. I take a quick look at them. They're onboard. My first problem has been solved.

My outline for the direct examination has three parts. First, I'll establish Gabriel's bona fides as a detective, then I'll segue to our dinner with Lauren and Richard. That will be the low point of the direct, playing into the defense's argument that Richard might be Lauren's murderer, so I want to get it out of the way early. I considered not addressing it at all, but concluded it was better for the jury to hear the story first from Gabriel. That way, when LeMarcus Burrows goes back over it on cross, it'll feel like old news. Once that's dealt with, the lion's share of Gabriel's testimony will catalogue the proof we have against Dana.

"What role, if any, did you have in the investigation into Lauren Wright's murder?" I ask.

"I was the police officer in charge of the investigation."

"Did you handle that investigation alone?"

"No. I was partnered with Dana Goodwin."

"The defendant?"

"Yes," he says. I had asked Gabriel to point at her when he said her name, but he's apparently forgotten.

"How did it come about that you and Ms. Goodwin were partners in the investigation?"

"She was Lauren Wright's deputy. The thought at the time was that she knew more about Lauren than anyone else in the District Attorney's office, and so it would be helpful to have her assistance."

"During the investigation, did Ms. Goodwin *ever* tell you that she had been engaged in a sexual affair with Lauren Wright?"

"No. She did not."

"Would that have been an important fact for you to know?"

"Of course. Among the first things we focused on was whether Ms. Wright might have been having an affair. Ms. Goodwin knew that she was, and yet she kept that highly critical information to herself."

So far, so good. I feel at home in court, handling a witness again. Like riding a bicycle. Then again, this witness is my boyfriend. It's bound to get more difficult.

"Did you know Lauren Wright before you were assigned to investigate her murder?"

"I did. My girlfriend . . . you, Ms. Broden . . . worked for Ms. Wright. I didn't know her well when you worked for her. After we started dating, you talked about her from time to time, and we had dinner with Lauren and her husband, Richard Trofino, on the night she was murdered."

I don't need to look at the jurors to know that they are paying attention now. I can feel the tension in the room rising. LeMarcus Burrows has done his job in setting up Richard as the alternative murderer to Dana. The jurors want to know how he acted that night.

"Please tell the jury everything—and I mean *everything*—that you recall from that dinner."

"As you can imagine, in light of the fact that I learned the next morning that Lauren had been murdered, I've given that dinner quite a bit of thought. So my memory is pretty clear, even though it's been more than a month since the event. I remember Richard and Lauren were already at the restaurant when we arrived. I had met Lauren before, but never socially, and I had not met Richard previously, so we exchanged the usual greetings. 'Nice to meet you.' 'What do you do for a living?' That kind of thing. It was all very normal. During dinner, I got the sense that Lauren was unhappy that Richard consumed as much alcohol as he did, but other than that, they seemed like any normal married couple."

"Tell the jury what gave rise to your impressions regarding the alcohol issue."

In my discussions with Richard to prepare him for his testimony, he steadfastly denied that there was any tension between Lauren and him that night. He said that he didn't perceive she was angry that he had a scotch or two before ordering the wine and claimed that was not uncommon for him. As much as I preferred Richard's version to Gabriel's, I knew that Gabriel had already shared his take on the dinner with Dana. It was therefore sure to come out on cross, so the smart play was for me to draw the teeth now.

"It wasn't anything either of them said. Just a feeling I got when I looked at Lauren. Maybe she rolled her eyes or something."

"Let's turn to the murder weapon, Lieutenant. Please tell the jury its make and model."

"It was a Glock Nineteen."

"Who was it registered to?"

"A former NYPD detective named Gregory Papamichael."

"Where is Detective Papamichael now?"

"Dead. About two years now."

"Did you or anyone under your supervision check to see if Ms. Goodwin had ever worked with Detective Papamichael?"

"We did. They worked together on a case approximately four years ago."

"Is that fact important to this case?"

"It is. We believe that Detective Papamichael gave his service weapon, the Glock Nineteen that was used to murder Ms. Wright, to Ms. Goodwin."

"How about Lauren Wright? Did your review of Detective Papamichael's work history reveal whether he worked any cases with her?"

"He worked only one case with her, but that was more than fifteen years ago, which was before the Glock Nineteen was manufactured. More recently, he worked several cases in the Special Victims Bureau, and Ms. Wright was the chief of that unit. But they did not work together directly. There would have been other ADAs who worked directly with Detective Papamichael."

I look over at the jury to get a preliminary fix on how I'm doing. There aren't any nods of approval, but no one breaks eye contact either, which tells me that they're at least engaged.

"How did it come about that Dana Goodwin was arrested for this murder?" I ask.

"We unlocked Lauren Wright's phone," Gabriel says. "Her text messages and voice mails indicated two things. First, that she and Dana had been engaged in a sexual affair over the past several months. And second, that on the night Lauren was murdered, Ms. Goodwin had texted—"

"Objection!" Burrows shouts.

Gabriel talks over him. "Lauren to meet her at the place where she was killed."

The cat is clearly out of the bag now. So much so that most lawyers in Burrows's shoes would stand down so as to not call more attention to Gabriel's testimony about the text. Burrows, however, is apparently not of that school.

"Your Honor, I've rendered an objection and request a ruling. The question assumes facts not in evidence."

Judge Gold scratches his cheek for a moment, like he's Marlon Brando in *The Godfather*. "Counsel, please approach."

We all join him beneath the bench, including Dana Goodwin, who Judge Gold has previously ruled is to be treated like counsel in these conferences. When we get there, the judge says, "Mr. Burrows, is this whole production because of the defense's theory that someone *other* than Ms. Goodwin sent the texts at issue?"

"It is," he says.

After a moment, but not much more than that, Judge Gold says, "Okay, here's what I'm going to do. I'm going to sustain the defense's objection, but only because the evidence at issue hasn't been introduced yet. What I'm also going to do is explain to the jury why they're not going to hear more about that text just now. Anybody got a problem with that?"

"No, Your Honor," I say. The last thing I'm going to do is be the person who says she doesn't want the jury to understand what's going on.

"Nor does the defense," Burrows says, because he's not going to be that guy either, even though I'm certain he would be much happier if the judge didn't go there.

"Excellent. Now step back," Judge Gold says.

When we're all situated in our usual positions, the judge turns to the jury and says, "Ladies and gentlemen, here's what just happened in the conference at the bench. As you know from Mr. Burrows's opening statement, it is the defense's contention that Ms. Goodwin did *not* send the text that Lieutenant Velasquez just testified about. That's why Mr. Burrows objected. I am going to sustain the objection because there's been no evidence introduced about who sent that text. Not yet, anyway. But that might change later, because the prosecution has a lot more witnesses to call in this case."

The judge's focus shifts back to me. "Still your witness, Ms. Broden. You may want to tidy this up a bit."

"Of course, Your Honor. Thank you." To Gabriel, I say, "Lieutenant Velasquez, please explain what you meant when you said that the message was sent by Ms. Goodwin to Ms. Wright."

Gabriel smiles at me and then turns to the jury with the same friendly expression. *We're all just trying to help here* is his silent message. *All except the nasty defense lawyer who's trying to trick you.*

"What I meant was that the text was sent from Ms. Goodwin's phone to Ms. Wright's phone. Obviously, I did not see her actually type the message into her phone. But it is my experience that when a text is sent from a phone, the owner of that phone is the sender."

I decide to gild this lily a bit. "And to be clear, Lieutenant, you read many texts when you opened Ms. Wright's phone, did you not?"

"Yes."

"With respect to the texts on Ms. Wright's phone that indicated that they came from Ms. Goodwin's phone, did you ever *see* Ms. Goodwin compose any of those texts and then hit the 'Send' button?"

"No. I never saw Ms. Goodwin compose any texts."

"Is that also true with regard to texts that were sent from Ms. Wright's phone?"

"Yes. I believed that the texts that indicated that they were sent from Ms. Wright's phone were sent by Lauren Wright. But, as I just said with regard to Ms. Goodwin, I also never saw Ms. Wright actually type out a text and press the 'Send' button."

"Even though you did not actually witness these texts being typed and sent, did you draw any conclusions about the author and sender of the texts when you reviewed Ms. Wright's phone?"

"Yes. I assumed that if the message indicated it was sent from Ms. Goodwin's phone that she wrote the text and sent it."

With that, I thank my boyfriend—still addressing him by his rank and surname. Then I pass the witness.

46.

DANA GOODWIN

My eyes ping-pong between LeMarcus Burrows and Gabriel Velasquez. Two very handsome men who are about the same age and very, very good at what they do for a living. Now one is an immovable object and the other an irresistible force.

I say a silent prayer that LeMarcus comes out on top. My life quite literally depends on it.

"Lieutenant Velasquez, my name is LeMarcus Burrows, and I am the lawyer representing Dana Goodwin in this trial. We've never met, have we, sir?"

"We have not."

"I feel the need to get that out of the way because I don't want the jury to think that you have a personal relationship with *both* the lawyers in this case."

It's a snarky comment meant as a dig at Ella, but LeMarcus delivers it with such charm that it provokes only a smile from Gabriel. The jurors are smiling too. I breathe a small sigh of relief with the thought that the ground Gabriel gained is going to be made up quickly by LeMarcus.

"Now, let's start from my favorite place: the beginning. In this case, at that dinner that you and Ms. Broden had with Richard Trofino and

Lauren Wright on the night Ms. Wright was killed. You said two things, in particular, that I want to focus on. First, Mr. Trofino had a lot to drink that night, didn't he?"

It's a clever opening gambit. By using the phrase "a lot," LeMarcus is being intentionally vague. Either Gabriel agrees with him, in which case LeMarcus has made his point, or Gabriel will spar with him over the meaning of the term, thereby looking defensive.

"That's correct. He had three or four scotches and a glass of wine. Maybe two."

Ella has prepared Gabriel well. I couldn't have crafted the answer any better. Admit the point so as not to seem argumentative, and then reduce the ambiguity. Of course, in doing so, Gabriel has acknowledged that Richard did consume quite a bit of alcohol, which is what we needed to establish. Drunks sometimes kill people.

"So he consumed somewhere between four and seven drinks, more than half of them hard alcohol, during your, what . . . hour or so dinner?"

"Dinner was longer than an hour, but your math is correct about the amount of alcohol."

"Thank you for your clarification. Second, when Ms. Broden was questioning you, I believe you said that you sensed marital discord during that dinner."

"No, I didn't say that."

"But you did think that Richard Trofino and his wife had been fighting, correct?"

"I didn't know if they had or they hadn't."

"Is that right? Did you think that theirs was the kind of marriage where the wife rolls her eyes at her husband as a matter of course in the company of someone she'd never met before socially?"

"Sometimes an eye roll is just that. I didn't come to any conclusions regarding the state of their marriage based on it."

"Fair enough, Lieutenant. By the way, I assume that you met with your girlfriend, the prosecutor, Ms. Broden, to prepare for your testimony. Am I correct in that assumption?"

"Yes."

"And am I also correct that Ms. Broden told you to tell the truth."

"Yes."

"But, still, she *practiced* how to present the truth with you a little bit, right?"

I half expect Ella to object. She's smart to hold her fire. This line of inquiry always sounds more sinister than it actually is. All lawyers prep their witnesses. Few suborn perjury, however. I'm certain that neither Ella nor Gabriel got even close to that line, but LeMarcus's questioning puts that possibility front and center to the jury.

"We did discuss my testimony. And that included her asking me the kinds of questions that she planned to ask me on direct, and also the types of questions I could expect you to ask during cross-examination. But she didn't suggest any answers. Those are all mine."

"But you did share with her the answers you planned to give ahead of time, didn't you?"

"Yes."

LeMarcus lets this sink in for the jury, but does so in the guise of not being sure what question to ask next. He walks back to the defense table, picks up a piece of paper, and then returns to the podium without once looking at me.

"You found the murder weapon, did you not?"

"We did."

"And where was it? Near Ms. Goodwin's home?"

"No. In a sewer on Park and Seventy-Sixth Street."

"Where does Mr. Trofino live?"

"Park and Seventy-Fourth Street."

"So the murder weapon was found in a sewer two blocks away from his home?"

"That's correct."

"Where does Ms. Goodwin live?"

"Astoria, Queens."

"I see. So not very close to where you found the murder weapon, then."

"She lives in Queens. The gun was found in Manhattan."

"Queens to Manhattan . . . that's too far to walk, wouldn't you say, Lieutenant?"

"I would say that most people don't walk from Queens to Manhattan."

"Did you check the footage from the toll plazas to see if there was any evidence that Ms. Goodwin came to Manhattan by car on the night of the murder?"

"We did. She was not on them. We suspect she took public transportation."

"I see. So, I assume you checked the train platform surveillance cameras and found her image there, then. It's the N train, isn't it, that goes from Astoria to Manhattan?"

"We did check the platform cameras for the N train in Astoria and Manhattan."

"Was she there? Did you see Ms. Goodwin?"

"No, though it's easy to avoid being photographed by those cameras."

"Is it, now? Then why'd you check if you figured it was easy to avoid them?"

"Sometimes we get lucky."

"I see. In this case you didn't get . . . lucky. But I think we can agree that you're not as *un*lucky as Ms. Goodwin, who wasn't on the cameras but still has the police thinking she took the N train anyway."

Ella objects, which causes Judge Gold to raise an eyebrow at LeMarcus. It's not on the record, but everyone knows he's telling LeMarcus that he's made his point and it's now time to move on.

"Lieutenant Velasquez, you testified on direct examination that the reason Ms. Goodwin was arrested was because of what was found on Ms. Wright's cell phone. However, you didn't discuss much of what happened before Ms. Wright's phone was reviewed. How many days passed between Ms. Wright's murder and the retrieval of the texts from her iPhone?"

"Seven."

"And during that time, is it fair to say that you were actively investigating the case?"

"Yes."

"Full-time, correct?"

"More than full-time," Gabriel counters. "Fifteen-hour days."

"You were partners with Ms. Goodwin during those fifteen-hour days, were you not?"

"I was."

"And so is it fair to say that you spent many of those hours in Ms. Goodwin's company?"

"Yes."

"Was there a single moment during those fifteen-hour days when you suspected that Dana Goodwin had killed Ms. Wright?"

"No, but as I said, she didn't tell me that she was sleeping with the victim either. If she had, my view would have certainly changed."

"Let's stick with what you were actually thinking at the time, shall we, and not any after-the-fact rationalizations you may have developed. So my question is: at the time you were investigating, *before* Ms. Goodwin was arrested, who did you think killed Lauren Wright?"

"We did not have a single suspect in mind."

"Who was in the running, then?"

In law school they teach you that direct examination requires non-leading questions, which means that the answer is not implied by the question, whereas cross-examination is all leading questions, the kind that on television portrayals of trials are punctuated with the phrase "isn't that correct?" But more experienced questioners know that if you can sprinkle your cross with open-ended queries, it's far more persuasive to the jury. The best way to do that is precisely how LeMarcus is doing it now. Allow open-ended questions when you know that *any* answer helps the defense. It doesn't matter if Gabriel mentions that they had a hundred suspects or only one, because Richard Trofino will surely be included.

By the look in his eyes, it appears that Gabriel knows where this is going. "With the understanding that it was still preliminary, we had focused on several suspects. The husband, of course, is always someone of interest—"

LeMarcus seizes on the opening. "Why was Mr. Trofino a person of interest?"

This time Ella comes to her feet. "Objection! Your Honor, the witness has not finished his answer."

"Is that right, Lieutenant?" LeMarcus says apologetically. "Was there more you wanted to say?"

"Yes, thank you. You asked, I believe, who we initially considered as suspects in the preliminary phases of our investigation. I needed to add that we were also looking at prior cases Ms. Wright had been involved in prosecuting, with an eye toward possible revenge motives. But also, we had some evidence early on that she was having an affair. We didn't know with whom, but a lover is *always* a prime person of interest."

Gabriel has just testified that I was also a prime suspect from the get-go, just like Richard. The only difference was that he knew Richard's name but didn't yet know mine. But good cross-examiners, like champion boxers, know never to show when they've been hurt. As a result, LeMarcus plunges straight ahead as if Gabriel hadn't laid a glove on him.

"I assume, given that Richard Trofino was a prime suspect from the start, that you questioned him right after the murder?" LeMarcus asks, ignoring the part of Gabriel's answer referencing other suspects.

"Mr. Trofino was questioned by the officers at the scene. Later that morning, we tried to question him further, but he was in no condition for further interrogation."

"Oh? Why not?"

"He got sick."

"Sick? Like he had the flu?"

"No. He threw up."

LeMarcus pauses, pretending that's the first time he's heard this bit of information. His quizzical expression conveys that he finds the prospect of Richard Trofino vomiting to be very odd. His head is cocked to the side, as if he's thinking through what it all means.

"And so . . . you just . . . sent him home?"

"Yes."

"Really? You decided *not* to question the man who, I assume you would agree, would be the most likely suspect in the first few hours after the murder. Didn't Ms. Goodwin disagree with that approach? Didn't she say that she thought Richard Trofino was being treated differently because of his money or his relationship with the mayor?"

"That's a lot of questions you've just posed. Allow me to answer your last one, because it's the one I remember. I don't recall Dana objecting to letting Richard go home, no. He had already been questioned by uniformed police officers at the scene, so we knew his version of events."

"Did Mr. Trofino vomit when the uniformed officers questioned him?"

"No."

"But there was something about the fact that you and Ms. Goodwin were questioning him that made the man sick."

"I'm not sure I would reach the conclusion that the people questioning him were the only variable. It was hours later. Everything was sinking in for him at that time. We were in an interrogation room, which is unpleasant and somewhat musty. Lots of factors contributed. I didn't take it personally."

"Who'd he throw up on? You or Ms. Goodwin?"

"I don't think he was aiming for either of us," Gabriel says.

"My question didn't call for you to speculate about the man's mental calculations, Lieutenant. *Who* did the vomit hit—you or Ms. Goodwin?"

"Mostly Ms. Goodwin."

"So you're saying that it never occurred to you that the violent reaction Mr. Trofino experienced upon the sight of Dana Goodwin—*throwing up on her*—was because he knew at that time that Ms. Goodwin was Ms. Wright's lover?"

"No. That did not occur to me."

Gabriel shows no sign of being outmaneuvered, but I'm certain he knows that LeMarcus has won the fight. Our sole objective is to remind the jury at every turn that Richard Trofino killed his wife. A key predicate we need to establish is that he knew about Lauren's infidelity. Even though Gabriel didn't say it, I'd wager that every juror now thinks the vomiting supports that conclusion.

"Lieutenant, you knew, did you not, that the day before Ms. Wright's murder, her husband met her at her office. In fact, he was meeting his wife there so that the two of them could go together to dinner with you and Ms. Broden."

"I am aware of that, yes," Gabriel replies.

If the situation were any other, I'd feel bad for Gabriel. He's being made to look incompetent. First it seems he never put two and two together to realize that the reason Richard threw up on me was because I was his wife's lover, and now he's going to say that it never occurred to him that Richard had the opportunity to take my cell phone during his office visit. Of course, I had never shared with him anything about my affair with Lauren, so there was no reason for him to consider any of it. But hindsight is twenty-twenty, especially in a murder trial.

"Do you know if during that visit Mr. Trofino took Ms. Goodwin's cell phone?"

"I have no reason to believe that he did."

"That wasn't my question, Lieutenant. Any reason you chose not to answer my question?"

"I thought I had."

"Really?"

LeMarcus has a way of making the word "really" sound like "bullshit." From the expression on Gabriel's face, he knows it too.

"Up until now, you've been very precise, Lieutenant. In fact, I bet that Ms. Broden, when she was preparing you to testify, told you to answer my questions, but only my questions, so as not to volunteer information that wasn't asked of you. She said that, right?"

Every lawyer preps their witnesses that way. Two cardinal rules of witnessing: tell the truth; don't volunteer.

"She said something along those lines, yes."

"Okay, so I'm going to ask you to follow Ms. Broden's instructions. I'm going to ask my question again. *Yes* or *no*, can you categorically deny that Mr. Trofino took Ms. Goodwin's phone during his visit to her office the night of the murder?"

"I will answer you the way I did before. I am not aware of any evidence that he did that."

"Come now, Lieutenant. That's not true. You *are* aware of evidence that Ms. Goodwin's phone had been stolen, aren't you?"

Gabriel's jaw tightens. It's subtle, and I'm sure not noticeable to the jurors, but I recognize the gesture as a sign that he's angry at himself.

"I know she *claimed* she lost her phone."

"The evidence will show Ms. Goodwin bought a new iPhone on the very day that she learned of Ms. Wright's murder. In fact, shortly after she was told about the crime. You're not testifying that her receipt from the Apple store is a forgery, are you?"

"No. I'm saying that—"

LeMarcus cuts him off. "Thank you, Lieutenant. So. Let's revisit this issue. You don't dispute that the Apple receipt is genuine, and that proves Ms. Goodwin bought a new phone on the very day that she learned of the murder. And you also concede that your investigation revealed that on the evening Ms. Wright was killed, her husband was in Ms. Goodwin's office, alone."

Ella rightly objects. By the tenor of her voice, I can tell that she knows that Gabriel is getting his clock cleaned.

"Assumes facts not in evidence, Your Honor," Ella says. "There's been no testimony that Mr. Trofino was ever alone in Ms. Goodwin's office."

Judge Gold agrees. "Sustained."

LeMarcus looks like a shark who smells blood. "Lieutenant, you did confiscate Ms. Goodwin's phone when she was arrested, correct?"

"Yes."

"Did it have a passcode on it?"

"No, it did not."

"I see. So you, or frankly *anyone else*, could read all of her text messages on that phone?"

"It was a fairly new phone, so there wasn't much on it."

"Again, Lieutenant, that wasn't my question. Let me ask it again. Could you *or anyone else* who had Ms. Goodwin's phone read her text messages?"

"It was not passcode protected, so I could."

LeMarcus smiles as if to say, *Now, wasn't that easy?* Gabriel does not smile back, as if to say, *Go to hell.*

"Lieutenant, sitting here today, do you believe that at any time during that visit on the evening of Ms. Wright's murder that Mr. Trofino was in Dana Goodwin's office alone? And by alone, I mean *all alone.* Without even Ms. Goodwin present?"

"I don't have any reason to believe that he was there alone."

"But if you did believe that, can we agree that you, as a fine investigator, would have questioned Mr. Trofino about whether he took that opportunity to steal Ms. Goodwin's phone."

"Objection!" Ella shouts again.

It's the same grounds. Facts not in evidence.

"Sustained," Judge Gold says again.

LeMarcus doesn't seem to care. Nor should he. The answers Gabriel provides have ceased to matter. This is all about his questions making the point that Richard Trofino should be the one on trial here, not me.

"You never asked Richard Trofino whether he took Ms. Goodwin's phone, did you, Lieutenant?"

"No."

LeMarcus returns to counsel table. Once there, he leans over to whisper in my ear.

"Not too bad, if I do say so myself."

I couldn't agree more.

47.

ELLA BRODEN

Wednesday and most of Thursday are the "science fair," the term prosecutors use to describe putting on forensic evidence. It's boring for everyone, including me, as it takes hours to make a single point. Establishing chain of evidence is no one's idea of riveting testimony. Nevertheless, I think the jury gets the highlights: Lauren Wright was murdered at the duck pond in Central Park, where her body was found. Her assailant fired two gunshots into her head at 1:27 a.m. The murder weapon is a Glock 19, and the gun was previously owned by Detective Gregory Papamichael, who never reported his pistol stolen.

I also put on the evidence of the affair, just to break up the monotony a bit. Although talk of secret hotel visits perks up the jurors, they fall back into their sleepy daze when they realize that there won't be any prurient details. Still, I establish that Lauren made a $300 cash withdrawal from her ATM nearly every week for close to six months, almost always on Tuesdays, with the occasional Wednesday thrown in. During some of those withdrawals, Dana Goodwin was captured beside Lauren by the ATM camera, and so I show the jurors the two of them together; sometimes their faces are much closer than I'm certain any jurors have ever gotten to their own bosses. The hotel clerk from the Best Western testifies that Dana and Lauren were regulars, and then he points them out on the hotel's grainy black-and-white surveillance footage, hand in hand in the lobby, wearing the goofy grins of high schoolers.

On cross, Burrows drives home one point repeatedly: none of the evidence I've put on directly ties Dana Goodwin to the crime. There are no fingerprints, DNA, or eyewitnesses that place her at the duck pond on the night of the murder. There's no record of her ever owning a Glock 19. Burrows doesn't even question the Citibank representative about the cash withdrawals or the Best Western clerks as he's conceding the affair.

A representative of Dana Goodwin's cell-phone carrier, a tired-looking man with heavily hooded eyes, testifies that Dana's phone was off for most of the evening of the murder, which was a rare occurrence for her. For that reason, there was no way to trace where it was, as he explains that even an idle phone sends pings to towers that indicate location, but not one that has been powered down.

"It went back on at about one o'clock in the morning, in the vicinity of Central Park," the witness says.

"Let me see if I have this right," Burrows says when it's his turn. "Your testimony is that by studying cell-phone tower pings, you know, beyond a shadow of a doubt, that Ms. Goodwin's phone was *shut off* while it was at One Hogan Place, at about six thirty on the night of the murder, and that it did not go on again until approximately one in the morning, or within a half hour of the murder. And you can further determine, conclusively, that when the phone went back on, it was in the vicinity of Central Park. Do I have that all correct?"

"Yes."

"Would this same ping occur if, for example, someone stole Ms. Goodwin's phone from her office at six thirty on the night of the murder, and turned it off at that time, and then that person turned it back on while standing in Central Park at one a.m.?"

"Yes."

"Please tell us, sir, where was the phone between six thirty p.m. and one a.m.?"

The phone company rep seems confused. "That's the whole point. I don't know."

"Oh. So you don't know if, for example, it was taken by Richard Trofino and brought to his home, correct?"

"I don't know who Richard Trofino is."

"And you don't know whether it was Mr. Trofino who turned off Ms. Goodwin's phone, after taking it from Ms. Goodwin's desk, and then powered it back on once he was in Central Park, ready to kill his wife. That's correct too, isn't it?"

The double negatives, as well as the repetition of a name the witness has already indicated is unfamiliar to him, renders the man speechless. I object, just to give the witness some time to get his bearings.

Judge Gold sustains my objection, even though he probably shouldn't. The fact that the witness is spared from answering the question, however, is of little import. The damage has already been done.

———

Yosef Izikson is the last of the science fair for a reason—he's going to be the means by which I get the text messages into evidence.

Izikson is a short, bald man, of slight build, who speaks with a heavy Israeli accent, even though he testifies that he's been living in this country for more than thirty years. He tells the jurors that he's the chief executive officer of a firm located in New Jersey called ABS, which does nothing to erase the jurors' glassy-eyed expectation that Izikson is just another nerd testifying about boring science.

It's only when he says that his firm specializes in security, and was responsible for cracking Lauren Wright's iPhone, that I hear the rumblings in the jury box of people starting to focus. But before I can ask my first substantive question about Lauren's cell phone, Burrows objects.

Rather than state his grounds, Burrows asks Judge Gold for permission to approach. The judge curls his fingers, inviting us to the bench.

When everyone arrives, the judge has already placed his hand over the microphone and is leaning over to hear us better. "Your dance. You lead, Mr. Burrows," Judge Gold says in a whisper.

"The last text received on Ms. Wright's phone is hearsay," Burrows says. "The prosecution is going to argue that these texts came from Ms. Goodwin because it says so on Ms. Wright's call log. But that statement—like any document—is still hearsay if it's being offered for its truth."

Black's Law Dictionary defines *hearsay* as a declaration made out of court presented in court for its truth. Therefore, in a technical sense, Burrows is correct. The phone's identification of Dana Goodwin as the sender of a text is hearsay, because it was not made under oath in open court and is being presented as evidence that Dana was the author and sender. But there are at least forty exceptions to the hearsay rule, ranging from excited utterances to business records to verbal acts. The king of these exceptions is that anything the defendant says off the stand is always admissible. That's how the prosecution can admit into evidence confessions made to police officers or wiretap recordings.

"Ah, were it that simple, Mr. Burrows," Judge Gold says, this time slightly more audibly. "I'm going to steal some of Ms. Broden's thunder here and jump in to make her case for her, because it seems to this old jurist that the text is a party admission, no different than if your client uttered the words she typed into her phone."

"That would be true if *Ms. Goodwin* typed those words into her phone," Burrows counters. "But she did not. And there's been no offer of proof that she did."

I enter the fray. "The offer of proof, Your Honor, is the text itself. It's self-authenticating. It literally says that the speaker is Ms. Goodwin.

There is no doubt that if Ms. Goodwin shouted her message from her window into Ms. Wright's window, those statements would be admissible as a party admission. The fact that the statement here occurred electronically doesn't change the law."

"She's right, isn't she, Mr. Burrows?" says Judge Gold.

"She would be," Burrows concedes, "but—"

"Ah, the distinguishing *but*." Judge Gold laughs.

"The critical *but*," Burrows says with a laugh of his own before he quickly resumes a more serious expression. "In Ms. Broden's example, in order for the statement to be admitted over a hearsay objection, the prosecution would have to put on some proof that it was Ms. Goodwin shouting out the window. For example, someone would have to identify Ms. Goodwin's voice, or testify to seeing Ms. Goodwin leaning out the window at the time the words were uttered. Here that corroborating evidence is lacking. We have no idea *who* actually sent the text. All the witness knows is that it came from a phone owned by Ms. Goodwin."

"Forgive me, counselor, but isn't that exactly the corroborating evidence needed for admission?" Judge Gold asks. "You can argue a different person actually sent it if you want, and maybe the jury will believe you, but that seems a question for them regarding how much credence to put on that particular piece of evidence, not one for me on admissibility."

"Respectfully, no, Your Honor," Burrows says. "A text is not entitled to any presumption of reliability because it is so easily manipulated. For example, sometimes my children text me using my wife's phone. When I get a text message from my wife that says, 'Dad, when are you coming home?' I assume it's from one of my children, not my wife, even though if you look at my phone it appears that the message has come from my wife."

"I love it when modern technology muddies what heretofore had been so clear," Judge Gold says. "I'm going to need more guidance on this before issuing a ruling. So I'm going to send the jury home and tell them to come back tomorrow at eleven. You all need to be here at ten and prepared to recite chapter and verse on the law on this issue."

48.

DANA GOODWIN

It's going to be a long night. LeMarcus gave me the choice of where to order from, but when I said I didn't care, he selected a pizza place. He also said he was open to any toppings except olives and anchovies, but I still didn't have an opinion, so he ordered the pie plain.

I usually do my own legal research, and I can see by LeMarcus's familiarity with the legal databases that he doesn't delegate this task to junior lawyers either. Our issue—the admissibility of a text message against a hearsay challenge—wasn't even a consideration ten years ago, which greatly limits the scope of the research. The "patient zero" of text admission cases is from Pennsylvania, a September 16, 2011, ruling issued by a "Bowles, J," according to the written decision. I can't tell if "J" stands for his first name or signifies that he's a judge.

To my utter shock, "Bowles, J" ruled that the text message in that case was inadmissible. I start reading from the opinion out loud, breaking what must have been twenty minutes without either of us making a sound.

"'As a matter of first impression, the appellant challenged the admissibility of the text message evidence and what is necessary to authenticate a text message' . . . blah, blah, blah . . . 'appellant claimed there was no evidence substantiating that she was the author of the text messages or evidence that the texts were directed to her because there was evidence that another person was using her phone for some of the time. The court noted that electronic communications, such as e-mail and instant messages, can be authenticated' . . . case citations omitted . . . and here's the key part . . . 'such evidence is evaluated on a case-by-case basis as any other document.' In this case, police could not confirm that the appellant was the author. The court found that, quote, 'authentication of electronic communications, like documents, requires more than mere confirmation that the number or address belonged to a particular person. Circumstantial evidence, which tends to corroborate the identity of the sender, is required.'"

LeMarcus has been listening throughout. "What's the court?" he asks.

All judicial opinions do not receive the same weight. Courts directly above the trial court—in New York that means the First Appellate Division, the Court of Appeals, and the United States Supreme Court—must be followed under the legal dictate of *stare decisis*. Decisions from other courts are used simply as guidance.

"Pennsylvania Superior," I say.

"Okay . . ." he says, but he might as well have said, "What's that?"

"It's an appellate court at least, but an intermediate one."

"Is the case called *Koch*?"

I scroll to the top of the decision I'm reading. "Yeah. *Commonwealth v. Koch*."

"I saw that too. You're right, it's good for us. But the facts in that case aren't that close to ours. It seems like some of the texts in question there *clearly* didn't come from the defendant. The opinion says that the prosecution conceded that, which seems to have cast doubt on whether the texts introduced as evidence were authored by her. And here's more of a good news/bad news situation. The case was affirmed by the Supreme Court of Pennsylvania, but on a three-three split."

Like the saying in baseball that the tie goes to the runner, a split in an appellate court means the lower court's decision stands. However, it doesn't provide the kind of judicial imprimatur of acceptance that we're after. If anything, it goes the other way. Three members of the Pennsylvania Supreme Court would have admitted the text message even with the undisputed evidence that other people were using the defendant's phone.

When the pizza comes, LeMarcus suggests that we stop our work to eat. The receptionist I met upon my first visit—who I now know is named Brian and serves a multitude of functions around the office besides greeting visitors, including being a paralegal and, in this case, a server of late-night pizza—brings out actual china on which to put the pizza, and crystal glassware into which our soda can be poured. More often than not in my late-night pizza days, I ate it straight out of the box, without even a paper plate.

Throughout the trial, LeMarcus has not asked anything about me that wasn't relevant to the case, and he hasn't revealed anything about himself. I am not sure whether that's because he makes it a practice not to get to know his clients on any personal level—the lack of familiarity no doubt easing the blow when they're convicted—or because it's part of his legal strategy not to be tainted with information that might create an ethical quandary for him if I were to take the stand.

Yet over our meal, his formal bearing eases up. LeMarcus says that he is the father of eight-year-old twins. After establishing that they are fraternal, I ask what they're like.

"Couldn't be more different, actually. James takes after his mother, both in looks and personality. He's the prettiest little boy you're ever going to want to meet, but shy. He likes to read picture books about dinosaurs and other fanciful things. Lawrence, sadly for him, is his father's son. A born lawyer, I fear. If you say *day*, he'll argue that it's night. Doesn't matter how high the sun is in the sky, he's got some explanation for why you shouldn't believe your own eyes."

I laugh at the comment, imagining a tiny LeMarcus Burrows. "Does he wear three-piece suits?"

"No. Not yet, anyway," LeMarcus says with a laugh of his own.

"My little guy, he's all about superheroes," I say. "Sometimes I envy that he can believe that there's this greater force that can save you no matter how much peril you're in. You know?"

LeMarcus looks puzzled by my statement. "I'm not sure if you're suggesting that I'm your superhero in this instance, or that you don't think my superpowers are up to the task."

"No, I'm sorry. It wasn't intended to be a comment about you at all. I know you're doing everything you can. But even you have to admit you've been dealt a bad hand."

"Don't give up on me yet, Dana. If we win tomorrow's motion, the prosecution will dismiss the charges. They'll have no other choice. Without the text, the only evidence that they have against you is the affair, and Judge Gold won't let them go to the jury with only that."

"They have Franklin Pearse," I remind him.

"That's still awfully thin," LeMarcus says after swallowing a bite of pizza. "I'd agree if the homeless guy identified you. Or if he provided a description close to resembling you, or even if he saw the actual shooting. But all he gives the prosecution is that someone around five and a half feet tall, maybe a man, maybe a woman, maybe black but maybe white, who was wearing a hoodie, was near the duck pond. Even though Richard Trofino is slightly taller, it's close enough to be a positive ID of him too."

"So you're saying that I'm going to be free this time tomorrow?"

I say this with a smile because I know that LeMarcus hasn't actually opined on how Judge Gold will rule. To the contrary, we both know that he's more likely than not to admit the text message into evidence. And if that happens, my conviction will be a foregone conclusion.

49.

ELLA BRODEN

I place the odds at fifty-fifty that Judge Gold rules the text inadmissible. A coin-flip chance.

Heads, the case ends today with Dana Goodwin going free.

Tails, she spends the rest of her life in prison.

When Judge Gold takes the bench, he appears to be well rested. He went to bed early last night, no doubt. By contrast, I was at the office until two in the morning, collecting virtually every written legal opinion I could find on the exclusion of text messages, e-mails, or any other type of electronic evidence objected to on hearsay grounds. It gives me some pleasure that LeMarcus looks as tired as I feel.

The jury has not been called, so their chairs are empty. Judge Gold is going to take the legal argument outside of their presence. He doesn't waste much time with preliminaries, aside from saying good morning.

"Mr. Burrows, please make your argument regarding the inadmissibility of the text message on hearsay grounds."

Burrows's pitch is not much different from what he said at the bench conference yesterday, but it takes much longer and includes a sprinkling of case citations. The good news is that he hasn't found any legal authority that I didn't. The bad news is that he *did* find the Pennsylvania case that excluded some drug dealer's texts. He's telling Judge Gold that the situation there was nearly identical to what he has before him, even though the two fact patterns bear virtually no similarities.

Burrows's point is a simple one—the standard is whether there are indicia of reliability that the owner of the phone sent the text message. If there is, the text should be admitted. If not, it should be excluded.

Judge Gold lets him speak for about ten minutes without interruption. When it's my turn, I take just as much time, with more of it devoted to the facts in the Pennsylvania case than I had originally planned. I emphasize that case represents the rare exception on the admissibility of text messages, and the judge there only excluded them because there was clear and uncontested evidence that someone other than the owner of the phone had used the phone, which is not the case with Dana's texts.

"And even in that situation, the Pennsylvania Supreme Court deadlocked on whether that decision was correct," I say. "Now compare that case with the one here. There is absolutely nothing to indicate that anyone *other* than Dana Goodwin sent the text message to Ms. Wright. There are no other messages on Ms. Goodwin's phone that were sent by others, which makes this fact pattern completely different than the scenario in the Pennsylvania case. And the only evidence that Ms. Goodwin did not have possession of her phone at the time of the messages is the say-so of the defendant. In other words, Your Honor, if you exclude the text message in this case, then I don't see how a text message or an e-mail is *ever* going to be admitted in *any* case. All it would take is exactly what the defense is doing here: making a bald claim that someone else might have had access to the phone."

Judge Gold is as solicitous of me as he had been of Burrows. When I'm finished making my argument, he says, "Thank you both. This issue quite clearly turns on the proof. I might hear evidence on that later, but for our purposes now, I'd like a proffer from you, Mr. Burrows, on what your witnesses will say regarding the access to Ms. Goodwin's phone."

A proffer of proof is a free shot for Burrows. He gets to summarize what his witnesses will say. I've never heard a proffer that came close to the nuance of actual testimony, especially after cross-examination.

"Your Honor, the defense proffers as follows: the evidence will show that Richard Trofino was present in Ms. Goodwin's office on the day of the murder, sometime after six. Lieutenant Velasquez has already testified to this, but we also expect that Mr. Trofino will confirm that fact when he takes the stand. We don't know if Mr. Trofino will admit to being alone in Ms. Goodwin's office, but even if he were to deny it, that denial will be rebutted by the testimony of one of the secretaries at the DA's office, who will say that she saw him alone in Ms. Goodwin's office for several minutes. So on that front, we think we have strong evidence of Mr. Trofino being alone in Ms. Goodwin's office."

Judge Gold interrupts to get to the point. "There's a big difference between proving that Mr. Trofino was alone in Ms. Goodwin's office and establishing that he took her phone. What evidence do you have on that score?"

"Lieutenant Velasquez has already testified that Ms. Goodwin told him that she lost her phone," LeMarcus says. "The receipt from the Apple store shows that Ms. Goodwin replaced her phone the day of the murder—"

"Why shouldn't I conclude from your statement that Ms. Goodwin sent the text and then got rid of her phone and bought a replacement?" Judge Gold interrupts.

"Because her husband will corroborate that she did not have her phone when she got home, which was hours *before* Ms. Wright was killed."

The look on Judge Gold's face indicates that he sees nothing wrong with LeMarcus's theory. When it's my turn, I tell him why it's very wrong.

"Your Honor, the prosecution has multiple objections to the proffer just made by Mr. Burrows, but the main one is that the testimony he's promised has absolutely no credibility. Specifically, Ms. Goodwin's testimony that she lost her phone *before* the murder is all based solely on her word. And her husband's so-called corroboration is just as self-serving. He can be expected to lie to protect his wife and the mother of his young son from a murder conviction. By contrast, the People's proffer is that Mr. Trofino will deny all of it. He will testify that he did not take Ms. Wright's phone and he never sent the text at issue."

"Talk about self-serving," Burrows says, trying to talk over me. "Every word out of Richard Trofino's mouth is a lie."

"Okay, thank you both," Judge Gold says, trying to reestablish some order. "I've heard enough."

He looks down at a sheet of paper in front of him. That means he decided how he was going to rule last night and has already written out his decision, which he's about to read into the record. This morning's argument—and indeed last night's research session—was largely just to put us through our paces.

Of course, I have no idea whether Judge Gold's epiphany last night was for or against me. I say a silent prayer and wait—like everyone else in the courtroom.

"This is indeed an interesting issue," Judge Gold says, "and one that has been well argued by both sides. As technology advances, the rules of evidence have to advance as well, or else they will become obsolete. I will issue a more detailed ruling on this issue because I think it is of scholarly interest and can be considered by others in different contexts from this one. But I realize that it is primarily of interest to the parties before me, and that my ruling will have important implications for this trial. Indeed, the text message at issue here is the lynchpin of the prosecution's case. So much so that excluding it from evidence could well result in a directed verdict, and double jeopardy having already attached, the prosecution would have no right to appeal my ruling. By contrast, admitting the text message will preserve this issue for the appellate courts to consider. Of course, that only occurs in the event of a guilty verdict, but if Ms. Goodwin is acquitted even *with* the admission of this text message, then ruling it admissible obviously had no prejudice to the defense. And so my ruling might be considered either Solomonic or cowardly, depending on your point of view. I will accept the text into evidence, and thereby preserve this issue for appellate review. I do so because I agree with the prosecution that the evidence that Ms. Goodwin did *not* send the text is uncorroborated, and therefore the authenticity has been sufficiently established to accept the text into evidence. I will, however, give the defense latitude to maintain its argument that someone other than the defendant could have authored those texts, and the jury is free to acquit on that basis."

Burrows jumps to his feet. "Your Honor—"

"Mr. Burrows, sit down. I've ruled. If you have anything to say about it, you're going to need to tell it to the appellate court."

50.

DANA GOODWIN

I try not to show it, but the last vestige of hope leaves my body with Judge Gold's ruling.

LeMarcus sits beside me wearing a similar poker face, but he too slumps slightly in defeat.

After announcing his decision, Judge Gold calls for a fifteen-minute recess. We all stand to watch the judge walk through the side door and back to his chambers. The moment the door closes behind him, the reporters reach for their phones, eager to tweet out this recent development.

I must be wearing my disappointment on my sleeve, because LeMarcus leans over to whisper in my ear. "We still have a shot, Dana."

"Yeah, slim to none—and slim just left town," I say.

"What?" he says, apparently not familiar with an expression my father used all the time.

"It means I'm going to be convicted."

"Not yet. Stay strong. I need you to project confidence to the jury."

I nod that I understand, but the introduction of the text message means that the prosecution is going to be able to link me directly to Lauren's murder. When court resumes, Ella will put on her evidence of the text messages. My adultery in all its glory. Not to mention the evidence that I lured my lover to Central Park, to her death.

After that ignominy, Ella will call to the stand a cleaned-up Franklin Pearse. He'll identify me—or at least someone fitting my description, general though it may be—as being the only other person he saw in the park at the time of the murder.

The final nail in the coffin of my defense will be the testimony of Richard Trofino, who will say over and over again how much he loved his wife. A repeat, no doubt, of his eulogy. After he finishes his song and dance, the prosecution will rest.

That will be more than enough for them to sustain their burden of proof, at least as a legal matter. Which means that I'm going to have to put on a defense.

LeMarcus has been circumspect with regard to his strategy for my defense. I know that's because he wants to avoid a fight with his client. He's been clear that Stuart will be our first witness, and that a lot rides on his testimony. Stuart provides me an alibi, and will corroborate that I did not have my phone after Richard Trofino left my office.

The part LeMarcus *hasn't* wanted to discuss with me is what role, if any, I'm going to play in my own defense. He knows I want to testify, but every time I've raised the issue he's responded by telling about the acquittals he's obtained without his clients taking the stand.

I understand his reluctance. Defendants are usually easy pickings for a prosecutor. Too many lies to keep straight, and all it takes is for one of them to be revealed on cross for even the most expertly established defense to fail.

"Being a criminal defender is like being a chef," LeMarcus told me. "You use every ingredient you have to put together your defense, but you have to take special care that nothing spoils the broth. And a lie, no matter how small, poisons everything."

At the same time, I think my testimony is critical. Richard Trofino is going to swear to the jury that he loved Lauren and would never in a million years have harmed her. I'm certain that to obtain my freedom, I'm going to need to say exactly the same thing.

I wonder what that will do to Stuart. He's convinced himself that my relationship with Lauren was a mistake that I regret. But to make my defense convincing, I'll need to say that I was in love. That there was no reason for me to kill Lauren because she loved me too. I'll need to be convincing that my happily-ever-after hopes involved being with her, not Stuart.

Just as this thought rolls through my head, Stuart approaches the defense table. He's allowed to watch the proceedings as long as they don't include witness testimony, which means he's seen firsthand that my hope of acquittal has just been dashed with the admission of the text message.

He places a supportive hand on my shoulder. "I'm sorry," he says. "I really thought the judge was going to exclude it."

LeMarcus suggests that we talk outside, glancing at Ella, who sits only a few feet away from us. She's looking down at her notes, seemingly oblivious to our discussion.

Without waiting for our consent, LeMarcus gets up and makes his way to the hallway. Stuart and I follow him out.

When we're in an abandoned corner of the hallway, away from prying eyes and ears, LeMarcus says, "Okay, here's how I see the rest of the day going. The odds are very good that the prosecution is going to rest today. Maybe even before lunch, if they finish Richard's testimony quickly. Stuart, that means you might take the stand as early as right after lunch."

"Okay," Stuart says. "I'm ready."

"Good. Your testimony is now absolutely critical. Remember what we went over during prep. You need to be firm that Dana did not have her phone the night of the murder. After that testimony, you'll provide Dana's alibi. It's equally important that you testify she never left your sight that night, and she definitely didn't leave the apartment. No hesitation at all on those points. Got me?"

"Yes. That's exactly what I'll say."

Stuart and I both know that his testimony will be littered with perjury. We've discussed the lies, making sure that he gets them right. His testimony about my losing my cell phone only requires that he move the timeline from the morning, when I first told him I couldn't find it, to the evening before. We decided to fix the time as right after dinner, the idea being that we had a lovely family dinner, after which I went to check my phone, and that's when I alerted him to the fact that I couldn't find it.

The other lie Stuart will tell concerns my alibi. Stuart and I didn't share a bed that night. I slept in Jacob's room. As a result, there's no way Stuart would know if I'd left the apartment.

"Thank you," I say to Stuart.

"No need to thank me. I love you."

51.

ELLA BRODEN

Judge Gold gives me more leeway than I would have anticipated for Izikson to explain the history of the law-enforcement battle between Apple and the federal government over the unlocking of iPhones. Specifically, the phone of Syed Farook, the San Bernardino shooter.

"If you go on the Internet, you see all sorts of theories," Izikson says. "Some articles claim that Farook's cell phone was cracked by freelance hackers. Others say that Cellebrite, a competitor of ours, did it. The cost of the work is also hotly debated. There are people who advertise on the web that they can do it for a hundred bucks, while the FBI director at the time said in a speech that it cost more than his entire salary for the remaining years of his tenure, which would be in excess of a million dollars. I don't know how Cellebrite, or whoever the FBI used, did it. But I know how we do it. And I know it isn't cheap, but it doesn't cost a million dollars either."

I ask him to explain how he does it, even though I know he's not going to answer. I just don't want to look like I'm hiding anything from the jury.

"I cannot answer that question," Izikson says. "It is not only highly proprietary, but a matter of national security. If it became known how we can get into cell phones that are locked, then terrorists and others could engineer around our methods."

Burrows objects, although I'm certain he knows he's going to lose. National security supersedes everything these days.

Judge Gold makes it official. "Ladies and gentlemen, ordinarily you are entitled to know how an expert performed his or her work," he says, facing the jury. "However, in this case, I side with the national security concerns and therefore rule that this witness need not divulge the steps that led to his conclusions. You are not to make any negative inference regarding the work performed by this witness based on my ruling. Instead, trust that he did this work in a professional manner, and that the information retrieved from Lauren Wright's phone that has been presented here is, in fact, the information that was contained on that phone."

With that green light, I spend the next hour going back through the key text messages. Obviously, Izikson has nothing to add substantively to Lauren and Dana's correspondence, but I lay the foundation that each one was indeed found on Lauren's iPhone, and that the time stamp is accurate, as are the sender and recipient information.

And then, at last, the moment that all of this has been leading to is at hand. The introduction of the last text message Lauren Wright ever received and sent.

There are eight screens around the courtroom, which makes it look a bit like a sports bar. Instead of a football game, though, the TVs project the text that is at the heart of the prosecution's case.

NEED TO SEE YOU ASAP!!! DUCK POND. I'M ALREADY HERE. PLEASE COME! IT'S URGENT!!!

And underneath is Lauren's response.

BE THERE IN 5

"Does Ms. Wright's phone indicate who sent the message asking that she meet at the duck pond?" I ask.

"Yes."

"And who sent—"

"Objection," Burrows says.

His tone is halfhearted. He's only objecting for the record, so that he preserves this issue for appeal. He knows it's going to be overruled, which it is.

I want the question and answer to be in sequence, so I repeat the question. "Mr. Izikson, once again, who sent this message to Ms. Wright? The message requesting that she meet at the duck pond?"

"Dana Goodwin sent it," Izikson says.

———

When it's Burrows's turn to conduct his cross-examination, he handles Izikson in the shortest amount of time possible. In fact, he asks only one actual question, although Burrows rephrases it numerous times.

The point he's trying to make, of course, is that no amount of security expertise can ascertain who authored a text. All anyone knows is the device it was sent from.

I had instructed Izikson not to fight Burrows on that. As a result, he concedes that he didn't see who actually typed the letters into the phone. All he knows is that it was sent from Dana Goodwin's phone.

———

In fictionalized versions of trials, they always make a point of putting homeless guys in fancy suits and giving them haircuts so that they look like bankers. In reality, that's not very effective because it comes out pretty quickly that that's what you've done and the jury feels like you're trying to pull one over on them. On the other hand, no one wants to be in the presence of a man who hasn't bathed in weeks. My practice has always been to have the witness shower and to launder his clothes, but otherwise not to change his appearance. That means Franklin Pearse takes the witness stand wearing clean clothing—blue jeans, a blue workman's shirt, and a light blue windbreaker. His hair is as spiky in parts as when we first met, but it was his decision to be appear clean-shaven.

I get Pearse's life situation out of the way at the start.

"Mr. Pearse, please tell the jury where you reside."

"Everywhere. Anywhere."

Pearse's voice is steady, although low. Judge Gold asks him to lean forward and speak into the microphone.

"What does that mean?" I ask.

"I normally sleep in the park. Unless it's too cold, and then sometimes I go to the shelter."

"In other words, you're homeless?"

"That's right."

"I want to ask you a few questions about one night in November. It's the night you saw and heard something in Central Park. The same night the police have asked you about before. Can you please tell the jury what you saw and heard that evening?"

"Okay. I go to the park a lot at night to empty out the garbage cans for recyclables. Near the duck pond is a good spot because they have that restaurant there, and they serve soda in cans. That night I couldn't get into the shelter because it was full, and it was really cold, so I was trying to stay awake. Anyway, I was at the garbage cans near the restaurant when I heard these two booms. Like *boom, boom*. Quicklike. And then I saw this person—not sure if it was a man or a woman because I only saw from the back. Wearing a black hoodie and running away."

"How far away were you from this person?"

"Not too far, but not close either."

"Tell us by reference to this courtroom. As close as I am to you?"

"No. Farther than that."

"As close as the door to this courtroom?"

Pearse considers this. "Yeah. A little closer than that, I think."

That places the distance between Franklin Pearse and Lauren Wright's murderer at farther than ten feet but closer than fifty. Next, I introduce into evidence a black hoodie sweatshirt and make a big show of telling the jury that the cops found it in Dana Goodwin's closet. I have a sweatshirt just like it in mine too. I suspect there's not a woman in New York City who doesn't. Still, it's evidence.

"The hoodie you saw, did it look like this?" I ask, holding it up in front of me like I'm the number-one draft pick of the NBA.

"Yeah. Black hoodie. Like that one."

"Mr. Pearse, were you able to tell how tall this person was?"

"I think so."

"Tell us, please."

"Not too tall. Not real short either, though."

Time for a little more court theatrics. "Your Honor, we request that Ms. Goodwin stand so that the witness can make an identification."

Burrows stands with his client without any prompt from Judge Gold. Burrows is a tall man, which is helpful for me and probably not something that occurred to him. He rose most likely out of reflex, something he always does whenever his client stands as a subliminal message to the jury of solidarity. But by doing so this time, he's going to allow Franklin Pearse to positively ID Dana as the same height as the murderer.

"Drawing your attention to the defendant's table, was the height of the person you saw similar to the defendant's, Dana Goodwin?"

"Yeah. Like the lady. Not the man."

On cross, Burrows establishes that Pearse can't say that the person he saw—"at a distance in the pitch blackness of night," as Burrows repeatedly reminds the jury—wasn't a few inches taller than the defendant.

"Have you met ever met a man named Richard Trofino?" Burrows asks.

"No. Don't think so, anyways."

"So the police never asked if you could identify the husband of the woman who was dead?"

"No."

"Do you know how tall Mr. Trofino is?"

"No."

"So, you don't know if he's approximately the same height as the person you saw—at a distance in the pitch blackness—in the park that night?"

"No."

"Well, he is," Burrows says.

———

My final witness is Richard Trofino.

I begin by expressing my condolences, and Richard nods and says thank you. The background portion takes fifteen minutes, long enough to establish with those jurors who don't recognize him that he's a man of power and influence in the city, but short enough to keep him from seeming like a borderline mobster.

Richard has made a point of calling me every night after the trial. I felt that I owed him this time, as the court's sequestration order meant that his only window into what was unfolding was what I told him on those calls and what he read in the news. Still, I dreaded talking to him. There wasn't a single conversation that didn't involve his screaming at me about how it was playing out. I told him that the defense wasn't getting anywhere with its strategy of blaming him, even as I wondered whether that was true.

Last night, I prepared him for this testimony. He was no more pleased with me than he had been during our phone conversations. Even my victory regarding the text didn't satisfy him.

The one thing that emerged quite clearly from these discussions was that, the more time I spend in Richard's company, the more it seems to me that he does in fact have the hair-trigger temper of a man who might just kill his wife. Needless to say, I am hoping to keep that side of him from the jury.

I begin my examination by asking Richard how long he and Lauren were married. This was intended to be a soft lob, but his back stiffens slightly. He pauses for a moment to rub his eyes before answering.

"It would have been sixteen years this coming February fourteenth," he says, acting as if he's still not accustomed to discussing her in the past tense, even though I've seen him do it countless times before with much less drama.

"Please describe the state of your marriage in the last year."

"I don't know quite how to answer that. I can tell you what I thought it was, and then I can tell you what I learned about in the course of this trial . . . the investigation."

We had rehearsed that I would ask a deliberately complicated question so that Richard could correct me, just as he did.

"Tell the jury your thoughts about your marriage in the past twelve months."

"I was very happy," he says through a strained smile, now looking directly at the jury. Again, just as we practiced. "But I'm not going to overly romanticize it. After as many years as we'd been together, we had our issues. Quirks that bothered the other one, that kind of thing. But that type of longevity also strengthens your bond and brings you into a period where you know that this person is *your* person, until . . . well, I was about to say until death do you part."

I would have preferred he not say that. Some jurors might conclude that was the only way Richard could get out of a bad marriage.

"And more recently, since your wife's murder, have you come to a different conclusion about the state of your marriage in the past year?"

"Yes and no," he says, again turning to face the jury. "Yes, in that I know that Lauren must have felt something was missing if she engaged in an extramarital affair. The fact that she became involved with a woman further indicates to me that she was searching for something that I couldn't provide her. That revelation . . . it was like losing Lauren for a second time. I'm never going to be able to talk to her about what drove her away like that. I'm never going to be able to make it up to her."

To my surprise, Richard begins to choke up. During prep he had done a similar speech, but always delivered it smoothly. I'm not sure if it's the realization of the fact that he's doing it for real that has brought on this rush of emotion or if he's putting on a show.

"You answered my previous question concerning whether the recent revelations about your wife's affair with Ms. Goodwin brought you to a different conclusion regarding the state of your marriage by saying yes and no. I think you provided us the yes part of your answer. What's the no part?"

"The no part is that I know that my feelings for Lauren were true. I loved her. And, although I can never be certain of this, I have to believe that she loved me too. The way I think about it now is that she got lost, but she would have found her way back to me in the end. I know that I would have welcomed her back with open arms. That's why her death . . . her murder . . . is so much more tragic. Not only because we've been denied the rest of our lives together, but also because I have to live with uncertainty about how she felt about me in the end. I know Lauren. She would have thought that taking away my faith in her love was somehow worse than death."

Richard's laying it on thick, that's for sure. I would have told him to tone it down if he'd shared with me that he was going to say that Lauren would view his uncertainty about her love as worse than death. That's something a narcissist says, not a grieving husband.

"When did you first learn that your wife had been unfaithful?"

"When . . . ironically enough now, Dana Goodwin told me. It was part of the police investigation. She was with Lieutenant Velasquez. They told me that there was circumstantial evidence of an affair. I honestly didn't believe it. And then, of course, when Dana was arrested, I learned of the text messages. There was no denying it any longer."

"To be one hundred percent clear, you had *no* idea of the affair until *after* your wife was murdered?"

"That is correct. Not only no idea—not even an *inkling* of an idea. It was the furthest thing from my mind."

"I take it, though, that your wife had spoken about Dana Goodwin?"

"Yes. They worked together."

"In the week prior to your wife's murder, what did she say about Ms. Goodwin?"

This earns a hearsay objection, but I suspect LeMarcus hasn't thought it all the way through. I'm not introducing Lauren's statements because they're true. Rather, the point is to show she was lying to her husband.

"Ms. Broden?" Judge Gold says, allowing me to unpack the reasoning behind my question.

"It is the defense's theory that Mr. Trofino had motive because he knew about the affair. He just testified that he did *not* know of the affair. What his wife told him about her relationship with Ms. Goodwin speaks to his state of mind, and therefore meets that exception to the hearsay rule."

"That it does," Judge Gold confirms. "Proceed."

"Please tell the jury what your wife told you about Ms. Goodwin in that last week of her life."

"The night Lauren was murdered, she told me that Dana was going to return to General Crimes."

"What was your reaction to this news?"

"I was surprised. Even though I'd be the first to admit that I don't know all the ins and outs of the DA's office, I understood that being a deputy chief was a promotion from being a line ADA. Later that night, I said this to Lauren, but she told me that it didn't always work that way, and that Dana missed doing trial work."

"Did you believe your wife when she told you that?"

"I did. It made sense at the time."

"And now?"

"Well, knowing that Lauren and Dana were lovers makes me think about Dana's decision to leave her job at Special Vics and to go back to General Crimes very differently."

LeMarcus objects. This time he's right.

"Mr. Trofino," Judge Gold says, "please limit your responses to your beliefs before your wife's murder. What you concluded after is not relevant." He turns to the jury. "Ladies and gentlemen, I'm sustaining that objection because there's been no evidence entered that Ms. Goodwin was planning to leave her job. Mr. Trofino's testimony is only that he was told that by his wife. I know it's a bit confusing, but this testimony is only relevant to the extent it addresses what Mr. Trofino was thinking *at the time* because the defense has put his mental state into issue, claiming that he knew of the affair and therefore had motive to commit the crime for which Ms. Goodwin stands accused. But Mr. Trofino's speculation now, after evaluating the evidence, about what it all means is no more relevant to Ms. Goodwin's guilt or innocence than yours or mine. And because we can't ask Ms. Wright if she told her husband the truth, it cannot be considered by you as the truth. Please proceed, Ms. Broden."

I quickly consider whether the jury realizes that the only reason Lauren would have told her husband that Dana was leaving Special Vics was because they had broken up. It seems obvious to me, but juries can be dense about anything not explicitly laid out. I decide to weather some judicial ire to drive this point home.

"Thank you, Your Honor," I say. "Mr. Trofino, do you now believe that your wife was saying this to you because her relationship with Ms. Goodwin had ended?"

Burrows is back on his feet. "Your Honor, you just cautioned that Mr. Trofino's state of mind *after* the murder is of no relevance."

"Sustained," Judge Gold says, an edge to his voice. He knows I did that deliberately. "Move on, Ms. Broden."

My last area of inquiry is to recount the last hours of Lauren's life. I begin with Richard's visit to Lauren's office.

"What caused you to visit Lauren that evening?"

"We had dinner plans—with you, Ms. Broden, and your boyfriend. It was Lauren's idea that we arrive together at the restaurant, so I met her at her office."

"Did you see Dana Goodwin on that visit?"

"I did. Lauren brought me into Dana's office and we talked for a few minutes. I didn't think anything of it at the time. I knew Lauren and Dana worked closely together. In fact, Dana and her husband had invited us to dinner at their home, and we reciprocated by having them out for the weekend at our house. Which is to say it was not as if Dana's existence was a secret Lauren was keeping from me. And so it made sense that when I visited my wife, I'd say hello to Dana. I think, if anything, Lauren did it because that's what she would have done if Dana and she had just been platonic work colleagues. So, rather than there being an implication that there was something odd about it, I think Lauren was guided by the fact that it would have been out of character for her if she *hadn't* done it."

"Were you ever alone in Dana Goodwin's office?"

"I honestly don't remember," he says with a sigh. "I know that this is an important issue in this trial. That the defense is saying I killed my wife and took Dana's cell phone to frame her for it. And so I know it would help me to swear that there's no way I was in her office alone. But the truth is that at the time, it was just a visit to one of my wife's colleagues. I wasn't thinking that every detail of it would be important later. So as much as I'd like to deny being there alone, it's more important that I tell the truth. And the God's honest truth is that I just can't swear that there wasn't a moment that Dana and Lauren stepped out and I was left alone. I don't think so. I don't remember that. But I can't swear it didn't happen."

This answer was born of compromise. Richard originally *did* swear it didn't happen. Over and over again, in fact. It was only when we spoke with Rita DeSapio, the secretary who sat between Dana and Lauren's offices, that he was persuaded to change his tune.

"Did you take her cell phone?"

"No. That I can swear to without any reservation. Never happened. Ridiculous that anyone suggests otherwise."

"Did anything out of the ordinary happen at dinner?"

"No. It had been a particularly stressful day for me at work. And the fact that I had to leave earlier than usual to meet my wife's friends . . . well, it's something I did for my wife."

"Were you drunk after dinner?"

"No. Again, because I didn't realize how important that dinner would later become, I didn't count my drinks that evening. And, I'm not particularly proud of this fact, but one thing I've done over the years is build up a pretty good tolerance to alcohol. So, if I had three, four, five, even six drinks that night, I would have been fine. I wouldn't have driven a car, mind you, but I would have been in complete control of myself."

"Please tell the jury what happened when you came home from dinner that evening."

"It was just a regular night. We got home at . . . I think a little after ten. We watched some television, and I was asleep before eleven. The next thing I knew, I was receiving a call from our doorman saying that the police were there to see me. And this I remember so clearly. I was groggy when I spoke to our doorman, but then I rolled over to tell Lauren that the police were there. I mean, she deals with the police on a daily basis, so I assumed they were there to see *her*. That's when I saw she wasn't in bed. And that's when I began to panic."

"Last question, Mr. Trofino. Did you kill your wife?"

He clenches his teeth as if he's disgusted that he has to dignify the question with a reply. Then he says, "Absolutely not."

52.

DANA GOODWIN

LeMarcus has a herculean task before him. There's no way Richard Trofino is going to crack on cross-examination. That means that LeMarcus has to make his points through his questions only, at the same time expecting that every answer from Richard will knock us back.

He goes straight for the kill, without any setup.

"Mr. Trofino, you lied when you testified that you didn't know about your wife's affair, because you most certainly knew about it. Isn't that correct?"

"No, that's not correct," Richard answers calmly, exactly the way a witness should on cross. No matter how hot the questioner, you remain cool.

"You're going to sit there and tell this jury that your wife *didn't* tell you that she was in love with Dana?"

"She never said that, and I don't believe it's true."

LeMarcus's voice is so loud that he's yelling, while Richard issues his denials the way you would address a lunatic—so as not to agitate them further.

Richard testifies that he did not take my cell phone, that he did not leave the apartment that night after he and Lauren came home from dinner, and most important, that he did not kill his wife, even as LeMarcus's every query suggests the opposite.

LeMarcus closes by asking for permission to have Richard's height measured. It's a risky gambit, as anyone who saw the prosecution ask O. J. Simpson to try on the bloody glove knows.

"Five foot eight, and maybe a quarter inch," the court officer says.

As the court officer is walking away, Richard says, "I know it's my fault. I know it."

It's an obvious tactic. I can tell from LeMarcus's expression that he knows it too.

"Mr. Trofino," LeMarcus says, "there was no question pending, but if I heard you correctly, you just confessed to murdering your wife, is that right?"

"Objection," Ella says.

She sounds hesitant. I suspect she doesn't know where this is going either.

"Sounded like a confession to me," LeMarcus says.

"If I may, Your Honor?" Richard asks, looking up at Judge Gold.

"It's not my decision, Mr. Trofino," Judge Gold says. "Mr. Burrows, still your witness."

"I have no more questions," LeMarcus says.

"I have some redirect," Ella says.

The party offering the witness always gets a chance to clean up the testimony after cross-examination. In this case, I have no doubt that Ella will go where LeMarcus was too afraid to tread.

"Make it quick, Ms. Broden," Judge Gold replies.

"It will be. In fact, I just have one question. Mr. Trofino, please explain to the jury why you just said that it was your fault."

"I didn't kill my wife. I swear that I didn't. But I see now that when I told Ms. Goodwin at her office that we were having dinner that evening with you, Ms. Broden, Ms. Goodwin must have thought that Lauren was going to replace her with you. By committing this murder, Ms. Goodwin must have hoped that she'd not only avoid getting fired, but that she'd get a promotion to Lauren's job—which is exactly the way it initially turned out, and it would have stayed that way if she hadn't been arrested."

LeMarcus is shouting "Objection! Move to strike!" over Richard's answer, but the jury's already heard it. That kind of testimony can't be unheard. Richard Trofino has just given the jury the previously elusive *why*.

Usually, the prosecutor gets the last word. There is no second cross. But that's a matter of the court's discretion. Judge Gold recognizes the importance of what's just occurred. Although it's cold comfort, he allows LeMarcus to question Richard again, on this one point.

LeMarcus doesn't say anything at first. Someone who didn't know him might think he was formulating his question in his head. I've seen the routine enough to know he's just being dramatic.

"Is that it, Mr. Trofino?" he finally says.

"I'm sorry, I don't understand the question," Richard replies.

"I wanted to know if you had anything to add. Maybe you want to tell the jury that Ms. Goodwin confessed to you?"

The jurors now get the joke. Most of them are smiling. Richard is not, however. He looks angry. Like a man using every ounce of his self-control to not spring out of the witness box and knock those smiles off the jurors' faces.

"Please answer my question," LeMarcus says.

"What question?" Richard says, still gritting his teeth.

"I'm asking you quite simply, Mr. Trofino, if you now want to testify, under oath, that when you were in Ms. Goodwin's office, at a time when you claim that you did not take her cell phone to put your own plan of murder in motion, that instead Ms. Goodwin told you that it was *her* plan to use her own cell phone to text your wife later that day to meet her in Central Park and then, when your wife showed up, to murder her."

Ella objects. "Argumentative."

LeMarcus smiles broadly. "I'll withdraw it. I think we all know it doesn't matter what Mr. Trofino says."

———

After Ella rests her case, LeMarcus makes a halfhearted motion for a directed verdict. Judge Gold quickly rejects it. Although that ruling isn't unexpected, it still jabs at my heart. The judge has ruled that the prosecution has met its burden of proof. In other words, that the evidence is sufficient for the jury to conclude beyond a reasonable doubt that I murdered Lauren Wright.

"Does the defense plan on putting on a case, Mr. Burrows?" Judge Gold asks.

"We do. Our first witness is Stuart Goodwin."

Watching my husband walk to the witness stand for some reason causes me to flash back to my walk down the wedding aisle. Aside from the fact that Stuart's blond curls are now almost entirely gone, replaced by a shiny, bald pate, he doesn't look much different. He's the same weight as he was on our wedding day—something he's quietly proud of—and Father Time hasn't laid a hand on his face. He doesn't even have crow's feet around the eyes, whereas mine tell the world that I'm no longer in my thirties.

With his hand raised, Stuart swears to tell the truth, the whole truth, so help him God. He looks nervous in the chair and fidgets a little to get comfortable. His hands rest in his lap, and he rubs his fingers together like a nervous Nellie.

No matter how much you practice with a witness, you can't break them of their little tics. More often than not, who they are comes through to the jurors. The twelve men and women who are passing judgment on me probably already have a fair impression of my husband before he utters a single word.

He's weak, I imagine them thinking. *The kind of man whose wife might just prefer female sex partners.*

LeMarcus begins the direct with the normal background questions, eliciting that Stuart and I have been married for six years and have a five-year-old son.

Then it's time for the lying to begin.

"Mr. Goodwin, on the night of Ms. Wright's murder, where was your wife?"

"With me. At home. From about seven o'clock, when we had dinner with our son, until the following morning when she left for work."

"Any time during that period when she was out of your sight for more than . . . let's say ten minutes?"

"No. We have a small home, and we spent the evening together. First reading in our living room, then watching television in our bedroom, then asleep. Wait—I should amend that. There was one period of time when she was out of my sight."

I hold my breath. This wasn't in the script.

I know LeMarcus doesn't want to inquire further, but he has no choice. "When was that?"

"If memory serves, Dana read to our son that night and put him to bed. That process normally takes anywhere from twenty to forty minutes. So during that time, Dana was with Jacob, and I was cleaning up after dinner."

"Understood," LeMarcus says, no doubt as relieved as I am that Stuart's going off script has been effective.

"Did your wife have her cell phone with her on that evening?"

"She did not. I remember that very clearly because we searched throughout the house, and it was nowhere to be found. I assumed she'd left it at the office. But of course, when she was arrested and they told us that text had been sent from her phone, I knew that someone had stolen it."

Ella objects, but she's a beat too late to stop Stuart. Judge Gold sustains the objection and instructs the jury that Stuart's speculation as to what happened to my phone is to be disregarded. Then he directs the court stenographer to strike Stuart's last statement—the line about someone stealing my phone—from the record.

LeMarcus finishes his direct at four. If he'd timed this better, he would have run out the clock, giving him the weekend to work with Stuart on how to handle cross-examination. But stalling for an hour will be too transparent. Besides, I know LeMarcus has already spent hours with Stuart. They're well past the point of achieving anything more than they already have—only diminishing returns would be achieved through further preparation. Still, my husband is not a man who does well under attack.

53.

ELLA BRODEN

Back when I was an ADA, I joked that I'd cross-examined more lying spouses than any lawyer in America. It must be something in the DNA of sexual offenders; unlike most defendants, they *like* to take the stand. A police shrink once told me that she believed it gave them a feeling of power, the same rush that caused them to become predators in the first place.

Stuart Goodwin is a different kind of lying spouse. He isn't the bad guy here. He's doing what many people would say was the honorable thing: exposing himself to a perjury prosecution in order to protect the mother of his son. But my task is no different than with any other lying witness. I'm here to rip him to shreds.

From the look of him, I don't imagine that will be difficult.

"It must have been something of a . . . shock to learn that your wife was engaging in a months-long extramarital affair with another woman," I say.

He flashes a little grin—more baring his teeth than smiling. "Yes. It was shocking to me. I would have never imagined it in a million years."

"Prior to learning about the affair, would you have said that your wife kept no secrets from you?"

"That's right. Or I from her."

"Do you own an iPhone, Mr. Goodwin? Or any cellular phone?"

"I do. And it's an iPhone."

"Do you have a passcode on it?"

He pauses for a moment. I suspect that his phone habits are not something discussed in prep with Burrows.

"I do. I use my thumbprint to unlock it."

"So even though you trust your wife implicitly, you still lock your phone. Is that right?"

"It's not because I don't trust Dana—"

"You would say, wouldn't you, that your wife deals with much more confidential information in her job than you do in yours?"

Burrows objects. I'm sure it's to throw off my rhythm, to give his witness some time to regroup. He knows I'm entitled to this information. Judge Gold looks as if he can't be bothered to issue a ruling and asks me to rephrase instead.

"Let me ask it as two questions, Mr. Goodwin. First, what do you do for a living?"

"I'm an art teacher."

"At the college level?"

"No. Elementary school."

"I see. So, finger painting, arts and crafts, that sort of thing?"

I might as well have called him a wuss. Still, he doesn't look the least bit ruffled.

"We do other things too, but you have the general idea."

"Can we agree that your wife, as an Assistant District Attorney, had access to much more confidential information than you do as an elementary-school art teacher?"

"Yes."

"And yet you kept *your* cell phone passcode protected. It's your testimony that your wife, who dealt with a significant amount of confidential information in her job, did *not* have a passcode on her phone, and thereby allowed whatever was on it to be accessed by anyone who happened to get hold of it?"

"Dana only used her BlackBerry for work. She often gave her iPhone to our son to play with. He's only five. That's why she didn't put a passcode on it. There was nothing confidential on her iPhone."

This is a small opening. But that's where a good prosecutor makes her living, off the crumbs that defense witnesses leave behind.

"Nothing?" I say with as much sarcasm as possible. "Not *nothing*, Mr. Goodwin. On her iPhone is a running record of her long sexual affair with her boss. Isn't that *something*?"

He still looks unperturbed, which means that I need to provoke him further.

I begin to read the texts aloud. "My love, my life, last night was incredible. I have never come so many times . . ."

"Objection," Burrows says.

"Sustained," Judge Gold says. "The texts are admitted into evidence, Ms. Broden. No reason to read them aloud."

I tilt my head in a slightly rebellious acknowledgment of Judge Gold's ruling. He's not wrong, but I want the jury to know there was a lot more X-rated material where that came from.

"Mr. Goodwin, don't you think that your wife viewed these texts—where she goes on about the sexual prowess of Lauren Wright being so far superior to your own—as confidential? Don't you think they were something she wanted to keep you from reading?"

"Yes."

"And yet you are telling us that she didn't passcode-protect her phone?"

"Yes."

That's when it hits me. Like a thunderbolt, although it was there all along. Maybe Stuart Goodwin is not lying. Maybe his wife's iPhone never did have a passcode.

And maybe he did read her texts.

54.

DANA GOODWIN

Judge Gold breaks for the day at 4:45 sharp. It's a union thing. Overtime must be paid to the court officers and stenographer if they work past five, and Judge Gold, for all his power in the courtroom, probably doesn't have authority to authorize the additional expense without the chief judge's sign-off.

No one looks disappointed by the early start to the weekend, of course. At the end of all the previous court days, LeMarcus and I left together as if we were a couple, although it was always to head back to his office to prepare for the next day. Stuart went home alone to tend to Jacob. Tonight, however, in view of the weekend, LeMarcus tells me that we should reconvene tomorrow morning at his office, so Stuart and I depart together.

We maintain appearances, holding hands as we leave the courthouse. The flashing of cameras as we exit the building is sufficiently blinding that it's difficult for me initially to discern the location of the car that LeMarcus has ordered for us. But it's double-parked on Centre Street, a sign in the window that says "Dana L.," as if leaving off my last initial would fool the press.

As the car begins to pull away from the shouting reporters, Stuart says, "I think that went okay."

From the look in his eye, it's clear to me that he doesn't understand what's actually occurring in the courtroom. Perhaps that's because he hasn't heard the testimony firsthand, but I actually think it's because Stuart can't shake his fantasy that we're destined to live happily ever after.

"Stuart, you need to prepare yourself for the fact that I'm going to be found guilty. You're going to be the one who has to explain it to Jacob. The minute after the jury's verdict, they're going to revoke my bail and take me away in handcuffs."

I'm trying to scare him straight. But I can tell that my words don't have the slightest effect.

"I know you're worried. But I know—not just think, but know, and know from the bottom of my heart—that it's going to be okay. The people on the jury, they understand how much we love each other, and that we have a little boy who depends on us . . . on both of us. They know that nothing they do is going to bring Lauren back to life, but if they convict you, they destroy three other lives."

"From your lips to God's ears," I say, even though I have little hope that God is going to listen to Stuart's plea.

———

When we arrive home, Livie tells us that Jacob has already eaten and taken a bath. "He's in his bedroom. He'll be excited you're both home."

Livie's comment about dinner reminds me that I'll need to figure out my own meal tonight. Since the trial has begun, I've survived on whatever takeout LeMarcus had served me.

I look over at Stuart. As if he can read my mind, he says, "I'll either whip something up for dinner or order in. You should go see Jacob."

I don't have to be asked twice. I literally run up the stairs to my son's bedroom.

Jacob is wearing a Batman costume as his pajamas. It's complete with a cape, but thankfully not the cowl.

"How's my best little man today?"

"Good."

"How was school?"

"Good."

"Anything you want to tell me?"

"No. Anything you want to tell *me*?"

"That I love you."

"Oh. I thought you meant about school. I love you too, Mommy." He scrunches up his little face. "Mommy, do you know why Batman became Batman?"

I do, of course. I suspect that my son's posing this question tonight is not coincidental. I wonder what has brought this to the fore.

"No, why?"

"When he was a little boy, his mommy and daddy were killed. And he decided that he would become a superhero so that he could save other kids' parents."

I'm doing my best to hold back tears. The last thing I want is for Jacob to see me cry. He must already know, or at the very least sense, that he's in danger of losing me. I could ask him directly what's brought all this on, but like waking a sleepwalker, I fear that may give rise to consequences I'm not prepared to accept.

"It's wonderful that, when something so sad happened to him, he was able to dedicate himself to helping other people."

"Yeah," Jacob confirms. "I think if something ever happened to you or Daddy, that's what I'd do too."

I want with all my heart to tell him that he's not going to have to be a superhero. That nothing is going to happen to me.

But of course I can't say that. For all I know, I'll be out of his life forever by this time next week.

55.

ELLA BRODEN

I'm exhausted at the end of the day. A week of trial is as grueling as any physical endeavor I've ever undertaken. Hiking up Half Dome in Yosemite or running a marathon are cake by comparison.

"Do you want to go out to dinner?" Gabriel asks once we're in a cab on the way back to my apartment.

"No. Bad optics if we're photographed in the middle of the trial. Let's order something in and open a bottle of wine."

Once we arrive at my place, I go straight to the wine rack. Gabriel heads to the computer to place our dinner order. Forty minutes later, the Chianti I opened is half-gone, and the food from UpThai has just arrived.

"I can't get Stuart Goodwin's testimony out of my head," I say as we begin eating.

Gabriel is still sequestered from hearing witness testimony. As a result, he relies on my evening summaries to assess how the trial is progressing. In the cab on the way home, I told him that Stuart provided the expected alibi for his wife. I didn't yet, however, share with him my darker thoughts about his testimony.

"What about it?" he asks.

"I'm not sure if it's about his testimony as much as about him, to be honest. But something doesn't sit right with me. He went on and on about how much he loves Dana, even after he learned of the affair. It came off . . . I don't know, kind of obsessive."

"Maybe he was just compensating too much for the jury."

"I thought about that too. But I've seen men like him on the witness stand. It's just a hunch, but he wasn't putting us on. He really feels that way about her. The kind of love that he thinks is all-consuming, but it's really suffocating. And it made me start to think. What would he do if he *did* see the text messages that his beloved Dana had been sending to her boss?"

"What are you saying?"

"That maybe we're prosecuting the wrong Goodwin."

Gabriel looks at me as if the thought's not been too far from his mind either. I wonder if he had suspicions about Stuart Goodwin before today. I know he's on record as doubting Dana's guilt, but he hasn't said a word to suggest I might be prosecuting an innocent person since the day of her arrest. That's more likely because he wants to be supportive rather than due to any change of heart, however.

"We never gave him a serious look," Gabriel says. "As soon as we learned of the affair, we made the arrest."

That made perfect sense. The last thing the cops want to do is send the message that they may not have gotten the right person. Actually, that's the second-to-last thing they want. Even worse is finding evidence to point to someone else without conclusively making the case.

"A lot of the case fits against him too," I say. "If he knew about the affair, he has motive. If he thought his wife was going to leave him for Lauren, maybe he decided to eliminate that option. And Stuart testified that she didn't passcode-protect her phone. I have a hard time believing that he never took the opportunity to see what was causing his wife to work all those late hours."

Gabriel nods in agreement. "So where does that leave it, then?"

It has never been my job to prove someone other than Dana Goodwin killed Lauren Wright. Which is why I know many prosecutors who would have let the conversation end there, secure with the thought that convicting the person on trial was the only task at hand. But I've never been that kind of prosecutor. There are things more important than winning. We need to be right.

I smile at Gabriel to let him know that I haven't gone totally over to the dark side. He smiles back, telling me that my message has been received and he concurs.

"I'm sure the husband has never been arrested," Gabriel says. "So we're not going to have his fingerprints in the system or his DNA on file. Which leaves us with surveillance footage."

He's saying that even if Stuart left evidence linking him to the crime scene, we wouldn't be able to prove it because his fingerprints and DNA aren't in the database. Normally you'd get a court order to compel him to give samples, but doing that now would destroy the case against Dana, so that's a nonstarter. Which leaves our only other option: hoping that he turns up on surveillance footage so we can put him at the scene of the crime.

Gabriel and his team reviewed thousands of frames of video to see if Dana had made the trip from Astoria to Central Park the night of the murder. Footage from the bank and the bodega around the corner from their home, hoping to catch her walking to whatever mode of transportation she might have taken; from the N-train and Lexington-line subway platforms, in case she had decided to come to Manhattan via public transportation; from the cameras at the tollbooths at the bridges and tunnels, in case she traveled by taxi. Her image never appeared. And they knew she hadn't driven the family car into the city because they'd run the license plates, which hadn't shown up at any of the Manhattan entry points that night.

It took more than a hundred man-hours to comb through the various tapes the first time through. Back then, Gabriel had the manpower to put five uniforms on it. There's no way anyone is going to authorize overtime again. Not to pursue what's little more than the fact that Stuart Goodwin gave me the heebie-jeebies.

"I'll help," I say. "And we should also track Stuart's phone."

Gabriel nods at my suggestion. Richard Trofino's cell phone was on at the time of the murder, and the pings indicated it was in the general vicinity of the duck pond. That wasn't much evidence, because his phone would have pinged the same way if it was sitting on his night table, given the proximity of their apartment to the same cell tower. But if Stuart's phone pinged in the vicinity, we could show he was there on the night of the murder.

Of course, it's a safe bet that Stuart knows this too. If he was smart enough to turn off Dana's cell phone, I'm certain he knew enough to turn off his own phone. Or he would have left it on in Astoria so that it looked like he stayed at home.

That's when another thought hits me. "Dana's phone must have been turned off at the office, right? Otherwise, it would have pinged after six and shown us where she went after work. But it didn't. How could Stuart have done that? There's no evidence he was anywhere near Dana's office on the day of the murder."

Gabriel smiles at my concern, as if to tell me that this is not something to worry about. "When I was a kid, I was into model making," he says, a seeming non sequitur, but one which I'm sure will reveal its purpose soon. "I don't think anyone does that anymore, but I could spend hours. I was really good at following directions and piecing things together. Shocker that I became a detective, right? But my point is that, when I finished, I'd always have some leftover pieces. My model would look exactly like the picture on the box, and the directions didn't say that there were extra pieces, in case you lost one or something, but there they would be, just sitting there, mocking me. Once, I even took a model back apart. I literally broke it after I'd finished it, because it was glued together. But I just had to know if I'd missed something. I hadn't; there were just some pieces that didn't fit. They weren't even duplicates.

They were . . . extras. Maybe pieces from a different model even, that had somehow found their way into my box."

"And that's relevant to the murder why?" I say.

"Sometimes all the evidence doesn't fit either, Ella. Maybe Dana's phone lost its charge. That's not something Dana would remember, right? She'd just take her phone home and plug it in. But when she got home, maybe Stuart took it off her nightstand and made sure it was turned off. In that case, the evidence fits without Stuart needing to be some criminal mastermind thinking through every angle. He's just a guy who got lucky. Or more likely, he saw the opportunity and took advantage of it."

56.

DANA GOODWIN

"My guess is that it's to explore a plea," LeMarcus says from the back of a cab on our way downtown to meet Ella Broden.

It's at least the third time he's expressed this view since Ella called about a half hour ago and requested that we meet with her right away. I don't know why Ella suggested this meeting, but I'm reasonably sure it's *not* to offer me a plea. The case is going too well for her to cut me a break now. Something else must be going on.

"Yeah, maybe," I say.

There's no reason to rack my brain with possibilities, however. I'll find out within the hour why she's asked us to come see her on a Sunday morning.

It's odd returning to the DA's office. I knew it would be, of course, but I'm surprised at the power of the emotions that confront me. I feel shame in reentering the only office in which I've ever worked. Shame and heartache.

On the weekend, a skeletal security force works downstairs. Still, I know them all. Coming in on a Sunday was more the rule than the exception during my career. But none of them makes eye contact with me.

I'm surprised when Leon, who is manning security today, tells us to go to the sixth floor. I had assumed that Ella took either my office—previously her office—or Lauren's, both of which are on the seventh floor.

"You okay?" LeMarcus asks as we take the elevator up.

"Just great," I tell him.

Ella is waiting in the corridor as the doors open. You have to do that to escort your visitors past the first set of locked doors.

The ground rules we established are that everything said today is off the record. Nonetheless, LeMarcus told me that I'm not to say anything unless he gives the okay.

We follow Ella down the hallway, not passing another person. The office lights are all off. It's so quiet that I assume we're the only people on the floor.

The room Ella directs us into has a temporary feel to it. There's nothing on the walls, no photographs or mementos on the desk. In fact, it looks almost vacant. Whenever I was preparing for trial, my office resembled a crime scene, like it had been ransacked to the nth degree.

Gabriel Velasquez is sitting on a sofa. Beside him is the young woman who is second-seating Ella at trial. I still have never heard her voice. The notepad in her lap tells me that she won't say anything today either. Her purpose is to transcribe what I say, which gives the lie to the idea that anything in a murder trial can ever truly be off the record.

There's a small, round conference table in the corner of the office. Nothing is on it. I imagine that this is the first time Ella has ever used it. She motions for us to assemble the adjacent chairs. She hasn't offered us water or coffee—a sign that she expects this to be a short visit.

Gabriel joins us at the table, but the other woman stays put on the sofa. There are only chairs enough for the four of us.

"Let me get right to why I wanted to meet," Ella says, speaking directly to LeMarcus as if I'm not even there. "We have reason to suspect that Dana's husband was involved in Lauren Wright's murder. We're not certain whether he acted alone or in concert with his wife, but we're willing to give Ms. Goodwin the opportunity to explain the situation to us."

"What evidence do you have?" LeMarcus asks.

"I'm not going to share that. But this is an opportunity for your client to tell us what she knows."

In a conspiracy, every member is equally liable. So long as there's an agreement beforehand, coupled with a single act in furtherance of that conspiracy, even if that act itself is perfectly legal, everyone involved is equally culpable. Getaway driver, shooter, even someone who just makes a phone call—or sends a text—luring the victim to the location of the crime, are all, in the eyes of the law, guilty to the same degree. The reason for this, among other things, is that it relieves the prosecution from having to prove each member's particular role, which would be next to impossible. All that is required is to show that each participant acted with intent to engage in the conspiracy and committed just one overt act in furtherance thereof, even if that act is perfectly legal.

"Can we have a moment?" LeMarcus asks.

"Of course," Ella says. "We'll give you the room."

"That's okay. You can stay put. We'll confer in the hallway."

LeMarcus rises and motions for me to follow him. When we're in the corridor alone, my lawyer peers down at me. The consternation in his face makes me feel a bit like a child about to be on the receiving end of a parental lecture.

"Why didn't you tell me?"

It's odd that LeMarcus, who would normally be skeptical if a prosecutor told him that the sun was going to rise tomorrow, has accepted without question Ella Broden's theory that my husband murdered Lauren Wright. Stranger still that he's leaped to the conclusion that I've long known the truth.

However, in this instance, LeMarcus is right. On both counts. So his question is an apt one.

I could remind him that his very first instruction to me was not to share with him anything he hadn't expressly asked me, and he never asked me if I knew who killed Lauren. That wasn't the real reason, of course. Not even close. "It's complicated," I say.

"It seems pretty damned simple to me. One of you is going to jail for the rest of your life. Do you want it to be him, or you?"

How many times did I attempt to scare witnesses in exactly this way? A hundred? Five hundred? Probably even more. I'd tell them that if they didn't cooperate with law enforcement, they were going to go to jail for a very long time, but they held the key to their own freedom, if only they would tell the truth. When that didn't work, I emphasized that if their own well-being mattered so little to them, they should at least consider the welfare of their children.

LeMarcus's expression makes clear that he'll tolerate his client lying to his face, but not throwing her life away. It's almost as if he takes personally my refusal to turn on Stuart. I remember feeling that way with witnesses too.

"I can suggest that you wear a wire," he says. "All you need to do is tell Stuart about their theory and see what he says." He must see reluctance in my eyes, because then he adds, "Dana, if you don't help them, they can't help you. You know that. And it's my professional opinion that you're going to be convicted. Your only way out is to help them to prove that Stuart is guilty."

———

"How'd the meeting go?"

For a moment I'm worried that Stuart can read my thoughts, or is having me followed. I didn't tell him that LeMarcus and I were meeting with Ella Broden and Gabriel Velasquez today. Then I realize that his question doesn't refer to them. He doesn't know about *that* meeting. He's just asking his usual question about my day with LeMarcus.

"Fine." Then I shrug. "I don't know how anything is going anymore, to tell you the truth."

He nods in solidarity. He believes we're still allies in the fight for my freedom.

What would he do if he knew otherwise? Would he kill *me*?

Stuart committed murder to protect our marriage, and yet I'm far from certain that he wouldn't kill me to save himself.

"Is Jacob in his room?" I ask.

"No. He was at a playdate with Ross today, and Ross's mother asked if he could have dinner at their house."

I'm sorry that my son isn't home, especially when I'm now cognizant of how little time I might still have with him. Then again, I need to be alone with Stuart tonight. I wonder if he sensed that somehow too.

"Come into the living room," I say. "I need to discuss something with you."

He follows me obediently. I stop at our sofa, and he sits beside me.

"What is it?" he asks.

"I haven't wanted to talk about Lauren's murder, but there's one thing that we need to discuss. And I want you to tell me the truth, okay?"

"Of course. I'm happy to discuss it. The only reason I didn't was because you said you didn't want to."

"Well, I need to talk about it now."

He looks at me, waiting.

Having gone this far, I know I need to finish the journey, but I'm frozen in place. I realize the living room might not have been the best venue for this discussion, as it places me twenty feet away from the front door. Stuart could easily get there before me. As I imagine being brutally murdered by my husband, Stuart waits patiently for me to tell him what I'm struggling with. Most likely so that after I tell him, he can provide the solution to this conundrum that has eluded me.

"I have to assume that you never expected that Lauren wouldn't have brought her phone to the park. Please tell me that's what happened. It would be too much for me to bear that you wanted me to be punished this severely for having an affair. I guess what I'm saying is that

I understand *why* you killed Lauren, but I'm just asking you to tell me that you didn't also intend to frame me for her murder."

My husband, the man with whom I share a child and have built a life, doesn't respond. At least thirty seconds pass in silence, which feels like an eternity.

I reflexively look to the kitchen, the most likely place for him to grab a weapon. But rather than get up, he scoots closer to me, until our thighs are touching.

"I swear on Jacob's life that I didn't want you to be blamed for this," he says. "I looked for her phone so I could take it with me. And when I realized the phone wasn't there . . . I threw the gun away near their house. My hope was that Richard would take the blame, not you. I killed her precisely because I couldn't fathom life without you. That means that the very *last* thing I'd ever want in this world is for you to go to jail. How could you even think that I'd want that?"

He's begun to cry. At first slowly, and then a rush of sobbing. I'm not completely certain, but I think the cause of his anguish is not that he murdered Lauren but that I've questioned his love for me. His head is pushed against my arm, but I can't summon the will to comfort him with an embrace.

He straightens up and wipes his eyes. He's staring at me. I feel myself welling up too.

I didn't know my affair would end with Lauren's murder. But it's cold comfort to say that, in a strictly legal sense, I am innocent of that crime. I did know that my infidelity would have far-reaching consequences. Even if I never imagined that death would result, I always knew that suffering would almost certainly occur. It always does when you disregard your sense of morality. And while I've seen plenty of wives blame themselves for their spouse's crime—and always felt anger at their pathos—I understand now why they felt that way. At the same time, though, I feel the judgment I heaped on those women fall squarely upon me.

57.

ELLA BRODEN

The Fifth Amendment of the United States Constitution contains a host of provisions. The most famous is the right against self-incrimination, which states that no person may be compelled in any criminal case to be a witness against himself. But elsewhere in the amendment is the clause "nor shall any person be subject for the same offence to be twice put in jeopardy of life or limb."

The so-called double-jeopardy clause prohibits anyone from being tried twice for the same crime. Double jeopardy attaches as soon as the jury is seated; therefore, this is the one and only time Dana Goodwin can be held accountable for the murder of Lauren Wright. Dismissing the charges would mean that Dana Goodwin could confess to me on the way out of the courtroom that she actually acted alone, and there would be nothing I or anyone else could do about it. Worse still, if we brought Stuart Goodwin to trial for Lauren's murder, nothing would stop Dana from testifying that *she* committed the crime. As a practical matter, therefore, unless Dana Goodwin was a witness against her husband, letting her go free means that Lauren's murder will go unpunished.

And Dana refused to cooperate with us.

But the simple fact is that Stuart Goodwin, or at least someone looking a lot like Stuart Goodwin trying not to be photographed, was captured by the security cameras in front of the Sherry-Netherland Hotel, on Fifth Avenue and Fifty-Ninth Street, at 12:31 a.m. on the night of Lauren's murder. The N subway line, which has a stop in Astoria, has an aboveground exit directly in front of the Sherry-Netherland.

We found Franklin Pearse at the shelter on Lexington and hoped that he would settle the question for us. After providing him with another roast beef sandwich, he repeated what he'd been saying from the beginning: that he only saw the guy from behind, so he didn't know if the person he saw in the black hoodie was the same person as in the photograph we showed him. And, as I suspected, Stuart Goodwin's phone was turned off all night, so we could not place him in Central Park that way.

Stuart Goodwin will claim it isn't him. Or, at the very least, that no one can be certain beyond a reasonable doubt that it's his face on the surveillance footage. Gabriel said he was sure, but I think he was seeing what he wanted to see. I'm not certain. But the one thing I do know for sure is that I now have reasonable doubt that Dana murdered Lauren.

"All rise," the court clerk bellows.

Everyone in the courtroom stands to watch Judge Gold walk in. When he's seated, he commands that we all do the same. Then the same ritual is observed when the jury enters, but this time I remain upright.

"Your Honor, before we begin today, I would like to be heard," I say.

He tilts his head slightly. "We're all ears, Ms. Broden."

I can feel the eyes on me. It reminds me of how I feel before the music starts at Lava. Now, as when I prepare to sing, I allow myself a moment alone and shut my eyes. Charlotte is there, and Lauren too. They both approve of what I'm going to do. I'm certain of that.

"The People move to dismiss the indictment against Dana L. Goodwin."

The gallery erupts. Aside from Kayla, Gabriel, and Richard Trofino, no one knew that I was about to utter those words. Actually, my conversation about it with Richard was one of the calmer talks we've had. I explained my reasoning, and he said that he understood and was in no position to question my judgment. "Nothing is going to bring Lauren back," he said, "and as much as I want justice for her, it's got to be the kind of justice she believed in for it to matter. I know this sounds terrible, but it's easier for me to accept that Dana's husband killed Lauren, and not someone she loved."

Drake McKenney was not given a heads-up because I knew he'd try to talk me out of it. I didn't even tell LeMarcus, not out of any sense of drama, but because I wanted to leave myself the option to proceed with the case to verdict until I was certain. But my brief moment of solitude has brought me home.

Judge Gold gavels twice. Although his judicial temperament usually keeps him poised, he looks shocked.

"Care to share your reasons, Ms. Broden?"

"The People have recently come into evidence that casts doubt on Ms. Goodwin's guilt."

The judge nods and smiles at me. It might be the first time this trial he has.

"I am a staunch believer in the wisdom of the great William Blackstone, who said that it is better that ten guilty go free than that one innocent suffer," Judge Gold says. "That sentiment, erring always on the side of preventing even the smallest injustice, is found throughout all civilized codes of law. And so let me be the first to say, Ms. Broden, that you have acted in the interest of justice today."

I nod to accept the judge's thanks. I'm certain Drake McKenney will not agree. If I had brought Dana Goodwin to a guilty verdict, the Special Vics bureau chief position would have been mine. Now, earning a living as a singer will likely be my only career option. Unless I want to go back to work for my father, which I most certainly do not.

"Ms. Goodwin," Judge Gold says. "I hereby dismiss all charges against you. In the eyes of the law, you are not guilty. Therefore, I wish you Godspeed."

Two more gavel strikes follow, but they do nothing to silence the din of the gallery. Judge Gold dismisses the jury and, after they leave the courtroom, he exits to his chambers. It's only when the door shuts behind him that I turn to Dana Goodwin and see that she's embracing LeMarcus Burrows.

Having made his way to the well of the court, Gabriel puts his arm around me. "I'm so proud of you, Ella."

LeMarcus Burrows interrupts. "Excuse me," he says. "But I just wanted to say, on behalf of my client, thank you."

I acknowledge his praise but don't offer the usual response that he's welcome. Dana Goodwin doesn't owe me her thanks. I didn't do this for her, after all. I did it for Lauren.

LeMarcus must pick up on my reasons because then he adds, "Not every ADA would have done it, Ella. Though everyone should. That's what I'm thanking you for. For making certain that justice has been served."

Over my shoulder, I again spy the defense table. Dana Goodwin is receiving an embrace from her husband. I hope to God that I've done the right thing.

58.

DANA GOODWIN

My first thought as a free woman is about Jacob, of course. My sweet angel boy.

Then I feel Stuart's arms coming over my shoulders from behind. "It's all over, Dana. I never doubted for a second that you'd be set free. And now . . . now we can begin the rest of our lives together. You, me, and Jacob."

I don't respond to his fantasy about living happily ever after. Instead, I pull away from his embrace and cross the six feet to the prosecution table. Ella Broden is surrounded by her second seat, LeMarcus, and Gabriel. The trio parts to allow my approach.

"Thank you," I tell her.

As a prosecutor, it always frustrated me not to know precisely what happened during a crime. I never feared I had the wrong defendant, but not knowing exactly how it all unfolded always bothered me. Those elusive pieces and their sequence were forever secreted in the defendant's mind.

That was never the case with Lauren's murder. I know how everything fit together, and have for some time.

I didn't think Stuart knew about my affair. When Lauren was killed, like everyone else, I believed that Richard was guilty. I had assumed that despite my plea to her in the park on our last night together, she did exactly what she said she would—went home and told Richard everything. And knowing Richard, or at least thinking I did, it seemed more than possible that he would have killed her for her infractions.

But when the gun was found and traced back to Gregory Papamichael, I realized that it had to have been Stuart. Gregory gave me the Glock 19 shortly after Jacob was born, right after the case we worked together ended, when Stuart insisted we keep a firearm in the house. When I handed Papamichael's old service weapon to Stuart, I told him that I never wanted to see it again.

And then, whatever doubt I clung to that it might all be some type of mistake—that maybe Papamichael had given a weapon to Lauren too—was erased when the text messages Lauren received were shown to have come from my phone. Richard *couldn't* have sent them. My iPhone—the one used to lure Lauren to Central Park—*was* passcode protected. Richard, of course, did not know my passcode was Jacob's middle name: Benjamin. But Stuart did.

"I didn't kill Lauren," I tell Ella. "I loved her."

Ella looks at me skeptically. I'm uncertain which part of my statement she finds false: that I didn't kill Lauren or that I loved her.

"Do you think Lauren would forgive me?" I ask.

I suspect my question has surprised Ella. I'm certain that she gave considerable thought to how Lauren would have reacted to her decision to dismiss the charges against me, but I'm equally certain that she has not considered at all what our boss would think about my failure to turn on my husband.

At least twenty seconds pass. I'm content to wait for as long as necessary for Ella to respond.

"I think she might *understand*, but forgive . . . I just don't know," she finally says.

This is a generous response. I'm not sure Lauren would understand. She dedicated her professional life to helping women find the courage to testify against their abusers. I'm certain that she'd wonder why I haven't done everything I could to make my husband pay for his crime.

I lower my voice, move a little closer to Ella. "If it were only about me . . . but I have a little boy to think about."

Ella nods as if she understands.

Of course she doesn't. How could she?

"Don't stay with him," she says.

With that, she begins to back away, to return to her people. I reach for her arm and hold her in place for a moment more. I step forward, closing the gap between us so I can be certain that only she can hear what I'm about to say.

"Hold on to Gabriel, Ella," I whisper into her ear. "You might think I'm the very last person on earth to take relationship advice from, but this is something I do know about. There's nothing more important than being with someone you truly love."

She reflexively turns around to look at Gabriel, who's watching us. He nods at me and favors me with a smile.

I stood trial for a crime I didn't commit for one reason: self-preservation. Simply put, accusing Stuart of killing Lauren would not have served my case well. Spouses pointing at one another is one of the oldest defense ploys in the book, and such claims are almost always rejected by juries. That would have certainly been true for me. I lacked any evidence of Stuart's guilt, and the only result I could have achieved by implicating him was my own conviction. If I admitted that Papamichael gave me the gun, then I'd be putting the murder weapon in my own hands, something the prosecution could not otherwise prove. More importantly, Stuart was my alibi; if I had told the police *he* committed the crime, I couldn't have taken the stand to say that we were both home, together, that night.

Perhaps, if I had asked him to take the blame he would have, but I doubt it. His loyalty to me was a product of the belief that we'd always be together. Once he realized one of us had to go to jail, I strongly suspect he would not have sacrificed his life for mine.

I could have worn a wire, and that way obtained the proof of Stuart's guilt. But I didn't know he would confess so readily, and I feared that if he figured out that I was turning against him, he would turn on me. That was a price I was unwilling to pay. Me in prison, and Stuart full of hate. He could have erased my very existence from Jacob's mind. At five, my son is still young enough to be fooled that way. Within a year, probably less, he'd believe that I'd left him at birth and never once read him *Mike Mulligan*.

"I told you we would live happily ever after," Stuart says as he moves over to me again.

"That's not going to happen, Stuart. You need to find somewhere else to stay tonight. I never want to see you again."

"No . . ." he says, looking confused. He actually reaches for my hand, not in an aggressive way, but as if we're still a couple.

"Don't make me scream," I snarl. "There are a dozen cops who would like nothing more than to shoot you. And I swear, if I see you anywhere near the house, I'll shoot you myself."

He relaxes his grip and smiles at me, his expression totally out of sync with reality.

"I understand," he says. "This must be incredibly emotional for you. Take some time to be alone with Jacob. You've earned it. We can talk about this tomorrow."

I watch him leave the courtroom. It's not until he fades from view that I'm able to breathe again. I'm going to take Jacob away—tonight. Somewhere I can start again.

59.

ELLA BRODEN

Dana Goodwin's words still ring in my ears when I turn to face Gabriel again. She was right about one thing: she is the very last person on earth from whom I should take relationship advice. Then again, I think she's also right. Nothing is more important than being with someone you love.

My father has come through the railing separating the spectators from the participants. He came to watch what he assumed would be the closing arguments.

"I'm proud of you, sweetheart," he says.

It occurs to me that this will be his first time meeting Gabriel. At least as my boyfriend. They met during the investigation into Charlotte's murder, but never since then. Even on Thanksgiving, we agreed to go to our separate families. My thinking at the time was that it was too soon after Charlotte's death to subject my father to guests; Gabriel had said that he understood, even though I could tell he feared that I still didn't view him as meet-the-father material.

"Dad, do you remember Gabriel Velasquez?"

My father shakes Gabriel's hand and offers him a big smile. "Of course I do. So nice to see you under better circumstances. Ella has told me so much about you."

"She speaks of you all the time too, sir."

My father laughs. "*Sir?* No, that will not do. Clint, please." To me he says, "Ella, after you finish up here, I'd like very much to take you and Gabriel out to celebrate. Would you both do me that honor?"

When he's nervous, my father can be overly formal. *Do me that honor?* I find it sweet that being around Gabriel makes him uneasy. I don't recall him ever acting that way around Jeffrey or my other boyfriends. There must have been something in the way I've described my life with Gabriel that has given my father reason to believe this relationship has legs.

There actually isn't much for me to finish up after court. In my prior life as a prosecutor, other cases piled up while I was on trial, so as soon as one verdict was rendered, I was right back in the salt mine. But this time, I have no other cases. I have no job, in fact. I chuckle to myself that the only post-trial things I have to do are to reach out to Karen and get another spot at Lava and make sure that Allison hasn't given away my Wednesday and Thursday appointment slots.

"Yes," I say to my father, "Gabriel and I would be happy to do you that *honor*."

"Great. Per Se at one?"

"Dad, not Per Se. Please."

"My treat, my choice," he says.

———

Per Se is probably the last place on earth I'd ever take Gabriel for a meal. Not only because of the $375-per-person price tag—before alcohol, tax and tip, so it's closer to $500, all in. I'm also relatively certain that if they have beef on the menu, the chef will refuse to cook it more done than medium, no matter how much we're paying for the privilege.

I prepare Gabriel for the fact that it's not going to be a burger-and-fries situation. In fact, he's not going to be able to order at all. Per Se serves only a nine-course tasting menu. It changes every day, and no single ingredient is ever repeated throughout the meal.

"Fantastic," Gabriel says. "Is there a McDonald's close by, in case I get, you know, hungry?"

"You'll eat your five-hundred-dollar lunch like a man," I say back. "Oh, and you need to wear a suit jacket, I think. Do you have one in your office?"

"This keeps getting better and better," he says. But he's smiling.

Needless to say, my father gets a prime table, even though I'm certain he made the reservation earlier today. Despite its astronomical price tag, Per Se is among the toughest reservations to secure in the whole city. The room befits a restaurant of grandeur. Not only is every last detail attended to, but also nearly two hundred feet of the eastern wall is glass, providing a view out over Columbus Circle to Central Park.

My father has taken the liberty of ordering champagne. As soon as we're seated, a waiter attentively fills each of our flutes.

"To . . . justice being done, and to those who did it," my father says, his glass raised.

After completing the toast, we each take a sip of the champagne. I know it's not Gabriel's favorite alcoholic beverage, but he plays along.

The first course arrives with much fanfare, as no fewer than four waiters accompany the three dishes. They are placed before us simultaneously, with the odd man out describing what's on the plate.

"The title of this dish is Oysters and Pearls," he says. "It is sabayon of pearl tapioca with Island Creek oysters and sterling white sturgeon caviar."

I catch Gabriel's sidelong glance, and it makes me giggle like a girl.

"What?" my father says.

"Nothing," I say. Then to change the subject, "So, do you think I'm the only unemployed singer in the restaurant?"

My father glances around at the other tables. Nearly all of them are occupied by men, no doubt on expense accounts.

"I'd say the odds are even higher that I'm the only cop here," Gabriel says. Despite the remark, I can tell that Gabriel is enjoying this.

"Well, I have some news I think you'll find very interesting about your employment status, Ella," my father says. "I had a conversation with Richard Trofino after court today. I've known Richard through the years professionally, and he said that the most fitting tribute he could make to Lauren's memory would be to see you installed as her successor as the bureau chief of Special Victims."

I laugh. If there's one thing that I *am* certain about after today, it's that my career as a prosecutor is over. Making an enemy of the sitting District Attorney is never the road to advancement.

"Does Richard also plan on becoming District Attorney? Because I'm pretty sure that after today, that's the only way I'm ever going to get that post."

"There's another way," my father says. "He's going to suggest to Drake McKenney that, if you're appointed, the mayor will support McKenney's reelection bid. If not, the DA will find himself running against a very well-financed primary challenger next year."

"Really? He'd do that for me?"

"Well, not entirely for you. I suspect that, in exchange for backing McKenney, the mayor will require McKenney's support for his own reelection. But Richard said that he's vetted the plan with the mayor, and he's on board."

I look at Gabriel. He's all smiles. I know that he's thinking that I can have it all. Chief of the Special Victims Bureau by day, rock-star Cassidy by night.

"That is certainly exciting," I say, "but it pales in comparison to the news I'm about to share."

"What's that?" Gabriel says before my father can inquire.

"About our moving in together," I tell him. "Although the address has yet to be determined."

"Well, then," says Gabriel, "I guess you're not the only one at the table who's getting what they've always wanted." He's beaming, which makes me beam right back at him.

My father reaches for his champagne. Raising his flute once again, he says, "To getting what you've always wanted."

"Hear, hear," I say.

We touch glasses as one to complete the toast.

ACKNOWLEDGMENTS

You've made it this far, why not go a little farther?

Please send me an e-mail at adam@adammitzner.com and tell me what you thought of *Never Goodbye*. I truly love to hear from readers, and I always—ALWAYS—write back.

After you've told me what you think, please tell the world by posting a review on your favorite site. Amazon, Goodreads, Shelfari, your own blog: they're all good places to let your opinions be known.

Never Goodbye is the first time I've attempted a sequel. I had previously resisted because I thought the stories in my prior books had reached a natural conclusion, but with Ella Broden I knew that there was more story to tell when I finished *Dead Certain*. I suspect that *Never Goodbye* will not be the last you've read of Ella's pursuits.

But before looking to the future, I need to thank all of those who have done so much so that you could experience *Never Goodbye*. In no particular order, my most sincere heartfelt thanks go to Jessica and Kevin Shacter, Jodi (Shmodie) Siskind, Clint Broden (yes, there is a real person with that name and he's even an extremely well-regarded criminal-defense lawyer!), Bonnie Rubin, Beth Miller, Matt Brooks, Ellice Schwab, Lily Weitzner Icikson (for giving her name), Joseph Icikson (for giving his name), Silvia Serpe (for giving her name), Abby Doft, Rita DeSapio (for giving her name), Sara Sadinoff (for giving her name), Jane Goldman, Gregg Goldman, Maeve and Grant Goldman (for giving the name of Mr. Big Tiger), Leslie Wright (for giving her name), Margaret Martin, Ted Quinn, and my parents, Linda and Milton Mitzner, and our dog, Onyx (for giving her name).

The people at Thomas & Mercer have absolutely been incredible, and the best publishers/partners an author could have. Special thanks to Liz Pearsons and Ed Stackler, who provide invaluable criticism and support, which made *Never Goodbye* better than I could have hoped. There are many people behind the scenes at Thomas & Mercer, nearly all of whom I've never met or spoken to, but I know that they contribute on so many levels, from proofreading to cover to design to marketing, and so a huge thank-you goes out to them as well.

Special thanks to Scott Miller, my agent at Trident Publishing since my first book. Also thanks to Jon Cassir at CAA, and Emily Siegel and Jessica Varney, all of whom are working hard to bring my books to film. And to the people at Audible, who make it possible to listen to my books.

My law firm, Pavia & Harcourt LLP, has been nothing but supportive of my writing, and I am thankful to everyone there, but especially George Garcia.

Last and certainly most, is my family. Each and every member contributes in so many ways to my writing. My daughter, Rebecca, replies "Yay!" when I text her something about the book, and her sister, Emily, will discuss any plot point with me and provide me her unique insight into the world. My stepson, Michael Plevin, provides me with interesting tidbits about the world at large, and his brother, Benjamin Plevin, is usually my first reader and offers what he calls "constructive complaints" throughout the writing process.

My greatest thanks go to my wife, Susan Steinthal. She not only edits the manuscript multiple times, saving me from embarrassment with each critique, but encourages me when I've hit a wall. She doesn't gloat too much when readers render criticisms that she made long before and that I wrongly ignored. But, of course, my real thanks to her have nothing to do with my writing at all, but are for being my partner, my friend, my everything.

Never Goodbye is my sixth book, and I am incredibly blessed to be able to share what I love to do with so many people. So my final, but extremely heartfelt, thank-you is to you—the people who read and listen to my books. Thank you.

ABOUT THE AUTHOR

Photo © 2016 Matthew Simpkins Photography

Adam Mitzner is a practicing attorney in a Manhattan law firm and the author of several acclaimed novels including the #1 Kindle bestseller *Dead Certain*; as well as *A Conflict of Interest, A Case of Redemption, Losing Faith,* and *The Girl from Home. Suspense Magazine* named *A Conflict of Interest* one of the best books of 2012; and in 2014, the American Bar Association nominated *A Case of Redemption* for a Silver Gavel Award. Mitzner and his family live in New York City. Visit him at www.adammitzner.com.